ISBN: 0998902608
ISBN-13: 978-0-9989026-0-9

First Printing, 2017
Printed in the United States of America

Author, Latashia M. Holmes
Editor, TeErra J. Johnson

Contact @frxshinc for book covers

So Inspired Publishing Co.

www.soinspiredpublishingco.com

ACKNOWLEDGEMENTS

First given honor to God my Alpha and Omega for being a God of second chances. I can honestly say my faith in God carried me thru to enable me to write Made U Look while incarcerated and eventually Self publish the book. I would like to thank my three beautiful children Tamia, Damarko, and Zion for loving me in my absence times of being a mother. I'll love you three until I take my last breath. And my four heartbeats Devin, Damare, Dylan and Jae my grand babies And to my Bomb Ass book editor Miss TeErra Johnson you are heaven sent and unmatched. There is no one I would have wanted to be apart of this journey with but you. From our first conversation you brought tears to my eyes and joy to my heart. I admire, respect, and adore you. Thanks for coming along this ride with me XOXO and special thanks to Monie Johnson, my colleague who introduced me to her daughter TeErra. And to the Matriarch of my family my 87 year old grandmother who in the last several years has lost her memory due to Alzheimer's disease and it's taken a dramatic effect on me personally and she doesn't remember me at all. But if she did she would have been my biggest cheerleader. I wish I could go back in time and show you I did something positive with my life and I know you would be very proud of me. I love you Leeesther Moore and I thank you for never giving up on me. Your prayers have finally been answered. And thanks to both my parents, thank you to my book cover editor @frxshinc You're amazing and my photographer Juan Hernandez love you and lastly to my BFF Latasha Johnson for your patience, love and understanding you held me down like no other.

MADE | U | LOOK

inspired by true events

THE BEGINNING OF IT ALL

India Smith

BAM! BAM! BAM!

"Who the hell is knocking at the door this damn early in the morning like that? They must have lost their minds!"

BAM! BAM! BAM! again.

"Shit whoever it is, they're going to wait until I finish using the bathroom," I said aloud, smoothing out my hair in an attempt to fix myself up a bit. *I don't know if it's this pregnancy or the drinks from last night but one of them has put my bladder to work.*

"Bitch you ain't shit," after looking in mirror I couldn't help but laugh at myself, my reflection resembled something of a fatigued lioness but with a lion's mane. After washing my hands, I sluggishly walked to the front door to open it but to my surprise, it was about ten police officers with their guns drawn. I wonder what would have happened if I shut the door in their faces and went back to bed as if this was just all a dream. But I didn't and I was wide awake so we'll never know that scenario. I put my hands in the air and said,

"This had to be some kind of mistake, this is my parents' home and there are no murders, or guns up in here. My parents are very well known respectable citizens," my heart was racing at this point, "this has to be some kind of mistake!" I repeated.

"Who's in the house with you ma'am"? The woman officer asked, in a strong and harsh voice that opposed the hips hiding und her uniform.

"Umm I'm not sure, my parents are out the country, s guess it's just our housekeeper and chef."

Ma

"Where are they?" The officer asked, unwavering from her stance, she was still sync with the other surrounding policemen as if they were prepared for battle.

I was starting to get pissed, "Are you implying that our housekeeper or chef did something so malice that you had to come to my parents' home, bamming on doors with your guns drawn and shit like you're looking for a serial killer or escape convict? Do you even have a search warrant?" I asked.

"Have a seat ma'am, we have it right here," he pulled out a yellow piece of paper tucked in his vest and handed it to me. The writing was so small I could barely read it but I saw something with my name on it.

"Where is your room Ms. Smith?" The officer asked, "we have a search warrant for the premises and we need to know which room is yours."

I laughed to myself, *these are some lucky motherfucka's because normally I would have never been here at this time of the morning.* Today is their lucky day, literally. Bastards. I was so drunk last night that I couldn't drive home and my girl who I partied with just happens to be our next door neighbor from childhood. She drove me to my parents home instead of driving me all the way to my house on the other side of town.

"Ma'am, where is your room?"

"Oh," snapping me out of my revive, "my sister and I share a room upstairs on the right. A sign is hanging on the door, it says 'India and Asia's Room'," I shook my head. I don't even know why he asked because from the sounds of it, apparently they had already found the room and were already tearing shit up. I tried to walk upstairs but one of the officers stopped me.

"Please Ms. Smith, just stay right here this should only take a few moments," he said, smiling and looking at me. I don't know what the fuck he was smiling about because my parents were going to make sure him and his commands were bent over, holding their knees while a dick was rammed up their asses, wearing a shirt with a knot tied in front when they got through with them. *They just don't know who they were fucking with.* Snapping me out of my revive again, they escorted our housekeeper and chef into the den and order for them to take a seat next to me. They both looked distressed and agitated, I returned with a venomous stare and looked at them crooked eyed.

I could only imagine what was running through their minds, both of them had seen it all and been through everything with us - the good, the bad, and ugly. This shouldn't have been too much of a surprise, but then again we've never had a bunch of cops running around my parents house either. And all the while they were flowing throughout my room, the Hennessey and Champagne from last night was flowing through my system and had me urging to go to the bathroom like crazy, especially with this pregnancy. I had to pee again. Damn.

Two female officers came in with a paper bag and whispered something to another officer who walked outside and got on his radio. I could hear him say 'we found something' while leaving out. I asked one of the officers could I use the bathroom and there was one in the den. Shit for all I cared they could have come in, wiped, and flushed. I just needed to go and badly.

"Go with her to the restroom," one of the officers said to another. I jumped up and ran to the bathroom, leaving the door open so they could see that I wasn't with no bullshit. When I finished and sat back down again this whole fiasco was finally over, approximately thirty-nine minutes give or take. They collectively appeared in my parents den, looking straight at me as if I was their next target.

"Well Ms. Smith we have some bad news for you."

Since they were on this formal last name shit, I wanted to pause everything and take out the whole damn police squad like they did in the Mr. and Mrs. Smith movie, but I couldn't move. I was too drained from last night's events.

"We have a warrant for your arrest."

"Can you please stand and put your hands behind your back."

Why is it when the police arrest someone they always ask 'can you please etc. etc.'. What if I said 'Fuck No!! I don't want to stand or put my hands behind my back!', then what happens? But I guess we'll never know the answer because, I did as I was told, sighing. I asked our housekeeper of twenty years to call our family attorney and contact my parents. She shook her head in agreement with tear filled eyes and said,

"Yes Madam India, I'll call Mr. and Ms. Smith."

I chuckled because the 'Mr. and Mrs. Smith' she was referring to wasn't white or TV stars. Well in a way they were famous, my father was Head Trauma Surgeon at General Hospital and my mother was a translator for the House of Representatives in the state of California. I'm sure you've seen an assembly, sitting around a large round table with microphones and headsets, discussing economic issues and politics. That was her job. She serves as the primary translator for various countries, she speaks french fluently from her creole background. She is one of those French black people with the 'good hair' and colored eyes, we didn't fall too far from the tree.

My sister Asia and I often got compared to the Fresh Prince of Bel Air's wife, the petite cutie from Jason's Lyric. We were always complimented for our celebrity look-a-like's. People asks us are we related to such and such and we would lie and say yes. Especially with Jada, I guess it was because we're caramel complexion with hazel eyes. But we didn't see any harm in it, why not lie and say you're related to a celebrity, we all wanted to be one growing up. Being a celebrity was a privilege.

Now, it was my chance to shine but not in the positive light. This form of celebrity status I was about to receive was spreading across newspapers, newsstands, and on TV as breaking news:

"Famous power couple, well respected surgeon Dr. Smith and wife, California House of Representatives Ms. Smith, daughter India Smith was taken into custody by Federal agents for what's assumed to be several millions of dollars in identity theft, bank fraud and robbery, with crimes suspected as far as across fifty states. The twenty-four year old India Smith graduated from Stanford University with a business degree. Her parents are very prominent and well respected in the community. Today, she's being arraigned in federal court with a bail set at five million dollars. They say the accused has robbed over 250 banks worldwide and stolen hundreds of identities. Stay tuned for future updates."

Wow, now I'm really a celebrity per say. But if only what they were suggesting were true. Because it's not. Don't believe the hype. It wasn't until the feds took me down to some high rise building, directed me to sit in some worn seat and asked me if I want something to eat and drink, that it finally hit me. I was caught the hell up.

If the feds came knocking at your door it wasn't to say that you've just won the Publisher Sweepstakes. You know the commercial where they come sneaking up to white people's houses with balloons and cameras everywhere with a gigantic check in hand. Well, that's not them sorry. I sat there listening to the questions but couldn't believe I was really there. It was like having a outer body experience. I know I watch this stuff on TV like Law and Order, the First 24 or 48 and shit like that but this was really happening to my black ass. I was being interrogated by two white male cops in a small stuffy room with a glass window, with two more officers probably standing behind it, waiting for me to sing like Mahalia Jackson, the famous Gospel singer. 'Hit the high notes baby!' is what they wanted to say, 'crack the glass just sing us something good.' They even had the audacity to play good cop, bad cop like I haven't seen that episode before. When it was finally my turn to speak I asked the million dollar question.

"What do the feds want with me? I'm nobody actually. Why were y'all even wasting your time? Y'all went after big time drug dealers and high profile murders and shit like that. Why waste your time with lil ole me? If anything, I'm just a misdemeanor, maybe a felony charge but not really even that. The shit I've done, and I'm speaking past tense with emphasis on past tense, was nothing. Not enough for the feds radar unless y'all are helping the local police out for extra pay or something because nothing else is popping off exciting these days in the Federal Bureau."

They laughed at me hysterically, "Oh you got jokes!" the bad cop says.

"Nooo I'm very serious," I retort.

"We'll to give it to you frankly Ms. Smith, we know you're not the big fish but you know who is and whoever the fuck you work for, pardon our French maybe that's not a good way of wording it. Whoever your partner in crime is, whoever your associates are, we need to know their names and exactly where you're getting these profiles from."

Now I see why they wanted to talk to me. They think I know something about this so called identity theft ring that's going around tearing shit up, hitting the banks, and jewelry stores while using other people's identity to do it with. But I have news for them, well maybe I don't have news for them but I'm not as dumb as I may look sometimes, maybe that's an understatement as well. Intentionally, I decided to utilize my higher education etiquette on their asses.

"Pardon me, federal agent sir. I would like to exercise my constitutional right to have my attorney present before answering anymore questions," I said, adding a hint of sarcasm to my comment. Their white stoic faces turned beat red. I had one up on them or so I thought anyways.

"May I have my one phone call please?" They both looked at me with disgust, walked out, and left me sitting there for hours. Finally, my attorney arrived and they moved me to another room. I suppose they have certain rooms for different shit. I know it's illegal to record my conversation with my attorney so maybe that is what prompted the move.

My attorney sat there writing notes, he said the officers wanted me to 'cooperate with them and things could go away quietly', which means they wanted me to snitch. As he prepared himself to speak to me, I just looked at him with a I-don't-know-what-you're-talking-about expression before I responded,

"HELL NO!" screaming.

He agreed, but had obligation to inform me however he didn't have too much more to say until he went through with the investigation that the feds had presented him with. He promised to be in contact with me in a couple days and told me to 'hang in there' until then.

I felt a little bit of relief for some apparent reason, why I'm not sure. I just wanted to lie down, I was exhausted from last night and today's events. I know everything happens for a reason, sometimes it just takes a while to figure things out. It will come to pass. God has a divine purpose for all. Sometimes people tap into their calling and some never do. But it's not because it was never there, some of us just don't know how to navigate ourselves to our destiny. I drifted in and out of reflective thoughts while being moved into my temporary new home at the federal building, in a 5x7 cell, locked behind a glass door. I sat on the top bunk and began to reminisce about my life. I wanted to go to sleep but my mind kept telling me no. And not the song either. I guess I felt overwhelmed with guilt, shame, the unknown, fear, embarrassment and all of these emotions from a-z going into overdrive. Taking me on a little ride.

A roller coaster if you will. *Fasten your seatbelt and hold on tight because this may be a bumpy ride from here on out.* God was punishing me and I kind of laughed to myself at the thought. And God laughed back a little louder. I was placed in a two man cell with a woman who talked to herself in her sleep, kept passing gas through out the night and slept naked to top it all off.

I laid on my bunk, lying on my back and went back in time to when this crazy life of mines began. Well, I didn't go as far back as to being an infant or anything like that but as far as I could remember. I remember sitting between my mama's legs, getting my hair combed and crying.

"Ouch mama that hurts!" I yelled as the comb raked through my scalp.

"Be quiet girl and get this hair done so I can get to your sisters who's over there playing in my makeup - ASIA! Get out my makeup bag and wipe off that lipstick and come over here and wait your turn."

Ignoring Mama as usual, Asia was the stubborn twin who never listened from day one. She was the oldest, born three whole minutes before I came and those three minutes mattered to her believe me. 'I'm the big sister, not you! Now listen to what I say or else!', she would say, as if she was three years older rather than minutes.

"Momma just give me two ponytails please, that hurts!" I said. But before I could stir any pity I was gently hit on my head with the brush, which meant to be quiet or else. She would comb our hair on Sunday mornings before church and we would keep it up normally for a week because Momma had to go out of town pretty often and Maria, our housekeeper, didn't speak the best English back then but she knew how to get paid every week.

Ever since I was a little girl, I hated anyone who would come near my head but Asia was a different story altogether. On Monday's when Momma was on a plane off to wherever she was going this time, Asia always took out her two or three ponytails and let her hair down, literally.

She would say, "India."

"Yes, Asia?" I would reply, half asleep before breakfast.

"You want me to comb your hair and put some makeup on you so you can be pretty for school?"

"No," I replied every day, "and Mommie said to stay out of her makeup. Daddy is going to punish you Asia."

"No he's not. He has gone to work, only Maria is here and

she doesn't talk like we do."

Our daddy was always gone to work before we left for school most days and Maria hadn't learned to speak English well enough yet.

"Why do you always play in Mommie's things all the time? Daddy says that's her personal stuff?" I questioned.

Her reply was always, "I don't know what personal stuff is!" and she would stick her tongue out at me.

We were only about six or seven years old but Asia knew she was something else, even back then. Exploring the playground of our mother's make up became her ritual every day and she became good at it too. In slumber we were two twin girls, when we arose, one would emerge with a little eye shadow and pink lipstick to compliment her long curly hair that hung down her back. But me, I faithfully wore my two or three ponytails until Momma came back home.

Plus our daddy wasn't big on discipline, he left that part up to our mother. But he would sit us down and say, 'Babies remember to carry yourselves like little women, mind your manners and respect all adults.' I guess that's what Asia was doing, being a little lady. No one could really fault her because that's what we heard on a daily basis before he kissed us and said he loved us both. Every child has their own way of interpreting what the world feeds them and how they absorb their environment. This would explain Asia and I, the similarities and dichotomy of the two personality differences.

I admired my father, I knew he was an important man, he would always have a dress shirt with a tie, dress pants and a white lab coat with his name 'Dr. Smith' on it. He also had a pager, I didn't know what it was at the time but I knew when it went off that daddy had to leave in a hurry. Even if it was when Miss Maria and him were in my parents bed wrestling. If we were downstairs and it went off, I would run upstairs and open the door without knocking, the one thing he told us to always do.

"Please India and Asia, always knock on a door before entering, it's called courtesy and respect," he would say.

"Ok Daddy," we would say at the same time like we rehearsed it. But we were used to doing everything together so I guess it came natural.

One time I burst into my parents room, "Daddy, Daddy the machine is going off on your jacket you have to go to the hospital!" I said excitedly.

"Thank you sweetie," and kissed my forehead, "but what did daddy tell you about knocking on the door first India?"

"Ok Daddy, I'll remember next time I promise," I said. I knew my daddy was fucking Miss Maria back then, I don't care what anyone says.

"You're a child India you really didn't see that or hear that." Daddy would say, "I'm showing Maria how to make up a bed sweetie."

And I would respond, "She makes me and Asia's beds up nicely daddy but I guess because you and mommies bed is so big she needs help?" then walk away confused.

I know what I saw and heard every time my momma was gone out of town, and that was the majority of our childhood. But Daddy never complained and neither did we. Asia actually liked that Mommie was always gone, she said 'Mommie too mean to be a mommy. All of our friends parents aren't mean like Mommie. Why do we have to be in bed at 8pm and why do we have to take swimming lessons, and piano lessons? Why? Why? Why?'. I didn't mind because those things kept us busy. But Asia hated everything but shopping. That brings me to how all of these crime sprees came about.

Let's start from the very first time when we were ten years old, we stole Barbie doll clothes from the toy store. Our mom would give us ten dollars a piece to spend every week. This particular week while shopping, I had my one Barbie doll and new outfit in hand but Asia had about twelve outfits and a Ken.

I said, "You can't get all of that stuff Asia, that's more than ten dollars...I think. Mommie said we only had ten dollars to spend."

"Shut up, I know what she said India but we need all these

clothes. Barbie needs to change clothes more than once, plus her closet needs to look like ours to make her real. And she needs to have a husband like Mommie."

Although I approached this situation in pure innocence, I would soon succumb to her overbearing rationale, "I already picked out my stuff and I'm not giving you my ten dollars."

"No India we can put these in our backpacks and nobody will know."

I didn't want to do it but me being so naïve and Asia being the big sister, I agreed. She put them in my backpack and we left the store after paying ten dollars for the barbie's.

When we got home with our scandalous souvenirs, our mom wanted to see what we purchased this week. She knew we didn't have enough money for all the new stuff we mistakenly showed her. In hindsight, we had more toys than the average child but our mom was no fool. Like most kids, you put away the old and play with the new. So she knew what we already had, therefore, we couldn't fool her and she knew we hadn't paid for everything. She made us take everything back to the store, apologize to the department, and donate our old toys to charity. She said we 'would learn to appreciate the benefits of being two spoiled brats who had to have whatever we wanted, even if it meant stealing it'. I was livid with Asia and didn't speak to her for a few days. But I couldn't stay mad at her for too long, after all, she was my twin sister.

My mom would reiterate over and over again, 'you two are bonded together for life'. And she wasn't lying either. My sister was the chosen one for many things, whether it was in fashion or men, but none of us would have guessed that she would chose our career path also. The career path that has me sitting in this jail cell, reminiscing. They say, 'choose a career you love and you'll love to do the job and do it effectively'. I swear we truly loved our jobs, per say, but I guess we could have been more diligent on the 'effective' part.

Everybody loves to shop at the expense of someone else and

that's what we did for a living. And we were good at it for almost four years. Our job was called 'Identity Theft LLC.' We sponsored trips to the banks, malls, car dealerships, and jewelry stores, all assuming someone else's identity. Who says that crime doesn't pay?

And how is it a crime when you get away with it? It's all insured anyway. No one gets hurt in the process, so where's the crime at? And we've never gotten caught impersonating someone, nor did it affect them personally considering the people whose identity we used didn't have a clue at the time that we were using their names and credit. Sometimes they didn't find out for months and by that time we were on to the next, the next state and next store with a new identity, mission accomplished. We would even fly to our destination of choice. It was different locations every time so with our skills we've been all over the world, basically in someone else's name, with our fake I.D.s. So technically, India and Asia Smith were never there. So if anything did jump off, we would be under the identity of our victims and not ourselves. So who was to validate that we weren't that person? Fortunately for us, we've never encountered any mishaps. Because they say, the more you practice the better you become, and we had plenty of practice. Both of us had performed thousands of identity theft schemes over the past four years. Thinking back, I would say we were damn good at what we did for a living. We could be considered an expert in that field. Well, up until now. Every good thing comes to an end right? Don't believe the hype.

2

MEET THE PARENTS

Carliess François Smith

After Maria called our suite in Europe and told us the whole story about India, I just couldn't sleep. We weren't able to get a flight home until tomorrow morning, so I was up and sitting in our hotel restless.

"Honey, I'm about to take a shower and lie down because we have an early flight in the morning and a long flight back home," looking distraught.

"Ok, Robert" is all I could say at this point.

It's not like we had long conversations anymore. Our marriage was simply for convenience now with no love loss, it just wasn't there for us anymore I suppose. To keep our 'happily married' appearance in tact, we always attend public functions together, like fundraisers and events. You know how some celebrity couples will be separated for years but never divorce and when you do read about it you always say you 'couldn't tell that anything was wrong'. They say it's cheaper to keep her. I wouldn't say I agree with that statement but I guess it depends on how much of your dignity your willing to sacrifice to keep a good reputation.

I looked out the window on the 18th floor penthouse suite with my thigh resting on the marble finishings, it was dark outside with little to no lights on in the city, reminded me of how I felt inside. You haven't seen the power of a mother until something happens with one of her offspring. Yet in the midst of the darkness, it was still peaceful here. I wish I could close my eyes and wake up and this would all just go away. But that wouldn't be reality now would it. Or the real damn world, so to speak. I heard the shower turning off as the water ceased making rhythms against the floor so I knew Robert will be out soon. *I better run downstairs to the bar before it closes because this is going to be a very long night.*

I closed the double doors behind me, the hallways were empty and quiet. But what else should I expect at 11pm in Europe? I guess my skeletons are finally starting to haunt me after all. While taking the glass elevator down to the lobby that led to the bar, I couldn't help but think of the inevitable so I took a deep breath to calm my nerves before this alcohol did the job, *my girls are going to be the death of me.*

"Louis the 13th, please," I tell the bartender while sitting down. It's my second favorite drink besides the Jewel of Pangea, which is only available in Singapore and puts you back about 26,000 in the local currency which is the equivalent of approximately 19K a bottle. But I swear it's worth every sip, it's exclusively for the rich and famous. This high priced concoction includes: gold flaked Hennessey 1985 Vintage, Krug champagne and sugar garnished with triplex 1 carat diamond. Absolutely amazing. I looked around at the place only to realize it was empty tonight besides myself and two older gentlemen sitting at the velvet seating booth. The music was nice however and very soothing. The bartender returned with my drink, he smiled and looked at me in the eyes. I smiled back. I got that a lot from men, always have. To be truthful, my eyes were my secret weapon. They had the power to hypnotize you the moment you looked at me. At first, I didn't know how to utilize them to my benefit but now I've become a dangerous weapon to be reckon with. I'm forty-eight years young but I can say with confidence that I don't look a day over thirty-five. I'm the exact color of honey with just the right amount of sweetness.

I consider myself short. I'm 5'4 but with stilettos, I stand at a perfect 5'6 with 36D set of twins and I'm not referring to my daughter's. I wear a size eight in clothing, but that depends on whether the designer is European or American made but that was only after I hit my forties because I wore a size six in clothes and shoes my whole entire life. Adding to my physical allure, when people looked at me most of them couldn't tell my nationality, especially because I have bone straight hair that reached my buttock like women from Asia. I've never had it cut, only trimmed and I have grey eyes like a cat. I am representative Carliess François Smith. I grew up in New Orleans, where all the women spitefully called me 'Care-Less' because I could care less about anyone's feelings but my own. But my name is pronounced Care-e-liss.

The two men in the velvet booth kept looking in my direction and waved at random times whenever they caught my glance. *They must be good and drunk by now.* I wave back and smile. *Such kid games, but hey, it could be worse, hell it is worse,* my mind drifted back to India. I asked the bartender for one more drink before I headed back upstairs and tried to figure this situation out about my daughter. I knew my girls were doomed from the womb. It's an inherited circumstance passed down from generation to generation. My mother had three daughters and my grandmother had two daughters and I have two daughters and we all have these colored eyes that got us into trouble, usually with men. We can normally get whatever we want without even saying a word. We let the eyes do the talking for us. People say our eyes does voodoo on men, their greatest pleasure and cryptonite.

They say women from the south had the power to do that shit. Maybe there was some truth to that, who knows but what I did know is that the women in my family were very driven, determined, intelligent, sexy and persistent creatures who were going to get exactly what we wanted by any means necessary. No questioned asked. I shook my head at the thought. So funny, but true. After finishing my last drink, I paid the bartender two hundred for my two drinks and tipped him one hundred dollars for his service.

He replies, "No ma'am, your drinks have been paid for by the two gentlemen sitting over there at the booth," he pointed to the booth on my right with a smirk on his face like the men he targeted with the tip of his finger.

"Oh is that so," I replied. "Well please be so kind and tell the gentlemen I never let a man pay for my drinks unless I plan on taking him to bed. But if you like, you can keep the money for being the messenger," I winked against his melting smirk and excused myself from the bar. That was rule number two that was taught to me as a young girl. My mother would always say, 'Never let a man buy you a drink while you're out socially, because at the end of the night, he will expect something in return. Always go out with your own money so you can enjoy yourself without any worries. If you choose to allow a man to buy you a drink without buying you a meal, be prepared to repay that man. Because he's not going to take 'no' for an answer, even if he only wants a phone number with hopes that eventually he'll take you to bed'. And the lessons didn't stop there, she was generous with her feminine wisdom as my older sisters and I grew into womanhood.

My mom would also say that, 'It's better to have your own money and make your own rules, don't be needy in any areas in life, especially when it comes to a man'. If she had a preference, she would put her all into rule number #1, numero uno. 'Always let a man want and care about you more than you do them. And if you have to second guess if a man loves you then he probably doesn't'. And how would I know that? I'll give you an example. I met my husband over twenty years ago while college interning in Washington, DC. He went to Howard University there. I was interning at the assembly building where votes are vetoed, a summer program for students majoring in politics. See early on I knew that politics is where I wanted to be. All the major players were there, including the President of the United States. It doesn't get any better than that. But most young women my age at the time wanted basketball players, football players etc. Which is ok if that's what you're into but I wanted a real 'shot caller' type of man. The one that makes sure that the ball players' checks are being printed and paying their taxes at the end of the year. A head-honcho-shot-calling type of man. This type of man maneuvered amongst giants with the title to match - Congress, Mayors, and the men that can shut the lights out over the city or hold court in the streets, start wars, declare the country was bankrupt or send billions to refuges. That type of power in a man is what I wanted and I knew exactly how to get it, hands down. But I didn't marry my 'type', per say, because I didn't have to.

But the moral of the story is I met my husband at a local bar one Saturday night while sitting at a table laughing and talking with a few other lady interns. We were just enjoying ourselves when a group of young men asked if they could join us. There were only two available seats at our table but three prowling bachelors. My future husband decided to let his two friends sit down while he stood there like the perfect gentleman that he is. He was a very nice looking man and very chocolate with a round face, stocky like a football player, about 6'1 wearing a baseball cap. I couldn't tell if he had nice hair underneath but it didn't matter. He was extremely handsome and polite. I didn't give him too much attention, we barely had a conversation outside of what was discussed amongst the group - what school we attended, our major and things of that sort. But what got my attention was the other two men who kept looking at me while talking with lust filled eyes but Robert's eyes were all over the room, observing of the environment respectfully. And when he did say something to me, I had his undivided attention with no lust in his eyes at all. We talked as a group for awhile and said our goodbyes and ironically enough, no one even exchanged phone numbers. I didn't see the man who would be my future husband until three years later after that and honestly, I didn't remember him at all.

We met again after three full orbits around the sun in the emergency room at the county hospital in Atlanta, Georgia. Robert was a resident doctor and as fate would have it, the doctor who was treating me that day.

He asked, "So what brings you in the emergency tonight Ms. François?"

"I haven't been able to sleep for three nights straight, I've been having pain in my lower back. So I need something to help me sleep please," I said while looking at the stethoscope resting on his wide chest.

He said, "You don't remember me do you?"

I met his eyes, "Excuse me? Should I? Have we met before?"

"Yes," he replied, "a few years back , that's probably why you don't remember."

I sat briefly with my thoughts and ran my rolodex, *did he go to school with me? No. I think I would remember his face. Is he one of my sisters friends? Or one of my girlfriends friends? I wonder who he is.*

He laughed at my lack of memory and ordered some lab work before he said, "I'm sending you to have a x-ray and when you're done with everything they'll bring you back to the exam room."

"Ok," I said but that was all I could muster because I couldn't remember who he was if I tried, I was in so much pain.

After finishing my x-ray and other medical examinations, I returned to the exam room and Robert came in shortly after.

"Still don't remember me huh?" he asked, laughing.

'Stop antagonizing me' is what I wanted to say but I was still in too much damn pain. Instead I said, "No and what's wrong with me? And can I please have some pain medication?"

He laughed and said, "Yes. Actually, we're keeping you for a couple of days, the pain you are experiencing is a tubal pregnancy and you need to have surgery to terminate it, I'm sorry."

I laughed, *he has to be joking, I'm not pregnant!* His facial expression was without humor and now I had to digest the circumstances. Well after it sank in, "The fact that I am pregnant by that asshole Frankie who happens to be my boss and who happens to be very married." I said mistakenly, I thought I was just thinking it but it actually came out of my mouth. *Oh shit, he must be thinking I'm a slut or some type of home wrecker or worse.*

"Can you give me something to knock me out please? I don't want to feel this pain or anything else at the moment."

He looked at me strangely but didn't say a word on the subject, "You're scheduled for surgery in the morning, I'll order you something to sleep and I'll check on you again after your procedure," he said professionally and closed with "goodnight," before walking out.

Where did I know him from? I asked myself but at this point it didn't even matter. Following my surgery and recovery, it was time to go home after two days in the hospital. My sister came to pick me up and while I was getting dressed and ready to go, the mystery doctor came to check on me.

"I hope you are feeling better and take care of yourself Miss François."

"Again, thank you for everything doctor and this is my sister Lita," I said without breaking eye contact.

"Hello Ms. Lita pleasure to meet your acquaintance," extending a hand, "are you two twins?" he asked.

"We hear that all the time," laughing.

"No, I'm a few years older but thanks," Lita replied.

Shaking her hand again, "Can you please pick up your sisters medication on your way out."

"Yes, which way is it?" she asked.

"I'll escort you there," he said and waved bye to me as they both walked out.

Once we got home and settled in, Lita made us some hot tea fresh off the stove before girl talk began.

"Your doctor friend said he met you in D.C. at a bar one weekend while you were interning for the assembly," she said before cautiously sipping the steaming herbs, cuddled into the couch across from me, "but he said you didn't remember him but he never forgotten about you."

I sat there trying to remember and when I did, I laughed in disbelief because he really didn't seem that interested in me at the time. However, present day, after three long years - he finally mustered the courage to exchange phone numbers. Well, not exactly. The doctor gave Lita his phone number for me and said when I was feeling better 'to give him a call and if not, no worries'. So after a couple of days of resting, I decided to call the doctor.

"Hello Dr."

"Oh. What's up Ms. François, how are you feeling?"

The baritone in his voice over the phone was the only remedy I needed, he could have done away with medical school and just used his voice for prescriptions, "Much better today thanks for asking Dr."

"So Ms. François do you remember me now or do you still have amnesia?" he said, laughing, "I wanted to talk to you that night at the bar but I didn't know what to say. I felt like it was love at first sight whatever that feels like," he laughed again but this time I joined him.

He continued, "You know when I got offered residency in Atlanta, I prayed I would see you again. I didn't know how to contact you but remembered that you said you went to school in Atlanta, so I knew my chances were good. I also knew that it was a long shot but I gave it a try anyway. Plus the opportunity at this hospital was excellent, but who knew we would meet again and under these circumstances?"

After the small talk and a few more laughs, I told the Dr. that it 'was over before it even started', referring to the guy I was pregnant with, and the rest was history. Twenty something years later, we're in Europe waiting to go see about our daughter.

To reiterate, the moral of the story is, as my mother would recite while applying her lipstick, "Rule number one always applies. Let a man love you more, first and foremost and I can guarantee you longevity." I sighed at the memory of her voice and accuracy of her proverb, and walked into our suite, snapping me out of my revive.

As always the good Dr. was resting peacefully as I peeked in the bedroom. *I'm glad someone can sleep*, I walked into the living room and sat on the sofa. Memory lane must have been full of traffic today because I started to reminisce a bit more, looking over my life.

Time passes by so quickly, my girls were the cutest little things as young children - caramel complexion with long curly hair, one with hazel eyes and the other with green, built with skinny frames until puberty hit. They were so well mannered and I loved to show them off. Everyone would say, 'Why don't you put them into modeling, they are so cute?' I would say, 'Thank you' but I really wanted to say 'Hell no!' I didn't want to make that type of decision for them or force my girls into doing something that they didn't want to do. That's child labor in my eyes and to add insult to injury, they would have to travel all over the world with perverts drooling over their innocents. Also, there's not a lot of little black girls modeling in the business, mostly white, except for a chosen few. I heard it was a real racist profession to be in and I simply wanted them to choose their own destiny, that's how I was raised. If that's what they wanted, they would have to choose that on their own. Plus, my mother hated models, especially the white ones. All she would ever say was, 'How did she become a model? My girls look ten times better than they do. She's too damn skinny anyways, they need to eat some southern food.' I laughed at the memory. My mother sure had a way with words. My poor daddy, Rest In Peace, never had a chance.

The more I've matured into my own woman, I reminded myself of my mom - same mirror, different generation. My poor husband didn't even see it coming. Since we've been married, I've slept with hundreds of men to get where I am today. My pheromones have mixed with foreign cologne that seeped off judges, mayors, governors, politicians of all kinds, and shit I could have slept with our last president if I wanted to. He loved everything about me from the moment we met.

I was presented with the opportunity to meet the head of state at a private dinner for Congress, while shaking my hand, I noticed he held his grip just a little too long, staring right into my eyes.

"It's a pleasure to finally meet you Mr. President, my name is Carliess Smith, I will be translating for the French Embassy at the meeting tonight," I glanced a smile along with my brief elevator pitch in an attempt to redirect his attention to the moment.

He couldn't even respond. He just shook his head in astonishment. After the meeting, he arranged for me and a few others to go out for a night cap. He eventually loosened up after a couple drinks, shedding his presidential ego and with his inhibitions weakening, he couldn't keep his eyes off me. He was looking at me with a lack of discretion, like he could have made love to me right there in that room. His energy was so strong I probably would have given into him if he so desired but he had gotten himself so intoxicated that secret service took him to his hotel suite. And we didn't see much of each other after that other than on occasion, at meetings and a few functions where he would always ask me to address him in French. He said it was an attractive and intelligent skill to be bilingual. Catering to his wishes, at the following meetings and events, I spoke to him in French. But that was typical for me, I was used to it. Since I began this profession, the majority of the men I've encountered wanted me to speak in French

- especially in bed, it was a turn on.

We can neglect the fact that most men can't understand the French language, they just like how it sounded coming off the tongue. Adding to my skill set, I have a remarkable tongue technique along with my fluency.

I've always had an advantage when it came to my oral capabilities. This opened the door to receive checks written by the mayor from the city's budget, luxury cars that I drove to see governors, numerous diamond rings, necklaces to thank me for my services, shopping sprees in Italy and Japan, and even a trip to Africa, which was supposed to be business not pleasure, was paid for by the diplomat of the continent. I've had a billionaire tycoon offer me my own island. Yes that's right, my own island. So to all the women chasing drug dealers, try getting one of them to buy you an island or something of real value that doesn't depreciate once it's purchased. This why I only wanted a certain type of man. I didn't want the police or DEA to be able to seize all my luxurious gifts. I like men who hustled legally and paid their taxes on time. Everything that was given to me was mine to own, to cherish. The men I chose to associate with can never be touched, this makes for a good night rest. So always choose your men wisely. There's still a lot of good, hardworking men out there with benefits. I've tried to instill this concept of a mate in my girls. This is why I was gone a lot while they were growing up, trying to secure their future. It was hard climbing up the professional ladder. It took a lot of dinners and French lessons, if you know what I mean, to get where I'm at today. Being beautiful gets you through the door but what you can accomplish will ultimately keep you there.

I've accomplished a lot over the years. My girls have always gone to the best schools, education is the key. They've always been involved in sports, took swimming and piano lessons, and all the extra curriculum activities that money can buy. With flourishing careers and salaries, my husband and I were far from broke, some even considered us well off. There were trials and sacrifices to be made but we made it, even with having children young, paying off school tuition and books, and having enough expendable income for our chauffeur. My girls needed a means of transportation because me my husband and I were gone most mornings before school started and not home when it ended. Plus our careers were really taking off and becoming more time consuming, so we arranged to have a live in nanny, a housekeeper and a chef. My husband traveled to medical conferences and I traveled for work and my other work.

Over time we had to understand the depth sacrifices. However, it seemed like I'm learning that now more than ever. Especially since the feds came and ran through my house like a welcomed guest and arrested my daughter. It was time for me to stop concentrating on myself and my career and be there for my girls. A mother has to give up some things and I should have learned that a while ago. I yawned, and took a glance my Cartier watch. It was almost three in the morning, I've been practically reminiscing all night. *I guess sometimes cleaning the mind is good for the soul.* I silenced the running thoughts before I fell asleep on the sofa, drifting to a more peaceful realm.

3

GETTING OFF THE HOOK

Asia Smith

"Where the hell is India's ass at? Her fucking plane landed almost an hour ago," I said, sighing from frustration. Kelly sat in the passenger seat, she wasn't tripping nor paying me any attention, glued to her phone.

"Her plane landed almost an hour ago," I repeated with no response from Kelly yet again. Looking over at her, "Hello I could have come by myself," I said with a little more bass in my voice. She looked up briefly and laughed.

"I'm tired of circling this stupid airport."

"Maybe her flight was delayed. You know that happens a lot," Kelly said, finally speaking.

"Oh you can speak," I said sarcastically, "I know that's a possibility but did you have to say it and jinx us bitch?" I sighed heavily again, as if the air could some how cool my temperament.

'SUPER FREAK, THAT GIRL'S A SUPER FREAK'

"Asia is that your ring tone?" Kelly asked, "you ain't cool!" laughing.

"Hello? Where you at India? I've been circling this airport for what feels like hours...ok here we come," I said, hanging up.

"Your sister finally made it huh?"

I looked at Kellie like she was crazy, "Why do you ask rhetorical questions all the time?" shaking my head, "never mind please don't answer." I couldn't believe this girl was in college sometimes.

"The airport is packed. I'm glad I filled up before picking her ass up."

"You think a lot of people flew in for the celebrity A-town party?" Kellie asked.

"I don't know but I sure hope so. I know that's India's reason for flying in with her slow motherfucking ass.

HONK, HONK! I waved my hands out the window at India.

"Over here!" I screamed, yelling out the car. She was finally here and standing on the curb in her travel attire, looking all cute. *This girl really came to party in the ATL. It's going down this weekend.* I smiled at the thought.

She walked up to the car and climbed in the back seat, "Hey there big sis! What's good?" smiling.

"Shit, glad to finally see you," I smiled too, "You finally made it. Where are all your bags at?" I asked.

"I only brought these two, we're going shopping, I thought," India said, looking perplexed.

"Of course we are," I glanced back at my twin sister in the rearview mirror, she looked good. *She must not be stressed about school like I am.*

"You're cute heifer!" winking back at India, "are you hungry?"

"What you think they served me some filet mignon on the plane or something," she said sarcastically and we all joined in laughter.

"Your sweatsuit is hella cute India!"

"Thanks. You know I have to fly comfortable, I even have on my Chanel flip flops," she kicked her feet up for show and tell but I could barely see while driving.

India reached up, touching Kellie's shoulder in the passenger's seat, "Hi girlie, sorry for being so rude and not saying hello. How are you?"

"I'm straight India and that sweatsuit is hella cute."

"Awe thank you girl, but we should thank Bloomingdales and most importantly, thank my parents," India joked, spreading more laughter around the car.

"India you're too much!"

"Ok, ok I'm starving though. Asia where are we going to eat at?"

"You want to order some soul food," I asked, looking in my rear view again.

"Sure, why not?"

"Mom and Dad says 'Hello' and they send their love."

"Did they send you their credit card also?"

India laughed, "Didn't you get money deposited into your account this month Asia?" solemnly speaking.

"Yes Ms. India, I did. But hell after my car note, insurance, food, gas, clothes, parties and shit, it's never enough," laughing.

India Smith

"No one told you to get a stupid ass car note anyways. What was wrong with your Lexus Asia?"

She opted to be sarcastic, "Nothing."

"Mine still runs fine and looks brand new. Shit our cars were brand new when we got them. It's only been two years," shaking my head. Kellie started laughing.

"What's so damn funny?" Asia asks looking at Kellie, "I wanted a different car alright," she was getting a bit agitated.

"I told mom from the beginning that I wanted an Infiniti truck or a Mercedes CLK550 but no she didn't listen. So now I have what I always wanted...my Mercedes." she smiled, looking content.

"And now...you have a car note." I said teasingly.

"Stop all your complaining," Kellie chimed in, "well I can tell both you rich bitches, India and Asia, y'all should be grateful for getting a car for graduation. Shit my grandmother couldn't afford to buy one for herself, let alone three bastard kids that her stupid ass daughter left her stuck with." solemnly speaking.

Kellie continued, "And I'm the first person in my family to even graduate high school and go to college. So it's a blessing to have parents, especially two parents who love and support you," she started sounding serious.

"Kellie you just preached a sermon but you're absolutely right. But that's not me always complaining, that's Asia's nothing-is-never-enough ass," I shot her a look, rolling my eyes.

"Fuck both you bitches," Asia said before turning the music up loud. We rode the rest of the way engaged in our own thoughts until we reached the restaurant.

When we arrived at the soul food spot, Asia was tasked with pulling her car into the tightest parking space because the place was packed. She was damn near about to give me claustrophobia.

"Asia let me out before you park and scrape the shit out of this Hummer and Range Rover you're trying to fit between."

Before she pulled all the way in, I opened up the back door and jumped out. *This bitch is nerve wracking, it's going to be a long weekend*, shaking my head.

Kellie walked up to me and put her arm around my shoulders before whispering in my ear, "It's going to be alright lil sis, you know how she's a straight bitch," laughing. I started laughing too. Asia just rolled her eyes and walked right passed us like she didn't know who we were. Once we were inside, we saw how the place was filled to the max but we knew that from the looks of the parking lot.

"It's hot as hell in the A," I said, making conversation while waiting for our seats.

Smart-mouth Asia who always had something to say interjected, "I told you that on the phone the other day. But no, you never listen."

I can't with this bitch. I started looking around the place with an observant eye, it was packed with mad black folks and it wasn't even two in the afternoon yet. It's quite interesting how we are still drawn to what was originally food created solely for survival and a lack of resources, yet our ancestors were inventive and essentially created their own cuisine that exist in our generation and I'm sure for generations to come. Ironically enough, we were still in the south and the south has a past of its own.

"I hope we don't have to wait long," I said.

"I know," Kellie responds, "but this is my type of spot," she said, winking.

I wink back, "Mine too," and we both burst out laughing in unison. There was a fine ass dude that spotted Kellie and said 'what's up' with a head nod. Kellie waved back and he gestured for her to come his way.

"I'll be right back," she said before getting up and going to see what's up with ol' boy. Ten minutes later, the waitress was able to seat us.

"Good we get a booth with a window view," I said while sitting down, bouncing against the cushion to the far left corner of the table. Before the waitress returned to take our order, Kellie walked up smiling like she just found her prince charming or something better.

"What are you smiling about?" I asked.

Before she could even sit down, Kellie started singing, "We got tickets! We got tickets!"

"Oh," I said, not really understanding what the fuck she was talking about, "tickets to what?" She handed us each a ticket that read, 'Entry Ticket for the Celebrity VIP Party'.

"These are VIP tickets," Kellie was still smiling from ear-to-ear, "to the big motherfuckin' event tomorrow night, we in the house! It's going to be off the hook and we are too!" she looked at each of us enticingly and continued.

"My brother's friend, Big Mike, knows all the celebrities in the ATL and he has access to get tickets for all the major parties as a perk."

"Sooo why are you just now saying something about Big Mike?" Asia asked, sounding a little upset, "We should have been getting at him from day one!"

"Asia I didn't know until now!" Kellie said, her face giving an expression like 'hold up bitch who you talking to like that'.

"When he called me to the table, that's what he wanted to talk about. I haven't seen him in a while. He's my other brother's friend from the block. But anyways he said 'Who are those two baddies you with?' I told him who y'all were and he said 'They top notch, I'm giving you these tickets because it's going to be a few niggas with some real dough in the building and maybe you can hook a nigga up with one of them with their fine asses!'. I told him, I'll see what I can do and thanks for the tickets,' and walked away, laughing with the tickets in hand."

Asia's flame dwindled and she was now fired in, Kellie continued ever so confidently, "He will probably offer to buy all of our drinks tomorrow night," winking to seal the deal.

"You ladies ready to order?" the waitress asked. We all knew exactly what we wanted, we were no strangers to this.

Even though we're considered small framed, we could eat, certified foodies. Asia and I were both only 5'1" with caramel complexion, a full set of 36C breasts, and we wore a size four in clothes and six shoe like our mom. Lately, Asia was wearing her hair bone straight and it has grown long past her shoulders. And I was rocking my natural curls, which also past my shoulders that bounced with the wind. We were, as my girls would say, 'slim thick wit' yo cute ass', but we were also greedy like teenage boys. Since little girls, we loved to eat. Kellie could eat also and had a sexy physique. She was big boned and very curvy because she carried all of her weight in her ass. She was a beautiful girl with a short, classy haircut. She was also caramel complexion, just a tad bit darker than us with big, pretty eyes and a round face. She was a true 'southern gal' as they would say, which essentially meant she was thick. She stood around 5'6" and weighed about 150 lbs-ish. She wore a size nine in clothing and her ass could sit a cup on it easily. She kept niggas with their tongues hanging out their mouths.

With this combination of women, to see the three of us coming would feel like time stopped, frozen in our coaxing beauty. We were familiar with men of all spectrums drooling over us like we were celebrities, pointing, catcalling and the like. Even when they were with their women, our beauty invoked they boldness and many would get hit upside their heads or cursed out. Asia would always say, 'There's a lot of beautiful women in the world but I guess they just know we're the women with the good pussy,' sarcastically yet egotistically. And we would all just bust out laughing. 'Amen!' I would say, 'and I second that emotion' was Kellie's line.

While finishing our food, the itis creeped in like a thief in the night and I started feeling hella sleepy. I was full and jet lagged, the fatigue on my body was no joke.

"What's planned for tonight Asia?" I asked.

"I don't know lil sis, I was planning on getting into something indefinitely, what's good? You hangin' tonight?"

Knowing damn well I wasn't, I always felt sleepy after a flight, "I need a power nap."

Asia and Kellie both looked at me crazy. "Don't start that tired bullshit again India, that's all you ever do is want to sleep when you get here bitch."

"You didn't fly all this way to go to sleep did you?" Kellie asked.

"No. I just need about 30 minutes, that's all," I said persuasively, laughing at my own attempt.

"Humph!" Asia grunted.

"Well, we definitely have to make it to the mall tomorrow morning. No matter how tired, I'm not missing the party. I planned on meeting me a live one, no holds barred. I'm literally going to let my hair down." The waitress stopped by the table, dropping off the tab, "Oh, I got this," I announce as I pay the bill.

"Thanks girl."

"Yeah, thank you sis," they both replied.

"You two lovely ladies are welcome, now please drop me off, I'm tired," I say humorously but dead serious.

Asia flew home like she was driving a private jet, but ever since she passed her test at the DMV, she was a fast driver. When we finally pulled up to the spiral driveway, I smiled. This was our parents first home when they got married. They stayed in Atlanta for five years before they moved to California when our dad received an offer to be the assistant head trauma surgeon at General Hospital. Because they were both business savvy, they decided to keep the property and rent it out, which they did for years, and even had it remodeled. When Asia and I finally became of age and she decided to go to school down here, the house had been empty for a year, it was perfect timing.

Asia and Kellie were roommates, and because the house was already paid off, my parents made an arrangement that Asia would pay the utilities and use the money she received from Kellie's rent. In reality, Asia essentially didn't pay anything because my parents put money into both our accounts every month, like clock work. And even if we run low, they'll put more in if we made that call.

As I walked into the house, I remembered running up and down the stairwell as a child. Every time I came here, that memory popped up, taking me on a nostalgic trip. I headed towards my room, dropped off my bags and belly flopped on the bed as if It was going to make a huge splash. *Damn it feels good to be back,* and fell asleep in the comfort of my childhood home.

When I finally woke up it was two in the morning, I walked down the hallway to Asia's room only to find the lights off and the room empty. Kellie's room reflected the same dim vacancy. *I wonder where these heifers are at?* I couldn't take the suspense and didn't want to worry about them so I gave my sister a ring.

"Hello, where are you at? Hello, where are you Asia?" I asked but instead of her voice I heard a cacophony of noises, "It's hella loud!," I yelled, screaming into the phone.

"India, I am going to have to call you back, I can barely hear you, we're at the club," she said before hanging up.

"Figures," I uttered as I walked back to my room and ran some bath water in the tub. When the water was hot and ready, I put one foot in to test the temperature. *Perfect.* Like a personal playground, I slid myself down into the bubbles and laid my head back against the towel for comfort. *This feels good, I wonder why I don't like going out to clubs and kicking it around town like my sister.* Closing my eyes and continued with my thoughts, *maybe I'm a homebody like our dad and Ms. Asia is adventurous like our mom and always on the go. Yes! That's it, it was in our genetics,* and I concluded with that assumption. *What is vibrating? Oh, my phone*!

I laughed at my own foolishness before answering, "Hello India, I won't be coming home and neither will Kellie."

"Ok," I said, playing in the suds that rested on the bathtub's surface.

Asia added a bit more details and exclaimed, "I'm going to breakfast and Kellie left hours ago with her friend. So we will see you in the morning sis. Don't wait up!"

"Be careful Asia…" I said, firmly. It was interesting how over protective we were of loved ones when they were in our presence or in town. I was always aware of Asia's lifestyle but I never carried that mother-bear mentality when I was back home in California. I guess in person, you bear a certain amount of responsibility.

"I'm always careful India, oh and don't answer the house phone," she said, "just let it go to the answering service."

"Why would someone be calling here at this time of the morning anyway?"

"Just don't answer it, ok!" she screamed, catching me off

guard, "Goodbye," and then she hung up in my face.

These bitches are too much for me. Back to bed I go, alone, I found humor in my solitude. The next morning Asia came in with a vengeance, opening blinds and shit in my room.

"Get your ass up sleeping beauty, let's get ready to go so we can hit the mall."

I looked over at her with one eye open and the other was hanging on to the last scenes of dreamland, "What time is it?"

"It's 11:30 so hurry up. I have a hair appointment at 4 p.m. and I have to get my entire beauty treatment: eyebrows, nails, and a pedicure!"

"Ok, I'm getting up now Asia."

A fly on the wall would have thought I was the one that hung out last night. I was still tired and this tramp was up and fully dressed. Well, I wouldn't say fully dressed, she barely had any clothes on. But she was dressed and ready to go, in attire fit to face the humid battlefields of this southern city. When I finally got up and dressed, we headed to Lenox mall.

"Where's Kellie, Asia?" I asked, stepping out the car.

"Oh her friend is taking her shopping. She will meet us at the hair salon later."

"Oh," is all I could say.

"I have to go to Bloomingdale's. I saw a cute, short ass dress that I must cop for tonight. I can't wait for you to see it India! I'm going to be a fast one tonight," she winked and laughed.

"Well I want to wear some bootie shorts," I replied, laughing simultaneously.

"That's what's up," Asia replied, giving me a high five, she liked the sound of that.

Asia continued to delve out the plans for our busy day ahead while walking up to the entrance of the mall, "We have Mac appointments at 2:30 to get our faces beat," she said wiping a hint of sweat from her forehead, "but let's knock out this shopping so we won't be late."

We hit the mall like we hit the lotto. I bought the bootie shorts I wanted, plus a whole lot of other shit I didn't need and Asia bought her short ass dress from Bloomingdale's. She wasn't lying, it came just beneath her ass but it was hella cute. I bought one too but in a different color. We both purchased shoes from the Gucci store and was forced to change our Mac appointment because we were running late as usual. After our little shopping spree, we headed to the salon so Asia's hair would be laid even if we didn't make it for make up.

"Hi, Anastasia, what's up girl?" I flashed a genuine smile, I hadn't seen her in ages. Black women and their hairdressers was a best friend and savior by another name.

"Hey India, you in town I see! You came to get your groove on huh?" she asked before displaying a brief twerk.

"No doubt, I need some good old southern hospitality," we both started laughing.

"Come on Asia, let's get your hair washed," she said, waving bye to me and walking to her booth. I sat down in the waiting area and watched BET to pass the time. And then walks in Kellie, Ms. Queen Bee with hella bag like she was carrying groceries for the family reunion

"Hey India, how long have y'all been here?"

"A couple of minutes, I see you've done some shopping ma'?" flashing her a playful smirk.

"Just a lil somethin' somethin'," laughing, "this nigga wanted to spend his cheddar so I went crazy like a hungry mouse." We both joined in laughter.

"I'm going to leave my bags with you while I get my hair washed India, is that ok?"

"Yes that's fine, that way I can look through all the stuff he bought for you like it's Christmas morning," laughing.

"Go ahead, I'm already hella late for my appointment," she said before walking to the back.

"Damn," looking at her receipts, "she wasn't playing with his ass," I smiled at her accomplishments. In this day and age, with the prominent presence of matriarchy in our society, it was nice to see the woman reaping the benefits of a man, rather than the other way around. The term 'fuck these niggas' was never a reflection of hate for the king, rather a cry for help, an S.O.S, or 911 call to the gender hotlines.

Three hours and a few BET episodes later, Asia and Kellie were done. Their hair was whipped, looking like they were ready for a photo shoot with more bounce for the ounce, a head full of hair just touched by Atlanta's finest stylist in midtown. Our next stop was the nail salon and finally we headed to our appointment at the Mac studio - we were now ready to show out.

"You know how I act a fool when I have an audience," Asia said, flipping her hair dramatically from side to side, "I can't wait to get my groove on. I need to stop and get a drink!"

"Didn't y'all get your groove on last night at the club?" I asked.

"No India we went to the strip club last night, not a club-club," she shook her head, laughing.

I can't believe these two, they're amazing. I didn't even respond to Asia's condescending comment because I didn't want to know what they were doing there.

"Turn that up, that's my shit," I said, snapping my fingers, *'That's what it's made for,'* I began to sing along, "*That's what it's made for.*" I knew the words almost better than Usher himself but my vocal talent was nowhere near his.

"I sure hope his fine ass is there tonight. He sure can show me what it's made for," laughing.

"Me too," Asia says.

"Me three," Kellie joined in for the count.

"Well we might as well have a threesome tonight then, because if he's there, it's on and popping."

"You mean foursome India, but that's cool. Team 'Kidnap-

His-Ass' in progress!" Asia says.

"Word...word!" I reply.

"Y'all some nasty twins, I should call y'all 'Freak One and Freak Two!' Kellie said, laughing.

"Shut up hoe," I replied and continued to sing my heart out.

When we pulled up at the house there was a car parked out front, "Who's car is that?" I asked Asia.

"Nobody's," she replied, sounding a bit flustered.

"That's her man," Kellie interjected, giggling under her breath.

"Her man?" I asked, perplexed.

"Well he thinks he's her man."

Asia added more context, "We only fucked once and now he keeps popping up and shit!" she was becoming more livid as she realized his car wasn't moving. She then popped her trunk, exposing the goodies from our shopping venture, and continued on about her life as if there wasn't a stalker afoot.

"Get your bags India and walk in the house, I'm just going to ignore his bitch-ass like I always do."

We grabbed our bags and walked past his car to the house as if he wasn't there, watching us like a hawk, waiting for his moment to pounce.

"Can I talk to you for a minute Asia?" He yells out the car window. She opens the front door and slams it. No response, no emotion.

"You're not going to talk to him Asia?" I ask dumbfounded and nervous.

"No, I have a restraining order against his stupid ass and I'm calling the police. I could kill that bitch ass nigga and get away with it because he's on my property. He better be glad I'm going out or else I would need a body bag and gloves tonight. Just let his ugly ass sit there until they come, his ass is gone learn today!" locking the door behind us.

"You never told me about him Asia."

"It was nothing to tell India. I met him at the strip club one night, we kicked it, I didn't like his ass and I never dealt with him since. A one night stand, that's it. End of story."

"Ok, then why is he outside then?"

"He was at the club last night when I left with my friend, soooo I guess he mad," she says laughing, "and I don't really give a fuck but he will stop popping up at my crib," dialing 911 as she finishes her statement.

"Hi operator, I have a restraining order against this guy name Travis Brody and he's outside my home...Yes, yes, 211 Shelter Creek Dr...Ok, thank you."

"Get dressed India and don't worry, he's harmless," she said walking upstairs.

"That's what people say until someone turns up dead Asia."

"Fuck that crooked dick ass nigga, he can't even fuck right, I'm not scared of his ass. Get dressed!" she reiterated while walking to her room. I guess he was 'harmless' because Kellie walked to her room also and didn't pay the situation no mind either. I was just glad I was only visiting because they do too much and always have some type of shit going down.

I intentionally took a quick shower so my makeup wouldn't get smudge or messed up. Next, I started putting on my brown leather bootie shorts with the cream stitching and a leather sleeveless vest I picked up at Neiman Marcus. I opened it just enough to tease anyone who took a peek, they would see the lining of lace bra of course, adding a little hint of sexiness.

I always thought Neiman was an old lady's store that only sold Gucci bags. I wasn't solely at fault because every time we went there with our mom, that's all she said. 'Can't find shit in this old people's store.' But she always left out with a nice hand bag with a price tag similar to what people pay in rent. My mom's a trip, I laughed at the thought. To top of my outfit, I put on my brown strap heels with the

'G' emblem in the middle, bling-blinging. *Gucci should be ashamed of themselves for making the baddest shit. These put me back $750 dollars easy, but I had to have them.* My curly hair got drizzled in the shower. I applied styling mousse, shine, and hair perfume because a man rubbing all over you can change the smell of your hair. I brushed the front of my hair and put some big waves along my edges and left the back curly.

I'm ready. My makeup was done, gold shadow and dramatic lashes, blushed cheek bones with some lip-gloss, perfect. I grabbed my red Gucci clutch and sprayed myself down with Versace Pink Crystal, this was my favorite fragrance at the moment and it completed my outfit, now I was good! And looked even better.

I gave myself a final look over, *Damn I'm shitting on these hoes tonight. I pray there's no drama.* I put action into my thoughts and seriously started praying - you just never knew with these two, especially Asia.

I walked into my sister's room, she had the music blasting, getting everyone pumped up to match the energy in the room, listening to Tupac's 'Toss it up' while she danced in her bathroom, smoking a blunt.

"Want to hit this sis?" She asks walking out the bathroom, passing me the joint.

"No, I'm good playa'," laughing.

Kellie walked in, as if on cue, looking like a million bucks, "Pass the weed my nigga," holding her hand out to take the freshly smoked blunt.

"Y'all both cute!" I said, not wanting to blow their heads up but it ended up having an adverse affect.

"Cute? Bitch 'cute' is for puppies, I'm BAD!!" Asia boasted, blowing smoke out her mouth - and she was right.

I had to give it to her, my sister was bad to the bone. She wore her off-the-shoulder, money green, satin, Gucci dress, it was short like a shirt and hot off the racks. If she bent over, her ass would be a live sunrise to any bystander, round and bright. It was that serious, my sister was a rare star. Her hair was bone straight, silky and she wore it with a part down the middle, hanging halfway down her back. She complemented her green eyes with green eyeshadow to match, ready to hypnotize a fallen prey the minute they looked into them. If you weren't beauty struck by the bounce of her hair and contour of her dress, her shoes would surely be your downfall. Asia had on a badass pair of gold Gucci heels with the signature print that Cinderella would have killed for.

And Ms. Kellie dyed her hair blonde at the shop today. She cut it hair short and had a little flip thing going on, it was hella cute. She reminded me of a sunflower, blooming in the summer with it's yellow petals blowing in the wind. Her body maneuvered every so smoothly like a jaguar in her black fitted dress with spaghetti straps, she wore nothing underneath and you could tell. She topped her outfit off with some red Jimmy Choo stilettos and a matching red lip. Hoes was going to be mad tonight.

"Let's roll!" Asia said, high as hell, "India you're driving," throwing me the keys.

When we got there, the party is packed outside,"It's ridiculous out here! Now this is what I'm talking about!" we say in unison. There was nowhere for us to park so we decided to valet. "This shit is off the hook!" Kellie said, "I need a drink ASAP!"

When we walked in, all eyes were on us and we hadn't even made it to VIP yet. Everyone was on their prowl tonight. We started bouncing to the music and feeling the vibe in the club while we walked upstairs to the VIP area.

We handed the security guard our passes, he stood about 6'5" and resembled something of a former linebacker.

He looked us up and down and said, "Now this is going to be interesting..."

"Huh?"

Ignoring me, he unhooked the velvet rope to the entryway,

"You ladies have a wonderful time," turning his head to avoid any eye contact.

"Did I miss something?" I ask Kellie, "what's 'interesting' supposed to mean?"

She didn't answer me, but instead she grabbed my freshly manicured hand and led me to the bar. Asia was right on our heels, smiling from ear to ear. When we got to the bar area, it's smothered with celebrities, ballers, and of course bitches of all types trying to catch them a man for the road. It was live as hell and they were bumping the music just right. Everybody was pumped, you could feel the energy throughout the building.

Amongst the rhythmic chaos, there was this one group of niggas at the end of the bar that stood out, it was like the lights shined upon them. I would even say it was a mirage, a half a dozen powerful men, looking like nothing but money - tailored shit, Versace, Ferragamo, Gator boots, mink hats and bottles. It was this one in particular whose skin melted in dark chocolate with hazel eyes, 6'2", 200 lbs, and dressed to impressed from head to toe with a fedora hat and cigar in his mouth. He was talking to this dark-skinned chick with a pink dress on. She was way too thick for that dress, but her bad.

Asia Smith

He had our mouths wide open and our nostrils too, I could smell money, power, respect and the most exotic cologne lingering in the air. Breaking my trance, I felt Kellie pulling my arm.

"Let's go to the bathroom Asia," she said, "and India, you come on too."

I didn't want to go to the bathroom, fuck the bathroom, I didn't have to pee anyways, "No, you and India go, I'll be right here when you get back." I stole another glance at the alpha male in the room.

"No Asia, I have to tell you something important."

Her incessant nagging was taking my focus off the finest creature God created but she was my girl and this seemed notable so I obliged. We walked to the bathroom and Kellie's breathing started to dissipate.

"What's wrong Kellie?" we both asked her, standing in a triangle like formation behind the bathroom door, alone. I wanted to know what the fuck was really going on, it started with the suspicious ass security guard and now it was Kellie's frantic behavior.

"Girl, them niggas are balling out of control! They are some of my brothers partners...the dark one name is Vance, he's the CEO of the crew. He's hooked the fuck up with them Colombian niggas. He's stupid rich! He has most of Atlanta sewed up with people into just about everything. The dope game, banks, you name it he's a part of it."

I started looking at her sideways, I was in disbelief but not in a good way, "You mean to tell me all this fucking time we've been friends, you knew all these ballers and never introduced me to anyone of them? That says a lot about our friendship Kellie..." I was really pissed now and from the looks of it, India was too.

"No, Asia it's not like that, they are my older brother friends. The brother that's in jail for life. And those cats are dangerous!"

I had heard enough, I uncrossed my arms and grabbed the doorknob, "Well let me find that out the hard way, now let's go back to the bar so you can introduce me and India." I walked out the bathroom and they followed. When we got to our destination, I gestured for Kellie to make her move and nudged her like 'do your thing.' I heard one of them say, 'Kellie is that you?' *'Bingo', I think we're in.*

"Look who's here, all grown up! This is Rico's little sister, Kellie, you remember her dog?" Mr. Fine asked, he was standing with one of his homeboys who was about the same height but half the handsome.

Kellie waved innocently like she was shy and shit, "Hi Vance, how have you been?"

"I'm straight, you're in college now, right Kellie?"

"Yes, and these are my two best friends India and Asia. India just flew in from Cali to kick it with us for the weekend."

As the introductions were taking place, I could feel the growing presence of eyes and egos awaiting to approach us. We were looking like dime pieces so all the niggas at the bar was on our line or trying to get in line.

Vance licked his lips, sliding the tip of his tongue across what looked to be soft and full chocolate pillows, "Umph double trouble huh? It's a pleasure to meet you both," he reached for my hand and kissed it, his mere touch alone sent electricity through my body.

Fireworks and fantasies were going off in my head, he had me star struck. I didn't know if it was the alcohol or weed, but this man was moving in slow motion and it was so enticing.

"So you're Asia?" He says, looking me up and down. One of his boys didn't waste any time and was all over India, as if they were past lovers, *she said she was letting her hair down tonight's, I hope this is what she meant, mission accomplished.*

"What you drinking Mami?" He asks.

"Whatever you're drinking Papi," I retorted.

He looked me over again and said, "Damn a nigga just died and went to heaven, who knew I would make it through the pearly gates," shaking his head.

"It's even lovelier inside..." I responded with a wink and he laughed.

"I don't drink, my dudes are drinking xoxo and ordering bottles. But you can have whatever you like," he winked back.

I smiled, "Thank you."

I didn't want to seem too flirtatious or interested, or this could threaten the chase, men were creatures born for the hunt. *Momma's lessons were about to come in handy*, I usually rested on my beauty and quick tongue to get what I want, but he was different. This required a few more tricks of the game.

"No, thank you Asia for being so damn beautiful," he flashed a smile.

I liked the fact that he was complementary. Don't get me wrong, I was praised daily for being pretty but in this moment, with this man, his compliments were as welcoming as a toddler's first words to a mother's ear.

After my drink arrived at the bar, he took my hand and led me to a table with an infamous 'RSVP' sign sitting on top. Two other men within his crew were sitting at the table too, they weren't entertaining any women, just their waitresses for more bottles.

Before we could sit down, Vance arbitrarily stated, "This is going to be my wife and she's going to have my babies," excitedly. I smiled but didn't respond, the show was just getting started.

The more vocal of the two said, "Damn she bad nigga, if you don't wife her, I will."

We all laughed and Vance put his arm around me, claiming his newfound territory, and continued, "I'll give it all up for her and never look back." He said jokingly yet it sounding a bit serious at the same time. One of the men extended their hand and introduced himself but the other one just kept staring, with lust filled eyes, sipping his bottle of champagne.

Vance finally came to my rescue, "Stop staring at her nigga," with a laugh.

Mr. Lusty Eyes responded, "I can't help it, I'm at a lost for words" and we all broke out in what seemed to be silent laughter, as the music drowned out our collective humorous release.

The show was finally over so I searched across the room, looking for my sister and Kellie who both happened to be on the dance floor, breaking it down.

Vance asked me, "You go to school with Kellie?"

"Yes but I'm from California."

He didn't respond, he just kept looking at me smiling. There was always something men found intriguing about a 'Cali girl'.

He ordered me a bottle when the waitress came to the table, and I politely said, "Thank you." But what I really wanted to say was 'I would like to walk around for a bit', but I wasn't sure how he would respond. For the first time in my life, a nigga had me lost for words. And damn he was fine. He had the prettiest white teeth with platinum bottoms and his skin was so smooth and chocolate like a Hershey's kisses. And when he smiled, I noticed he has dimples. This dude was definitely 'all that and some'! And his presidential Rolex and those fat ass karats in his ear didn't hurt either. *I wonder does he have dick just as good as he looks.* Now that would be incredible if he did, but I doubted it. He couldn't be blessed in all areas could he? The song, *'It's like that and that's the way it is'*, came up next and I couldn't help myself but start snapping my fingers.

"That's my old joint," I said, still bobbing my head to the beat, he joined in right on queue before I excused myself, "I'll be back, I have to go dance with my sister."

When I got up from the plush couches, they all stood at attention, as a sign of respect and especially because the I was now associated the alpha amongst the wolves. I made my way from Vance's reserved section, in my Gucci heels, prancing to the beat, and synced up with my twin so we could tear up the dance floor like we always do.

I could feel all eyes on me and I loved it. I dropped it to the floor and brought it back up, turned my ass in circles and shook it on the nigga my sister was originally dancing with and let him have it. India was showing out too. Vance just sat there watching me like a hawk and his boys eyes were sequentially aligned. So I gave their asses a show, but this time it was my show.

When the song was over, this dude approached me with that 'Can we talk' bullshit. I smiled and pointed in Vance's direction, who was still looking at me. I said 'bye' to the guy who desperately stood there for my attention and turned around to walk away but he grabbed my arm.

"What are you doing? Let me go!" I said. I was hella irritated but when I turned back around, Vance was right there.

"Man, it's disrespectful to touch another man's property. Plus I saw the lady tell you that she was with someone...so I'll advise you to walk away nicely while you still have a chance," he said intimidatingly and even though he was face-to-face with the guy, he still managed to flash a smile my way, showing his platinum teeth and dimples while exerting his overt masculinity.

The guy let my arm go and walked away. I said, "I'm sorry, I didn't mean to cause a commotion."

"No need to apologize baby, I know you get that all the time," he blew me a kiss.

Yeah I do get that all the time, but I didn't want to tell him that. Plus, I would have just cursed that punk-ass dude out and the crew would have come running. But most of the time, I usually had to make all these false promises and niggas left quietly.

I blew a kiss back, flirtatiously, and that opened the door for his next bold move. Vance grabbed my pinky finger and pulled himself in close, with his lips gliding along my ear he says, "Let's get out of here for a minute, it's too loud and I need some air." I could feel my shoulder pressing against his strong chest, and the warmth of his body soothed me, *how could I deny this invitation?* Plus he wasn't ask me, he was telling me.

As we were leaving out, the chick in pink stocky dress strutted over to Vance. *Now this is going to be interesting,* I see what the security guard meant now and I shook my head. She looked me up and down, and then back to him.

Her voice penetrated the ear-piercing music and loudly said, "Vance can we talk for a minute?" If she hadn't announced who she was speaking to, the surround five people who turned around would have assumed she was yelling at them.

"No, not right now. I'll be back in a few," he turned, looked at me, and said, "You ready shorty?"

I replied, "I was born ready." He laughed, grabbed my hand

and we walked out of VIP, downstairs, and out the club, "Where are we going?"

"Nowhere really, we're just going to sit in my truck and talk. Is that alright with you?" I nodded 'yes'.

The valet came and said, "One minute boss." About sixty seconds later, he pulled up in a midnight blue Range Rover with red leather interior.

Now that's what the fuck I'm talking about. Bitches better watch out because there's a new sheriff in town. Before we got in the car, he opened my side of the door and tipped the valet with a hundred dollar bill. He was playing all his cards right, a humble gentlemen. We drove down the street for what seemed to be five minutes and parked by the lake.

"It's nice down here," I said.

"Yea it's nice at night," he played some slow jams but turned the volume down low, making it the perfect get-to-know-you setting.

He shifted his weight towards me, targeting his light brown eyes at mine and asked, "So Ms. Asia, how do you like Atlanta shorty?"

"I love it, now that I've met you..." teasing his ego.

He laughed, "Oh is that right? I could be a bad guy for all you know."

"I could be a bad girl," I replied, and we both started laughing.

"Asia, I know you hear this a lot, but your eyes baby...when I saw you at the bar I damn near stopped breathing," grabbing his chest.

"Well Mr. Vance, you had the same effect on me and you have some beautiful eyes as well." He didn't respond he just kept looking at me.

I was starting to get nervous about the situation until he touched my face and said, "I'm going to make you my wife. I was taught you can have anything in life you want with hard work and determination. And I'm determined to have you ma'," and just like that, he kissed me.

I kissed him back, sticking my tongue in his mouth like a reptilian, he did the same. It felt like I had never been kissed before. This shit was unexplainable, my whole body went completely numb.

"You alright ma?" I shook my head 'yes' and he said, "Well say something then?"

I think the words 'I love you' came out, I couldn't believe I said that shit, but I did.

He said, "Is that right, you serious ma? If my kiss is all that wait until you get this dick!"

That snapped me out my trance and we both broke out in laughter. His phone rang, he answered it and said a few words before hanging up.

He turned back to me, "That was my dude, he said your sister is looking for you so I'm going to take you back before she gets worried."

"Oh I left my phone in the car by accident so she can't reach me," I said.

He just smiled, "You ready wifey?"

I smiled back and said, "Yes, future husband," and we went back to the club.

When we pulled back into the valet, before we got out the truck, Vance said, "Do your thing ma' just be respectful to a nigga…," with a wink, "the night is still young."

VIP was still jumping when we got back and the club was packed. I pushed myself through the crowds of people dancing, standing around enjoying themselves. The music was so live and loud it was like walking through a maze trying to locate my sister and Kellie. Every few steps I took, a different guy would approach me asking to buy me a drink.

"No thanks." I said about fifty times. I finally located my girls at the bar downstairs.

"Where you been Asia?" India asked, smiling.

"Oh I just went for a lil' ride, order me a drink."

"Ok, these niggas been buying out the bar all night. It's going down!!" Kellie just shook her head laughing. We ordered some drinks and partied like rock stars. This dude came and summoned India to VIP area for some celebrity cat.

"Damn, like that India!" I say.

"I'm good," she says and turns her back to him and continues to talk to us, laughing in the process. But there was so many celebrities in the building, it was ridiculous. A few basketball players, football and even a few professionals from the major league. The moment couldn't get any better, it was like we were skating on thin ice around this joint. It was like Baller Heaven. And some of the finest men on earth was out tonight. I would occasionally look up at VIP and see Vance looking down at me, he would wink. And I would wink back. *What kind of game is this we playing? Hell whatever it is feels good!*

"What you smiling about Asia?" asked Kellie.

"Your brother's friend." I reply steadily, twirling my finger around my hair.

"Ok Asia be careful, he's cool people with a lot of dough but he's older with a lot of women chasing behind him." Kellie firmly states, "You really want that headache and heartache?" She looks at me. "But I know you so, I'm just putting it out there, be careful though."

"I love you too Kellie Morgan, you look damn good tonight, might I add." I say, smiling.

"Thank you bitch, so do you!"

"I know, that's how I was able to pull the biggest fish in this bitch," bouncing to the tute of my own horn.

"What you know about that?" dancing and singing to the song. Let's finish fishing." I said, sipping a drink.

We walked back up to VIP, one of Vance's boys was on Kellie real hard but she wasn't feeling him. But he started sweating her, damn near begging. "Come on baby, let's dance."

"No, I don't like this song, plus me and my girls about to go to the restroom. Please excuse us." Kellie began walking away, "Damn some people just can't take no for an answer," and we all laughed, we were all too familiar.

When we come out the bathroom, I see Vance in the corner with what looks like a heated debate with the chocolate girl wearing the pink dress. He glanced in my direction but continued his conversation. I kept it moving. *Where's India?* I wondered. *She can't still be wrapped up with that basketball player, with his cute ass*...before I could finish my thought, India appeared holding a bottle of champagne and sipping out of it with no remorse.

"Hi. Y'all ha-having fuuun?" India ask, slurring her words a bit.

"Fa' sho." Kellie responded.

"I won't be coming home tonight," India says smiling. "I have an early breakfast date."

I mouthed, "The young ball player?"

"No, he was cute though," India regained her balance, standing in heels.

"I'm telling Mommy!" I yell playfully, laughing. We started walking towards the stairs when Vance came and asked can he talk to me for a moment.

I looked at India and Kellie and said, "I'll see you guys in a few," they continued downstairs.

Vance walked me over to the small table we were at earlier but this time, it was empty. "I know you saw me talking to my lady friend but don't let that discourage you ma'," he playfully tapped my elbow, "I did have a life before we met," smiling.

"I understand, trust me it didn't faze me one bit," forcing the confidence in my speech.

"But it really did though. I just want to be totally honest with you Asia. You do understand that." Vance cautiously awaited my response.

"Yes Vance, I understand, but you being honest probably will take an entire weekend to explain everything," I ease the tension with a smile.

He smiled back and said, "I got you ma', my IOU's are legit," still smiling.

I smiled too. When the party ended, India left with who-knows-who and Kellie and I went home alone, but satisfied. *Oh how the tables have turned.*

Walking in the house, I say to Kellie, "That party was off the hook!" dancing as if the music was still playing, "thanks girl for the tickets."

"You-you know you my girl Asia," slurring her words.

"Bitch you drunk as hell, go to bed!" I say laughing at her.

"Yeah…unfortunately alone," she replied, ruefully.

"Goodnight Captain Hook," Kellie stumbled briefly, walking towards her room and laughing. I couldn't help but laugh too as I motioned towards my bed and passed the fuck out.

4

PARTY'S OVER

Asia Smith

Vance and I spoke several times on the phone but never went out on a date. *It had been two months already. Maybe I'm too young for him or maybe he's in love with that other chick from the party.* All sorts of crazy ideas surfaced in my head. School had begun so we cut back on all partying. But India had such a good time at the party that night, she claimed she might come and move out here to finish school after next semester. But I doubt it. I was lying in my bed watching T.V. falling asleep when my phone rung, '*Super freak -*'.

"Hello?"

"Hey baby, are you sleeping?"

"No, who's this?"

"The nigga you're in love with..."

I paused, but I wanted to respond right away. I looked at the caller I.D. but it was a blocked number so I had to answer with caution because I couldn't catch the voice.

"I'm sorry, I was lying down I didn't mean to be rude," I said but he started laughing and I caught the voice.

"Vance why are you calling playing, it's 10 o'clock at night."

"You had no idea who I was, you were just going with the flow. I like your style girl," still laughing.

"Well if I don't see you soon your not going to be the love of my life," I said solemnly.

"Well what are you doing right now?"

"Huh? Right this moment?"

"Yes."

"Lying down, watching TV."

"That sounds cozy, you want some company?"

"If it's you," I utter, smiling hella hard.

"Ok I'll be there in about an hour."

"Ok see you then."

I called Kellie's phone even though she was just two doors away, "Kellie what's up? You sleep?"

"Sorta."

"Is that a yes or no?"

"Yes, why Asia?"

"Oh, because Vance coming over."

"Really when?"

"NOW BITCH!" I say excitedly.

"Oh I see someone is eager. Ok Asia don't worry about me, I'm going back to sleep and have to leave out at 6am to take my granny to the airport."

"I'll try not to make too much noise and wake you up," I say laughing.

"Goodnight crazy girl, have fun."

"I will, bye!" I jumped up and got in the shower and put my hair in a cute pony tail because I hadn't combed it all day. I had just the right nightie to put on, my mom bought me and India some lingerie from La Perla for Christmas. *Perfect!* I sprayed on some 'Angel' perfume by Thierry Mugler, it was my favorite scent right now. Luckily, I had my eyebrows and feet done yesterday, so I was ready for whatever. And the fact that I hadn't had any dick in a while just intensified my taste buds even more. I kept hoping and praying Vance would call to ask me out, but when he did, it would be brief or if we did talk, it was be late and I would have school early in the morning. But "it's Friday night.." I caught myself singing over and over. My phone rung, I didn't let it ring but once.

"Hello."

"Hey baby, I'm pulling up, this is a nice house you have."

"Thanks, I'm coming downstairs to let you in." Opening the door I saw a Black 500 Mercedes pull behinds mines. I was too lazy to pull into the garage. His chocolate fine ass got his Louis V. overnight bag and the sight of him alone got my pussy moist. *Damn this dude is fine, 'calm down Asia',* I kept telling myself.

"Hi baby, you look ready for bed," he said with a smirk then gave me a hug. And he smelled good, *damn, I'm going to lose it.*

But I managed to say, "You look good," giving him a peck on those baby soft lips.

As we walked into the foyer, he said "This place is really nice. You say your parents gave you this joint?" he asks as we walk into the living room, with the lights dim and candles burning. He sat down on the white leather couch, dropping his bag beside him.

I sat next to him and crossed my baby oiled legs, "Well my parents actually own the house but since I go to school down here, it didn't make any sense for me to pay rent anywhere. The house was vacant for about a year before I moved into it."

"So your twin lives in California with your parents?"

"No she has her own place that my parents own also."

"Like that huh?"

"Your parents are balling in real estate."

"Well they own several investments and rental properties."

"That's cool. Are they into real estate? I mean, for a living?"

"No my dad is a surgeon and my mom works for congress, politics and stuff. She actually translates for the government worldwide. She speaks French fluently."

"Wow, so you're half French and black, that explains those bedroom eyes," smiling.

"No, I'm not half French, my mom is though and my dad is black, he's dark like you."

"So that's the attraction then. You *love* dark men." Vance laughed, over emphasising the 'love' in his statement. His dimples greeted me once again.

"Well what's your story? You have green eyes also."

"No I don't, they're brown."

"Yea but light brown."

"They are?" He inquired.

"You know they are!" I rolled my eyes at his sarcasm and this time we both laughed.

Looking at me, he says "You're even more beautiful than I remember,"

"You too."

He briefly looks left and then to his right, "So show me around."

Damn, I thought he was going to kiss me, shit, "Ok."

I motioned to get up and showed him around the house, except for Kellie's room. When we got to my room, the master bedroom, he shut the door.

"This room is huge for one lil' lady," he says.

"Then why don't you move in with me and occupy some of the space."

He laughed. "I'll think about that and get back to you." He pulled me close and kissed me, again, like the very first time. I almost lost my composure. When he stopped, he led me down on the bed and gazed at me.

And I gazed in return. We shared that moment for about ten minutes, it was intimacy in its purest form, a soulful connection joint at the pupils.

Concerned, I asked "What's wrong?"

"Nothing's wrong baby. Absolutely nothing." He found his voice, You're flawless, everything is perfect with you, where did you come from?"

"California." I said.

He started laughing, "I didn't mean it like that."

"Oh." I shook my head at my own amusement. He laid down beside me and picked up where we left off, star gazing in each others eyes.

"Asia I couldn't stop thinking about you since the night I met you." He cleared his voice. "I tried but I couldn't. My boys laughed when I would start drifting off sometimes. They would say 'You thinking about that broad from the club huh?' He chuckled. I'd laugh because I knew I was busted. I never knew it could be love at first sight but I guess that shit is real huh?"

"My dad said the same thing about my mom and they have been together for over twenty years." I say proudly.

"Word." He adjust himself slightly.

"Yes."

Then he kissed me again, but this time he let's his hands do some exploring. He starts with my breast, caressing them gently, playing with my nipples until they harden like a rock. He starts sucking on my neck, showing attention to both sides. He continues to navigate my body with his tongue, taking the southern route towards my breast, it felt like a wet torpedo igniting the nerve endings in my body.

I moan, "ohh, ohh". Then he slips his finger into my soaking wet pussy and plays with my spot, he enters another finger and I'm almost about to lose it. But suddenly yet ever so smoothly, he pull his fingers out and replaces them with his tongue, licking my clit, opening me up. He proceed to lick the walls, spreading my legs and speeding up the process. He's licking and sucking like he invented this shit. He made me arch my back and grab his head, and like a bull going for the red flag, he was trying to push it inside of me and I happily obliged, guiding him by his ears.

"Oh Vance it feels so good baby." My reaction triggered him to speed up, taking me way over the top!

"I'm coming baby --"

Skillfully, he slurps my juices like he was dying of thirst, "You like that baby?" He asks sensually. I can't even answer, I'm caught in a daze.

He laughs, "I hope that means 'yes'," walking into the bathroom. *Oh God, please let this be my husband. I pray. I haven't even had the dick yet.* He came out the bathroom with the smell of fresh toothpaste on his breath and lied next to me.

"Baby you ok?" He asks half concerned, half laughing.

I took the moment to just look at him, allowing the moment

to linger before I answered, "No. I think you gave me vertigo," playfully touching my forehead. "Where did you come from," I utterly softly, partially speaking to myself.

He smiled and said, "ATL baby!" He kissed my forehead, "I'm going downstairs to get some water, is that ok?" Vance motioned to get up, "Can I get you anything while I'm down there?" I just looked at him, giving him a face that reads boy-don't-make-me-hurt-you *and please don't ask what you can give me...down there.* I shook my head at the thought.

"Asia? Asia?" Vance calls out for me before I busted out laughing.

"Oh no I'm good thanks baby."

I can feel it, I'm going to be sprung off his ass. I'm in trouble. I get up, turn on some music and dim the lights. As I began to pull the sheets back, he walks up behind me and whispers in my ear. My back was facing the door so I was unable to witness his entrance or hear his return.

"Put your hands up, you're under arrest." I do as I am told and then this nigga puts handcuffs on me. Literally.

I turn around to face him and say, "What is this?" referring to the handcuffs. Vance let out a laugh he seemed to be holding in. I joined the laugh in return.

"This has to be some kind of joke, right?" I proclaim, questioning his intentions.

"They were in my bag, I forgot I had them but they could come in handy." He replies with a sly look on his face. Suddenly, I couldn't help it, I swiftly put my handcuffed hands around his neck and kissed him. He stopped mid-way through and walked back to the bathroom again.

"Vance are you going to take these off?" He winked and shut the door in my face. I walked to the bathroom door and called his name, again. He opened the door in his birthday suit.

My eyes glanced right at his protruding 9" inches. I guess

Vance thought I looked like a deer caught in the headlights, at least that's what I was able to gauge in between his laughter.

"Do you want them off or what baby?" he turns me around and removed the cuffs. It was like I went into shock. I didn't know what I was expecting, but seeing believing.

He dangled the cuffs in front of me before throwing them on the bed, "I'm getting in the shower, you want to join me?"

Every action of his had me captivated at his brazen behavior, *this is a bold ass nigga*. Releasing all inhibitions, I stepped into in the shower. After lathering each other up, we started kissing again. This time I made my way downtown and did a little shopping myself. Just seeing that chocolate banana all wet did something to me. I took him in my mouth and rotated like I was devouring the last popsicle on a hot summer day. I licked and sucked like there was no tomorrow. It felt so good to him that he decided to straddle up. He took my ponytail out and ran his fingers running through my hair, massaging my scalp like a masseuse. The shit felt good to me too - giving pleasure could be just as good, if not better, as receiving it. It was something about the power and control, the exchange of masculine and feminine energies and roles. The peak of a woman's dominance was if she saw a grown man crying from her performance. In this case, I know he actually wasn't crying, but the illusion became more realistic as the water began running down his face. That shit was crazy. I started speeding up, sucking like I was removing the blackness and turning his dick albino. Faster, faster then he finally released himself after moaning my name.

"Asia...Asia...oh Asia..." The sound of the water hitting the shower floor coupled with my name running off his wet lips made me cum too. He pulled me up and kissed my forehead.

He kissed my belly button and continued down. This time kissing my dripping vulvas, but he kept going lower. He sucked in between my thighs until I thought I was going to pass out. It felt so good. Sliding off the bed, Vance navigated to another edible part of my body and put my toes in his mouth, one by one. *This shit should be against the law, I swear.* It should be a crime to make someone feel this good. He had me screaming for him to quit, and that was only the first foot. After he finished them both, he turned me over and stared over my back. He observed my tattoo I share with India, identical body art. It read 'Only Death Can Separate Us' with a sword going through a heart, drops of blood adds to the imagery along with fact that each drop had our names. He kissed that too. He made his way to my buttocks and kissed them both, one at a time. My legs began to open from his guidance as he placed the tip of his dick at the center of my opening. He allowed the tip to explore in and out a few times, teasing me.

In between moans, I'd say, "Put it all the way in baby," but he wouldn't prevail. So I got on my hands and knees and backed that thang' up. He saddled up and rode that ass like a jockey going to the finish line. I was moaning and screaming so loud I thought my parents could hear me all the way in California. Then he flipped my ass over and put my legs up in the air like a TV antenna. Vance displayed his skillful penmanship by spelling his entire name inside of me, in cursive writing. He touched everything inside my body like he had me open performing a surgery.

"This feels so good baby!" In between moans. "Does it feel good to you?"

He looked me straight in my eyes and said, "Yes-yes, this pussy is the bomb baby." At that moment, I lost it. I had my very first organism and he came right with me, inside of me. He put my legs down, turned me over, and laid me down on his chest.

He kissed me and said, "Get some rest, because this ain't over."

We didn't sleep at all that night. We fucked until it was daylight outside. When we finally did stop for air, I couldn't even walk to the bathroom. I tried but I couldn't do it. So I laid back down looking at Vance, who was knocked out cold, sleeping like a newborn baby and looking like one too. *Just beautiful.* We slept until 2pm the next day.

He woke up first and got in the shower. Finally, I was able to walk again without feeling like my pussy finished boot camp for the marines.

I went to the guest room, took a shower and brushed my teeth. I brushed my hair into a cute ponytail again and put my robe on with nothing underneath. When I walked back into my room, he was on the phone, lying down on the bed. So I just laid beside him and put my head in his lap. He reached down to kiss my cheek and continued his conversation. When he hung up, he said "Good afternoon baby!"

I responded, "Good afternoon, energizer bunny." We both laughed in amusement. "You hungry? I can make us something to eat."

He pulled me up from beside him so we could face each other, "You can cook too?" He asked, seriously.

"What's that supposed to mean?" I made an inquisitive face.

He retorted, "Good looks, good body..." he playfully bit my bottom lip, "umph umph good pussy and you can cook. Something can't be right." He proceeds to shake his head.

"Well baby, I'm like the whole package, is that a problem?" I asked, gently kissing the right corner where his two lips met.

He held his hands up, mid-laugh, like he was surrendering, "I don't want no problems!" he said but his demeanor changed and he paused for a bit, "can I ask you a question baby, don't take this the wrong way but why don't you have a man?"

Don't panic Asia and please don't say 'because I was a hoe in my previous life', "Good questions baby, I really don't know why, I guess God was saving me for you." I said aloud, happy I didn't blow it with any word vomit, *whew that was close!* The host on jeopardy would have been proud of that answer. Vance smiled, confirming my thoughts.

"Yeah maybe that's it, or maybe men are intimidated by you, baby." Vance hunched his shoulders a bit. "Your looks, you're intelligent, kinda' independent and young. Some men can't handle that combination. It's just too much." He paused. "They prefer you to be cute but needy, or cute but not so bright. Or ugly and a hustler."

Like the girl in the pink outfit.

"But you're bad baby." clasping his hands together like I just sealed the deal.

"Thank you, you're not so bad yourself Mr. Vance..." I left my remark opened ended, as if it were lingering in the air, awaiting a response for his last name.

He smiled and said, "Smith...Vance Smith"

He's playing right? Somebody must have told him my last name was Smith or this is one hell of a coincidence, "Are you serious?" I ask.

"What you mean baby girl? Why would I lie about something like that?" Vance looked puzzled. "That's my government name it's on my birth certificate."

I got up and went inside my purse and handed him my driver's license.

He laughed after glancing at for a second, "Hand me my pants."

I gave him his jeans and he took out Louis V. wallet and slid me his license. And sure enough his was a 'Smith'.

"Well atleast you don't have to change your last name if we were to get married," he snickered and tapped my ring finger.

"That's true," I laughed back.

"Throw something on, we'll go out to eat and then come back to make love all night," he smacked my ass and jumped of the bed.

We both got dressed and headed to get something eat, it was great timing too because I was starving. As we walked out the house, the sun greeted me brightly and shined the light on my transportation for the day.

"Nice car baby!" I say, complementing the car and stroking his ego at the same time.

"Thanks ma'." He smiled, "You have a nice car too, it's kinda small though but those are made for women."

"Um you think so?" Vance shook his head as he unlocked the doors of his car, using a keyless remote.

"Yes, men like big, fast cars baby!"

As we headed on our route, Vance played *'They Don't Know'* by Jon B. I wonder if this was a hint or something, a subliminal message he was trying to convey. When we arrive at the restaurant, Vance pulled up to the valet.

Getting out the car, a man approached us in a suit, "Hello Vance," taking his keys, "same spot?" he asked.

"Same spot. Thanks Curly," he grabbed my hand and led our way in.

Everyone knew him - the greeters, the waiters, shit probably even the cook. From the familiarity of his steps through the restaurant, I take it we sat down as his usual spot.

They knew where to sit us without even asking, and brought out a bottle of champagne without a mere inquiry. When they did ask me what I would like to eat, Vance recommended the crab, although, he said it was my choice when the waiter took our order. Impassively, I went with his recommendation, obviously he knew exactly where he was as if he had done this all before.

"You come here often?" I asked, waiting for him to lie.

"Yea about two or three times a week, sometimes even more if I have to."

"What you mean if you have to?" I was hella confused.

"Sometimes I have to stop by if there's a problem or something like that."

My thoughts start drifting, *What is he saying? Maybe he's a plumber*?

"Oh," is all I could say and I left it at that. I would find out the truth sooner or later. They brought out some delicious clam chowder and the best homemade rolls I've ever eaten.

"Good, huh?" he said, in between bites.

"The best!"

"I'm glad you like them, they're an old family recipe."

Oh now I get it, his family must own this place, "So your family owns this restaurant?" I asked.

"No, I own this place."

"Oh." Is all I could muster, once again.

"I own two other restaurants and a sports bar also." Vance grabs another biscuit. "The party we met at, I own that building too. I rent it out for parties and celebrations," he takes a bite and begins devouring his biscuit. I didn't know what to say. *Dang I really didn't know this man even though i just slept with him.* You should really get to know a person before sleeping with him, I began to drift off into my thoughts. But, oh well.

5

THE BIG FIGHT

Asia Smith

Vance pulled up to my school – we really hadn't been on speaking terms because he was trying to play me. For the past few weeks he would call and say he was coming by but never showed up or he would say he was going out of town for a couple days on business. It had gotten to the point where I didn't care if his ass ever came back around. But today of all days he decided to surprise me and pop up at my school and pay me a little visit.

Unbeknownst to me, I hadn't noticed when he pulled up because I was all up in this dude's face, talking about an assignment I missed. I can't say how long he had been sitting there, nor do I care, but he eventually honked his horn to get the attention he had been waiting for.

Normally, I wouldn't have turned around but my classmate said, "Asia your man is honking at you." I turned around and briefly looked at Vance, then turned back and continued my conversation a little longer to make him wait like he had been doing me lately. I finally said my goodbyes and gave the guy a hug to give Vance a show. After I finished the scene, I strolled over to the driver side window of his car like I wasn't tripping.

"What's up Vance? What brings you up to the school house, you're not trying to enroll are you?" sounding sarcastic.

"Get in Asia!"

I must have looked perplexed, because that's exactly how I

was feeling, but I got in anyway and he drove off immediately.

"I have another class Vance, what are you doing?" my perplexed face was now transitioning to one of concern.

"We're going shopping."

Those magic words soothes the soul. We rode damn near in silence, only lending our ear to the oldies he had playing on his radio. I knew immediately something was bothering him. Jogging my memory briefly, he said he always listens to oldies to relax him.

At the stop light, he looked at me and said, "Why were you doing all that fantasy shit at the school, hugging that lil boy?" he paused, "you think that kinda' shit gets to me Asia?"

Obviously it did, you mentioned it. I thought, but kept it to myself.

"I don't know what you're talking about Vance. I just gave him a hug and said 'thank you' for his help." I said, slowly releasing my breath, hoping some of this stress would go with it.

"What did he help you with Asia?" he quickly glanced off the road and back to me.

"I missed an assignment, so he gave me his notes and the questions to the lab test," Vance waited for me to continue.

"And that's all! Why Vance?"

"Umph, so you're telling me that everybody that *HELP'S* you, you're touchy-feely with?" His voice began to rise, overemphasizing the word 'help' in his statement.

"I thought that didn't bother you a minute ago, now you want to argue?"

"I'm asking the questions and you're answering them, that's not arguing!" The rise continued, his voice now competed with the Oldies playing the in background. "My point is that you did that shit on purpose and you better not ever disrespect me again or make me wait on your dumb ass."

"I didn't even – "

"Be quiet Asia!" he screeched, cutting me off.

"You didn't let me finish Vance." I said subtlety, trying to regain control of the situation.

"There's nothing else to say, just BE QUIET!" This time, his voice rang in pure victory, completely tuning out the oldies playing in the background. Any hope for this calming remedy had failed in this ordeal. We arrived at the mall shortly after.

Before getting out the truck, Vance said, "We're going on a trip, that's why we're going shopping."

"Where are we going!?" My astonishment evolved to pure excitement.

"Jamaica, Asia."

"When?"

"We leave Thursday night, that's your last day of school for this semester and we'll be back the following week."

I was too excited at this point. I forgot all about being mad. We hit the mall with a vengeance. We hit up Gucci, Saks, Louis Vuitton, Burberry, Fendi and Ferragamo. All in that order.

As we passed the Tiffany's store, Vance asked, "Why don't you wear the Tiffany's set I bought you?"

"I wear it sometimes but I need an upgrade!" I say, laughing.

"Upgrade?" Vance gave me a look like I was tripping but whatever.

"I have to call India and tell her the good news," changing the subject and smiling at the same time.

Back in the truck, Vance asked me, "You hungry baby?" This is the first time he called me 'Baby' all day.

"Yes, I want some Mexican food," starting to put on my seat belt. He knows this bomb Mexican spot with bomb drinks.

"Ok baby..." and there it was again, "let me make this quick run first and then will go eat."

I didn't mind a little business before pleasure. When we pulled up at the set where his boys hung out, a few of his friends I recognized from the club that night approached the truck.

"What's up Asia! How you been?"

"I'm straight Boobie, how are you?"

"I'm straight, just need to holler at your boy," he says, bouncing a basketball, suiting his athletically built frame.

"Baby I'll be right back, I'm going to run in this house and when I come back, we're out!"

"Ok, baby." I retort. *Let me call India and tell her about my trip.*

The phone only rang but once, "Hello?"

"Hey lil sis, what you doing?"

"I was studying for finals this week," India sighed, "I'll be glad when this shit is over."

"I know, my last day is Thursday and me and Vance are going to Jamaica!"

"Seriously, Asia?" she matched my excitement. "You're so lucky! Bring me back everything! Even a man!" we start laughing.

"Where's ole' boy you were seeing?"

"I'm cool of his ass, all he wanted to do was fuck all the time! No romance, no flowers. I can fuck myself if that's the case. I need a man like Vance. Let's switch places. He won't know!" laughing again.

"I know we could easily flip the switch, it ain't like we've never done it before," we were flexing our ab muscles left and right from this comedic reunion. *I missed my sister.*

"Yea Asia please don't remind me, I hated that shit! Anyways, how long are you going to be in Jamaica?"

"A week…" as I finished my statement, I watched Vance come out the house and that chocolate chick from the party walked up to him, "hold on India…this bitch is walking up to Vance."

"Who?" She asked.

"Remember that chocolate girl at the party that Kellie said was his woman?"

"Oh, her…"

Instead of listening to India, I drifted off and started paying attention to their conversation. I rolled the window all the way down to hear clearly.

"Why is that little bitch sitting in your truck Vance?"

"Monique don't make me beat your ass out here. Get back in your car and go home, I'll holler at you later."

"No! Answer me Vance, I'm serious! I'm going to snatch that hoe out your car and beat her ass!"

She was yelling just as loud as she did in the club, only this time there was no music to mask her voice. *Who does this ugly bitch think she is? Beating my ass is exactly what she's NOT going to do. Don't let my petite looks fool you.*

He grabs her arm, "I said go home with all of this B.S."

I was so caught off guard be this whole ordeal that my heart started racing, "India, I'm going to have to call you back..."

"Asia wait! – " She yelled into the phone but I had already hung up.

I watched this chick yank away from Vance, trying to get loose. Some girls were walking up and edged a bit closer to this unexpected confrontation. At the same time, Boobie and his boys came outside to witness the same commotion that alerted us all. I guess the girls were apart of her crew because they were all saying 'Vance you're hella wrong and blah blah blah' and before I knew it, she had gotten loose and started running towards the truck. Instantly my reflexes took over. As she reached for the door, I opened it and kicked the bitch in her chest. She fell back, I jumped out and punched her again in the face.

Vance grabbed me as I was mid-punch, "Baby stop!"

"Bitch why fight over some dick, he still gonna' fuck with both of us!!" Vance was performing his best attempt to restrain me, "So, don't let Vance be the reason!" I screamed. "You're only mad because you're about to get eliminated," still yelling. "Your spot is taken bitch!!" Vance staggered, he was balancing both our weight as I continued to pop off while adrenaline flowed through me fiercely. "I'm good looking, good pussy with a 'I-don't-give-a-fuck-attitude'! You ugly bitch!"

I managed to say as many threats as possible before being put back in the truck. I must have mistaken Vance's staggering for his swift maneuvering to get me in his car, out of the street, and off Monique.

"Don't move Asia and I mean it!" Vance said and walked back towards the crowd.

I couldn't believe this shit. They had me all out of my character over some weak ass dick. *Well it wasn't weak but you know what I mean.*

To calm my nerves, I called my sister back, "Hello? India you're not going to believe this!"

"You had to fight Asia?"

"How did you know?"

"Because I know you, what happened?" She asks, but before I could answer, Vance got back in the driver's seat.

"Baby I'm sorry, I didn't mean to put you in this kind of predicament."

"What is the extent of your relationship with her Vance..." pausing, "it has to be some heavy shit if it had me fighting in the street?"

"It's complicated Asia."

India started pushing buttons on her phone to remind me she was still on the line, but I just hung up instead. *I'll just have to call her back.*

"Well you need to explain something to me Vance, I mean you at least owe me that much."

"Let's go eat first baby, then we can talk."

I didn't say a word, the incident alone spoke volumes. All of my unanswered questions and speculations have been confirmed. When we got to the Mexican restaurant, I'm wasn't even hungry anymore and I didn't have anything to say.

We got seated and Vance asked, "You mad at me baby?"

"No!" I responded.

"Then why did you just yell?"

"What are you talking about Vance," I say rolling my eyes.

"You were quiet the whole ride Asia," Vance started to sound concerned, concealing some of the guilt in his voice.

The waitress comes to take our order, before she even utters a word, I asked for a drink, "May I have a double shot of Hennessey and hold the ice please."

She walked away and Vance began to testify, "Baby it's like this, me and Monique have history from way back," he says slowly, "she was like one of the boys. Me, her, Boobie, Dre and Mike all from the same block. Anyways...when we started hustling, she did too."

The waitress returns with my drink. "Thank you," I say.

"Are you ready to order? Do you need a minute?" she asks. Vance throws up one finger, and she walks away.

"Baby I didn't know you knew how to fight, that shit was crazy," he says laughing.

Sipping on my drink, "I don't find that shit funny Vance and I guess there's a lot about each other we don't know," I say with sarcasm. "So Vance, what does Monique mean to you?" I asked again.

He takes a deep breath and continues with his confessional, "We've fucked around for about ten years. I was her first, when we were about sixteen, and when we got deep in the game, she was one of my biggest hustlers. She has a crew of broads, they all get money for me and move heavy weight. I wouldn't call Monique my woman but she's more than a friend." At that very moment, I lost my appetite.

"Then when I met you, shit just really got hectic."

His phone kept ringing during our conversation but he kept sending whoever it was to voicemail. It didn't matter though, I didn't want to hear anymore. I thought I was going to be sick.

"Vance I don't feel good, can you take me home please?" making an exhaustive expression to compliment my request.

"Let's order something to-go then we can leave." He says.

I excused myself and went to the restroom. *Asia what have you gotten yourself into,* looking in the mirror, *this shit going to get out of hand.* When I came out the restroom our food was ready and so was I.

When we got in the car, my drink really started to kick in. I kept looking over at Vance driving, *damn this nigga is fine.* The combination of alcohol and anger had me feeling horny, or at least, my mind was dancing at the idea of it. To satiate my boiling hormones, I slid my hand across his dick and it responded instantly to my touch. He looked at me, smiled, and started to say something but before he could, I put my fingers over his lips to 'shhh' him. I unzipped his pants and started to caress his dick. Massaging in a rotational motion, slow and fast, giving him gripping sensations across the spectrum. His penis was my piano and I stroked them keys like a professional. His dick liked it, growing in girth after each tug to the boat. It wanted more, so I started stroking as fast as I could.

When he couldn't take it anymore, he pulled over like a highway patrolmen in training. I put him in my mouth, trying to take it all in before he could bust. After a few twirls and head twist at the tip of his penis, I straddled his lap and lifted my skirt. *Good thing I wore this outfit today, easy access.* He let the seat back and enjoyed the ride.

When we were done, we wiped ourselves clean with baby wipes - he always carried them in his truck. We adjusted our clothes and I went back to the passenger seat, laid on the headrest and dosed off. He drove me back to the school parking lot to get my car.

Shaking me gently, "Baby you cool to drive?"

I looked at him and smiled, "Yes, I'm good. I just needed a power nap."

"So, I guess you're not mad at me anymore," he said, laughing.

"I was never mad, just disappointed," I said sternly, "there's a difference."

He grabbed my face and kissed me, "I love you girl."

"Love you too," I retorted, "I'll meet you at the house, ok?" getting out the truck.

"See you there," he confirms.

I got in my car and drove off. During the drive, my subconscious mind took over. *I need to step my game up a notch with Vance. He's going to have to do better than Jamaica to make this shit ok - Mr. Casanova with two and three bitches and shit.*

I loved him but I wasn't about to let him walk all over me like a doormat. I knew it wouldn't take me ten years to realize that shit either. There were far too many women who adopted men with their rose-goggles on. Some could see the flaws and red flags, yet still decide to stay with hopes they could change what the world and past relationships had already fucked up. Other women, well, they just refused to take the goggles off, and lived in a garden abundantly, many failures disguised as flowers - pretty red roses.

I needed to have a heart-to-heart with my Mom, *I'll call her tonight.* Pulling up to the house, I saw both cars parked outside. I assumed Kellie must have let Vance in. *I wonder what he would do if I didn't come home tonight,* I laughed to myself at the thought. He better be careful because if he kept pushing my buttons, he was going to see what I was really made of. I got out my car and thoughts kept running through my head like the olympics until I walked up to the house.

"Hey baby, where's Kellie?"

"She left a minute ago with her friend"

"Oh...I'm about to take a bath and go to bed, I'm exhausted."

"I'm watching the game, go ahead," he says.

About twenty minutes into my bath, Vance comes kneeling down by the tub, staring me right in my eye, "What's up baby?"

"You know I love you right girl...don't you?"

"Yes, I know. I love you too - " I barely finished uttering those precious words before his precious lips pressed against mine.

He smoothly pulled away, "Now, hurry up!" he yelled

playfully, flicking water in my face.

When I got out the tub, he was already in the bed smiling, "Come here girl," motioning his fingers back and forth, with open arms.

I walked over to him, climbed on top, and start running my fingers through my wavy hair, "What's up baby? You miss me," I flash a smile, using my womanly charm.

"Always," his dimples greet me. I don't know what you've done to a nigga these past couple of months girl. It feels like you put a curse on a nigga or something," laughing.

Kissing his chest, I started making my way down to the prize, "It's called love, baby," I say and continue making my move. Kissing his body going lower and lower, and there it was, waiting for me with a grinning round tip.

"Umph, Asia, I do love you...oh baby," rubbing my hair as I motioned up and down, "get it baby, get it."

I stop, and come back and kiss his lips.

"I love you too," I say. He lays me down and reciprocates, sucking and licking like his tongue was on fire and begged for my dripping waterfall to put it out.

"Put it in baby," I'm moan, "ohhh Vance baby, I want it inside of me," upon my command, he slides right in and it's a perfect fit.

"Oh yes baby, right there."

We were going at it like two heavyweight boxers, pound for pound. Vance was my opponent, bobbing and weaving in the ring, hitting all the right corners.

"This my pussy Asia?"

"Yes!"

"Tell Daddy it's his pussy."

"It's yours baby...yes, yes! It's your's. I'm coming baby."

"Come for Daddy baby," he was hitting my shit like he was going for the knock out. I came all over him like a melted ice cream. I was still riding my orgasmic waves when he took me from the bed and placed me against the wall and put my hands up, balancing his weight against my wrist stacked on top of each other. This was domination and submissive erotica at its best. He slid right back in from the back side and continued to do his thing. *Damn I didn't think it could feel any better.* In and out, faster and faster. I laid my head back on his chest, this was the only other part of my body I could move other than my ass cheeks that were flapping against his thighs.

"I love this pussy girl," Vance said in my ear.

"Ummm, Vance baby I'm coming again," letting go.

"I'm coming too baby," stroking 100 mph, releasing my wrist and grabbing my waist. We both came together, tasting sweet orgasmic ecstasy - that humanistic sexual peak within us all. I left a puddle of juices on the floor. We just stood there for a moment, regaining ourselves. Vance kissed the back of my neck, then he grabbed my hand and led me to the bed. We didn't even clean up the mess off the floor, we were too exhausted.

As I laid in his arms falling asleep, Vance softly says, "Don't ever think about leaving me Asia or I'll kill your ass," he kissed me, and I started drifting off. *This must be some dangerous pussy.* I welcomed my slumber with sexual satiation and bodily exhaustion at the front door.

We never again spoke about the Monique incident. But we did have a hell-of-a week in Jamaica, living it up like the celebrities. It was a quintessential vacation, we did everything there was to do - we ate everywhere and everything there was to eat, we shopped at every mall, boutique, and outside vendors who were in town - you name it, we did it. And without question, we made love all love over that foreign island. It felt like a honeymoon, although, I had never experienced one before.

On our way back home, Vance slept most of the plane ride and I kept thinking about the conversation I had with my mother a few days before we left.

***

"Hi Mommie."

"Hello sweetheart, how's everything with you?"

"I'm good Mommie."

"Wonderful dear, I love you Asia."

"You too Mommie. I just wanted to say I love you because you have a tendency of hanging up, and I didn't want you to before I even got the chance to tell you...Mom I'm going to Jamaica in a couple days with Vance..." *silence,* "I know you don't care for him –"

"Correction sweetie, we've never met him Asia. To assume I don't care for him is incorrect."

"Ok Mom, let me finish please?" Her silence insinuated I had the floor. "He's a little older, 26 with no kids."

"That's nice Asia."

"He owns a couple of restaurants – " before I could finish, she interrupted me.

"Legally Asia? I hope...because if not it's just a front when the feds come knocking. They'll take all of it."

"If it wasn't assumed legal – "

"Asia listen. Let Mama give you some advice. I know you and your sister are grown now but you'll always be my lil' girls. I want both of you to enjoy life to the fullest, with all it has to offer. But don't let illusions like trips and cars, even money for that matter, become your false hope. Educate yourselves. I'm not saying don't accept gifts because if you're dealing with a person and giving him or her the most important part of yourself, you should be rewarded. But make no mistake that what comes with those gifts, especially monetary gifts, the giver wants some sort of control. You and only you should have control of your own destiny. And please don't get yourself pregnant without being married first. A man can make millions of babies by millions of women. But the woman he marries with his child or not will ultimately mean the most to him."

Her words of wisdom continued to flow, "Don't let them fast-talking-hustling-men fool you. The picture is perfect until it all comes tumbling down. Then all sorts of women pop up, your gifts get taken away and you're back where you started from. Square one. Like, what was it all for? I don't want you to get caught up with that 'glitter is gold' nonsense. Be very conscious of what you already have and that is strong sense of family values. And lastly, don't give yourself completely to one man, unless he's doing the same with you. I'm not encouraging you to sleep around, but I mean don't give your heart and mind away until he's ready to reciprocate. Pay attention, you're a beautiful and intelligent young woman Asia. So enjoy your trip and your friendship with this young man. But take it slow with your heart and retain all this information for future usage."

"I will Mommie, thank you."

"You're welcome and call more often, we miss you."

"I miss you too."

"Love you sweetheart, enjoy." *Damn, I love my Mommie, she was the shit! She had to be connected to the Cleopatra lineage in her ancestry somehow...and that meant we were too.*

6

LET'S GET IT STARTED

Asia Smith

"Hey Essence girl, looking fly as usual," she turns her head to see who's looking at her.

"Oh, what's up Asia! You're fly too," excusing herself from a group of girls, "what's been up with you lately?"

"Nothing much just trying to keep my head above water with this school shit. Some of my classes are hella hard," I said, adjusting my book bag which seemed to bear as much weight as the stress of school itself.

"I know, Asia. My freshman year I almost gave up but you have to persevere. Plus you're already passed that stage so you got this boo!" laughing.

"I know Essence, my parents would be devastated if I

dropped out of school. They're big on education."

"Now see, that should motivate you more. Both my parents were killed in an accident when I was three and I was placed in foster care until I was eighteen."

"I'm sorry to hear that Essence," I didn't know what else to say, none of students walking past would have knew we were having this deep conversation.

"It's ok, I'm over it plus I did some research and located some family members. So it's cool," smiling, "do you have anymore classes?"

"No, I'm done for the day."

"Do you want to take a ride with me? That's if you don't have any other plans."

"Sure, I'll ride. I don't have anything else to do. My life consists of the same routine every day. You smoke?" I asked her.

"Sure do." She retorted. Walking out to the student parking lot, Essence's hits her alarm and starts up her car with a little button.

Getting in the car I say, "That's tight! That's some alarm system you have."

"Yea it is. It's top of the line but expense as hell."

I take out my stash and roll up a blunt, "This is some good shit I got, my man keeps me supplied," laughing.

"I heard that. My dude lives out of state in Philly, I try to go see him as much as possible but between school and hustling, it gets hard sometimes." I almost choked on my blunt when she said 'hustling'. I started coughing and couldn't stop.

"You alright over there?"

"Yea girl! I told you this some good weed. But what do you mean 'hustling'? You move work?" and by 'work', I meant coke.

"Naw, nothing like that. It's better than that...safer."

I pass her the blunt, she takes a hit and says, "This some good shit Asia. I might have to buy some of this," after blowing out her smoke, she gives me the game with all trust barriers bowed down, "I rob banks and go into stores with other people's identity. You know about identity theft?"

"Yea, I've heard about it. How does it work exactly?" She had my undivided attention. I felt like a student listening to a professor when she ran it all down to me - as it turned out, I did have another class today.

"Well for starters, I get different 'profiles', that's what they call them. I buy them at $250 dollars each, per identity. A profile contains their full names, and maiden name for females, birthdate, social security number, address, phone numbers and if you get a good one, their credit history and score and bank account number. The profiles I buy usually comes from somebody who works inside a bank or a car dealership, that's how all their information is available. Then, I write down all the information for a driver's license and my boy makes fake I.D.'s. They look real as hell too. You can even fly with them. You know how security puts it under the light? Well, they're looking for certain characters on the I.D. that only the department of motor vehicles, supposedly, puts on them. But my boy puts those same characters on his too. I know a few other people who make I.D.'s too, but theirs won't pass the light test and they're cheaper. I only use the cheap one's for instant credit. But when I fly or go into the banks, I have the I.D.'s that take the light. They cost $500 and the one without cost $250. But it's worth spending the extra few dollars because your return is greater, at the bank that is. That's where I get my money at. I make around thirty thousand a month, alone. I split it half way with my business partner."

I was looking in disbelief, a deer caught in the headlights. But these headlights were the money, the scheme, and this wealth of knowledge I just received. I couldn't believe what I was hearing. I didn't respond. I just shook my head in agreeance while she continued.

"It goes like this Asia...just say I have all of your information, like a profile of you. I'll get an I.D. made in your name with your birthday, address etc. Then I just have to remember your social security number when I go into a bank that you bank with, like Bank of America. With your account number, I'll fill out a withdrawal slip in the amount of, let's say, $5,000. If you asks for more than that at once, they need a manager's approval, that's standard in all banks. So I never go over $5,000 at a time. The less help I get, the better. I'll say I'm traveling and don't have my ATM card so they'll ask for a second piece of identification and I'll show a fake passport that's aligned with the same profile, my boy makes passports too. And voilà, they give me the cash and I walk out."

I was amazed at this point, Essence had me wide open with this shit, "So Essence you're telling me that you can assume anyone's identity?"

"Girl yes, I've done hundreds. My boy put me on about three years ago. He's major with this shit. That's how I paid for my education. Once you're through with foster care at eighteen, you're basically on your own. So I had to do what I had to do to get through college. I damn sure wasn't going to be no stripper," laughing.

"I heard that, but to each his own."

"If that works for some, I'm not knocking their hustle. Plus them bitches get paid and come up with the plug most of the time. Feel me."

"Yeah," is all I could say.

"I only go into banks Thursday, Friday, and Saturday. If I check someone's account and they have $50,000 in it, I know I'm taking the majority. I go three days in a row and pull out $5,000 each time – "

It can't get no better than this. We finished the blunt but I was on a new high and needed to know more, "How do you know how much money a person has?" I asks.

"Well usually the profile I buy contains that information. If not, I call the bank and check my account. You see I say 'my account' because I've now became the person," laughing, "I usually don't like talking to a live person, but if I have to, I will."

"I'll call and say I've wrote a check for a large amount and wanted to see if the check cleared and from there I can get the balance of the account, it's that easy Asia. I swear."

"You're a genius Essence, I'm really impressed," I said, we were now driving down the freeway without any music, just the sounds of Essence's coaching.

"Yea It's crazy, I know. But when I finish with the bank, I open credit in that person's name and if they already have an account open like Saks Fifth Ave, all you have to do is show your I.D. and give your social and they can pull up your account without having the card. And all of their open accounts are displayed in the profile as well. But if a store isn't open, that's cool too because I'll open it. Like Neiman Marcus, they gave me big limits and I used it all. You can buy whatever because the limits are huge like twenty, thirty thousand. I buy myself nice shit though, always."

"So Essence, you're never scared that you'll get caught?" I asked, she was just too calm and fearless talking about her fraudulent affairs.

"Scared? No. My adrenaline is working overdrive. Plus they can't say you're not the person because you know all the information and if they think it's a problem they'll just deny the credit. That's all, and I keep it moving. Plus, not too many people are up on this lick yet, it's all good right now but the same rules applies to them. They don't know the person personally. Unless, it's the branch where she actually banks, so they typically think I'm the person and my picture is on the I.D. I once had an young, amatuer teller verify the signature. But the real person scribble-scrabbled her name so I did the same and it worked. Once you get used to it, you can do it in your sleep. Plus I always flirt with the tellers, men or women alike. Always give compliments and shit. Whatever you have to do, just PAY ME damn it!" laughing.

I laughed at her dramatics too, "I can't believe this shit is real. It sounds too good to be true."

"Yeah it is unreal to me sometimes too." We pulled up to the brand new lofts downtown and Essence hit the underground garage opener.

Pulling into a stale, my suspense couldn't rest any longer, "You live here?!"

"Uh huh, come on," she said and we went up to the sixth floor.

"How long have these condos been up?" I asks.

"Three years. I bought mine in the first phase of construction. So I got mine at a cool price."

"Now, they're kind of ridiculous with the amount they are asking for."

We step out the glass elevator and walk towards her door. She opens it and I can't believe my eyes. This place looked like something on MTV 'Cribs'. With my first glance I saw a baby blue leather sectional with a baby blue, yellow, and white rug. As my eyes continued to introduce themselves to the immaculate interior design, they were met with a sixty or seventy inch flat screen on a marble wall, a glass bar fully loaded with beautiful paintings, photography and artwork. I was in awe as I made my way over to the handmade vases and marble fireplace.

"You want to look around? Go right ahead," Essence smiled modestly, as if she were being complimented about her decorative skills for the first time, "My hungry ass is going to make something to eat."

Essence strolled her way into a huge, stainless steel kitchen with granite counter tops everywhere. I walked into one room, I guess it was the guest room because it wasn't too big. There was a queen size leather bed with two end tables, beautiful lamps, a glass TV stand, another flat screen TV and nice pictures on the wall. The bedspread was purple suede, it was very nice I must say. The adjoining bathroom was decorated in purple and silver. Walking down the hall, I came upon another room with a desktop, Apple computer, phone, fax machine, paper shredder and a black leather sofa with a black and white zebra rug. This was very nice as well. But that was just the beginning, the master bedroom was the bomb, the other rooms were mere warm ups.

She had a king size mahogany canopy bed with a black and white comforter and to top it all off, her initials were engraved. The bed was highlighted by roughly ten throw pillows in red, black, and white. In the corner stood a black leather chair and matching ottoman with a mink rug, resembling the color scheme of the room. Another sixty or seventy inch flat screen sat on the wall, joined by an oil portrait of Essence, in the nude, with a see-thru robe. The portrait painted a romantic fantasy with a chocolate covered strawberry in her mouth and a glass of champagne in her hand. She sat ever so elegantly in a King's chair, a throne and topped off her regal appeal with a Tiara on her head. And like many great kings, this powerful portrait was hanging over the bed where she rested. She even had a fireplace in her room with a bucket of champagne and two flutes. The color scheme was not shy to the bathroom either. It was red, black and white Chinese print, adding a foreign touch. *This is what the fuck I'm talking about. Living and shit. I need something like this.*

"Asia you ready to eat?" she yelled from the kitchen.

Essence was sitting at the island where she placed my plate.

"Your house Essence... is bomb girl!"

"Thank you, I'm glad you like it,"smiling. "I hope you enjoy the meal, it's my specialty. Grilled salmon with lemon pepper, baked potato and a seafood salad."

"Looks delicious," I say, eyeballing the feast that awaited my devour. I take a bite, "Um and taste delicious!"

"Good, now eat up!" she says, pouring us both a glass of wine.

"So Essence you bought all this nice stuff off people's profiles?" I asks.

Shaking her head, "Yes, I opened credit at the furniture

stores too. Instead of having anything delivered, I picked it up. I rented a truck in the profile name and went to get my shit," laughing.

"You're a mess Essence. How can I be put on? I'm sprung already and haven't even done shit yet. But *this* is what I'm talking about," waving my hands in the air, pointing at everything so she understood my point.

"Well Asia, I only got involved because I actually needed the money to put me through school. But this shit is addicting like crack. One good hit and you're sprung," taking a sip of wine, "...and bank hits are good hits."

"I can imagine, you don't put all that money into your account do you? I mean, since you're a college student and all, wouldn't that draw attention to yourself?"

"Noooo! I only keep around seven to ten thousand in my account at a time. But I have several accounts and I mostly invest in stocks and bonds - they guarantee money for the long haul. Plus, I'm planning on retiring soon. I don't want to get too far ahead of myself and get caught up. I'm comfortable, and plus, when I start medical school, I won't have time for this shit anymore."

"Oh, so you're majoring in Medicine?" I asked, trying to balance between listening and eating - somehow they seemed one in the same, I was being fed multiple ways.

"Yes, I changed my major, it was business at first. I might make it my minor though."

"That's cool, my dad is a surgeon."

"Is that right? Poor little *rich* girl..." Essence said, she was now curious about my motives, "So why would you want to get into the game? You come from money."

"I know, but I want to get my own, on my own terms. You know?" looking her in the eye, so she could receive me.

"Yeah well I was forced to get mine."

"Well Essence you've done good for yourself, you've 'moved-on-up' like the Jefferson's honey!" singing, "but seriously, this would be a good look for me. You know my dude hustles too."

"I know that fine-ass-nigga Vance you got. I've seen him at the school a couple of times. That's why I was comfortable with telling you because I knew you could relate. But make no mistake, no one knows anything about me, not even close associates. I had a couple friends when I first started and they started acting shady and shit. Like they weren't happy for me. They knew what kind of struggles I had been through, but jealousy and envy is a mothafucka'. So I had to let them go. I see them from time to time in passing and I just toot my horn and do it moving." I was looking at her in awe, *this chick really got game*.

"But if you're serious about being put on, I can hook you up. But you can never tell Vance it was me that put you on...him and my people are real cool and he speaks highly about you," I unconsciously flashed a quick smile and she continued.

"'My lil' mama this, lil mama that'. I don't think he would approve of you dipping into this thug life," she laughed and threw up a few mock gang hand signs.

"I'll never cross you up Essence, trust that. And what he doesn't know won't hurt him, right?" raising my glass. She raised hers. Then we toasted.

"I'll drink to that."

7

I'M A HUSTLER BABY

Asia Smith

The first time I went inside of a bank with a fake I.D., Essence was right by my side - partner in crime, literally. The previous day, the roles were reversed and I observed the skill in detail to see exactly how it was done. She was the Denzel of my training day and she was right, the shit was like taking candy from a baby, sweet.

"May I help you?" the bank teller asked, she looked to be about middle-aged and ready to end her shift. I handed her my withdrawal slip and I.D. without a blink. I smiled at how I finessed her, I was well prepared for my first time in the field and Essence had made sure of that. I even remembered the social security number, just in case she asked, but she didn't.

"You don't have your bank card Mrs. Sutherland?"

"Oh no, I'm traveling and usually don't carry cards with me, only travelers checks in case of an emergency. But I do have one major credit card," I retorted.

"May I see it for one piece of identification please?"

"Sure," I pulled it out of my Gucci wallet and handed it to

her. She looked at it and handed it right back.

"Thanks," she said. "How would you like your cash? Big bills or small?"

Jackpot, "It really doesn't matter, they all spend the same. Whatever you have in your drawers is fine."

She counted out $5,000 cash and put it in an envelope, "Have a nice day Mrs. Sutherland."

"Thank you kindly and you do the same." I wanted to bust out laughing but I didn't. Essence and I walked out the bank and into the car I rented under my profile's name. We drove off and enjoyed the high.

"You did good Asia, I mean Mrs. Sutherland," laughing and rolling down the window to feel the fresh air, "you didn't look nervous at all," she said proudly.

"I really wasn't. I just wanted everything to go smoothly," I said, taking the freeway en route to our shopping spree - I gave her $2,500 because it was her work we used and it was only right to split. And with that money, we headed to the mall.

"Do you want to do more banks tomorrow and Saturday?" she asked.

"Hell yeah! I'm pumped now." Essence laughed again, only this time at my excitement.

"Well, the next two you can do by yourself. Do you feel comfortable?"

"I feel like that Devry commercial. 'You can do it!'" We started laughing in syncrasy

"You're so crazy Asia. That's what I like about you. You're fine as hell like me, sexy, with a gangsta swag."

Did she say 'fine' and 'sexy'? Oh no, I hope she don't swing my way. I changed the subject quick, "Where do we shop first?" I asked.

"I want to go to Kenneth Cole, there's an outfit and boots I want. They have some nice shit in there."

"I like their stuff too," I say.

After the Kenneth Cole store, we hit Saks. I dropped a thousand easily in there but hell, it was worth it. I was celebrating my new profession. And plus I'll make more money in the next few days. I dropped Essence off and told her I'll see her tomorrow morning. She waved 'bye' and got out the car. *Boy this has been a helluva day. I'll call India later to fill her in on my little adventure.* I was tired and I know Vance was probably home waiting for me. What a day. The next twenty-four hours was the same thing, different day, same scenario. The banks were hella cool. We were killing them and my confidence was through the roof. It felt like I had been doing this for years. Essence has so much work that I could actually be doing this shit for years. But I decided that only a few more hits should suffice, then I'll chill. But like she said, 'one hit of this and you're addicted'. *Man I'll probably end up needing rehab. But am I willing to go? Hell naw!*

8

CHILLING AT THE BAR

India Smith

My mom and I were out back sitting by the pool, doing a little catching up, "So, India have you spoken with your sister lately?"

"Yes, Mom. She's actually in town on her way over here, we're going shopping. You want to come with us? We haven't done that in a while?"

"No thank you, sweetheart. I have a dinner date," she said, sipping her a glass of white wine.

"A date with who?" I questioned, "Mom, you're married. Or did you forget?"

"I haven't forgotten anything, it's not what you think lil' lady," laughing.

"Oh, sorry Mom."

"It's ok, we're all judgmental at times," crossing her legs in her deep colored red dress, it was almost burgundy, matching the stain of her lips. I was blessed to come from a woman who carried this err of class and sexiness on a daily bases. But along with her sass, came an attitude to match, just like Asia and that's where the two butted heads.

"Mom please try not to argue with Asia when she gets here ok?"

"I can't make any promises India. Your sister can be so rude and obnoxious sometimes. It's hard to believe you're twins. Such opposites."

"I know right? Just please mom try - "

"Try what?" Asia asks, sneaking up on our little powwow.

"Nothing Asia...you finally made it! You were supposed to be here hours ago," I say.

"Hello Asia, you look nice," Mom said, complimenting Asia - it didn't matter how much they got into it, a mother could not deny her daughter's beauty.

Giving Mom a kiss on her cheek, "Thanks Mommy, where are you going Boss Lady? Looking all good?"

"Boss lady?" she looked confused. Mom continues, "What type of slang is that Asia? What does that mean exactly? We started laughing.

"You're a boss mom, it's nothing bad."

"Umph, I bet. It probably means 'bitch' or something,"Mom said, tightening her lips.

"No it doesn't, calm down. Where's my daddy?" asked Asia.

"You know perfectly well where Dr. Smith is at this time of the day," rolling her eyes.

"Oh yea, boning one of those student nurses, huh?" laughing, "I'm..playing..mom," she tried to say as the laughs continued to flow.

"No you're not Asia, that's not funny!"

"But he probably is Mommie," I interjected, joining in on the joke but that backfired immediately because Mom cut her eyes at me, "why are you looking at me like that Mom?"

"It's because you and Asia are just alike," smacking her lips, "whatever you say India," she said but her attention had already redirected to something else. She was not paying much attention to me anymore because she was preoccupied by the arm candy on Asia's arm.

"My dear Asia."

"Yes Mom?"

"Who bought you that Presidential Rolex and the ring, they're absolutely beautiful," reaching for the jewels.

"Thanks Mom, you like that huh?" Asia extended her wrist so Mom could get a better look of her new bling.

"Vance gave them to me for my birthday."

"Oh, Vance...what school did he attend again Asia?"

"Liberty," Asia snatched her hand away and crossed her arms defensively.

"Where's that college located Asia?"

"It's not located anywhere! It's actually not a college at all Mom...it's a high school."

"Oh Asia, you couldn't get yourself a nice young man with a degree? Making legal money?" she was revved up now, ready for battle. She hated to see her daughters falling short of the wisdom she bestowed, and drug dealers where the bottom of the barrel in her eyes when it came to successful, powerful men.

"I knew you were going to start mom..."

Asia was defeated at this point, "How about I print him a degree off the internet for you? Some people make them all day long, ready to go. And Mom, I don't even have a degree yet, so why should he?"

"Well that's your choice Asia, but you do attend college. I know because I pay for it, and you need to get your act together. Psychology is a wonderful major to be in right now. You can find yourself a nice psychiatrist or something like that."

"Mom you need a psychiatrist, ok. And Vance makes more money than any M.D., PH.D, D.D. or whatever initial you want to put in front of a 'D' that gives him some type of worth suited for your liking. We're straight Mom."

"Well Ms. I-don't-have-a-degree, just make sure you put some of that money aside for his bail because you're going to eventually need it," laughing.

"Oh you got jokes Mom, huh?"

"Asia let's go," getting up and throwing her my keys, "my head hurts and y'all are too much sometimes...bye Mom." I utter through the pain and our mom just sat back with her leg peeking through the slit of her dress and sipped her wine nonchalantly.

"Bye Mom," Asia says rolling her eyes and walking away with a mission.

"Your mother is going to make me hurt her one day, I'm serious," Asia said, getting in the car.

"And that's going to be the day you die bitch if you fuck with my Momma." I say sternly, in a serious tone - *who's the serious one now?* "What took you so long anyways? You left my house this morning around 10 a.m."

"I know, I had some stuff to take care of." I started looking at her like, what stuff?

"What you looking at me like that for India?" Asia paused and took a deep breath, "...Rusty called me."

"Oh, I should have known, can't get enough huh? You playing with fire Asia, why?"

"Why, what? I'm grown. Stay out of grown people's business."

"Ok grown ass, don't call me talking about I'm pregnant and I don't know by who?"

"Bitch please we used protection!" Asia snapped.

"What kind of protection? Asia? Bike helmets so you wouldn't get a concussion from hitting your head on the head board!"

"You play too much," she said, trying to brush me off.

"I'm serious, don't call me!" I yelled but Asia started laughing as if was all a joke, as if she wasn't fucking with real niggas who did real shit of they felt any sense of disloyalty, "It's not funny, where are we going anyways?" I asked.

"To Neiman Marcus, I saw a bag I wanted and I needed to go to Gucci for a few things."

"You have some work Asia? I don't want to spend no money if I don't have to." I admired Asia's grind but I wasn't surprised by it either, I knew she always had a little 'bad girl' in her ever since the Barbie incident years back.

"Yeah, you know I got some work!" she said confidently.

"Well let's get to work then," I laughed and realized how crazy it was being twins sometimes and how quickly we could transition from yelling to loving in a split second. I guess that was just the extension of a woman's temperament, hot and cold, or lukewarm and room temperature - you just never knew what you were going to get.

"First, India, let's stop at CJ's. I need a drinnnk," Asia dragged her words exhaustively.

"You want to go to the bar before we go to the mall?"

"Yes, what's wrong with that?" she asked a bit taken back.

"Oh nothing, I suppose Asia," *she finds any excuse to drink.* The last time her and my mom got into it, we went drinking but that's because they blew up at one another. I began laughing to myself at the memory.

"What's so funny over there?"

"I was just thinking about the last time you and Mommie got into it."

"Oh yeah, that time she put me out," Asia shook her head.

"Remember her yelling 'Asia don't walk away from me while I'm talking to you young lady."

***

Asia Smith

"Mom, I don't have time for this shit," I uttered under my breath, or so I thought.

"Did you just say a curse word at me?" My mom asked, fully estranged by my last comment.

"Yes Mom, it slipped out."

"Get your disrespectful ass out of my house!" she yelled, at a higher octave than normal.

"Mom did you just say a curse word at me?" I said, with a tone of sarcasm.

"Can't we all just get along?" India yelled.

"India never disrespects me Asia, you forget I'm your mother," walking up to me.

"No I haven't forgotten Mom! And India be thinking it but she doesn't say it...believe me," my mom walked past me and slammed the door behind herself in full fury, she was too through.

***

India Smith

"Yea that was funny, Mommie was furious," Asia said, slowly stepping back into the present as the nostalgic memory fades.

"And so was I," I say laughing because we could laugh about it now, but back then it was another story.

"You two are just alike, age is the only difference between you two and that's it," laughing.

"Fuck you India," pulling up in front of CJ's, the most popular bar in town, "I'm glad it's early so we don't have to park real far."

Getting out the car, "How long are you in town for Asia?"

"I'm leaving tomorrow."

"Oh," is all I could say.

Walking in the bar, waving at a few familiar faces, "Let's sit at the bar, I don't want a table. I can't stand that waitress."

"Who can you stand Asia?"

Our good friend, who happens to be the owner walks up, "Hey beautiful twins, what's good?"

"Hey CJ, why are you behind the bar?"

"I own it don't I?" laughing.

"Yea but you're bartending today?"

"Sam had an appointment today, what are you having? The usual?"

"And you know this man!" we all broke in laughter.

"Coming right up," he says, walking to the back.

"India what's wrong with your Mother?" Asia asked, redirecting her attention to me.

Shrugging my shoulders, "I don't know, she's crazy I guess and that's your Mother too Asia, we're twins."

"Fuck all that twin ish, her own mother don't even bother with her."

"That's not true Asia. Mommie talks to Granny all the time. I talk to Granny more than you two put together India."

"I call her at least once a week. And she always says the same ol' thing. 'Is your stuck up mother still crazy? Acting like she's all that?'."

"Granny would spill all the beans, 'Is she still walking around like she didn't fuck her way to the top, shit I remember when that lil' hoe was screwing her sister's man and by 'sisters', I mean it in the plural sense. I wouldn't trust her with my cat. And your snobby twin sister doesn't care either. She acts just like her damn Momma. Is she a lil' tramp too?'."

"Granny didn't say that Asia, you're making that up," I snapped.

"She did India," laughing.

"Well if she did say that, did you kill her?"

"Kill her? What are you talking about?"

"Well Asia she could have just died instantly from a major heart attack when you told her you were actually the twin that's a hoe, not me," laughing. "Plus when I call Granny she acts all happy to hear from me."

"That's because she doesn't want to hurt your feelings. For real, she doesn't like you two bitches," pointing at me, kiddishily.

"You play too much Asia."

"No, your grandmother loves you but she can't stand Mom."

"That's because they're just alike. All three of ya'll. Look alike and act alike."

Asia started looking at me crazy, "And who do you look like India?" with a raised eyebrow.

"Shut up and order us another drink."

"Thanks CJ," we acknowledged him with a head nod when he gives us our second round.

"So how are you and Vance this week?"

"You know, same shit. Different day or night, nothing's changed much. But Monique's running around saying I'm 'trying to take her man'. Bitches always trying to say somebody stole their nigga." Asia shook her head.

"I would say that too, if a man leaves you and has a whole relationship elsewhere! And we know *if* you let him come back, he'll leave again. Mommie said if you let a man disrespect you once, he'll do it two, three more times. So if a man doesn't want you, why not move on? Because it certainly won't be right the second time around. Why would you even want him back after he left you the first time? Bitches are crazy man I swear," laughing and synchronizing my head shake with Asia's.

"Shit they be back and forth, up and down like the stock market." Asia said, "After the first time he fucked up, I would say 'to hell with his ass', and get my fat ass child support check and hook up with the next hottest thug popping," slamming her hand on the bar counter.

"Shit some of these chicks are so far in denial, it's scary." I said.

"If my nigga wrote a song about his ex-that he doesn't even have a baby with, that should be a key indicator – '*Bitch move fast, quick and in a hurry!*'" Asia rapped.

"I think that song went platinum too," adding to her dramatics and laughing.

"She needs CD's and collectables of that record in her house, car, iPad, and cellphone as a reminder - '*If you like it, then you should put a ring on it*," laughing.

"Damn that's cold Asia, but you're right. She's kinda cute though and faithful," I say sarcastically.

"I'll be *faithfully* asking for my checks every month, but flossing with the next nigga like a real one. Maybe she has a side nigga she's keeping secretly?" Asia hunched.

"Secretly, why? All his shit is done openly. How many relationships did he have during her? And his new chick is bad as fuck...," I proclaim, looking over at my sister.

"You right, it's totally over for her now. There's no get back, no comparison. She crept in and the next thing she knew, she was the one...just like me. But that was back when they were young, years ago." Asia said.

"Well Asia, some women just don't get it." I said.

"I see but they have the audacity to call us 'hoes'. No boo, boo! But if the tables were turned, it's ok for a man to leave you when he's tired. Well I'm a woman and I'm leaving you when I'm tired too. I leave just like they do but first. Except it might be with your business partner if I'm trying to upgrade, it just depends," laughing, "but I'm a 'hoe' though. Whatever...my pussy clean, no disease, bomb pussy and head. He's going to be the one in denial."

"Yes Asia, your right and speaking of black couples, I do love Puff and his new boo together - she's hella bad, cute, swaggy and got her own with no kids, hand down wifey material. She's another baddie and you have to love her," smiling. "her style is impeccable and I don't care how many motherfuckers she's been with Hollywood, NY, or wherever, they were all spying on her ass anyway." I said.

"That ass though, just hot!" Asia said, "If that's what that nigga likes, and with all that money she gets a month, she should get some ass implants if that's what his fine ass likes. Let me be seen with his fine ass. The tabloids would become rich off us. Because if he does have it going on down there like I think, they'll have pictures of us making love in the club, at the bar, and in the car," laughing.

"I'm serious, shit is going down, literally. And you know how

I love to suck dick, I'll be yelling 'nigga pull my hair so the tabloids can see this'. The picture is only going to be my mouth because the dick go be all in it. Evaporated," laughing. We were hollering in laughter at this point in the bar now. Everybody was looking at us crazy.

"Hell India, I'm going to be posting pictures all on social media and let all them hatin' ass bitches know what's up," Asia said.

"Stop it, you're making my stomach hurt," trying to finish another sip of my drink through the jokes.

"You wouldn't do the same India? Tell the truth." Asia said.

"Of course big sis. Shit, that fine ass nigga can take my virginity in my ass," laughing. "and make me like it."

"You nasty India!" slamming her drink down, from my raunchy response, "but see that's what's up. Now I know you're my twin sister because at first I had my doubts. You've been impersonating this whole time and shit," laughing.

"Fuck you Asia!"

She held her finger up like she was about to walk out of the preacher's sermon, "Excuse me India, my phone is ringing." Asia said.

"Hello. Hi baby what's up?" smiling, "Baby I'm going to put you on speaker, tell me that again," pressing the speaker button on her phone.

"I wish you were here to suck this big, hard, black, long dick." Vance uttered.

"I was just telling India about sucking dick baby. I wish I was there too. I would suck that dick so good, the skin will be sucked off. I'll suck it so much that it'll be albino when I'm finished with it baby," laughing.

These two freaks are perfect for each other. He started laughing, Asia and I couldn't even hold it in anymore, we fell out like somebody was tickling us. This lady who was sitting at the bar looked at Asia like she was disgusted. I knew what was coming before I could say anything.

"What the fuck are you looking at me like that for?" Asia

sternly questioned the lady, catching her off guard, "Don't be mad because you don't have a nigga's dick to suck tonight, and that you're just jealous because you have to come to a bar and try to pick one up. Stupid ass bitch!" The vicious words riddled off her lips like bullets exiting the barrel of a gun. I had to jump in and speak before Asia loaded up for the next round of fire.

"Asia stop, that's enough." I said.

"No, fuck her stupid ass," shots were fired once again.

"Baby!! Baby!!" Vance was yelling on speaker. The lady was obviously embarrassed because she moved, shit, I was embarrassed too but that shit was funny as hell. Asia is a fool foreal.

After our third drink, we left and barely made it to the mall before it closed, but we still managed to do some damage. Essence gave Asia a black American Express card with the name 'Ling Ling', it was obviously a profile from an Asian woman. Asia had an I.D. for extra legitimacy but she said, 'Them fuckers better not try to ask me for my I.D. with this AX, they never ask when the signatures match. Plus, it's a black card and it comes with perks. For all they knew, I could be married to an Asian. Fuck them, they better not discriminate against me!'. And when we got to the register, they never asked her, not in one store.

We had so many bags, we filled up the trunk and the back seat. Once we got to my house I was ready to pass out. Asia started packing, she had to purchase another Louis Vuitton luggage set for all the new stuff she brought for her and Vance. I just put my bags in the spare room with all the others that I hadn't gotten around to yet. I needed a mansion, like on cribs, for all the shit I had. I felt like a celebrity or something, but Asia was even worse.

Between her and Vance's closet, they were able to donate clothes during Christmas to five local churches in Atlanta, four battered women's shelters, seven goodwill stores and three drug rehabs centers across the city. And they only wore designer clothes. Could you imagine a homeless person in Dolce & Gabbana, holding up a sign, asking for money? Nobody would give them a dime, I know I wouldn't. But that's just goes to show you how much stuff they had to give, the community and streets were definitely thankful of their charitable deeds. But if their wardrobe was considered large, it was incomparable to the amount of love and synergy they felt for one another. That's why, even with all of that shit Asia talks, I know she ain't going nowhere and neither is he. He might as well get a tattoo like ours and join the club.

9

THE BLACK EYE

India Smith

Why is my house phone ringing at three o'clock in the morning? "Shit!" I say, scuffling to answer the phone.

"Hello India? Yes, it's me Asia you sleep?" she asked, I couldn't tell if her voice was trembling or she was just half asleep like me.

"What you think I'm doing at 3am in the morning?" I said, laying in bed.

"You by yourself?" Asia asks.

"Yes Asia, if I wasn't I damn sure wouldn't be answering the phone," rolling my eyes under the covers.

"I have to tell you something, promise me you won't get mad...." Asia's voice trailed off awaiting my response, my declaration of loyalty.

"What Asia?" my heart began to beat.

"I have a black eye." Asia said, in a tone that I was unfamiliar to. Now I was awake, body erected and sitting up bed. My relaxed demeanor faded.

I needed to confirm what I was hearing, "A what?"

"You heard me, I just sent you a picture to the cell phone that you're not answering."

"Hold on, let me get it out my purse," I say, still processing what my sister just told me. "Asia you're not bullshitting, Vance hit you?"

"Yes he did. So please curse him out." Asia said.

"Why did he hit you Asia? And why did you let him? He's not dead is he?" I ask, my heart beating faster.

"NO HE'S NOT DEAD!" Asia yelled loudly, "He's right here and he won't leave." Asia said.

"Are you scared? You want me to call the police?" I ask.

"NO! And don't tell the Huxtables either." Asia said.

"I won't. Daddy would have a heart attack, Mommie would probably say 'that's good for you'," laughing. "So I guess that's what I would look like with a black eye huh?" looking down at the picture Asia sent me.

"Yes, but not as cute." Asia said.

"What you mean not as cute? There's nothing cute about that," her ego was insane, I was worried about her safety and she's still in a beauty contest.

"I mean, I'm cuter than you India. So you wouldn't be as cute."

"You so stupid." I said.

"Vance who's cuter? Me or India?" Asia asks.

"You baby, you know that." I hear him say in the background.

"Tell Mr. Tyson to shut up! Half of the time he can't even tell us apart with his stupid ass! I'm flying down there tomorrow on a black eye (opps), I mean redeye..."

"Fuck you bitch," Asia laughed.

"So tell Vance not to have his ass there. Where's the other bitch anyways? That's who he should be hitting in the eye!" I yelled, I had so many mixed feelings about the situation.

"You stupid India, you want to talk to him?" Asia asked.

"Hell no bitch. That's you who kisses and make up. I'm still mad, like you should be. And why did he hit you Scarecrow?"

"Scarecrow? What does that mean India?" Asia asked.

"You act like you have no fucking brain. That what it means. I'm going to take you to see the wizard," trying to laugh off some of this steam, I just couldn't make sense of the situation.

"Fuck you," Asia said.

"He shouldn't be able to live without a breathing machine. So why did he hit you?" my curiosity heightening as the moment progresses.

"India please," laughing, "because he called me a 'No class, triflin', disrespectful bitch'. And I responded 'Negro I've sat down and had dinner with presidents, mayors, and congress members all my life. I do have class, I was raised by the classiest woman I know, literally.

You're momma is the bitch with no class wearing blue weaves and the last time I saw that bitch, she was digging in her nose, with them long ass nails, flicking the shit off and had the audacity to not wash her hands. Now where is the class at in that? And you talk about me not having no class and being disrespectful. If that's not a blatant statement coming from you, I don't know what is, you punk ass nigga!' Next thing I know, star spangle banner..." laughing, and that was Asia's storytelling skills at it's best.

"Were you at a restaurant Asia?" I asked.

"Of course, you know that fool ignorant as hell. He wouldn't care if we was at social services main office, especially if I start talking about his twenty-year-old mama with them red streaks in her bangs," laughing.

"You better shut up before he hit you again and you have to wear them stunner shades like his mama be wearing," we both started laughing.

"She does doesn't she? You remember that huh?" Asia said.

"Yes, the last time you took me to her house, she had them on. I was looking like, *this has to be some kind of a joke* but it wasn't."

"India she refuses to grow up for some reason. Last year, he asked me what to get her for Christmas. He already bought her young ass a new car for her birthday, mind you, she also has a new house so I said, ' a gift certificate to Toys-R-Us'," we both started laughing again.

"I agree with him, you don't have no class and you are disrespectful, I'll call you back when I wake back up. I'm going back to sleep. I love you, bye!" hanging up in her face because she would have continued to talk. I was laughing to myself, trying to get comfortable so I could fall back to sleep.

A gift certificate to Toys-R-US, that girl needs some help and fast. This past year has been crazy with them two, I'm so glad I'm not going through that, falling back to sleep. When I finally wake up, I call Asia back to check on her.

"Hello, what's up India?" Vance answers.

"Hello Mr. Tyson, can I please speak to my sister with the black eye," he laughs and gives her the phone.

"Hello India." Asia said.

"Hey pirate, what's up?" I say jokingly.

"India what did you say to make him laugh?"

"I called him Mr. Tyson, that's all."

"You're stupid, but, you're coming right?" Asia asked.

"Yes, I'm about to pack and be on time because I hate waiting at the airport," I say, looking over at my empty suitcase and a closet full of clothes.

"I will, I promise. I'm going back to sleep, I'm tired." Asia said.

"Oh, you're tired now?"

"Yes, goodbye," hanging up.

"Rude bitch, I'm going to punch her in her other eye," I say to myself and finally roll over to get out of bed.

10

SHORT BUT BRIEF

India Smith

When I finally made it to ATL, Asia was already bossing me around, "India please don't mention shit about the incident, I'm trying to put it all behind me," she said, looking stupid as fuck.

How could she be so foolish? 'Behind you'? It only happened yesterday? I heard her plea but at the moment, I couldn't hold in my genuine feelings about 'the incident'.

"You sound hella stupid but whatever. Plus, it's really not any of my business nor do I want to get involved with your bullshit. I'm not into getting my ass kicked! I just wanted to make sure your dumb ass was ok," by the end of my statement Asia was looking at my crazy.

"Why you looking at me like that? You're the crazy one, not me," rolling my eyes, laughing, "plus I'm not staying long, my friend wanted me to fly down to help him house shop. So, I want be in your way too much anyways," Asia was still penetrating a menacing stare, "and stop looking at me like that with your one good eye," I said.

"Yes, whatever India, fuck you!" Asia retorted.

"I know...but it's true Asia, I'm over it already. Can you drop me off at the W Hotel please?" I asked.

"Oh you're not staying at the house? I thought you were making sure I was ok? What if I was really hurt?" Asia asked. I was trying to read between the over dramatics and her matter-of-fact reaction, somewhere in between lied the truth.

"Well Asia if you don't care, I sure in the hell don't. Plus I thought you were putting this 'behind' us. Just drop me off, my friend is picking me up at three this afternoon. I'll stop by after we come from house hunting and shopping."

I took a deep breath and continued, "And let me say this and I'm done! NO-FIGHTING, please! This is an advance warning. I didn't come here to watch a fight. If I want to see that shit, I'll go to Vegas to be entertained."

"Bitch, please. We're good, plus he didn't mean to hit me anyways," she said, sounding stupid once again.

"How do you accidentally hit someone?" I ask? "Oh my bad, nevermind, please don't answer that, I don't even care to know," sighing as we pull up to my hotel. Kissing Asia on the cheek, "Give my love to Vance," and I grabbed my bag and got out the car.

"You don't want me to come up with you?" Asia asks.

"No I need to hurry before he gets here, I'll call you when I'm done ok? Love you girl, see you later," I wave 'bye' and watch her drive off. Once she was out of sight, I waved for a cab and headed back to the airport. *I can't with this bitch and her antics. She's cool and back in love and shit. I'm going back home and not answering my phone for her dumb ass. This bitch is too stupid for me right now. I should have just told her I missed my flight in the first place. I don't know why I fall for her shit every time.*

The cab driver asks me, "What airlines?"

"Oh, Delta please."

Thank God for my Delta miles, I had a free roundtrip. I was glad I didn't waste my own money on this trip. *Oh well, until next time. Bye, bye ATL and Asia with the bullshit.* I couldn't deal with her right now. Hopefully she wakes up, because right now, she's still very much asleep mentally.

10

THE CONFRONTATION

Asia Smith

"Get dressed Asia, I'll be there in thirty minutes, we're going out to eat so be ready."

"Ok, I will. I'm about to jump in the shower." I said.

"I'm not playing Asia, be ready."

"I said ok Vance, damn," hanging up, *I don't know what's wrong with him but lately his ass has been acting funny.*

I got dressed really cute, wearing an off-the-shoulder sweater, wide leg trousers and knee high boots, even though you couldn't see how far the boots went up. To top it off, I wore my fedora hat. It not only made my outfit more playful but it covered up my hair, which needed to be washed. I switched bags for today too, lately I've been carrying my L.V. but with this outfit I wanted to carry a small signature Gucci. I put on some makeup and sprayed myself with Versace perfume. Some people may think name brands made them who they were, I on the other hand, carried these designers on my shoulders. It was my very essence that was captivating, versus, the nominal recognition of brands I surrounded myself in.

I'm ready, kissing myself in the mirror. I walked back to Kellie's room to tell her I was leaving but she wasn't there as usual. *She must be really feeling this nigga Chris because she's never home anymore. But anyway, where is this nigga Vance?*

"'You better be ready' and shit." I mock to myself. I look out the window and see him pulling up. Right on time. I walked out to the car, smiling.

"Hey baby," I say, getting in the car. I dropped my hip first, flirtatiously, so he could see my ass poking through my trousers. He reached over and gave me a kiss as I settled.

"What's good? You look nice as always," Vance compliments me, as expected.

"You too baby," I say back in admiration. He knows he's the finest thing in Atlanta. I'm honored to be his woman. His outfit was on point too. He had on an all white ATL fitted cap, white button up collared shirt, with a white L.V. tee shirt underneath a black L.V. puff vest, and a pair of L.V. denim jeans and black L.V. sneakers with that smooth chocolate skin, hazel eyes and deep dimples. I had to hold my composure every time I saw him. The boy was fine and all mines. Well, with the exception of that bitch Monique who was still hanging around like wet laundry and it's almost been two years. But she was nothing to me. She doesn't even get anytime with him and whenever she does, I make sure he's nice and wore out to even give his best performance. So, she can have some sloppy seconds if she wants. That's her bad. Even though she did have him first, she's ending last. I've moved in her spot, first place.

11

JAZZ LOUNGE

Asia Smith

We went to a jazz lounge that served dinner, it was nice and peaceful. I enjoyed it.

"Baby we need to talk about some things, so after we eat we're going somewhere quiet to talk," solemnly speaking.

"Ok Vance, whatever you want baby," I say in between sipping on an apple martini.

I really have to stop drinking every time I go out. After dinner, we head up the interstate, listening to some slow music once again. *Oh, something's bothering him, I* make the connection. He takes the exit heading towards the pier.

"We're going towards the pier baby?" I asks.

"Um hmm," he retorts. We pull into what looks to be loners lane by the water. It's beautiful until Vance says, "Asia what have you been into this past year and haven't told me about it? And before you answer, I just want you to know that if you lie about anything, you will find yourself in that ocean at the bottom with a few others that lied to me. I just want to make myself clear on this."

My mind was everywhere at one time, *'What the hell is he talking about'? This is some ol' Monique making shit up B.S.* I choose my words carefully before I spoke

"Baby I've never lied to you about anything nor have I've done anything that would hurt you. I talked to Rusty last week but I told him to top calling and he hasn't called back since," trying to be as truthful as possible.

"Ol' boy still calling huh? Asia I'm not tripping off you talking to him, just don't do nothing stupid, that's all," with a smirk on his face, "but that's not what I'm talking about ma'," Vance says.

"Come again? What then? I haven't done anything," then it hit me.

"Asia baby, you know I have eyes and ears in these streets. There's nothing and I mean nothing you can do, without me finding out. But you already know that though. And yet, still you choose to start robbing fucking banks and shit without telling a nigga nothing!" yelling.

"Why are you raising your voice Vance?" I asked.

He started looking like he would kill me right here in the truck and throw me in the river after, "Asia I'm going to ask you one more time and if you don't answer correctly, I'm going to beat your ass out here." he threatens, "even if I don't want to, I promise you I'll shoot you in your back and leave you for dead." his anger heightening as he continues to talk. "Stop fucking playing with me Asia!" Vance was screaming at this point.

"Well Vance, for starters if you shoot me in the back, you'll kill your baby. I was going to surprise you when we got home with the ultrasound pictures. So go ahead and shoot me Vance, that's double homicide," the secret was out.

I had just found out I was eight and a half weeks pregnant, thank God. He sat there, froze for a moment, just looking at me. Vance had never been a man lost for words, but tonight he was.

"Vance you ready to shoot me or what?" I asks fearlessly.

"Don't play with me Asia please," he said in a low tone, "Are you really pregnant?" He asks.

"Yes baby, I am. I went to the doctors after I missed my period two months ago and my doctor confirmed it. Then I went back to have an ultrasound to see exactly how far along I am. They said I'm about eight and a half weeks." I say, happy to finally get this weight off my chest, until Vance suddenly hit me with the next weight.

"So why have you been drinking with my baby Asia?" Vance asks.

"Well at first Vance, I wasn't sure I was going to keep it," I say.

"You weren't sure huh?" He asks, shifting his emotional temperament.

"No I wasn't."

"Well if you weren't sure, you shouldn't have told me because there's no way in hell you're killing my baby!" Vance yells, again. "Then I would kill you, seriously Asia. I don't have any kids so why would you want to do some stupids shit like that anyways?" he asks concerningly.

"Because Vance, my parents are going to have a heart attack when I tell them that I'm pregnant and not married. They are very old fashioned, especially my dad. It's going to be a disappointment," I was in rare form, at this moment, I resented the perception my parent's had of me and I would hate to further agitate it with this news.

"Disappointment my ass Asia. What about me? You didn't take the time out to think I would be disappointed?"

"Yes, that's all I've been thinking about lately, it's been weighing me down," I say.

"I love you Asia, but make no mistake about me removing you from this earth about mines. I'm almost thirty with no kids! Why wouldn't you want to give me that blessing, huh?" his voice sounded hurt.

"I do but just not now Vance," I said.

"Asia once again, you are not killing my shortie. Is that understood?" Vance asked.

Putting my head down, "Yes."

"Put your head up Asia, this is something to be proud about. You're the one that captured my heart girl, and you're the one who's having my shortie," smiling. "You already know you're going to be my wife. So why you trippin' ma'?" Vance asked.

"We never talked about marriage before Vance," speaking softly.

"That's because you're dumb ass running around town robbing banks and shit. I haven't forgotten about that subject either. Stop that stupid shit Asia. I have more than enough money to take care of you, stop trying to keep up with these other bitches. You talking about your parents are going to be disappointed, how are they going to feel when your ass goes to jail for robbing banks? Answer me Asia! Don't just sit there looking stupid," Vance demanded.

"I should slap the shit out your ass for playing me all this time. But you get a pass because of my shortie. When's your next appointment?" Vance asks.

"In a month, I think? I have all the paperwork at home," sounding defeated.

"Look at me baby...kiss me, I love you girl," embracing me and grabbing my chin so he could look me in the eye.

"I love you too," I say, returning his embracement, wrapping my hands in the nap of his neck, and leaned in for a kiss.

"We're going to have a shortie," smiling again, as if the thought was marinating and hitting him for the first time, "wait until I tell my niggas! I have to go celebrate. Shit, I might even get a commercial slot announcing it. You can buy that shit for about forty, fifty racks. I did it once for my restaurant when I first opened it," he was too damn excited for me.

Yes, we were going to have a baby, but the whole world didn't have to know. I guess this meant I was in this for the long haul with his ass. But i wasn't ready to stop hustling. And I wasn't about to stop. *I'll just take my business elsewhere where he doesn't know anybody.*

For the next month Vance stayed up under me, he wouldn't let me breathe. He would leave every morning and come home every night, and we were fucking and sucking like dogs in heat, non stop. My pregnancy had reached four months and I was scheduled for another sonogram at my next doctor's appointment and Mr. Daddy just had to tag along.

"Good Afternoon Miss. Smith, you here for your sonogram today? Have you had one of these before?" the doctor asked.

"Yes," I replied.

"Then you know how it works, it doesn't hurt at all. There's maybe a little discomfort. Is this young man going to escort you in or shall he wait outside?"

From her comment alone, Vance temper kicked in and he instantly got mad - glaring at her like, *bitch you're going to wait outside and I'll do the damn sonogram if that's the case.* But he didn't say a word.

I guess she read his mind, because before I could answer, she said, "You two follow me."

I changed into the blue gown with the back open and laid on the exam bed like she told me.

"You ready to see your baby?" she said.

Vance answered, "Yea!" She turned the lights down and put the cold gel on my stomach and moved it around a little.

"You comfortable?" she asked me. I said, 'yes' but I really wasn't.

"See there's the baby," she pointed on the screen and started explaining everything to us: the heart, lungs, fingers, toes, head, eyes, everything. My baby had their thumb in it's mouth, I thought that was cute. Vance asked can we find out the sex of the baby.

"Why sure if he or she allows us to find out and open its legs." the nurse complied with our inquiry.

After she hit a few buttons and measured to see if everything was accurate, she moved the tube and it went between the baby's legs. She didn't have to tell us, it was like Vance and I intrinsically knew it was a boy.

"Congratulations young couple, looks like you two are going to have a baby boy!" the nurse confirmed our unspoken assumption.

Vance was too excited and as a means of expression, he had tears in his eyes. The first time his tears welcomed me to witness their fall. The entire ordeal almost made me cry. After the appointment we went to eat and see his mom to tell her the news. Vance was too juiced. He couldn't stop smiling.

"Asia we're having a boy!" he kept reiterating.

If it wasn't real for me yet, it was definitely sinking in now, "I know baby."

"Vance Jr. We'll call him V.J.," he said 1000 times.

His mom was excited as well. *I wonder when was I going to get excited?* But low and behold, I felt Monique would somehow try and rain on my parade. And when it rains, it pours. Vance came home that night and laid on the bed. I was almost asleep.

He kissed my cheek, "Baby we need to talk."

"Ok," trying to close my eyes.

"Right now Asia!" Vance demanded, forcing me to wake up.

I sat up in bed and looked him in his eyes, communicating an heir of skepticism. He looked pitiful, "What's wrong Vance? Did something happen?" I thought someone got killed or something like that.

"I want to be the first to tell you before you hear it in the streets. Because that messy-ass hair salon you go to, knows *everybody's* business!" Vance emphasized.

"What Vance? You're scaring me," I said.

"Monique..." as soon as he said her name I knew, and suddenly his pitiful look was quite fitting, "...she says she's pregnant too." I just looked at him crazy.

"You know I haven't been fucking with her like that, I've been here with you every night. I don't know if it's true or not but she called me today and told me that shit!"

I was still looking at him like, *am I supposed to feel sorry for you nigga?* Finally, I spoke but the tears came rolling down first, "Vance fucking 'with her', and 'fucking her' are two different things! You mean you haven't taken her out to the movies, dinner, or what the fuck? I would have appreciated that much, instead of you fucking, but it is what it is. I suppose. I guess my son will have a sibling his age to play with," wiping the tears away.

"I'm sorry ma'," guilt riddling along his words.

Why do niggas always say they're sorry when they fuck a bitch? Let me say I was pregnant by another nigga and say 'I was sorry'. I would be 'sorry' alright, at the bottom of the river.

"But you, you're not sorry Vance, you're a pimp for that shit nigga. Two bitches pregnant at the same time. What's next? We have our baby showers together, too?" I was getting more upset as I was talking and the scenarios of humiliation were replaying in my head.

"I guess you're going to marry this bitch, huh? A polygamist, right? I mean y'all only been together for like 100 years. Please get the fuck out my house!" I'm asking nicely but still boiling with anger.

"Baby I said I was sorry, what you want me to do? I mean that's her body, I can't make her get an abortion," Vance was making his plea and failing miserably.

"I thought you didn't believe in those or at least you had me believing that shit. I might as well get one – " *POW!* I grabbed my face in shock.

"You slapped me Vance?" I asked in disbelief, as if his words would comfort the wound he just opened.

"I swear to God Asia, you say some stupid shit like that again and it's on. You ain't killin' shit of mine. That's my nigga in there," pointing at my stomach. "So stop talking that B.S.! You're trippin'!"

Still holding my face, I continued with my original threats, "Nigga get the fuck out my house now," Vance got up and walked into the bathroom to get a cold towel for my face.

"No matter of fact, I'll leave, and you stay," I say under my breath, as I'm getting out of bed, putting on my grey sweats I had on earlier. I grab my purse and run downstairs. I heard him coming out the bathroom behind me so I sped up to get a much needed head start. I jump in my car, lock the doors and drive off. *Where can I go, shit I left my phone. Fuck it, this way he can't reach me.*

Before I knew it, I was at Essence's house hitting her buzzer, "It's Asia, can I come up?"

She buzzed me in. When I got inside, I started crying and told her the whole story. She couldn't believe it. I told her to get me a glass of wine.

"My doctor said a glass of wine won't hurt the baby," lying out of my teeth but this was more beneficial to my emotional temperament, than it would be detrimental to my son's health. The truth is, I hadn't even discussed this with my doctor. A few tears and pours later, we both winded up getting drunk.

"You can sleep in my bed if you like Asia, I just want to comfort you. You shouldn't be be alone at a time like this," Essence said.

I didn't care where I slept, I just needed to lay down. She helped me to her bed and took my clothes off. I laid down on what felt like clouds. Her bed was so soft and comfortable. And next thing I remember, she was sucking my breast, and the shit felt good too.

"What are you doing Essence?" I asked, in between moans. I couldn't believe his shit was really happening.

"Just making you feel good, relax. I won't hurt you," then she slipped her fingers between my legs and made her way down. I wanted to stop her but couldn't for some reason. The shit was kind of kinky, kinky as hell actually. She found my spot with her tongue and went to work like a nine to five job.

The bitch had skills like a man, but better. There was a difference in her touch, feminine yet strong and she navigated my clit like it was her hometown. I guess a woman knows what a woman wants. She did so many different things to my body. She even put whip cream on me and licked it off. I'm not bisexual but I can see why so many women are. The shit was crazy. The following morning when I woke up, I had a slight hangover and headache.

"You awake sleepy head? I made you some breakfast. I'll bring it to you. Just stay put," Essence ordered. She came back with fresh orange juice, pancakes, eggs, bacon and strawberries with whip cream on the side. Then I had a flashback about the whip cream incident, just a few short hours ago. It was funny how after pleasure filled nights, your body reacts days following. Whether it was visual memories, physical flashbacks, aroma triggers or even postponed orgasmic shakes.

"Essence, thanks for the hospitality but last night was considered rape," I say picking up a piece of bacon.

"What?" Essence asked, a bit taken back.

"I'm kidding," laughing, finally breaking a smile, it had been closed dormant since last night's incident with Vance and his newfound baby momma drama.

Essence laughed too, "For a minute I thought you were going to call the police."

"No, but don't try that shit again," I said solemnly.

"Was that your —" Essence asked.

Before she could finish I said, "Yes! And, last time! I'm on dick, long, big, fat, black dick. You should try it, you'll like it. Believe me."

Essence started laughing again, "I like dick too but it's the best of both worlds," she said.

"I'll have to remember that," I replied.

I finished my breakfast, showered and left. Driving home I couldn't stop thinking about yesterday's events. People will take advantage of you if you let them and I wasn't going to play victim card because somewhere in the back of my mind, I knew this could happen. I just didn't know when. Essence had given me plenty of warning signs throughout our business trips. It started innocent like complimenting me, holding my hand a little too long and even kissing me on the lips. She went as far as buying me gifts and stuff. And Vance, let's not even go there.

Over the last couple of years, although he's spent the majority of his time with me but he didn't live with me nor did he stay every night. I knew he still messed around with Monique. After all, she did work for him. But she was the stupid one though, no bitch could come and remove me from my position. If I can't be at the head of the class, I drop out. That's my motto. Pulling into my driveway, I noticed his car isn't here. *Good, go be with your other baby mama.* I didn't want to have a confrontation anyways.

I take a hot bath, throw on a sweat suit, pack my luggage and book me a one way trip to Cali. *I'll show his ass not to play with me,* smiling. I pull my car into the garage and call a cab to take me to the airport. *I'll call India when I get there. She loves surprises anyway.* I slept the entire plane ride. I hadn't gotten much sleep the night before thanks to Essence freaky ass. *Damn, what a night of events.*

12

CONFRONTATION #2

Asia Smith

When I landed, I rented a car and drove to India's house. I had a spare key. I took a quick shower, ordered some food for delivery, laid on the couch and made myself comfortable. I turned my phone off so if Vance tried to call it would go straight to voicemail. India didn't get home until late. When she came through the door, she jumped.

"Damn Asia you scared me. Why didn't you call me to let me know you were coming? Any other time you call?" India said, adjusting her startled demeanor to a more welcoming one.

"Hey lil sis! It's going down in the ATL. If I didn't leave in a hurry you would be coming to bail me out of jail for murder in the first degree!" I didn't want to hesitate and it was quite apparent from my presence in this house, unplanned, that something was up.

"What happened now Asia? It's always something with you," India shook her head worrisomely.

"Well India, you already know I'm pregnant," I said to trigger her memory and set the stage.

"Ok Asia, I know that part, what else?" India asked.

"Guess who else is pregnant?" I asked rhetorically.

"Asia, no! You have to be joking!"

"So our babies are like twins or something. Isn't that some ol' ghetto shit? And the nigga act like it's nothing. I'm not fucking with him ever again. I'm good, just run me my money every month and we're good," I said.

"Does he know you're out here?" India asked, sitting down on the couch, I guess this was heavy for her too.

"I don't know, I sure as hell didn't tell him. Fuck him, let him be over there with the Hershey's kiss looking bitch, rubbing her ashy feet for nine months. I'm done India, I'm serious." I said, pushing my phone away from me.

"When are you going to tell Mommie and Daddy?" India asked.

"I'll take them out to dinner and break the news. That way they can't scream or holler and embarrass themselves out in public. And don't talk to Vance when he calls!"

"Like I said the first time...and I'm not playing, I don't want to be a part of your baby daddy drama," India said.

"I'm already stressing over school, that's why he would think I'm coming home late. I have a study group that I attend after class to help me pass my exams," I said, confessing my academic struggles.

"Well I don't know why you're having problems in school. You never did before, you were valedictorian all the way through high school?" India questioned.

I became somewhat defensive, "But this isn't high school India. This is college and the shit is a lot harder! It's more information to retain. Plus, I want to do well, in case I go for my PH.D."

"Whatever smartie pants and what are you doing about school anyways Asia?" India asked.

"I'm not doing anything because I'm not going," I said.

"Oh our parents are really going to be pissed, wasting their hard earned money! You better tell them before they find out. I would tell them about the pregnancy ASAP. So maybe they will at least feel some sympathy for you."

"Anyways India, did you think about what I told you about? The business I have with Essence?" I asked, changing the heavy subject.

"Yes, I did give it some thought, it sounds too good to be true," India said.

"I know, that's what I said. But it's the real deal. You see all that stuff I've been sending you, that evidence alone and it's all off the work –" I paused, I thought heard some noise in the background, "is that your house phone ringing?" I asked.

"Yes but I never answer it, most people just leave a message."

"If he calls India…I'm serious," I said.

"Now I think that's my cell phone," looking at the caller ID, glancing down at her phone, "Oh shit Asia it's him," India yelled, confirming my worst nightmare at the moment.

"Don't fucking answer it!" I screamed.

"Ok, ok calm down. I'll let him go to voicemail. But I don't want to be a part of this, you understand?" India reiterates her initial point.

"Does he have Mommies house number?" India asked.

"No, thank God! But knowing him, he could get it," shaking my head.

"Well in that case you better let Maria know what to say if he calls," giving me advice.

"She's going to say I'm 'not there' because I'm not!"

"Ok Asia, you have all the answers. But if I was you, I would make sure everyone was on the same page."

I gave her a blank look, "Well I'm going to bed, some of us have to get up in the morning. Since you're staying here, you better get some groceries because the refrigerator is empty," India said, laughing.

"I know, that's why I ordered some food. I left you a plate in the microwave," I said.

"Thanks but I ate before coming home. See you in the morning. Goodnight!" India made her way to her room.

"Goodnight India, I'm right behind you," yawning.

Two weeks had passed by and I still wasn't accepting any of Vance's calls. India talked to him a couple times. She said he called when she was in class so she had to answer and told him she would call him back.

"Asia I had a long talk with Vance today, I can't keep avoiding his calls and you shouldn't either. Just tell him you don't want to be with him and come to some resolution," India confessed.

"No!" I yelled, this situation has had me on edge. "I don't want to talk to him. But what did he say?"

"He said that he was flying out here and dragging you back to Atlanta by your hair and that you think he doesn't know where you are but he does," India said.

"Did he sound serious?" I asked.

"Yes he did. He said you had a doctor's appointment and you missed it. He's mad as hell Asia. Just call him," India is pleading at this point.

I wondered why she cared so much, "Hell no if he think he knows where I am, I'm going to stay at Rusty's house," I said.

"Now why would a pregnant woman stay at her ex-boyfriends to get away from her current boyfriend? That doesn't make any sense to me Asia," adding her judgmental two cents.

"Well none of this makes sense, does it India? fuck him – " I yell briefly before India cut me off.

India Smith

––

"Hello?" Asia answered the phone, "Hold on India," placing one finger in the air as a clue. *I can't believe her.*

"Rusty, what's good?" Asia said.

"I'm ok. I called you back, I know you're in town" Rusty stated.

"Yes, and I want to see you too," Asia said flirtatiously.

"Now? Ok I'm on my way." Rusty said and India hung up.

"India I'll be back in a couple days." Asia said.

"Asia please don't do this. This isn't right. You shouldn't be sleeping with your ex-while you're pregnant, that's nasty," making a face of disgust.

"All I'm going to do is go sleep India, I'm exhausted and you worry too much. I love you, I'll call you tomorrow," walking out the door with her overnight bag.

I don't think we have the same parents, shaking my head. *Well that's her life, she's making her bed, she has to lay in it.* I run myself a bubble bath to relax my mind. My cell phone rings, *Who the hell is calling at 11:30pm?*

"Hello," I answered the phone blindly, not looking at the caller I.D., or else I would have known not to answer. "Hey Vance, what you doing up this late?" I say, rolling my eyes.

"Just thinking about your crazy ass sister, she still not answering the phone?"

"Just give her some time, she'll come around. It's probably just her hormones – "

KNOCK! – KNOCK! – KNOCK! "Hold on a second Vance, someone's at my door." *Asia must have come to her senses and forgot her key.* Getting out the tub, I wrapped a towel around my body and grabbed my robe. *It better be her ass because nobody else should be knocking at this time of the night,* walking downstairs. I fling the door open and I'm instantly shocked.

"Oh my god!" I screeched.

Walking in uninvited, "Hey India, you left me on hold," Vance laughed.

"Vance what are you doing in California? And how do you

know where I live?" I asked out loud, but all I could think was, *this bitch is in trouble.*

"Where is your sister at India? Is she sleep?" Vance asked, looking at me suspiciously.

"Umm, I think she's at my parents' house," his gaze overwhelmed me. How a lion would look if his pride was threatened.

"You think?" Vance paused as if he was waiting for a better answer, "Come on India, you know exactly where your sister is. If she's not here, where else could she be?" he had a sinister look on his face.

"Umm the last time I talked to her, she was getting ready for bed," I said, trying to mask my discomfort.

"Then why are you fumbling over your words? Is there something else I need to know Is there something you're not telling me lil sis?" he asked, intruding deeper into my home and towards me, step-by-step.

"Umm, no. I mean she's at my parents' house and you know they're very strict. So we can't go over there tonight but in the morning," I say trembling, my mask seemed to have evaporated, my voice started to sound like I was about to cry and his intimidating presence didn't help either.

"India, I didn't fly all this wa,y to wait until tomorrow to see your sister. I have a plane to catch in the morning," lying. His calm demeanor scared they shit out of me, literally.

"Can I use your restroom," he started walking towards it before I even answered his question.

Damn this girl has fucked up, what can I do to warn her stupid ass? I told her not to go over there! He came back with my phone in his, looking at the last number in my phone history. *Shit, she called me from Rusty's house phone to say she made it. She's busted.*

"Who called you at 10:30 India? From a 410-" before he could even finish, I told him everything,

Damn I told her I didn't want to be in the middle of this shit. Driving over to Rusty's house, Vance kept asking me why a pregnant woman would be at her ex-boyfriend's house at this time of the night?

"Has she been staying with this nigga since she's been in town?" Vance asks.

"No! I swear she just went over there tonight after I told her what you said. She packed up and took a cab. He has a spare room," I said. *I hope for her sake, he really does.*

"It's not what you think Vance," attempting to save my sister's life from this man's fury. His boy was with him and I didn't know what they were going to do. But lord knows if he hurts my sister, he has to hurt me, that's just the way it is. As we approach the house, I wasn't quite sure which one was his – I had only been here once at night to drop Asia off and that was a long time ago.

"I think this is the house," I said pointing to a two story house with the lights off.

"India, I promise you I won't hurt your sister just as long as she's not fucking or saying something smart," Vance said laughing.

"Ok Vance," I reply.

From his expectations, her chances were slim because she's probably going to be doing both, knowing her. I started crying and praying at the same time, the heat of the moment was starting to take over and consume me in my emotions.

I wish I could call my parents but they would blow this all out of proportion. Plus, Asia still hasn't talked to them or seen them since she got here.

Vance and his friend walked to the door and rang the doorbell. A light turned on and Rusty opened the door. *BAM.* Vance hit him so hard in face that he stumbled back, leaving an opening for his opponent. Vance and his acquaintance walked inside and closed the door behind them. *Damn I wonder what's happening.*

Once inside, Vance told Rusty, "Nigga don't you know it's disrespectful to harbor someone else's woman? And especially when she's pregnant with his child!"

Vance pulled out his gun and placed it in his mouth, "You

want to disrespect me nigga. Two continents couldn't keep me away from mine," Rusty's eyes seemed to have been bulging from the pressure of the gun and utter shock.

"I don't hear you saying nothing nigga," Boobie started laughing. Rusty was so scared that he pissed on himself.

"Watch this nigga Boobie while I go see where Asia is. And if this nigga look at you wrong, R.I.P. his bitch ass," Boobie nodded in agreement as Vance made his way upstairs, in search of his mother to be.

Vance checked the first room which happened to be the master bedroom. Upon close observation, only one side of the bed had been slept on. Vance then went down to another room, what looked to be the guest room and opened the door quietly. He couldn't see, his vision was impaired because it was pitch black. However, through the wavering darkness, he could tell someone was in the bed. He found the light switch and turned it on. There she was, knocked out cold. Vance let go a brief sigh of relief. *She better count her blessings because I probably would have smoked both these motherfucka's if they were fucking.*

Vance sat on the bed next to Asia and started stroking her hair. She moved a little then he kissed her cheek. She looked up, saw Vance and almost had a heart attack. She grabbed her chest, Vance placed his finger over her mouth and said, "Shhhh." Taking her by the hand, she didn't object to his touch, she was scared to fucking death and he knew it.

Walking downstairs, he told Boobie, "Let that sucka' loose!" Asia looked and mouthed "I'm sorry," and they all left out the door.

Getting into the car, I saw my sister from the backseat crying, "Asia you ok?" I ask, still trembling and praying.

Asia sniffled, "I was fine until Death-Row-CEO-wannabe showed up," wiping a tear that rolled down the side of her face.

"I told you not to go but you just don't listen. How's Rusty?" I asked.

"That nigga good lil sis," Vance answered, "maybe a little shook up though," laughing.

"You think that shit is funny don't you Vance?" Asia asks, fuming with irritation. "Disrespecting that man's house like that —"

Before she could finish, Vance cut her off, "No Asia, what's disrespectful is having another man's bitch that's pregnant sleeping at his crib! That's as foul as it gets. For all I know, y'all could have been fucking. So that nigga would have to put his dick near my shortie and shit!" getting mad while talking, "THAT'S DISRESPECTFUL!" Vance pulled off for dramatic effect, the tires screeched against the concrete beneath us.

"Oh now you're calling me a bitch, because I was at my ex-boyfriend's house..." Asia paused, "soooo what name would be appropriate for you then Mr. Viagra. The man that has two bitches pregnant at the same time?" Asia had a point, a reason to act out. Any woman would feel a sense of betrayal if they were in her predicament.

"Look baby, Viagra is for pussy niggas, so gone with that shit Asia and you act as if a nigga did that shit on purpose, shit happens! And I don't want to talk about that," Vance demanded.

It was just like a nigga to deflect any emotional responsibility for his previous actions, especially actions with other women. If all men faced trial for their wrong doings, they would be deemed innocent until proven innocent. They claim women are the weak ones or too emotional, however, it's truly men who can't bear the weight of anything but their ego or a dumbbell, let alone guilt.

As if Boobie and I were no longer in their presence, Asia and Vance continued their heated discussion, "Well what do you want to talk about Vance? How you put a gun in Rusty's mouth?" Asia asked.

"Asia, look it happened, it's over with. Done! But if that was me, a nigga couldn't barge in my shit and take nobody out," Vance's ego took over the conversation.

"I wouldn't care if it was the niggas wife and I tried to walk out of the door with his back towards me. It just wouldn't happen," he concluded with confidence.

"Well everybody ain't you, Scarface ass nigga!" Asia yelled.

"India I'm sorry you have to go through this," looking annoyed, I also buckled my seatbelt tighter because we we driving way over the speed limit down the highway.

"Are you dropping me off Vance or am I kidnapped?" I asked.

"Yes sis, I'm dropping you off. Sorry I had to put you in my business like that. But your twin is way out of line. Not just for being at the niggas crib, but her whole get down up until this point. She needs a refresher course in the respect department and I'm the one who's going to have to give it to her ass, literally," laughing as he got off the exit to my house.

"Vance please..." pleading, "don't hurt Asia. I know she does things irrationally sometimes but she really doesn't mean any harm," the tears began to flow as we were pulling up.

"Lil sis, I love you like a blood sister and trust me, I'm not going to kill her, just give her a lil' spanking to wake that ass up. Plus she's carrying my shortie, I can't do too much damage now could I?" Vance parked out front. "Now go upstairs and get you some rest. Try not to worry too much. She's in good hands," Vance laughed. "I'll be by to swoop you up around noon so we can go sightseeing. I've never been to the Bay Area, plus I need to meet your parents. I already had a long talk with your father, he seems pretty cool."

Asia and I look at each other like 'Oh shit!'

"Now go get your beauty sleep," Vance kissed my forehead goodnight, like a big brother seeing his sister off to college. I get out of the car in total disbelief. This was some motion picture shit forreal. *Well, Asia never listens, and never has.* When I get inside my house, I call Rusty to make sure he's ok.

"Hello Rusty, you OK?" I asks.

"Hell no India! Who were those two thugs that ran in my house like two mad men on acid or something?" Rusty asked.

"That was Asia's man Vance and his partner in crime so to speak. They didn't hurt you did they?" I asked.

"Hell yea I think my nose is broke!" Rusty was mad.

"I think I'm missing some teeth and let's not talk about my pride. Fucking with your sister sure has its benefits," Rusty said.

"I'm so sorry Rusty, I told her from the beginning I didn't think it was a good idea to stay at your place. But you know she doesn't listen. Plus who knew Vance would show up in California," venting. At this point, I forgot I called him to check-up versus me trying to digest the recent events.

"The things we do for love," Rusty retorted.

I laughed, "Yea you're right. Well I hope you feel better, go get your nose checked out."

"I am in the morning. Did you know that when you break your nose, you get two black eyes with it?" Rusty said.

"Damn, I didn't know that. So you can't even go to work huh?" I asked.

"I'm good. I have more than enough sick time. So I'll utilize it." He said.

"Ok I'll check on you tomorrow, and sorry again Rusty."

"Goodnight India."

"Bye," hanging up the phone.

I swear I don't want a thug for a man but who wants a pussy for a man? I wonder what my dad would have done if that happened to him. I already know the answer. He probably would be the 'surgeon' trying to save the man he just killed for disrespecting him. My dad is smooth around the edges but he also has razor sharp when provoked. *Naw, I guess I want a lil' ruffneck because you never know what can happen. Look as Asia stupid ass, perfect example,* yawning. I needed to write a book about my sister. I know it would be a best seller. But what would I name it? I know, *'Deceptions of a Diva',* I laughed at the thought until drifting off to sleep.

Pulling up at the hotel, "Asia wake up! We're at the hotel," shaking me.

"Ok, damn!" I look up to see that we're at the W Hotel. I wonder how he found this hotel. I guess the same way he found India and Rusty's house. Getting out the car, this night air feels good on my face.

"What you smiling about? You've been to this hotel before?" Vance inquisitive ass asked me.

"No I haven't! If you want to know why I'm grinning, it's because this air feels good. Is there anything else you would like to know Sherlock?" I asks.

"Shut your smart ass up before I slap the shit out of your sneaky ass girl!" Vance yells.

Getting on the elevator, Vance pushes twelve and Boobie presses the button for ten. *Different floors. Boobie must have someone with him, I wonder who.*

Vance slides the key card inside the slot, he paused for the greenlight and proceeded to open the door. *Oh my God, no he didn't.* I couldn't believe my eyes, they started watering immediate.

"Vance I thought you were going to kill me." I said.

"I did all this before I knew you were at that niggas house. I should kill your punk ass and use all these roses for your funeral." He said.

Vance had the entire room filled with red and white roses. Rose petals on the bed, a huge white teddy bear with a heart that said 'I love you', and two boxes sitting on the table gift wrapped.

"What are those?" pointing at the apparent gifts.

"What do they look like? Sherlock Holmes" Vance playfully asked.

"Can I open them?"

"Naw, I'm taking them back tomorrow. Have that nigga Rusty buy you some gifts. You fucked a nigga up tonight you know that right. I should have left you there and flew my ass back home and said 'fuck you'. You would have called when it was time to have my shortie. But for some reason I love your ass and you should be counting your blessings Asia. Because I could and still might hurt your ass for trying to play me. I don't care how mad you get, don't do that shit again. I'm dead serious Asia!" Vance said.

"Baby I'm sorry but you have to understand how I feel also," pleading, still taken back by the room itself.

"I do understand and a nigga ain't trying to hurt you. Shit just happened and no! Before you say it, I'm not in love with Monique. I have love for her and that's different. I'm trying to be real with you as I can. It's complicated Asia but I promise you this shit will come to an end. Just give me a little time that's all I asks," looking me in the eyes.

Damn I love this man. I put my arms around him and kissed him like my life depended on it.

He grabbed my waist and pulled me in as close as he could, squeezing and gripping along my hips. Then he slapped my ass and pulled away. "What was that for?" I said.

"Because you've been a very *bad* girl. You should be glad I didn't use my...," Vance paused, still looking me in my eyes. "You didn't fuck him Asia, did you?"

"Hell no! It's not like that. I keep reiterating we're friends, that's it..."

"Um hmm, I bet. Take your clothes off." Vance yelled.

"Huh?" still processing.

"I said take them damn clothes off...now!"

I strip into my birthday suit, body blooming just as bright as the roses that entrapped us. With an urge to tease, I twirl in front of Vance, showing off my own sweet flower, the contour of my body like the petals of a rose.

"Lay on the bed and show Daddy where you want him to make you feel good."

I lay on the rose petals, my back pressed against the bed, and spread my legs while I place one finger inside my treasure box and find my spot. I had forgotten how good I can make myself feel, it's been a while. It started feeling so good, I fiend for more and allowed another finger to join the party. *Two should take me there.* I rubbed my breast, circling my nipples and clit simultaneously. I forgot Vance was even in the room. Once I closed my eyes, I was in paradise. All the while, giving Vance an erotic show. Moving my hand, Vance slipped his finger inside me.

"Ohh baby," I moaned when he put another one. "You're going to make me cum," I whispered.

"Not yet," he said, "turn over."

"Your wish, is my command." I said while repositioning, and my plump breast shifted from staring at the ceiling to hanging freely beneath me, in the air, against the weight of gravity.

I got on all fours like a good dog should, anticipating his entry but to my surprise, he started using his tongue to lick me from the tip of my lower back all the way to my clit and back again. Long slow strokes, trialing the underlinings of my body. Vance decided to pull out a few tricks from his bag of fun tonight, the bag that every sexually advanced man has whenever he needs to remind his woman of how much of a king he is in bed. Monotony was not present tonight. Vance was putting his taste buds in places he had never eaten. Hesitant at first, I began to become more open to and it helped to have a familiar feeling equally as satisfying. Vance continued to massage my clit with two fingers, performing Mr. Miyagi's 'wax on and wax off' technique. Adding to this orgasmic complexity, he slipped his thumb in my pussy, pushing it in and out preparing me for the dick. My body responded to these sensations openly like the gateway arch of St. Louis. When he did enter my gateway, he shockingly entered the wrong hole.

"Awe Vance. That hurts."

"Take a deep breath baby, it only hurts for a minute," attempting to make me less tense.

"Awe Vance. Awe, it's too big!" but he kept pushing it in, "aww baby, aww Vance!"

Kissing my neck, "It's almost in baby, stop resisting, try to relax," then he finally got it in.

"Damn baby this shit feels good. It feels good to you baby?"

"No Vance it hurts," but the more he stroked in and out, it did start to feel good.

He lifted my upper torso and held me by my waist while beating my ass up, literally. After about fifteen minutes, I started to enjoy it.

"I love you baby!" I yelled.

"I love you too, damn girl this shit feels good. You like this baby?" he asked, maneuvering his hips rotationally, massaging inner parts of me that haven't been explored.

"Yes..."

"You miss daddy baby?" Vance asked, still stroking.

"Ohhh yes daddy. I'm about to...Ohhh Vance," he still had two fingers inside of me, now moist from the combination of pleasure portals pulsating.

"Cum for daddy baby..." his pumps became more consistent and deeper, you could hear my ass clapping against the walls in the room, "...oh shit I'm coming too!" we came together like an erupting volcano. I could feel his juices joining mine.

"Damn girl that shit was mad crazy," pulling out.

"My ass is sore Vance," turning over.

He started laughing, walking to the bathroom, "I told you I was going to whip that ass! You thought I was playing."

"That's not funny. I'm going to get hemorrhoids," shaking my head.

"Shut up and come get in the shower!" he said, stepping in with one foot, testing the temperature with his hands.

We took a nice, hot shower together and allowed the water to cleanse our pheromones. While we were kissing and touching, Vance said, "I love you Asia."

"I love you too Vance, but don't do that shit again. I'm serious, that shit hurt."

"It only hurt when I put it in, but after that didn't it feel good?"

"Yes, but it still hurt my butt is going to be sore." I said.

"Good! Whenever you get out of line again, I'm going to whip that ass!" laughing and slapping me on my ass.

"Stop boy, you play too much!"

"I ain't playing, I'm serious."

"I'm tired," I say, getting out the shower, the events of the night were obviously catching up.

"Baby me too," Vance said, following my lead, stepping foot out the tub.

He kissed my stomach, "What it do Shortie? Daddy can't wait to meet you. I love you boy and you have a crazy momma," the baby started moving, "I know Shortie, you know it's your Daddy talking, huh?" he said, rubbing my stomach but looking at me.

"Don't play any more games with my baby Asia. Let this be your first and last time doing some dumb shit. For real, for real."

I just kiss him and walk away, "I'm tired Vance," I say, getting in the bed.

He got in too and pulled me close, "I missed you."

"I missed your crazy-deranged-shit-talking ass too," falling deeper into his embrace.

"Goodnight bootylicious," laughing.

"Goodnight," he said and we laid in peace.

I woke up the next morning before Vance, who was knocked out with the covers over his head. I went and sat at the table, ordered some breakfast and a caramel mocha. The hotel's room service came with Starbucks. To pass the time, I started to unwrap the two gift boxes, beginning with the biggest one first. Peeling back the wrapping paper, I was met with a Gucci robe, with matching slippers, a red silk pajama set and my favorite body lotion. As I continued to dig, I uncovered bath gel, perfume from Versace, a Gucci diaper bag with a matching baby carrier and cute little Gucci booties for the baby. *He must have really been missing us when he went shopping.* I opened the smallest box, *it must be jewelry,* I inquired assumingly. Once I took the wrapping paper off the box, I could tell it was from Tiffany's. *This should be interesting. I love everything from the Tiffany's store.*

"Oh my God!" I started screaming. "Vance, oh my God. It's beautiful," my eyes are synced with a ten karat marquise cut platinum diamond engagement ring.

I ran over to Vance, "Baby! Baby!"

"What Asia?" trying to pull the covers back over his head.

"Baby thank you! I love you," kissing him all over his face. I put my ring on my engagement finger. "Look baby!"

I forgot I ordered us breakfast. Room service was knocking on the door but I hadn't heard them through my excitement, "Asia somebody's knocking at the door," Vance said, looking about.

"Oh baby, I forgot," I ran to the door.

"You ordered room service?" A tall older gentleman asked.

"Yes, thank you," I said.

He starting looking at my ring so I flashed it in his face, "That's nice ma'am. Do you wish to charge this to your room?" unphased by my showcase.

"Yes please, thank you."

I closed the door after giving him a tip and resumed my celebration. Vance was sitting up in bed and I ran to tackle him like a football player.

"Calm your ass down Asia," falling back from the impact.

"Thank you baby, I love it!"

"Nobody told you to open those boxes. I said that I was taking them back," trying to look serious.

"Baby, thank you! I love you," kissing him, "look at my ring. It's the one we looked at together!"

Instead of looking at my ring, he was looking at me crazy, "Asia calm the fuck down. It's going to be ok!

"I'm sorry baby, I'm excited. Does this mean we're engaged?" I asked.

"It means you're going to be the mother of my son and if you act right from here on out, you'll probably be my wife." Vance said.

"Probably my ass negro! I am going to be your wife!" I started doing the cabbage patch dance.

He started laughing, "Silly girl. Can you give me my breakfast please? Since you woke me up? We should eat now because we have a busy day ahead of us."

"I have something for you to eat..." putting my leg up on the bed slowly, seductively.

"Looks tempting boo, but I'll pass. You're on restriction. No head and no dick!" looking at me square in the eyes.

"For how long?" I asked.

"Let me think about it," rubbing his chin inquisitively, "I don't know? I guess until I feel like you deserve this dick and I'm going to make you work for it," laughing.

"Ok, but what about that bomb ass head of yours?" I asked, biting my lip.

"It's the bomb baby?"

"You know it is Vance, don't you? You make me explode every time," tilting my head back.

"You're classic girl, seriously. I don't know what I'm going to do with your hot ass," shaking his head.

"You love me though!" I say with confidence.

"True 'dat, I do. But don't take my love for you as a weakness and go running around with my heart in your hand. It's valuable, like a rare gem baby. Only a few in my life have encountered my love for what it is. Now, pass me my food before it get's cold, crazy girl!" laughing.

13

BAY AREA

Asia Smith

"I want to see the whole Bay Area before we go back home Asia."

"Vance, you sound like a tourist baby," giggling.

"Basically that's what I am, right?" looking up at me.

"No fool! You had a specific purpose for coming here, and it wasn't for no damn vacation," looking back up at him.

"Well let's make it a vacation then."

"No Vance, this isn't the place to be vacationing at. This city is boring as hell," I say laughing.

"Where do the thugs and gangsta's hang out at babe?" Vance asked.

"They're all around, it's like sets I guess. In LA it's crips and bloods but out here, it's sets. Like Bayview and Hunters Point. I know people that stay on Osceola, shout out to my cousin Darkskin!! It's popping over there. Then it's Fillmore, the 'Dirty Mo' is what they call it, Sunnydale, Lakeview and the T.L. -"

"What's the T.L.?" Vance asked.

"It's a set called the Tenderloin. That's where people go to hustle baby. They come from all over, from different cities across the bay like Richmond, Oakland. It's the mecca for hustlers. You can find just about every set down there trying to get their money," giving Vance the landscape.

"Oh. So that's the hustling spot, huh?" he asked.

"Yes, it's where the homeless, dopefiends and hustlers combined hang out like one big happy family," I said.

"That shit sounds crazy Asia. You have to take me down there so I can see it for myself," looking interested.

"Ok baby, but don't say I didn't warn you," I shook my head and we began to get dressed for the day.

"So which neighborhood does your parents live in?" Vance said, getting in the rental car to head to my parents house.

It's the suburbs. It's called the Excelsior district. It's in the back of Lakeview, in Saint Francis woods. It's hard to explain..." I paused, anticipating where the conversation was leading.

"You'll see. I'll take you all around the city and then you'll know what I mean."

"Well I'm strapped just in case something pops off. I'll show them how we do it in the ATL. How we really get down. Fuck what you heard. I'll show them some shit in 3D!"

"The shit I'm packing, niggas ain't never heard of. It makes a tech nine look like a tonka toy. One shot and blocks are wiped out, eliminated, no longer existing," motioning his hands as if he were aiming a gun.

"So why are you packing shit like that when we're going to my parents house Vance? My parents aren't the enemy," laughing.

"You never know baby, you never know," pulling into the circular driveway.

I see India's car, "I hope she didn't tell my parents about last night."

"Naw she's not that stupid," he said, giving me a sigh of relief.

"Leave your 'eliminator' in the car Vance, because my mom is touchy-feely and she's probably going to hug you," laughing.

"I didn't plan on bringing it in anyway," he said.

"This is a nice house," Vance admired as we walked towards the door.

I turned the knob and walked in, welcomed my sister's voice, "Asia we're in the den!" India yells.

"Why hello Mr. Vance. It's a pleasure to finally meet your acquaintance. I see why my daughter loves him, he's a fine specimen," my mom says as we entered the room.

"It's a pleasure to meet you as well, Ms. Smith," reaching in to give my mom a hug.

"Um hmm," clearing his throat. "I hate to intrude," holding his hand out.

"Oh Robert stop it!"

"It's nice to meet you Vance," my father says shaking his hand. "Now I can put a face with the voice."

"Same here Mr. - I mean Dr.Smith." Vance presenting his

best self, as expected.

"Welcome to our home, please be seated," my mom said, and as she was motioning for us to sit, I noticed she couldn't take her eyes off Vance.

"So Vance, I'm glad you called me because we had no idea Asia was even in town," sounding upset. "Our daughter has the tendency to pop up unannounced, without warning sometimes, and this is bad behavior. It's actually unacceptable to say the least."

"Oh Robert...don't start," my mom uttered, trying to keep the air clear.

"No Carliess! She didn't even have the audacity to call us and tell us that we were going to be grandparents. I found out from Vance when he called the other day worried about her!" my father's harbored emotions were now coming to the forefront.

"That's just being childish and naive on her end. I will not stand for blatant disrespect. I am your father young lady do you understand me Asia?" he said with his voice rising.

"Yes Daddy, I was going to take you and mom out to dinner and explain everything - " sounding pitiful.

"Well honey, now we know and that's all that matters. We're going to have a beautiful, healthy grandchild and that's a beautiful thing..." my mom interjected, attempting to lighten the tone once again.

"Umph. Well Asia have you started your prenatal care yet?" My dad asked.

"Yes Dad, I have." I responded.

"So Vance...what are your plans?" redirecting his attention.

"Vance asked me to marry him Daddy," interceding.

"And what was your response Asia?" looking at me like I was some sort of alien or something.

"Why are you looking at me like that Daddy?"

"Because I know you quite well Miss Asia, you're only twenty years old and you still believe you're missing out on life. When I was twenty, I was in school with ten more years to go. My life didn't begin until way after my thirties, with the exception of having a family, and we may have started young but we were prepared mentally. Yesterday, when Vance called me at work, I was prepped to do surgery on a young woman around you and your sister's age. The patient had been shot in the head by her boyfriend and she was also pregnant."

"Daddy did she make it?" India asked.

"Yes she's alive but we discovered a number of injuries related to abuse and a lot of bruises on her body. This wasn't the first time this woman had been abused by a man and the sad part about it is, we couldn't save the baby," my Dad paused, still processing the trauma.

"She wasn't that far along and statistics show that women in abusive relationships tend to never leave or if they do return to the relationship, it's because they believe it was partly their own fault or they'll make up excuses for the men they're with. The majority of abused women come from an abusive family. The father beats the mother while the daughter watches, and the cycle just keeps repeating itself. From generation to generation, like a generational curse. I'm not making any excuses for those women, but some women actually enjoy being disrespected and beat by men. The entire time I spent in the operating room, I thought about you two. I said, 'she's around my girls age, I need to speak to them more often and tell them that I love them. I want them to know that they are loved by a man, even if it's only their father'," sounding sentimental.

"We love you Daddy," I said, kissing his cheek, "and you don't have to worry about us, we're good in that area," trying to give him some reassurance.

"I suppose you're right Asia but sometimes you can make a person snap. I wanted to kill you myself a couple times," laughing.

"I'll second that!" Carliess said.

"Mom don't start please. We have company," I said.

"Vance is not company dear, he's family. So when's the

wedding?" looking at Vance.

"I'm not sure ma'am we haven't really discussed it in detail but it'll be after the baby is born," Vance responded.

"I see that nice looking rock you're wearing. It's beautiful. Nice choice Vance," still looking at him.

"Thank you," he retorted.

"Let me see Asia, you didn't show me!" India said. "Wow that is nice! It's from Tiffany's."

"Let me see dear," Dad asked.

"You like it Daddy?" I asked, seeking some sort of approval.

"Yes, it's beautiful," he said, admiring with his eyes from where he sat.

"I pray you're serious because you're about to become someone's mother Asia."

"I am serious Daddy. Where's Maria? I want to show her my ring," I asked, looking around.

"She's not here Asia."

"Oh. Is she sick?"

"No, she does take time off like every employee does. So Vance, I hear you and your family own a couple of restaurants in Atlanta?" Mom asked.

"Yes ma'am we do. My Grandmother was the matriarch of the family and we followed in her footsteps. I also own a club and a few office buildings that I lease out. I invested my money wisely," speaking with pride.

"Well son, it sounds like you have a good head on your shoulders. Keep up the good work. But you have your hands full dealing with our daughter," laughing.

"You can say that again Mr. Smith, she's full of surprises but I love her."

"Well it takes a certain type of man to do that...I think her Mother's side of the family performs voodoo on men. The believers are keepers!" my father mocks, laughing.

"Robert please! Don't start that voodoo crap. I did no such thing on you. I believe you did something to me," laughing.

"Carliess you did and I was the best thing that happened to you, don't you agree?"

"Yes dear." My mom responded but all the while was thinking – *You, the Congressman, District Attorney, Judges, and a few others were also 'best things' that happened to her.*

"I'm hungry Vance, you ready to go eat?"

"Yes, I'm starving," he retorts.

"Where are you taking him Asia?" India asks.

"Probably the pier, he thinks he's a tourist," laughing.

"He is," India retorts.

"We can all go out to eat, our treat," Dad says. "Let's go to Asebella's. I love that restaurant."

"Sounds good to me," I say.

"Asia, I'm riding with y'all. Daddy we'll meet you there!" India says.

"Ok sweetheart, we'll be right behind you. I need to change my attire," Dad motions to get up.

"Ok we'll see y'all there!" I say, and all the women walked out of the den, towards the door.

"Excuse me Ms. Smith," Vance approaches us.

"Yes Vance," Mom replies.

"You three, standing there all together, reminds me of the movie 'Sparkle'," he said, ending his statement with a charming smile.

"Why thank you Vance. I'll take that as a compliment. There were some beautiful women in that film," my mom replied while gazing at Vance.

"What movie is that Mom?" I asked, missing out on the inside joke shared between the two.

"Go buy it Asia and watch it tonight. It's about three sisters who were singers. My sisters and I used to get compared to them all of the time when we were younger, but in reality, we couldn't sing," my mom laughed as she took a lap around memory lane.

"What *were* you and your sisters good at Mom?" I asked, poking fun at her.

"Asia that's not nice," India smirked.

"We were good - No, *great* at a lot of things," my mom said and we all laughed.

After we packed into our cars, we headed to the city to share our first meal as a family with Vance and the baby present at the table.

14

CREEP CREEP

Asia Smith

I've been back in Atlanta for about a month now and shit hasn't gotten any better. At my last doctor's appointment, Vance and I got into it again. It was all because my phone rang and I didn't answer it.

"Why aren't you answering your phone, is it your little boyfriend?" I wouldn't even dignify him with an answer.

Lately, he's been starting shit for no reason. We've been looking at houses and he got mad because I didn't want a big ass house or mansion, but he felt the opposition. I wanted a house that I could clean by myself, without any help unless I chose to. He responded childishly and said things like, 'You're so ungrateful Asia, why don't you want me to treat you?' and all this bull shit. *I'm sick of his ass. Now here he goes again at my appointment, I wish he didn't come at all. What's the point? I can tell him all about it when I get home.* It was the same procedure every time: checking the height and weight, measuring the baby, and asking me, 'how are you feeling?' – nothing different. But he insisted on coming to all the appointments. I wonder if he went with Monique to hers. But realistically, who cared? Better her than me. I know she would love the attention if he did go.

"Ms. Smith you've gained twenty-five pounds in the few months of your pregnancy. I see that you're eating good," the doctor laughed while looking at my medical records on a clipboard.

"Yes, she eats everything and we eat out a lot," Vance replied.

I could have sworn she was talking to me. This shit has got to stop. After the appointment, we headed to a restaurant downtown and he dropped me off after.

"I'll see you later baby," kissing me on my forehead.

"I have some business to tend to," he said, releasing me from his grasp.

"Ok, I'll see you later," I retort, getting out the truck, closing the door and watching him drive off. *Good riddance. I'm glad he didn't want to come in. I'm still mad at him, for what he did to Rusty.*

Thank God Rusty forgave me. He said he understood why Vance did what he did and it wasn't my fault but he preferred that we keep our friendship at a distance. It was cool with me, just as long as we were still friends. I took a nice, hot bubble bath and listened to some oldies to relax.

"Hey girl how was your appointment?" Kellie asked after she creeped into my bathroom doorway.

"Same thing, different day. What's up with you?" I asks.

"Nothing, heading out. I have a date tonight that I'm meeting at the club," she said, holding her keys and purse in hand.

"I sure miss clubbing....I can't wait to drop this load, then it's on!" laughing and performing a mini-twerk in the tub as if someone was behind me.

"Well, have fun! I'll see you tomorrow!" I say, playfully smacking her butt as she walked out heading for the door.

"You might see me tomorrow but you'll hear me tonight because it's going to go down!"

"You so stupid Kellie," giggling.

"Don't even try it Asia with you, 'Oh hit my spot Vance-Oh Daddy that feels so good!'," Kellie said, mocking me humorously.

"Get out Kellie, bye bye," waving and splashing water in her direction as she exits. *Just wait until I can fit into my jeans and cute shirts.* Vance better watch out because it's on.

Getting out the tub, I lotioned my body down and massaged my protruding belly with coco butter so I didn't get stretch marks. I put on my pj's, lied down and watched T.V. *I hope that this fool don't come here tonight. I'm not in the mood for his B.S. There's nothing on TV anyway and it's almost 11 p.m. I guess I'll watch the news.* My phone beeped and said, 'New Message'.

I tapped the replay button and heard Vance's voice, 'Hey baby, I'm tied up and probably won't make it home tonight. You're probably asleep, that's why you're not answering, so I won't disturb you two shorties. Sleep peacefully, one love,' message concluded.

Good, he's not coming! After the news went off, I was still wide awake so I headed downstairs to find something to eat but there was nothing. Well, nothing I wanted anyways. *Damn I'm hungry.* I slipped something on and went to get something to eat. I intended on returning home quickly so I could just relax in my solitude.

But what do I want? Maybe some shrimp and fish but that's way across town. Fuck it, I don't have nothing else to do. Plus, I can stop by Essence's house, it's right by her spot. These are the hours she keeps anyway. After I get the food that I demolished, in what seemed like three seconds, I drove over to Essence's house to bring her a plate.

Is that Vance's truck parked out front? What's he doing at Essence's house at 12:30 at night? And then it hit me, *oh that's how he knew about the banks.* I knew that they knew each other but I didn't know how much they knew each other. Apparently, it was well enough for him to be at her crib this late. It's some funny shit going on. I waited for a minute, trying to get my composure together and that's when I noticed three dudes, in all black, getting out a van with guns. They all had on black beanie caps, *what the fuck!* They rang the buzzer and someone let them in. They left the lobby door open and ran up the stairs. Now shit is starting to register, somebody was about to be hit. It was a set up.

Oh my god, Vance. I jump out my car and run across the street. I'm trying to run fast but it feels like I'm moving in slow motion. *Please God don't let this be for Vance.* When I finally get inside the building, waiting for the elevator, I hear screaming and then gun shots like a semi-automatic weapon. *POP! POP! POP! POP! POP!*

"Come on elevator hurry up!" I say while hitting the button repeatedly like that will make it come faster.

When it finally opened, I was startled by the presence of those same three men, but this time their hats were over their faces, and before the elevator closed, they ran by and out the door. I stood frozen, wind from their pursuit passing against my face, heart racing. When I reach Essence condo, the door was wide open.

"Vance, baby? Where are you?!" I screamed but no one answered. I went into the living room first but no one was there. I heard something coming from Essence bedroom, that's when I almost passed out. Essence was lying in a puddle of blood on her bed naked. Her face was completely gone. I knew it was her because of her body, with her rose tattoo above her chest and Vance was on the floor, looking up and gasping for air. He had been shot in the chest and he was bleeding badly. I ran over to him, crying hysterically.

"Baby please hold on! I'm going to get you some help!" his eyes said 'yes' but nothing came out his mouth but blood. Instincts kicked in, I ran to the phone on Essence's dresser and called '911'.

I ran back over to Vance, "You're going to be find baby," rubbing his head.

"Just hang in there, help is on the way..."

"God please don't take my sons father. Lord please," praying to myself aloud as Vance drifted in and out of consciousness.

I kept kissing his forehead and begging him to stay with me, "Vance don't give up baby, you gotta be strong for your son. We need you!"

The paramedics came and took over, and asked me to leave out, "No! I can't leave him, he's my son's father. Please!" tears streaming down my face.

"Yes," one of the paramedics said, "come on," and took me into the living room. Finally they had him on a stretcher to take him out. Everything was moving so fast and going in slow motion at the same time.

"Can I please ride with him?" I asked desperately.

"Yes," one of the paramedics said.

I rode in the ambulance and overheard one of them say to another, "It doesn't look good and his chances are slim."

They radioed the hospital to give his status and vitals, and ten minutes later we were there. They took him to the back and told me to wait in the waiting room and that someone would come and talk to me momentarily. I was absolutely a mess at this point. *Why Vance? Please don't take him from me Lord.* I kept praying over and over without ceasing. It always seemed that during our humblest moments in life, we are so inclined to speed dial the holy deity to which we call God. We feel the powerlessness of our being as humans and turn to the only hope we know intuitively.

After what seemed like hours, a nurse came to see me.

"Are you related to the victim?" she asked.

"Yes, I'm his fiancé. I'm having his child," I retorted.

"Ok, your name?" she asked.

"Asia Smith," I answered, on the last edge of my patience. I should be the one asking questions.

"Ok Ms. Smith. What's your fiancé name and birthday?" she asked.

"His name is Vance Lawton Smith and his birthday is February 4th," I said, I was transitioning from patient to irritant.

"Is there anyone that you would like us to call?" she asked, finishing her twenty-one questions.

I had totally forgot about calling anyone, "His mother," I told her.

I gave the nurse his mother's name and number and she walked out. I reached into my purse, got my phone, called Boobie and told him everything that happened. He hung up and said he was on his way. I sat down and said another prayer. Fifteen minutes later, Vance's mom Sonia arrived and so did his dad. Sonia must have called him because I don't have his father's number. I told them the whole story as well. We all waited and cried, and kept praying that he was ok. Vance's sister came about an hour later, she put her arm around me and said 'it was going to be ok'. I really liked his sister, she was cool from jump. After the majority of the family arrived, Boobie and what seemed like the entire Atlanta Players Club showed up. The waiting area was packed.

"Where's my husband? My husband has been shot? Where is my husband at!?" someone was screaming.

"Ma'am you're going to have to calm down. Who is your husband?" a nurse asked.

"Vance Smith, where is he!?"

"Ma'am I'm going to escort you to his family. They're all in here," the nurse said, walking the screaming woman into the family waiting area.

Monique was screaming, "What happened? Where's my baby daddy at? WHO SHOT HIM?"

"Calm down Monique!" Vance's father finally spoke up. "He's

in surgery. We'll know how he is when the doctor comes in."

"Why is she here?" pointing her finger towards me. I was too distraught to even respond.

"Monique if you're going to act a fool while my son is fighting for his life, I'm going to ask you to leave." Mr. Smith said, speaking on everyone's behalf.

"I'm not going anywhere. Tell that bitch to leave, I'm his wife! I have every right to be here."

She had me believing that she was his wife. *Is she? Shit with all the surprises, I wouldn't be shocked if she was.*

"You're not his wife!" Boobie said, "And Asia ain't going anywhere."

"I am his wife, common law nigga!"

"Gone with all that noise Monique and your disrespectful ass! I swear if you weren't pregnant I would punch you in your mouth like Asia did. You just didn't get enough, huh?"

"Don't say shit to me, every again Boobie!" crying hysterically while she walked out.

A part of me felt sorry for her, but that moment passed quickly. Vance was in surgery for seventeen hours. When the doctor did come in, I was sleep on Vance father's lap. I woke up when I heard the doctor's voice.

"Well family, it's touch and go right now. He's alive, but barely. He was shot up pretty good. But it didn't hit his heart, only some major organs were damaged. It's up to him to fight to stay alive. I'm sure he's a fighter because whatever type of gun they used to try and kill him, should have. But he's still amongst us. So keep praying. I'll check back on him later on. If any changes occur, we'll keep you guys informed. I think you all should go home and get some rest. This has been a long night for all of us."

He also informed us that Vance would be under an alias for security purposes. We all thanked him, told him how grateful we were and he left. Boobie said that I wasn't going home, and that I would stay with him and his woman. Everyone agreed to be back at the hospital before dinner. Boobie took me by the house to get a few things and I told Kellie what happened. She said she wasn't going to stay at the house either. She would go to her friends. I called India and told her too. She said she would be on the next flight out. My mother was out of state and I didn't want to worry my dad. Plus, I was sure India would tell him. And as planned, India arrived the next day. Boobie picked her up from the airport and brought her to the hospital. All of the other relatives had already made our way back, his whole family and all of his friends. It was like a huge get together, family affair or something. When India came into the waiting room, his family looked like they saw a ghost.

"Asia we didn't know you had a twin sister."

"Yes I do," grabbing her and giving her a tight bear hug. "Thanks for coming," I whispered in her ear.

"You're welcome," she said. Letting her go, I took her by the hand and lead her to a seat by me.

"How is he?" India asked.

"We don't know too much but the nurse said he's still unconscious and he's on a breathing machine," I started to cry as my words become more realistic, especially in our current environment.

"It's ok Asia, I know he'll pull through. You have to take care of yourself for the baby's sake. Have you eaten anything today?" India asked concerned.

"Yes, Boobie made me eat earlier."

***

Boobie

Sonia asked me to take Asia out of this stuffy room and get something to snack on from the cafeteria.

"Ok Sonia, I'll take her, plus I need some water."

As if I could bear any of the emotional weight she was carrying, I reached out for Asia's hand to support her physically and proceeded to walk to the cafeteria.

"What would you like Asia?" I ask.

"Nothing, I'm not hungry." Asia said.

"Please eat something, you have a baby to think about. Even if it's just a piece of fruit," pointing to the basket of oranges.

"Ok, I'll get a fruit salad and bottle water," she said nonchalantly.

I ordered me a cheeseburger and fries. *I hope I can make Asia eat some of my food.* When my order was done, we went back to the waiting area. But to our surprise - a big, black, ugly gorilla looking chick with orange hair and three other girls were standing with Monique. We walked passed them and went to the seats where we previously sat. Monique rolled her eyes the millionth time and I rolled mine right along with her. *I wish she would try something when my sister is weak and stressed out, not to mention pregnant.* That's just how ignorant Monique was, which is why I've grown to favor Asia more. I never knew what Vance saw in Monique anyways. I guess because she knew how to get money but he should have broke her off with some dough a long time ago and sent her on her merry way. He told me that he started hustling at sixteen and made his first million at twenty-one.

Then he had his family who worked and invested into restaurants for him. He was a very intelligent brother despite not going to college. I guess some people are just street smart and others are book smart. I guess the latter of the two would be me. Asia fell asleep on my lap while we waited for updates, three long hours later, a nurse finally came in to deliver the news.

"There's no changes yet. You guys can go home, it's late. I'll call his parents if there's anything changes to his condition," the nurse headed back through the automated doors that separated the waiting room of relatively healthy individuals from patients who were just short of their luck.

We all gather our belonging in preparation to leave when Monique announced, "I'm staying. I ain't going anywhere until my man wakes up!" in usual Monique fashion.

Vance's dad said, "Shoot yourself! " and we all walked out.

***

India Smith

Boobie, Asia and I went to his house. He had a beautiful home in a gated community. When we got there, his wife or girlfriend – whoever she was to him, cooked and it smelled good.

"Asia, Introduce me to Lisa," I asked and we migrated towards the kitchen.

"Make yourself at home," she said to me directly. "It's a pleasure to meet you."

"Thank you, I appreciate your hospitality towards my sister and I," I said.

"No problem, Asia is like family. We love her," that made me feel better. We ate and talked the rest of the night. Asia ended up going to bed and Boobie just left.

"So how long have you and Boobie been together?" I ask, trying to understand their dynamic a bit more.

"About twelve years." Lisa said proudly.

"Wow that long?" I asked.

"Yes, just as long as Vance and Monique," she said with her nose turned up. "But see, that's why we love Asia because Monique never bonded with anyone. She's childish, loud, obnoxious and ghetto." For a moment, I thought we were talking about the flaws of Asia's personality but it seems like Monique is lacking a bit of polishing. At least my sister knows how to carry herself when she wants to, it's her temper that usually becomes her downfall.

"I knew when the right person came along he would leave her ass. She has no class at all, it's terrible," the conversation shifted momentarily from girl talk to Lisa venting.

"Yea I can see that," validating her. "She is a bit much. But I don't understand why he still deals with her then?" I asked, drifting into a pensive stare.

"Well, to be honest, I think it's because she knows too much. She's been around since we were teenagers. She started out selling dope for him and when shit went down, she was just like one of his boys you know. So she knows a lot more than some of his people's know. Plus I think he feels sorry for her."

"Sorry my ass! I don't want my sister to keep going through B.S. because he feels sorry for her," shaking my head, trying to find logic within this triangle affair.

"I know India, I understand what you mean. Boobie and I talked about it with Vance before. He said he's really in love with Asia and it shows. He hardly ever spends time with Monique. I think she got pregnant on purpose," laughing. "But he says he wants to get rid of her slowly and she could keep the house, cars, whatever. But she just won't go away. She's like a parasite," laughing again.

"Well hopefully she'll learn something from this and calm her ass down a notch," I say.

"I hope so too, before someone gets hurt," Lisa said.

"Right. Well, I'm tired Lisa, it's been really nice conversing with you. You're cool people's," grinning.

"So are you Twin Sister," playfully tapping my knee.

"See you in the morning, goodnight!"

I slept with my sister, all up under her like she was my man. It had been years since we've done that. I like to think that this was how we were in the womb. When I was younger and I got scared during the night, she would tell me to get into her bed with her. I was grateful we shared rooms.

For the next couple days, we went about the same routine.

Waking up to Lisa's homemade breakfast, going to the hospital visit Vance who was still unconsciousness, then we would return to their house to eat and go to bed. This particular day at the hospital, I was starving. I asked everyone in the room if they wanted something to eat. Everyone said 'no thanks,' but Vance's father said he would go with me to the cafeteria and I told Asia I'll bring her something back just in case.

When we got to the cafeteria, they didn't have anything Mr. Smith nor I wanted, "Let's run to get something from the restaurant down the street, it'll only take a few minutes," he said.

"Sure why not," my stomach felt like it was starting to do cart wheels. We walked to the parking garage damn near in silence. But I started noticing how much Vance resembled his father. He was dark with smooth skin, a mustache and goatee with pretty brown eyes. His hair was wavy with specs of gray - very handsome, sexy even. We reached his car and I was pleasantly surprised.

"Nice car," I say.

"Thanks sweetie, I barely drive it but since it's nice out, I figured I'll pull her out." It was a classic, I don't know the exact year of the model but I estimated a fifties or sixties two seater Mercedes, everything was original.

"I take it you're really into cars?" I asked him.

"Yes, I have a storage area full of luxury cars. You know anything about cars?" he asked.

"Not really, I only know how to drive them."

He chuckled, "That's ok, most women don't but I bet you can tell me about a designer handbag and shoe," laughing.

"Yes sir, I sure can," laughing also.

"Please stop with the 'sir' thing, I'm not as old as I look. I know I-we had Vance when we were only fifteen years old..." he said, slightly thinking to himself.

"Really? Wow. Babies having babies huh?" laughing.

"Yeah, that's a way of putting it," breaking his thought. "But

I'm glad we did because it made me become a man, I had to take care of my responsibilities."

"That was very mature of you because most men would have ran away or disconnected himself from the situation," I said.

"I can't lie, I was in denial at first because we were so young but once he came and I saw that he looked just like me, I handled my business," nodding his head with pride.

"My family owned a restaurant so I went to work for them and I hustled a little while to make enough money to open my own...and the rest is history."

"Oh now I see where Vance gets his business sense from, from you."

"I guess so. But he still has a long way to go to be like me. I didn't hustle to make money, I did it to support my family and once I opened my first restaurant I stopped hustling completely. Vance has a lot to be thankful for but he takes it for granted. He owns a lot of property and doesn't have to hustle any more but he still decides to do so."

His father was painting a picture a of Vance, "I hope so because he's about to be a father and a child needs their parents even if they aren't together."

"I agree," we pull into the restaurant parking lot, go in and order our food. I kept staring at Mr. Smith, he was starting to look good to me. I even felt my pussy getting moist. *Damn what's happening to me?* He was fine as hell but he's also Vance's father. I shake it off because I knew I wasn't attracted to him, *right? It's probably because I haven't had any in a minute, that's all. I hope that's it.* We get our food and head back to the hospital.

"Thank you Mr. Smith for taking me to get something to eat."

"Please India, call me Vance or Sr. that's what most people call me," smiling. He has dimples too. *He sure has strong genes. How in the hell did Miss Sonia get him?* She wasn't ugly but ghetto as hell and she wore any color hair she wanted to wear that day.

I guess it depended on her mood. Some days red, blue and on a good day maybe even brown. She was a very carefree person with no worries in the world. And she was loud at times. But by her vocabulary, you could tell that she was not very educated. But she was a cool person and she had a bad shape like a brick-house, even to be in her early fifties. And she had the prettiest skin I had ever see. She was high yellow with almond shaped eyes. Her daughter Vantrice looked more like her than Mr. Smith, I mean Vance Sr. but she took his color. Now Vantrice was my girl, she never took sides or tried to play the middleman. And if her brother was wrong, she admitted it and told him about himself. She actually was friends with both my sister and Monique, she even tried to keep the peace amongst them.

"You ok over there," Vance Sr. asks me.

"Yes, just thinking that's all. I probably need a drink."

"Same here. Well after we leave the hospital we can go have a couple drinks if you like," he offered.

"Well I love you too," I say jokingly, laughing. "I need to get my drink on."

"Me too," he said, laughing with me.

Back at the hospital, there weren't any changes. The family waiting room was still gloomy. Vance was still unconscious. Same thing, different day. Visiting hours were over at 8pm so we all gathered our belongings to get ready to leave because there were only ten minutes remaining. Everyone kissed and said their goodbyes.

"See you in the morning unless something changes," we all said. I kissed Asia and told her I was going to have a nightcap with Vance's father.

"Ok, I'll ride home with Boobie, see you when you get there," Asia said. We told each other we 'I love you' and left.

"You ready?" Vance Sr. asks.

"Yes," I retorted and we walked to his car but this time he had his arm around me. I felt uncomfortable at first but that went away as quickly as it came. I felt at ease with him. While in the car driving, I asked, "Are we going to a bar or a restaurant with a bar?" Because I wasn't really dressed.

"I thought I'll take you to one of my establishments, there's no dress code. It's a sports bar," licking his lips.

"Oh, I like the sound of that."

When we pulled up, I was amazed. The place was really nice on the outside, it had a sign that hung over the entrance with the letters 'V.S.O.P.' in neon lights. To top it off, the venue even had a security guard and valet parking. Inside was even more amazing than the exterior. It had flat screens everywhere in every corner with red leather booths, tables with red coverings, and pictures of all the Atlanta teams from football to basketball – it seemed like all the sports. He had a room with pool tables and another room with basketball games for adults. Adding to the sports bar theme, classic old school arcade games were stationed in another room – Pac Man, Centipede, racing games, shooting games with a gun and a motorcycle game that was shape like a real Harley Davidson. His place was nice. But what stood out the most was the huge fish tank that covered most of the bar area. It had to be at least twenty feet long with salt water fish swimming throughout. It was beautiful.

"You really have a nice place Vance Sr." I said softly, still in awe.

"Thank you pretty lady. I'm glad you approve," nodding his head. After he walked through and gave all of the men dap, the black masculine greeting, he took me to a private area in the back.

"We can be more comfortable back here unless you want to sit out there with those knuckle heads."

"No this is fine," I said, preparing to sit down.

A waitress who kept mean-mugging me continued to bring us drinks. Finally I asked him, "What's up with yo girl that's bringing us drinks? She keeps mean-mugging me. Are you two an item?" I asks, I started feeling myself since I had three Patron shots in a row, straight, with no chaser.

He laughed, "No we're not an item. I am actually single at the moment. My last relationship went down the drain months ago."

"What happened?" I found myself asking, the 80 Proof in Patron encouraged my audacity.

"Well let's just say she wanted other things in life that I didn't want."

"Such as?" I asked, the tequila was speaking on behalf of my curiosity.

He laughed, "Such as kids. I'm about to be a grandfather, what would I look like having a kid and a grandchild at the same time," pointing to himself.

"You'll look like a player," I laughed and he laughed too.

"Well we can't have that can we? I'll leave that to the younger men to handle. I hung up my hat years ago."

"That's too bad," I responded, *shit I'll let you give me a baby, some sperm or simply a nut at this point.* I wanted him in the worst way, I had to admitted to myself. I couldn't take my eyes off him. *Damn he's such a fine older man,* I kept thinking.

"India do you want one more before I take you home?" looking me in the eyes.

"Which home? Yours or mine?" the Patron had me thinking naughty things, until I realized those words actually came out of my mouth! *Opps!*

He looked at me and said, "Excuse me did I hear you correctly?"

At this point, there was no use of being a punk now, go for what you know, "You heard me correctly Mr. Smith – I mean Vance. I've been attracted to you all night," I said as he was still looking at me.

He smiled again with those damn dimples, "It's the drink talking India, not you. But thank you, that's a compliment coming from you," smiling.

"No hold on, I am drunk...but I know exactly what I want and right now it's you," matching his gaze.

"Let's get out of here," he said.

"Let's go," I grabbed my purse and finished what was left of my drink.

I wasn't sure what he was thinking because he didn't say another word. Not even in the car. But the song said it all, *'This is what I do to get you in the mood baby, I'll do it all to get you in the mood.'* The old school music he played gracefully blessed our ear and actually turned me on even more. When we got to his house, he punched in a code to open the big, black iron gate. To say his house was a mansion was an understatement. This thing was huge. It reminded me of the movie 'Dallas' those old school mansions that rich white people lived in. Once we pulled in close enough, the circular driveway lit up and the porch light came on. I thought my parents little five bedroom house in Saint François Woods was something. But his house made my parents' look like a doll house. He had his 'V.S.' initials centered on the front of his mahogany, wooden frontdoor.

Once inside, I thought I died and went to heaven. Everything was sparkling white with marble floors throughout the whole house. Whatever rooms didn't have marble, was filled with the plushest white carpet I had ever seen. Each room had its own theme – a formal dining room and living room, an Asian room with cultural aspects throughout. There was a red, black and green room with a velvet green sofa with throw pillows and plants everywhere. He had a huge picture hanging on the wall with cut up pieces of dollar bills inside it. Very unique. Then there was his den that took my breath away also. It had a fireplace shaped like a cave with a rug in front of it crowned by a tigers head. He had a portrait of Vance Jr. and Vantrice when they were children standing on each side of Vance Sr. who was sitting in a king's chair. He had a brown leather sectional sofa and two brown leather chairs and a smaller area in the corner with brown leather stools.

Adding a bit of fun to the room, there was a backgammon set and card table in one corner, and a chess set in another. It was a room you could relax in. The house had seven bedrooms and six bathrooms.

He had a heated pool in the back with a jacuzzi and a guest house in the back also. The patio had a barbeque pit built in and a wet bar. It looked like a kitchen but it was outside. And it was all lit up with lights. His master bedroom took the cake. A king size caramel and brown leather head board with a brown leather comforter. There was a rug that covered most of the room with brown, beige, red, and gold with designs. To my right was a long seat with an ottoman in the corner. In front of us stood a built-in fish tank with another fireplace directly in front of the bed. Towards the back was a sixty inch flat screen on the wall where you could see a patio on the opposite side. Adding a sensual feel to the room, tall candle holders stood firm in each corner and were already burning. The focal point of his room was a black art portrait of a man and woman making love above his bed. They were in the bed with covers over them but the man was on top of her staring right into her eyes. I fell in love with the portrait instantly.

"You have an exquisite taste in art," I said.

"I'm glad you like the picture. It caught my eye the first time I saw it also," he replied.

"You live here alone?" I questioned.

"Yes, except for my housekeepers. She occasionally stays over but during the day I have a few employees here," smiling. Those dimples greeted me again.

"Would you like another drink?" he asks.

"Yes please," he made us both another drink but before we could finish them he took me by my hands and led me to the fireplace.

"You're absolutely beautiful India," he said, kissing my forehead which sent electric jolts through my entire body, and then he kissed me and caressed my face. He gently slid off my wife beater and unfastened my bra, I had already taken my jacket off when I first got there.

He sucked on my breast like a newborn baby. I wish I had milk to feed him. He moved his way down and removed my sweatpants and to his surprise, I didn't have any panties on. I hated wearing them.

He just looked over my body as I laid on the rug next to the burning fireplace and lusted over me like a hungry wolf. He came out of his clothes quickly and when I saw how well-endowed he was, I knew I needed another drink and fast. His dick was the size of muffler, it was a tree stomp. I've never had a penis of this caliber before. I didn't know if I could handle it. But after he sucked and licked and sucked some more, he paid attention to every hole on my body and I do mean every hole. I was begging for him to enter me.

"Please put it in," I said over and over again until he lifted my legs up over his shoulders and entered with some resisting.

"You're tight baby damn but soaking wet," he moaned. He pushed again until he made it inside.

"Ohh," I said in his ear. He was stroking me like an Olympic swimmer going for gold. He was very experienced, I could tell by how he took his time with me. I matched his every move and came three times in this one position.

"Damn baby this some tight pussy," he moaned.

"I can make love to you every night, oh my God I'm coming again!" I yelled.

"Come for me baby, that's right make it rain on this dick," stroking steadily for the goal. It was more like a storm how I came, this time loud and hard. He turned me over and hit it from the back while kissing my neck, back, and ears with each stroke.

"Where have you been all my life," I asked in a whisper.

"Right here baby, waiting on you," he retorted. He picked up his pace and I would be damn if I didn't come all over his ass again. But this time I was screaming at the top of my lungs.

"I love this dick, oh-oh my god...don't stop!" He kissed my buttocks and then smacked both cheeks.

"You love this dick then throw it back at this dick!" I did what I was told – tired, sweating and all. Then he started to cum.

"Damn baby this pussy is so good. You're making me cum," gripping me tighter.

"Come on daddy, cum for me!" and that he did and the shit felt so good. He picked me up and carried me to the bathroom and laid me on the bench. He ran me a hot bubble bath and placed me in it. *I must be dreaming, this is utopian bliss.* He washed me up and dried me off with a big, fluffy towel and carried me to bed. We slept for a few hours, I suppose, and before I knew it we was right back at it again. He was the most considerate lover I ever had. Just when I thought I had mad skills in the bedroom, he had me beat hands down. Around ten in the morning, the housekeeper brought breakfast up to the room. How she knew I was there, I couldn't say but she arrived with two breakfast trays with scrambled eggs, wheat toast, sausages, bacon, and blueberry muffins. For drinks, she prepared fresh orange juice for me and coffee for him. As quickly as she entered, she swiftly left.

"I know I look a mess..." I said, barely awake.

"You look beautiful," he said smiling.

I smiled back then he sat up in bed and asked me, "Are you ready to eat?"

"Yes, I'm starving," I said as my stomach growled, reacting from the sight of the feast that lied in front of us.

"Well dig in, enjoy!"

Before I got a chance to taste everything, my phone started beeping, someone had left me a message. Biting my bacon, I asked Vance to hand me my phone because it was closer to him. He did and continued to finish his breakfast. *I knew it was Asia, she was probably looking for me because I stayed out all night.* I called her back as soon a I finished my food.

"Hello. Where are you at Miss Stay-out-all-night and had me worried?" Asia asked as expected.

"I'm with Vance Sr.," twirling my fork around my devoured plate.

"I know you said you were going to have a drink but where did y'all go to get it? Africa?" sounding annoyed.

Laughing, I said, "No sweetie, we're still in Atlanta, I think?"

looking at him puzzled. 'Are we?' I mouthed. He mouthed back 'yes', laughing.

"India don't tell me you fucked my baby's grandfather with his fine ass, did you?" yelling excitedly into the phone.

"Well I won't tell you then," laughing.

"Hoe quit playing. You didn't!" Asia said.

"I did. I'll talk to you when I get there, goodbye!" and hung up.

"So she knows where you stayed last night, that's not going to be a problem, I hope?" he said while reading the paper.

"I'm grown so it's not going to be a problem but what about us?" I asked, suddenly feeling awkward about the situation at hand.

"Well one of two things can happen: One, we can go with our feelings and let whatever happens, happen or two, we can kiss and say goodbye no hard feelings. It's up to you grown woman," laughing.

I didn't know what to say, my foot was in my mouth. Just looking at him, I wanted more. What's a girl to do? He came and sat on the bed next to me and looked me in my eyes.

"I don't want you to feel like I took advantage of you," solemnly speaking. Looking me in my eyes the way he did turned me on. I kissed him, laid him down and rode that black cowboy like a rodeo until we both climaxed. I didn't know what came over me. I just did what felt right at the time.

As I lay on his hairy chest, he kissed me gently, "I guess we have our answer," whispering in my ear.

"I guess so," I whispered in his.

We laid there for about an hour before we both took a shower and got dressed to leave. Riding in the car, my thoughts took the stage. I liked the fact that he was older and mature but still sexy. But he didn't act too old or dressed old fashioned. He put on a Gucci sweatshirt with Jordan sneakers and a baseball cap. I just smiled to myself. I could *do* him for a while. He was smiling back at me. I guess he was thinking the same thing.

When I got to Boobie's house, only Asia was there, "Where's Boobie and Lisa at?"

"They had some errands to run," crossing her arms, "so tell me lil miss hot pants how was my Father-In-Law?"

"Can I wash my ass and get dressed first before we go into details?" laughing.

"NO BITCH! Spill the beans!" Asia yells.

"Well your Father-in-law has a dick the size of a muffler," demonstrating with my hands.

"Oh India, you're lying!" her eyes enlarged, she awaited my confirmation and started getting excited.

"No I'm not. It's a water heater baby," laughing.

"He looks like he would be packing heat too. Can he put it down though?" she asked, I had her full attention like I was giving a lecture on the first day of class.

"Yes ma'am. He is a gentle lover, very mature and he makes love to your whole body."

"Damn I see where Vance gets it from. Like father like son," laughing.

"I sure miss my baby," Asia said, looking sad.

"He'll be fine Asia. I betcha' he'll wake up and be ready to leave the hospital that same day," I said, reassuring her and rubbing her back.

"I know," she said.

"I'll be glad when that happens, I miss him," she mumbled and started to cry.

"I know Asia, we all do. We just have to keep praying," I said, trying to be strong for her and wiping her tears.

"Mom called this morning, she's in Japan but she said she'll be back in a week and she'll come stay with me for a while. But I told her 'No, I'm good,' plus you're here," she said, looking back at me.

"How long are you staying anyways?" she asked.

"Well it's August so I can stay I guess until school starts back or until Vance wakes up. I don't know, I'll just ride it out with you because you need me here."

"Well, let's go get lunch and head back up to the hospital. Annnnnd don't be making goo-goo eyes with Vance Sr. either. Sonia's feelings would probably get hurt." Asia said.

"Whatever, Sonia better sit her tired ass down. She don't want it," laughing.

"Anyways, get dressed so we can go to eat at the new Chinese restaurant that just opened."

It had been a week since Vance was shot and it was starting to wear on Asia. She looked like she was going through it and that scared me. Especially since she was pregnant.

Asia's phone started ringing, "Hello, hu-huh? I'm on my way!" Asia's face lit up. "Let's go India, Vance is waking up. They said he opened his eyes for a moment but closed them back shut. MY BABY WOKE UP!" victory and relief rang from the depths of her larynx.

I drove 100 mph to the hospital and even ran a red light. Thank God no police were around. When we finally got there, everyone was pulling up. Sonia was leading the pack, she was already walking to the entrance, along with Vantrice. We all ran into the family waiting room to hear the news. Sonia was crying and Vantrice was consoling her.

"What's the matter," I asks. "Is everything alright?" The nurse came back in and brought a pitcher of water along with some cups.

"How's Vance? When can we see him?" Asia said without taking a breath.

"The doctors are in there with him now and his parents will be able to see him shortly and depending on how he feels, maybe one to two others. We don't want to over do it today."

We all shook our heads in agreeance. Boobie and Lisa had just walked in, and without hesitation we gave them the update. Vance Sr. arrived with his brother, who looked just like him, and some of

Vance's other friends. We were all laughing and talking about what we were going to say to him or what he might say until we were interrupted when Monique's loud ass came in crying.

"My husband woke up? Why was I the last person to know!" looking at Sonia.

"We called everyone basically around the same time," Vantrice said and started rolling her eyes, looking irritated.

"Well I should have been the first one called, not everybody else," she replied. No one paid her any attention and that only made her start up again.

"I don't know why you all keep bringing this half breed bitch up here," looking at Asia. "I'm his muthafuckin' wife!"

Boobie walked up to her and stood in her face, "I'm not going to tell you again Monique. You need to gone with all that B.S. you talkin'. My nigga never married your ass, you don't even have an engagement ring and that half breed you're referring to, her name is Asia and she has every right to be here just like you do. But if you keep it up, them rights can be taken away from you. Feel me?"

"You don't scare me nigga! I know what me and Vance have, we've been together for ever fifteen years, that's my husband. And I will say who can see him or not. Not you!" screaming.

Vance Sr. said, "That's enough. I'm sick and tired of your dramatics Monique. My son wouldn't want this to be happening like this. So either you calm down or leave and if you leave please don't bother to return."

"I hate all of you, I swear. Just wait until I see Vance," crying on the shoulder of her friend who looked like a linebacker. Then all of a sudden, she grabbed her stomach and started doubling over.

"What's wrong?" her friend asks.

"My stomach is cramping, call the nurse!"

A nurse ran in with a wheelchair and sat her down, "She's going to have to be seen in emergency," wheeling her out. She ask Monique was she experiencing cramps similar to menstrual pain. She shook her head 'yes' and they headed out. The two friends with her were looking angry as well. The doctor came back and said Sonia and Vance Sr. could see Vance but only for a few minutes at a time and with that, they both headed to the room with the doctor leading the way.

Asia Smith

I was so happy my baby woke up. I felt joy all over me. I think the whole room was excited. We all held hands and said a prayer thanking God for giving him back to us. *I can't wait to see him.* Sonia and Vance Sr. came back in the waiting room about twenty minutes after they left.

"What did he say? How does he look? Is he in any pain?" they were bombarded with questions.

"He's fine considering his condition and he didn't really talk much but he did ask to ask to see you Asia," my heart skipped a beat. My baby wanted to see me.

"Can you take me back there," I ask Vance Sr.

"Sure, come on," he said. We walk back through some double doors, holding hands and went to ICU. He pushed the intercom, stated his name and the door pushed open. I felt like I was walking on the moon. I took my steps carefully while a lump was forming in my throat. I started to get hot and light headed, I was beyond nervous. When we made it to his room, I froze. Just staring at him lying in that bed with all these tubes everywhere and a big machine sitting next to him with two IV poles connected to his arm, he looked weak. Just seeing him like that broke me down.

"It's alright Asia, let it out. But you have to try to be strong for him now and the baby you're carrying. O.K.," he said, giving me some fatherly advice.

You can do this, I said to myself. I slowly walked towards the bed trying to hold back my tears. I kissed his forehead and softly said, "I love you baby."

"I love you too," Vance said, but it was barely auditable. I took his hand into mine and sat in the chair next to the bed and put my head on his chest. He started squeezing my hand so I looked up. His pretty brown eyes were open.

"Hi baby, you scared us," I said.

"They can't kill a soldier baby, I was made for this kinda' shit," trying to laugh but instead he started to cough.

"Don't laugh baby, it's ok…don't talk, just rest baby. I love you so much Vance, I prayed every day that God wouldn't take you away from me and he answered my prayers," rubbing his shoulders.

"I love you too baby and remind me to thank God when I get up," smiling.

Then he closed his eyes and drifted back to sleep. The nurse came back in and said, "That's enough for today." I kissed my baby on the forehead again and told him I loved him as I walked out waving good-bye. Back in the waiting room, everyone was so quiet it was almost eerie.

"What's wrong?" I asks. It couldn't be Vance because I just left him.

Vance Sr. says, "Monique had a miscarriage, they said it's probably of the stress. They admitted her and she's having some procedure done to clean her up."

I didn't know what to say, what do you say at a time like this? We weren't friends but I wouldn't wish that on my worst enemy. Damn, she was my worst enemy. Sonia said she would go check on her when she got settled in a room and she would call her mother. She didn't want anyone to tell Vance yet until he felt stronger. *Wow, that could have been me.* Sonia and Vance Sr. said they would make a visiting list tomorrow to determine who would be allowed to see him. There could only be two visitors at a time. Boobie said he wanted to visit tomorrow and also his friend Dude, *Vance's friends had the most interesting names.* They said they only wanted to see him for a few minutes and then they'll just wait until he came home. Vance Sr. said it wasn't a problem and they could be first to visit tomorrow morning. Everyone said their goodbyes and went on their way. I kissed Lisa and told them I'll be there later. Then they left. A few of his other homies said they were just waiting for him to wake up and now that he was, they were cool and they left. The party was winding down. I saw Vance Sr. wink at India, and she didn't even think I noticed, but I did.

But it didn't matter anyways because my baby woke up. That's all that matters to me. We were all juiced about Vance, but tomorrow was Essence's funeral and I wasn't looking forward to that. But I had to pay my respects. *She was my friend right or was she? I don't know if she was fucking my man but I wouldn't know that until Vance felt better, much better. Then I'll confront him about it.* Until then, it was just an assumption. Should I let it go and be grateful my man was alive and let the dead rest in peace? Time will tell that answer because at this point, I didn't know what to think.

The next couple days, I stayed day and night with Vance. I only left to go take a quick shower and I came right back. We took turns visiting him - myself, his mom, dad, sister, and Boobie came twice but that was it. He said he had some business to take care of for Vance and he would see him when he came home, which would hopefully be in the next couple of weeks. He was getting stronger by the day, sitting up by himself with a pillow and he was starting to ask for real food.

"Mom can you bring some red beans and rice and oxtails up in here? This hospital food is for old people," we all laughed.

"I'll try and sneak some in here but I'm not sure your doctors wants you eating heavy food like that yet."

"He's not going to trip if I'm hungry. Shit, I need to gain my weight back. And those Ensure drinks they have been given me ain't go work."

"I'll see what I can do Vance but I'm not making you any promises," she said.

"Baby," he looked at me.

"Yes Vance."

"You do it then because scary-cat over there is buggin' out," he said, trying to laugh but coughed instead.

"Stop laughing Vance, do you want me to get you something from the cafeteria now?"

"Yes please, a grilled cheese and fries."

"Ok, does anyone else want anything while I'm there?"

"Bring me a Pepsi Asia and a cup of ice," Sonia said.

"Ok I'll be back."

While waiting on the elevator, I saw Monique's friend pushing her in a wheelchair towards Vance's room. I started to give my condolences, but for what? The bitch didn't like me and the feelings were mutual but our babies were going to be siblings. *Well actually...they're not now*. I even considered sending her some flowers but knowing her she would have thrown them away if they came from me.

India told me earlier, 'I'll give her some flowers alright, I'll take them from the grave site to give it to her punk ass. Because if the shoe was on the other foot, she wouldn't care about you or your feelings. Just leave it alone.' And she was right.

As the elevator doors opened, I stepped in and our eyes met, "What you looking at bitch?" she asked as the door was closing. She was just another sorry loser in my book. I was glad I didn't go out of my way for that miserable hoe. My stomach began to growl. *I'm starving too, shit did I eat anything today?*

I ordered our food, got our drinks, picked up my to-go boxes and headed back up to Vance room. Everybody was waiting outside. Vance is talking to Monique. I was certain that she was talking to him about the miscarriage. I just looked like *whatever*.

"How much longer is he going to be on the morphine

pump?" I asked to change the subject.

"His doctor said he'll probably need it a couple more weeks. They're going to try to wean him off because it's addicting but his pain is so severe and since he's doing so much better, it might even be sooner," Vance Sr. said. "And I sure hope so because I don't want him addicted to no damn drugs. He's a man, he can handle some pain. Shit a little pain is good for him. All he needs is some antibiotics so he won't get any infections."

"Daddy he is still in alot of pain. I can see it all in his face," Vantrice says.

His nurse walks past us to go into his room, "Is everything ok? You pushed your buzzer?" she asked him.

"Can you please ask my father to come here for a minute."

"Sure," walking out. "Sir, your son would like to see you." Vance Sr. got up and went inside the room.

"Dad."

"What's up son?"

"Please ask Monique to leave. She's stressing me out, I don't have the strength to argue with her right now."

"Fuck you Vance, I'm serious. If you're going to disrespect me and I just lost your baby nigga then fuck you!" yelling.

"Hold up, what's going on in here?" Sonia said running in, we followed closely behind her.

"Monique, my son ask you to leave, now it's time for you to go!" Vance Sr. said.

"Fuck all you muthafucka's!" Monique yelled as she was getting wheeled out the room. Vance sat in his hospital bed looking worn out. He hit his morphine button twice, trying to escape the pain.

"Baby you ok? I brought your food."

"I'm not hungry anymore, I lost my appetite but thanks baby," kissing my hand.

"What was that all about Vance?" Sonia asked, looking at her son.

"Monique with all her drama, she told me she lost the baby and tried to blame Asia and said I should make Asia get an abortion and some stupid shit. I asked her to leave, but she wouldn't. Mama I dont have the strength for her right now. Please don't let her come back to see me until I'm home. I just want to get out of this hospital strong enough to leave all this shit behind me. I'm tired and I'm taking a nap, but you all can stay if you want to. And Asia, don't go nowhere, you hear me?"

"Yes, I'm not. I'm going to be right here baby, like Bonnie and Clyde." He smiled and closed his eyes.

I don't think he was sleep but he was in deep thought. Sonia, Vance and Vantrice stayed for a while and then they decided to leave, "We'll be back in the morning Asia, I'll bring you both some breakfast."

"Ok Sonia, thanks," leaning in to give her a kiss. I did the same to Vance and Vantrice.

"Bye, see you in the morning," closing the door behind them and I went to lay on the couch bed in the corner of the room and went to sleep myself. I didn't wake up until the nurse came in to see about Vance.

"You want a blanket Asia?" she asked?

"Yes, please," nodding my head.

"I'll be right back with one," she said and walked out.

When she returned, Vance was woke, "Hi baby, you woke up."

"Here you go Asia," handing me a blanket.

"Thank's."

"How you feeling Vance? I mean your pain level?" she asked.

"It's about a six right now. I just hit my button and it usually takes a minute to kick in but I'm good, thanks."

"Ok, well if you need anything, just buzz me."

"I will...come here Asia," he reaches for me.

"What's up baby?"

"I just want to look at you, that's all. How's my shortie

doing?" Vance asked.

"We're fine now that you're better," smiling.

"I love you girl," he said, gazing into my eyes.

"I love you too baby."

"Come lay with me."

"Vance I can't fit in that bed with you. It's too small plus I don't want to hurt you."

"I need to feel you next to me, you won't hurt me just be careful getting in. Let the rails down."

I do as I am told, lifting my leg up and glided in as best I could without disturbing him. He was waiting with open arms but it was awfully tight. I lay down sideways, looking at him.

"Give me some sugar, I miss you girl," he said and we kissed so rough that we accidentally hit the nurses button.

She came running in, "Oh, sorry to interrupt you two love birds but Asia you can't be in the bed with him, it's hospital policy. Plus he has staples in his chest and under his arms. We don't want to interfere with the healing process or even take the chance of something rupturing, do we?"

"No ma'am I'm sorry," I retort, humbly bowing my head.

"No, it's ok. Just pull your couch closer to him. Come on, I'll help you," she offered, walking towards us. We move the couch as close as we could and left the railing down. Vance was laughing the whole time while I was being scolded, knowing it was his fault in the first place.

"Baby if Nurse Betty wasn't on our heels, we could do it in here, huh?" Vance asked as soon as the door shut behind her.

"You're nasty Vance," smiling at the thought, I missed his playfulness.

"Oh you wouldn't do it?"

"No, I can wait until you come home. As a matter of fact, we don't have a choice but to wait," giving him a stern look while I lay down into the coach.

"Shit baby, wait until I can get up and go to the bathroom. It's on," winking at me.

"Vance please, you should be thinking about getting better, not getting pussy," shaking my head.

"I'm thinking about both," he said, trying to laugh.

"You're going to pop those stitches, boy you better stop."

"Where's my food at?" Vance asked, looking directly at me.

"Over here, it's cold though."

"I don't care, I'm hungry and I need something in my stomach," he said, giving me sinister look that I couldn't make out.

"Ok, let me get it."

"Asia."

"Huh?" looking up at him.

"What about the meal between your legs," licking his tongue at me.

Rolling my eyes, "Vance, stop it." I get up to grab his cold grilled cheese sandwich, "You want me to warm this up in the microwave down the hall?"

"Yeah and hurry back before I miss you!"

"Whatever big baby," I say and make my way to warm his food up in the nurses lounge. After its hot and ready, I also bring him back some orange juice, "Eat up boy."

"Thank you baby. Did Vantrice do the paperwork for the house?" Vance asked.

"Yes, we close in about fifty more days. Just in time for you and when you come home. I haven't had time to do any shopping but we will have the bedroom set delivered in time. Remember they said six to eight weeks. It's been six weeks already, so it's perfect timing. That's all we need for now anyways. You can rest at home when you get out or do you want to stay at Boobies for a while?"

"Hello no! I'm staying right in my own gated community in my brand new six bedroom house, breaking in every room and bathroom in the place. Shit even the living room, dining room, den and basement. Hell, we don't need any furniture, just an air mattress everywhere," after he finished his boastful statement, he began reaching for another bite.

"Vance please. You're not going to be strong enough for all that you talking. The doctor said you still have to recuperate for a couple of months," handing him a napkin as he finished his meal.

"I'm my own damn doctor Asia, once I leave here they can kiss my black ass. Thanks for saving my life but I have a life also. Baby I'm a boss!" slamming his fork down to add a dramatic effect.

"Funny Vance, you are feeling better though, I can tell," I said aloud but it was more of an internal thought.

"I'm tired. I'm going to sleep and looks like you are too. I see you keep hitting the morphine button, boss!" laughing, "give me a kiss goodnight," I reach in and tongue him down.

"Goodnight, don't let those bed bugs bite," I say, grabbing my blanket.

"You don't bite do you?" he says playfully while winking at me.

"Boy, goodnight. You're so silly!"

15

DEATH SENTENCE

India Smith

It had almost been a month since Vance had been shot and I believe it had taken a toll on his father. For the last couple of days, he was under the weather. I offered to stay with him a few nights before it was time to return Cali for school.

Lying in bed watching TV, I played in his hair while he rubbed on my ass, "Baby how you feel?" I asked.

"A little better India, I hope it's nothing serious but I think I'm coming down with a chest cold because it's starting to feel tight in this area." I started rubbing his hairy chest and he smiled.

"I'm sure going to miss you when you're gone baby," he said.

"I'm going to miss you too," I say, kissing him. We formed something special in this little bit of time we spent together. He gave 'grown man loving' a whole new meaning.

He pulled me on top of him and removed my g-string, that was the only thing I had on. He started kissing on my breast, taking one in his mouth at a time. I slid myself on top of him and rode him real slow, gyrating my hips like a belly dancer.

"This feels good baby," I said looking at him. I must be putting it on him because his eyes were closed but he was smiling. So I put a little more rhythm into it.

"Ooh baby. I love the way you feel inside me," still working him, I picked up the pace. I reached down and kissed him but he didn't respond. I tried to stick my tongue in his mouth but he wouldn't open up.

"Baby what's the matter? It doesn't feel good?" Still no response.

"Vance answer me!" Nothing.

"Oh my God, what's wrong?" No answer.

I tried shaking his shoulders but he didn't wake up. I put my head on his chest to check his breathing, but there wasn't any.

I immediately jumped up screaming, "HELP! HELP! PLEASE CALL 911!"

I hadn't realized I was naked, jumping up and down, panicking. His housekeeper gave me a robe and sat me down on the chase. My heart was beating so fast I thought I was going to die. I couldn't stop crying and every time I looked over at him, I went hysterical.

When the paramedics arrived, they worked on him and tried to revive him but he was already gone. They put the blankets over him as best they could and waited for the coroner's office to come. I was so embarrassed because I had to explain to everyone who questioned me, exactly what we were doing and for how long. The paramedics believed he had a heart attack. I told them he had been complaining of chest pains earlier but he thought he came down with a chest cold. The more I told the story, the worst I became.

When they finally took his body out, he still had an erect penis. When I watched them remove him. I didn't know whether to laugh or cry. *Damn. Why me? Why am I thinking 'why me'? Why him? He's the one who died, not me.* My head started spinning and suddenly everything went pitch black. I passed out. When I woke up, I was in the same hospital Vance was in when he got shot and where Monique lost her baby and now where Vance Sr. body was probably held.

My sister and Vance were sitting right beside me, crying.

"You ok India? You went into shock." *I did*, this was the first time I've been conscious since the blackout.

"Yes, I'm ok. Vance I'm so sorry," I say whole heartedly.

"What you sorry for lil sis, you didn't kill my pops. He had a heart attack," wiping away a tear. "But damn lil sis, you must have fucked the shit out my dude. That's 'till death do you part' for real!" we all started laughing. A bit of comic relief much needed amongst us all.

"Shit that's a hell of a way to go out. You must have some killer pussy sis."

"Stop it Vance, this is serious," Asia said while trying not to laugh herself. "Are you feeling ok India?"

"Yes, I feel like going home. I need to go home."

"Ok, let's just wait until the nurse says you are good to go. Just relax until then," she reaffirmed me while rubbing my forehead.

"Who called you Asia?" I asked.

"Vance's housekeeper Rosie called Vance when we were about to leave Boobie's. We had dinner over there and a little 'welcome home' feast to celebrate Vance getting out of the hospital."

"So they know too?"

"Well, not in detail. We said we had an emergency, that's all and we would call them later."

"Good. Please don't tell anyone exactly how he had a heart

attack, please. Let's just deal with his death," whether consciously or subconsciously, it was evident that I felt a bit guilty and ashamed.

"Ok India, I understand. But there's nothing to be ashamed of," Asia hit the nail on the head, sister's intuition at its best.

"Asia's right India, it could have happened to anyone of us. Please don't worry yourself about this," with a look of approval.

"Thanks Vance, I love you guys dearly – " I say with another tear falling.

"We love you too lil' sis," Vance interjected.

"But I'm not sure how much more of this shit I can take, this would be the third death within a couple months," I said, feeling overwhelmed at the thought.

"They say, death comes in three's," Asia replied.

"Yeah, I guess...the baby, Essence, my old man," putting his face in his hands. "This shit is crazy."

Rubbing his back, "It's going to be ok. I know it hurts. God please help us, we need your strength," Asia prayed out loud. I said a silent prayer also. *When does the tragedy stop?*

Over the next couple of days, I was in and out of it. The doctor prescribed me some valiums to help me relax and that's exactly what they did, relax me. Vance and Vantrice had a memorial service for Vance Sr. at a hall. They had a poster size picture of him and some home video footage of his accomplishments. It was really nice with food and an open bar. They didn't want a big funeral because Vance wanted him cremated to keep his ashes. Vance said every year he would throw him a big birthday party with him attendance and also a memorial party on the anniversary of his death.

Sonia took it pretty hard, I guess she still harbored feelings for him. He was the father of her two children. She barely spoke to me or even looked in my direction but that was understandable because she knows about our relationship and how he died. Vance told his sister Vantrice and I know she told her mother. But Vantrice and I embraced one another and I gave her my condolences.

My plane was scheduled to leave at ten tonight, so I didn't stay too long, plus I wasn't in the mood for all of those people and their subtle grievances. Asia was ready to leave once Monique arrived with her ugly posse, being loud as usual. She kept crying 'My Father-in-law, oh my Father-in-law', very dramatic. It was almost like she was auditioning for a part in a movie – overacting is how some critics would judge this scene. Asia kissed Vance goodbye and told him she would see him later. I said goodbye to everyone and we left.

Pulling up to departures at the airport, "I'm going to miss you being around India, thanks for all your support."

"That's what sisters are for...to be there in a time of need. And I want to thank you for being there for me when I needed you. This whole trip was crazy, huh?" I asked.

"Yeah, I'm glad it's all behind us. Now we can get settled in our new house and try to get back on track before the baby comes," Asia said, looking down and giving her belly a rub.

"I'll be back for the shower, and Christmas is at your house this year right?"

"Right," Asia replied. "Mom and Dad are coming too. I spoke to her this morning."

"Um, I don't feel like talking to her but she's picking me up from the airport," shaking my head. I couldn't bear another ounce of stress, even if that was coming from the woman who birthed me.

"Goodluck!" laughing mischievously.

"Yeah I know I'm going to need it," I retorted.

We proceeded to grab my bags out the trunk, "I love you sis." Asia set my bags down on the curb to hug me. In her greatest attempt to hold me tight, there was still an occupied space where my future niece or nephew rested patiently.

"I love you more and take care of my baby inside your big belly," laughing and touching her stomach.

"I'll call you when I arrive."

We exchanged kisses, Asia drove off and back home I went

with new memories. *It's better to have loved than to not have loved at all.*

Back in California, I stayed at my parent's house for a couple days - I didn't want to be alone. But I still felt lonely because the day I got home, my mom was off to Washington, my dad works long hours, and Maria has a life outside of work. So basically, I was by myself and slipped into a deep depression. I didn't know how to climb my way out. Dark clouds smothered the west coast sunshine with chilling memories of the summer. School was about to start and I was excited about that. I would at least be around people all day and my study group was a mixed race of individuals who was off the hook. The first day of school was hard for me, I had to get my routine back in motion. I wasn't used to getting up early anymore and staying focused all day. So much had happened so fast, my body felt like it was trying to shut down.

"What's up India? Are you coming to the meeting at Taylor's house tonight?" Sam asked.

"I'm so tired. I need another cup of Starbucks, but yeah, I'll be there," I said, but immediately regretted my verbal RSVP exchange.

"Be on time, ok. We need to discuss how we're going to conduct this group this semester. Be punctual, it starts at seven p.m."

"Bye Sam, I'll see you there."

I went home and set my alarm for six-thirty, it only takes about twenty minutes to get to Taylor's from my house. When my alarm clock went off I washed my face, brushed my teeth, and ran out the door. I didn't want to be too late and hear all of their mouths, especially Sam. She nagged like a mother would sometimes, it was nerve rattling but she meant well. I stopped at a drive-thru Starbucks and headed to Taylor's. Sure enough, everyone was there and on time. All their cars were right in front, as usual.

KNOCK, KNOCK, KNOCK! Knocking on the door, Taylor answered, "Hey India, I'm glad you showed up," giving me a hug. "I missed you this summer." I didn't even respond. I guess the caffeine hadn't kicked in yet. I waved to everyone in the room, 'Hey India', everyone said. I sat down on the sofa where there was an empty seat.

"You look tired India," Tyrone says.

"I am, I've been to hell and back his summer and my body is weak. As much Starbucks as I drink a day, you would think I would never go to sleep. But I'm always tired..." I said exhaustively, arranging my body to get comfortable.

"Well we have something to help you stay up for days. I do it when I have exams and need energy to study all night."

Taylor, Sam and Tyrone all looked at me at the same time. I know they snorted coke and popped ecstasy pills occasionally, but I always declined. I thought it would kill my brain cells and me, and I would eventually die of an overdose or something like that.

That's how I always felt about drugs. But the three of them were all A and B students, acing every exam and not missing a beat. *What the hell was there to lose?* I watched my sister go through it with Vance being shot, I lost the man I thought I loved and even though it was only the beginning of the semester, school was already killing me physically and emotionally. I was a mess. *Fuck it, why not.* I ask Sam to show me how to do it. They had already prepared a record album on the table with some coke sitting on it. It looked like a pile of snow to me. She used a card that you play spades with and made a couple lines. She had a few colorful straws in her hand and handed me one. By way of demonstration, Sam put the straw to her nose and inhaled the coke. One whole line. She then tilted her head back a moment as the recreational substance filled her body. I was up next and she told me to try. I did exactly what I saw her do and waited a second for it to take effect. They were all looking at me strangely, or so I thought.

"How do you feel India?" Sam asked.

"Cool." I retorted. It wasn't as bad as I thought.

"Try another line," she said. I did, without being told twice.

"This is the shit," I said. "What do the pills make you do?"

"Calm down Smokey The Bear, one step at a time," Sam replied. "The 'E' pills are mood stimulators. Whatever mood you are in, they enhance it. For example, if you're feeling freaky, you'll be even more freakier. If you want to kill somebody, you would probably gain the willpower on an E pill. And if you're feeling down, you'll probably feel worse. It's just whatever mood you're in at the time. I only take E's when I'm going out clubbing or with my dude." During her debrief, I noticed everyone nodding their heads in approval at different points — reminiscent of their individual experiences.

"Well Sam, I don't have one of those so I probably don't need one," laughing.

"India it's not just for that, you can chill off one," finishing her statement and snorting another line.

"Tyrone takes them all the time for no specific reason," laughing.

"Fuck you Sam," Tyrone said while throwing a couch pillow at her.

Sam dodged it relatively quick before asking me, "Want to do another line?"

"Sure, why not?" I performed the three step process as I did previously but this time, there was a fourth step or rather reaction from performing the steps too many times. My nose started bleeding.

"That's normal for your first time, don't trip rookie," handing me a paper towel. "Just hold your head back and get that rush."

I'm high as hell now, "Why y'all didn't put me on before now?"

They start looking around at each other confused, "We did India, we asked you before and you basically stood on your soapbox for an anti-drug campaign. 'Crack kills' and shit," laughing.

"Well this isn't crack," I said.

"No, it's not but crack is made from coke, it's in the same family," Professor Sam continued.

"Well I don't care what family this is from, this is the shit."

I was feeling myself after the first line. And to my surprise the shit did keep me up all night. After my first hit that day, we did coke three days a week in our study group. I was getting back to my normal self, or so I thought. I didn't come to realize that I was becoming addicted and I even started popping ecstasy. Sam wasn't lying about it being a mood enhancement. Whoever invented this pill had to be a genius. It gave you the power to be able to control your mood to however you wanted to feel. *That's just plain genius to me. I love that person. And I wish I could thank them personally.* I started arranging for Sam to buy my own personal stash of coke and E pills. I was snorting at least twice a day and popping pills just for the hell of it. My depression was long gone. Bye, bye. But I had to welcome another side of India, another side of myself that came with this new lifestyle.

16

I GOT THE HOOK UP

India Smith

"Hi Asia, how are you doing?" I asked my sister. I hadn't spoken to her in a while. I was so busy with school and getting high, I didn't have time for her anymore.

"I'm good India, how are you? I haven't talked to you in awhile, schools keeping you busy huh?"

"Yes, that amongst other things," I said. 'Getting high' is what I really wanted to say but didn't. "I miss you."

"I miss you too. We finally moved into the new house, it's nice," Asia said.

"I bet. I can't wait to see it."

"It's huge, you know Vance. Mr. I-have-so-much-money-let's-buy-a-mansion," laughing.

"Well, be grateful you have a man and a man that bought you a home. I want to be like you when I grow up," I said, giggling at my own statement.

"You're crazy India."

We paused a moment, I didn't know how to ask her to hook me up with the dude who gets profiles for the banks because within the past couple of months, I went through all my money getting high. I was waiting for the right moment to ask her. I wish she would just bring it up.

Breaking the brief silence, "So how many rooms does it have?"

"Seven bedrooms and five bathrooms, a den, family room, two patios from the master bedroom and a guest room. It has a pool in the backyard and Jacuzzi, it's brand new."

"Sounds nice, I can't wait to see it. I guess one of the rooms are mine," I laughed and started to flip through one of my textbooks to calm my nerves.

"Of course, that's what Vance said when we looked at the house. 'This room is for my Shortie'. The nursery is going to be right next to the master bedroom even though the nursery can fit in our room, it's so big! And he said it's a room downstairs that could be for you when you come to visit. No one can sleep in there but you."

"How sweet! But check it, if I have my own room I need to decorate it myself to my likings…"

I took a quick deep breath and went in for the kill, "So I need the hook up on the profiles so I can get some extra cash to go shopping. Plus, I want to start buying some things for my nephew. I've seen all sorts of clothes and toys I want to get him," the bait was set, but my nerves hadn't subsided so I continued to flip through a few more pages.

"Oh yeah, you sound like Vance and his Momma and your Momma too. This baby is going to be like a Prince or King. Maybe I should name him 'Prince King' or 'King Prince'. Which one you like?"

"Neither. Unless he's going to be a singer or rapper," laughing. "And there's already a Prince, *'Purple Rain Purple Rain'*," we both starting laughing. I didn't know whether it was at the name or my singing, or both.

"What is purple rain anyway?" I asked, still flipping through a pages, unconsciously glancing at the words.

"Rain that's purple," Asia retorts.

"I guess he was smoking some purple rain when he made

that song huh? He was probably high," still laughing.

"Why not yellow rain or pink?" Asia jokingly asked.

"Because that's not what he was smoking," I said, still laughing.

"But seriously Asia, I need the hookup," hook, line and sinker.

"Ok India, I'll give you the dudes number and tell him I told you to call. Essence and him were real cool. He really doesn't deal with people directly, you would have to go through somebody but he liked me so I know it should be cool for you. Shit, you should try to pull his ass, the nigga is papered up. He's been having people in banks for over ten years. Can you imagine how much money he has? Shit, the year I was doing it with Essence, I brought in 180,000 by myself. And he has about ten workers going state to state in banks and using instant credit, now add that up by ten years. And never has he went inside a bank. It's all his work and he gets a percentage. The boy is paid. He owns hella property everywhere and he owns drycleaners, a hair salon and a few other things – "

"That nigga has to be ugly Asia!" I said, closing my book since the hard part was out of the way.

"He's not ugly India, he looks like a high yellow nigga with straight hair."

"High yellow, oh hell naw."

"No India, he's cute though. Let me get his number out my phone, hold on for a minute...kk I'm back. Write it down and call him, his name is 'Milo'. Call me tomorrow and let me know what he says."

Jackpot, "Ok, I will. Thank you!" Feeling relieved, I pushed the book aside completely and laid out on my bed.

"Thank me for what? You're my sister India, I love you."

"I love you too. I'll call you tomorrow," and hung up.

Well that went well and I'm glad she didn't ask too many questions about why I wanted his number. I just hope he's as cool as Asia says. High yellow though...I don't know about that one, laughing to myself. *I guess I should call him now and get it over with. I'll do a line of coke to give me some courage before I call.* As soon as I finished my thought, I set it up and snorted a line. I kept a personal stash in my room, on top of my nightstand and I put it inside my top drawer if anyone came over, which was rare. I had to have my coke in the mornings like some people needed their coffee. It was a must for me. I wasn't tired anymore while I was in class, I was focused. It was a win-win.

I typed in the number and dialed the line, *here goes nothing!*

"WHO 'DIS?"

"Hello, may I speak to Milo?"

"Who 'dis?" he asked again.

"This is India, Asia's twin sister," I was alert and ready to get to business.

"Oh yeah, she did tell me she had a twin. Are y'all identical or fraternal?"

"We're identical," I said, keeping everything short on my end.

"Is that right? So you're fine as hell too?"

"Well I guess so, if you think she's fine," I said as he was indirectly stroking my ego.

"You know you're bad, stop acting like you don't know."

This nigga is way too cool, I think I like him already, "Well it all depends on what your preference is. I'm not as wild and outspoken as Asia."

"That's cool, what's up though?" he inquired.

"Well Milo, by the way that's a nice name," I said, hoping the small talk would open some streams of trust.

"That's my nickname but thanks. So what's up with you? You said your name is India?"

"Yes."

"So it's India and Asia, that's cute for twins," his flattery continued.

"Thank you."

"So what you trying to do?" he asked, switching our conversation back to business.

"I'm trying to get with you on some work. But I live in California."

"You do? Why do you live way out there?"

"My parents live out here, Asia moved to Atlanta to go to school. Plus I attend college here in Cali too."

"Oh I didn't know she was from there. I have your sister's picture, you can use it because y'all look just alike. And I do have something, but do you know how we roll?" he asked.

"Yes, Asia explained it to me."

"Well, when are you ready?"

The pressure was on, "I'm ready now, do you have something I can do out here?"

"Yea you can do it anywhere, I'll come out there this weekend and we can talk and make something happen."

"Ok that's cool. Take down my number and call me when you get here. I'll pick you up and you can stay at my house instead of getting a hotel, if you like." I didn't know if this was strictly business because it was getting a little personal, especially with my generosity and opening my home.

"Alright, I'll call you tomorrow with my itinerary."

"Ok, talk to you later."

That went well, I guess I'm on my way. I just pray I can pull it off but shit that's what an E pill is for. I can do anything when I'm on one of them, snorting another line. Laying my head back on the pillow, singing *'We're in the money, I'm in the money'*! I headed to the bank after school to get a few dollars for the weekend. I'll have to buy some food for the house which I hadn't done in a while. Shit, I hadn't cooked in months it seemed like. All I did was eat fast food. Shit, I can't even remember the last thing I ate today. *Did I eat today? I'll run to Starbucks and get something from there, I'm not really hungry anyway.*

After leaving the bank, I look at my balance. *Fuck, I really need to make some money, I only have $200 dollars in my account. Where is all my money going?*

Milo called and gave me his flight information. He would be in Friday night at 7pm on United Airlines. *Cool, perfect timing. I'll stop by my connects to get me a fix. I might as well get enough to hold me over for the week and then I'll pick him up and take him to eat. I hope he offers to pay because my funds are running low. Maybe I can ask my dad? Naw, he's too nosey. He'll want to know what happened with my allowance for this month. I could ask Asia, I'll wait to see if I have to and if I do I'll her put money into my account for me. Shit, I need to do a line, my nerves are bad.*

I pull out my platter from under the car seat and snort a few lines while waiting for the light to change. I lean my head back but the car behind me started blowing their horn.

"FUCK YOU!" I yell out, "It's only a fucking light! What's your hurry?" I didn't know if it was from this summer's trauma or my new recreational use, but I've been a bit feisty lately.

I pull up to Taylor's for our study group and walked through the door, "Hey slow poke, better late than never!" Sam says.

"Hey you two, what's up?"

"Nothing just preparing before starting," laughing.

"Prepping all right...partying is more like it," I sit down on the couch and wait my turn for a line.

I loved coming to study group because they always had free coke and E's if you wanted some. So if I was low on funds, I knew I could still get some coke without having to buy any.

"You cool?" Sam asks me.

"No," I say, picking up the glass plate, snorting a line.

"So I take it you've been staying up in class lately," she asked, grinning.

"Yes, Sam. I'm staying alert in class...thank you for your

concern."

She was starting to get on my nerves with all this 'staying up' shit so I changed the subject, "Can we go over the review questions for the exam next week?" I ask.

"Sure, let me get my notes out my backpack."

We all sat around and went over questions and answers for the exam. We discussed it for about an hour then we all said our goodbyes.

"I'll see you guys Monday, have a good weekend. Bye," I walked to my car, feeling good and my thoughts started to drift - *I can't wait to meet this Milo person, I hope he's sexy shit. I haven't had any in almost three months. If he's ugly, I guess I'll break out the vibrator. I'll stop and get some batteries because I know I'm going to need them,* as I laugh to myself.

17

IN MY PROJECTS

India Smith

Milo took me to one of his spots in the projects of San Francisco. I was surprised that he had people in the Bay Area too. This particular spot was in the Sunnydale projects. I heard of this place before but never been here, never had a reason to until this day. It was filled with old, run down, barrack looking buildings that were connected by chipped, cracked concrete streets. I assume there were ten apartment units in one building. The building we went inside had black iron gates on the doors and windows for security purposes, I suppose. No need for Brinks or ADT security. When we walked in, I immediately noticed a steel, pipe furnace coming from the floor. I knew it was the heater because a guy said 'Be careful walking pass it or it will burn your skin off.' *Damn, they must not have any children living here,* I thought. But later I found out that I was wrong, and they had at least three more in the building.

When we got to the house, the guy who must have owned it told me to sit down on a couch that was covered with plastic. *Why do they cover their seats with plastic? Maybe because the kids eat in the living room, or maybe it's to preserve the couch?* Pensively thinking, *I would just have to ask Milo later,* making a mental note. Milo introduced me to his friend named 'Younger'. And he looked young enough for the byname or maybe he was the youngest in the family?

I was trying to not be mentally overwhelmed by the projects, but it was a whole world within itself. Outside, people were hanging out in front, listening to music, drinking, and smoking weed. When I first got out the car, they were yelling, 'Who's that piece? She's bad!' until they saw Milo.

"Ohhhh hell no Milo! You always get the bad bitches nigga!"

"Money talks, B.S. walks."

Huh? I thought to myself. His response caught me off guard.

So, I'm what y'all considered a bad bitch huh, I wouldn't dare say it out loud. Those thugs would have probably killed me where I stood. And they weren't alone, the women who were outside all looked at me and rolled their eyes in disgust. But I was used to that so it didn't bother me none. I just wanted to hurry up and get in the apartment and away from this crowd. You always heard about drive-bys and shootings in the projects. I know I looked nervous and paranoid because I kept looking around like a crackhead, seeing if anyone was driving too fast or walking around like they were going to shoot. I didn't know what to expect. I was so relieved when Milo finally grabbed my hand after his banter with the thugs and led me to the building. He said he had family that lived here. I couldn't imagine anyone being raised here and making it out alive. The place looked scary as hell to me. My neighborhood was like heaven with streets paved in gold in comparison to this. Thank God for my parents because I don't think I could've made it growing up here. But Asia is another story. She can adapt to any circumstance. She just jumps right in, head first. But me, I'm more cautious and resistive.

Milo insisted I come with him to meet his peeps. He said, 'You can't understand me until you understand where I come from. This is where I was made, what made me into the man that I am today'. Realistically, I could care less about any of that but I couldn't tell him that, I needed him to help me make some money quickly and a lot of it, and he was the man to do that. Bringing up his life struggles didn't affect me one way or another. It wasn't like we were all in love and ready to walk down the the altar, but whatever.

I popped a valium in the car to calm my nerves when he asked, "What are you taking over there beautiful?" He kept calling me beautiful and I hated it.

"A Motrin, I have a headache," I replied.

I didn't want to tell him the truth, for what? He didn't need to be all up in my business and shit. Plus we barely knew each other. If only he knew, I really wish I could snort a line or two, none of this shit would bother me at all. I'll gladly roll with the punches. But since I couldn't pull out my secret weapon, a pill had to do for now. I still couldn't believe how close I lived to these projects, it seemed like countries were in between our neighborhoods, not blocks. The suburbs and projects – different people, different mentalities, same city, same color.

I just kept thinking that if my parents knew I was over here they would die. What if something happened to me, they wouldn't understand why I was here in the first place. It kind of made me laugh because you never actually know how your children will turn out in life. It doesn't matter how prosperous their lives seemed with a perfect home, private schooling, and suburban life. They could still turn out to be on dope or living in these projects or become a famous basketball star or an attorney, you just never know. That's why I didn't want to have any children. Hell, mine probably would turn out to be a serial killer. Just reflected on my sister and I, *on paper we fit the status quo but if you dug a little deeper you will find drugs, fraudulent activities and more,* shaking my head. If my mother's constituents knew what her children did for a living, they would die.

Milo worked with hackers who tapped into credit card companies, he also had a woman who preformed phone sex and only accepted credit cards. With this combination, he always had credit card numbers readily available. His lifestyle was relatively lavish, a mere reflection of his accumulating wealth. He went to professional basketball games and sat courtside at football games, concerts and more. All courtesy of credit card numbers. He also transferred money off people's American Express cards into bogus accounts. The nigga was that good with this identity theft game. He had it sewed up, royally. Milo's so called 'work', in the projects, consisted of his partners making fake I.D.'s and credit cards from library cars and reactivating old credit cards by putting new strips on the back with other people's information. This way, you can use your own card with your I.D. but it would contain some else's credit. Pure genius. They also made fake passports, social security cards and some more shit. Whatever you needed, they had it or could make it, so to speak.

Milo gathered all his belongings, two briefcases filled with counterfeit materials and said his goodbyes before we were on our way. *Finally.* I impatiently sat there all the while Milo chopped it up, it wasn't my cup of tea. And I wasn't impressed, well maybe just a little. Milo was doing big things in the streets. I overheard him tell his boy before we left that this set of work was worth five hundred thousand dollars if it all went down the right way.

Damn, like that. He could just give me half and I'll be ok, these dudes were balling! But I couldn't let him know that his world fascinated me. I had to control my composure, keep my poker face, and 'never let them see you sweat' was my mom's motto. 'You never show fear, insecurities or defeat' was another lesson she told us when me and my sister were younger. If we walked or talked with our heads down my mom would yell, 'Hold your heads up high, women never look down at the ground unless they have low self-esteem or admiring her shoes. You're beautiful and smart, plus you're better than that'.

'You shouldn't look down unless you're tying your shoes, and you can even have someone else do that for you also, do you understand?' And we would shake our heads in agreement. I laughed at the thought.

Back in the car, Milo started bumping the classic 'Ready to Die' CD and that shit was bumping so hard that the windows were shaking. I was feeling it too, I started moving my head to the beat.

Milo looked over at me and said, "You're not the stuck up type after all beautiful?"

Stuck up? Is that what he thought about me? "Wow, that's what you think, huh?"

"Well because you're light skinned, with good hair and light eyes. You have to be stuck up?" He kept glancing over at me while trying to keep his eyes on the road.

"Why are you stereotyping me Milo? I don't believe I came across as the stuck up type, did I?"

"Naw beautiful, I'm just saying most chicks –"

I interjected before he could finish, "I'm not most chicks just like you're not the average man! How would you like it –"

"Ok, ok beautiful. I get your point, my bad love," smiling and cutting me off. "You're feisty just like your sister, I like that. You hungry?" he asked.

"Yes I am, I have a taste for some seafood."

"Um, I know the perfect spot beautiful. Have you ever been to Thanh Long in the avenues?"

I couldn't help but smile because that was one of my favorite restaurants in the city. They had the best roasted crab and garlic noodles. He earned a few brownie points for that suggestion. I shook my head 'yes' and that's where we headed after we dropped the work off to his associates in Hunters Point. Yes, Milo and I were making beautiful music together, life was good. Or so I thought...

18

BABY BABY

Asia Smith

"Baby, I'm miserable. This baby is killing me slowly," grabbing my stomach with one hand and forehead with another.

"Asia it's almost over, quit complaining."

"Don't tell me to stop fucking complaining Vance. This shit is all your fucking fault anyways," I yell while trying to get off the couch and head to the bathroom for the hundredth time today.

"Come on baby, let me help you," smiling.

"What you smiling about? Ain't shit funny!" I didn't know if Vance liked seeing me in pain or he just found pleasure in watching me carry his child – the good, bad and the ugly.

"Calm down, damn. I'll be glad when you have my seed ma' and then my old, sweet Asia will return," laughing.

Rolling my eyes at him, "I don't think so – ohhh baby, I'm having a contraction."

Suddenly it felt like my bladder turned into a blade and it was aiming right towards the womb. I stopped to hold the wall, stabilizing myself and regaining balance.

Vance Smith

"Ok...remember to breathe like they told you Asia," I said, I hated to see my baby in so much pain, she was miserable and me too, for that matter.

Asia Smith

"Ok it's over, let me go to the bathroom now."

While sitting on the toilet, another contraction came, "Vance!" I hollered loudly.

"I'm having another one," bending over and holding my stomach.

Vance hurried into the bathroom and said, "They are twenty minutes apart baby!"

"Call India and tell her and my parents to meet us at the hospital," I said. Earlier, they all went to our aunt's house to drop off some gifts, it was Christmas day.

"Do you need some help baby," Vance asked, rubbing the back on my neck.

"No I'm fine, just call them and your mom and have them meet us." After I get up and wash my hands, another one comes. The dagger returned.

Vance was on his cell phone, "Yes they are twenty minutes apart," looking at me in a way I wasn't too familiar with, "Baby you're having another one?" He asked worrisomely. I shake my head 'yes', talking would have been too much.

He continues on the phone, "Meet us there!" he says and helps me to the coach.

"Baby I have to run up stairs to get you and the baby's bag," he trembled over his words, looking nervous.

The Vance that I had known up until this point had never displayed any signs of weakness, even when he was shot and his father passed away. He always kept that masculine composure. But at the wake of life, the life he brought into this world, a life beyond his own, you could see the very humanity slip between his eyes.

He reaches for me, "I'll be right back," kissing me on top of my head. *This pain is too much. How do women continue to keep getting knocked up?* When Vance came back down the stairs, I had another contraction.

"Ok baby. When this one stops, I'll put you in the car," rubbing my head.

After the contraction settled, I took a few deep breathes to balance the pain. When I got inside the car, I started to feel as if I was sitting in a puddle – my amniotic sac had broke.

"Vance! Vance!" I screamed.

He was putting the bags and car seat in the trunk and ran over to the passenger side after he heard me hollering, "Yes baby, what's wrong?"

"My water bag just broke –"

"Oh shit!" he said, looking like somebody just surprised him, "Ok baby, let me go grab you a towel," running towards the house .

My poor baby has been ripping and running for two days straight. He has catered to my every need. He hasn't left my side since I started getting close to my due date, which just happens to be today. December 25th, wow that's crazy!

"Here baby, let me wipe your legs and feet."

As Vance goes to work, I become observant of the mess I just made. *Damn that must have been a lot of water, my interior rugs are soaked.* Thank God I had leather seats.

By the time we reach the hospital, I had two more contractions. Vance called my doctor and she said she was on her way. We pulled up and I saw my parents, they beat us here.

Opening my door, "You ok baby?" My father asks.

"No, Daddy it hurts!"

"I know sweetheart, but once it's over you'll forget all about the pain," he said as he was helping me sit down in the wheelchair that the nurse ran over to us.

"Thank you, Daddy."

Just as I said his name, I realized that in a short amount of time, I would become the parent of my own child. Reality was sinking in. And so was this child of mine who was making his way down to the birth canal.

"You're welcome baby," pushing me inside.

India looked scared, like she saw a ghost and my mother

looked beautiful despite the fact that she was crying. And poor Vance, I don't know what to say about him. He was running around like a chicken with its head cut off. He came inside with us but wanted to go get our bags. I told him that we didn't need them yet. But he said he packed my iPod in case I wanted it and he left the video recorder and his camera. He was just a nervous wreck. It was kind of cute though. They admitted me and put us in a private room.

We made an appointment just in case because we knew a lot of people would be showing up. I got undressed in the in-suite bathroom and put on the hospital gown. My doctor came in to check me and said I was five centimeters with five more to go. She hooked me up to a machine that monitors the baby's heart rate, and mines as well. There was another monitor setup that can determine when I was having a contraction. It showed up on the screen. She asked me if I wanted an epidural and I said 'yes'. The nurse called the anesthesiologist stat for me. Once I received my shot, it helped – I didn't feel any pain, the medication that was injected into my back was smooth sailing, or so I thought. Sonia and Vantrice arrived as well as Boobie and Lisa. Also, my mom's sister Tamia came. The whole room was packed. 'Merry Christmas' was written on the chalkboard across from the bed, along with the nurse's name. The ambiance was set.

"You ok baby?" Vance consistently asked me.

"Yes, I just wish this baby would hurry up," I said while squinting to get some of the sweat from running into my eyes.

"He's stubborn baby, just like his daddy." Vance said smiling. I didn't even respond I just smiled. Vance tried to kiss me at that point but I started having another contraction.

"She's having another one!" he said rubbing my head.

"Whew! That was a big one," I replied. My nurse came to check on me and said it was show time. My parents, India, Sonia and Vantrice all put on hospital gowns – adequate attire for the occasion. Vance already had his on from the beginning. Boobie and Lisa said they didn't want to watch and they'll be outside.

Vance was forming sweat beads on his forehead, "Well, this is it! My shortie is ready!" he said excitedly.

At least somebody was excited, all I could think was – *it's about time, shit! I've been in labor for two days and at this hospital for six hours, we arrived at 3pm and now it was 9pm.*

My doctor came in and checked me after the nurse, "Well Asia, let's make you a mommie," she said.

"Is it really time Alicia?" I asked. We were on a first name basis, she was my doctor but also a good friend of ours.

"Yes Asia, now I need for you to put your legs up as far as you can," I did as I was told but the baby still wasn't out yet. "You have to push," she encouraged.

I said, "Ok," and pushed. I pushed again, only this time it started to burn. "Alicia it's burning," I said.

"That's because you're dry down here, you have no lubrication. All your water dried up when your water broke."

Vance was rubbing my head and peaking down to see. Vantrice was video tapping. Sonia, India, my aunt and parents were my cheerleading squad.

"Come on Asia! Push your baby out!" Alicia stated, snapping me back into the moment and the task at hand. I pushed again and Alicia said, "I see a head full of hair!" I felt somewhat relieved. Vance had tears in his eyes.

He whispered to me, "Thank you baby, I wish my pops was here."

I retorted, "He's been here with us the whole time," and kissed his lips.

"One more quick push Asia!" Alicia said, interrupting our moment. I gave it one good push, straining my muscles when I heard Alicia say, "Congratulations! He's a healthy lil' thing!" He didn't even cry until she told Vance to pat his butt.

"His first spanking," Vance said in between tears.

PAT! PAT! He hit his butt and then, "WAAAAAH!" I heard

his first cry.

Finally. I closed my eyes and rested a moment while Alicia sewed me up. Everyone was watching the baby get cleaned and weighed.

My parents stepped away and approached Alicia, "Thank you so much, we appreciate your help!" they said, shaking her hand.

"Not a problem Mr. and Mrs. Smith. Congratulations to your beautiful, healthy grandson. And congratulations to you also, proud father," she said to Vance who couldn't stop smiling.

"Thank's doc. I have something for you in the car."

"You didn't have to buy me anything Vance, this is my job. This is what I love to do," she said, smiling. And she meant every word she said. She loved her job. They cleaned him up, weighed and wrapped him, and handed him to Vance.

"Congratulations sir," the nurse said. "He weighs seven pounds, seven ounces, thirteen inches long. You have a very healthy baby boy."

Vance took him in his arms and kissed him.

"Say cheese!" everyone said in a harmonic cadence, holding cameras in hand. Vance smiled and kissed him again.

"Let's go see Mommie lil' man," walking towards me. "Look V.J. that's your Mommie. She's tired from all the pushing she did to get you here. She's a very special lady and we love her," Vance said to his son. He kissed me on the lips, "I love you Asia."

I opened my eyes and looked at him, "I love you too Daddy."

He handed me our son, I looked at this tiny baby and couldn't believe I carried him for nine months. Someone said 'smile', I don't know who, there were so many cameras being flashed. I smiled and kissed my baby.

"Hi there lil' man, I'm Mommie."

Boobie and Lisa were back and a few other new faces, mostly Vance's friends. My parents took the baby and Sonia came over to give me a kiss on the forehead.

"Thanks Asia for my grandson, he's beautiful." I was overwhelmed. Before I could respond, I started crying and it was like a chain reaction.

Vance started crying and then India, a domino effect. After that, I passed out and fell asleep but the party continued without me, Vance held the baby all night. He wouldn't let the nurse take him to the nursery so they brought the crib inside our room. Vance said he didn't want him to leave the room in case they tried to do a switch-a-roo with his son. He was being overprotective but if he wanted to stay up with the baby, so be it. I woke up around midnight.

"Hi sleepyhead," he greeted me with a relaxed smile.

"Hi yourself, how long have I been asleep?" I asked.

"About three hours."

"Oh, where's the baby?" my heart skipped a beat as my instincts kicked.

"Right here, in the baby bed," looking to his right.

"Push him over here so I can see him," Vance had him on the side of him and he was laying down in the recliner chair. He moved the crib and place him in the middle of us.

"Thank you Asia for our son," looking at me in the eyes.

"Thank you Vance for my son," I retorted.

"I love you Asia, and my son being here completes me. You complete me. I can't wait to make you my wife."

I was choked up, I didn't know what to say. Vance has said this before but hearing him say it now, it held more meaning. I smiled at him and he smiled back, showing his dimples.

"I hope he has your dimples."

"He probably does, he looks just like me. My mom had my baby picture and it looks just like V.J.," he said smiling.

"What time did everyone leave?"

"They all left around 10:30 p.m., visiting hours were over at ten but under the circumstances, they let everybody stay until ten-thirty."

I glanced at the clock, observing time for the first time since my contractions began the day before.

"But they'll be back tomorrow. I also gave Alicia our gift that we got for her."

"Oh yea, I almost forgot about that. Did she open it?" I asked.

"No, not while she was here but I know she's going to like it."

We got her a charm bracelet with different baby charms: a bottle, rattle, pacifier, a stroller and a stethoscope. We also bought her a 'thank you' card, with a gift certificate to a spa that included a free guest. And it never expired, so I know she'll be pleased.

Vance drifted off to sleep. I was so proud of him. He was really supportive my entire pregnancy. He looked so peaceful lying in that chair – like a black hersey's kiss. 'Goodnight Daddy' I said to myself and fell back to sleep.

I was sleeping quite well until the baby cried and we both woke up. Vance started to feed him and the nurse came in to check on us, as she had done constantly throughout the night. She brought us some diapers and bottles because I couldn't breastfeed - my chi chi's hurt too bad. I watched Vance feed the baby and my heart smiled. He actually looked like he knew what he was doing, as if this wasn't his first time, he even burped him and changed his diaper.

"Baby?"

"Huh?" I answered.

"He's going to be hung down there like his daddy," laughing.

"Is that right?" I said.

"Well he better watch out because all the lil' girls are going to be knocking on our door. I'm just glad we had a boy first, now we can have a sister for him."

"A what? Vance you're kidding right?"

"Nope," he insisted. "As soon as you're six weeks are up, I'm breaking down those walls!" laughing.

"Oh nigga you got jokes! I'm going on the pill, getting the

shot, using a diaphragm and all that good stuff. You won't get me a second time."

"Why baby? You have a sister and so do I. He doesn't want to be an only child, that's weak!" Vance said sarcastically.

"Well for the record, my sister and I came as a package deal remember. And Sonia's crazy ass did it again but I don't know if I'm ready for that, especially so soon."

"I was just joking baby, but we are going to have another one," looking at me in my eyes.

"Ok whatever you say Vance." He laid him back down and came to sit next to me.

"You're so beautiful baby," Vance said.

"You are too."

"I'm glad you gave a nigga a shot."

"A shot of what?" I ask, laughing.

"A shot at loving you," he replied.

"Well, I'm glad you wanted a shot," pulling him by his neck to give him a kiss. We kissed long and hard.

Coming up for air, "This is how he got here."

"I know," I said laughing. And he was right, it all starts with a kiss but once our energy takes over, we have the capacity to create life. This is exactly what we did, nine months ago when our son was conceived.

"Let's get some rest, tomorrow is going to be a busy day," Vance laid back in his recliner and went to sleep. I looked at our son and reached over to kiss him, my night was sealed and drifted back to dream land...until he woke us up again a few hours later.

In the heat of all the excitement steaming from V.J.'s birth, I totally forgot we were in the middle of a holiday. I couldn't wait to get home to look at our white Christmas tree and sit by the fireplace and sip some hot coco and chill with my family and my newborn son. Life was good right now.

19

SAY IT ISN'T SO!

Asia Smith

Bringing V.J. home was the most exciting time of my life. We had a welcome home banner in front of the house, balloons and fresh flowers everywhere inside the family room. I was still sore from pushing his big head out, not to mention, I ripped during the process and had to get four stitches. The pain medication made me sleepy so I didn't stay up too long. My parents were staying with us to help out and I greatly appreciated that. My mom said for the first week, I didn't need a lot of visitors coming and breathing all over the baby. Plus she wanted me to get my rest in order to fully recover. Vance's mom came over every day too. This combination meant the new grandmothers got a chance to take turns with V.J.

Our first night at home, my mom helped me take a nice hot shower and she made some sweet tea to take with my pills and told me not to worry about the baby. She was going to sleep in the nursery with him and tend to his needs. She just wanted me to relax and get some rest. As soon as I hit the pillow, I was out. Vance and my father were downstairs watching the game and my mom was bathing the baby and getting him situated in his new home.

"You are grandma's baby," kissing his cheeks.

"Grandma's going to spoil you rotten with your gorgeous self. You resemble your father so much V.J. you're absolutely beautiful."

"He is a nice looking boy isn't he?" My dad crept in and overheard my mom on her soap box.

"Oh Robert, I didn't know you were standing there."

"Yeah I'm just admiring you with the baby, he's perfect. I can't wait to take him fishing and teach him how to play golf."

"You hear that V.J.? You're grandpa wants to share with you with grandma," putting his diaper on and applying baby powder.

"Give grandpa a kiss goodnight, its bed time," Robert kisses his tiny forehead. "Goodnight son, grandpa will see you in the morning," smiling.

"Goodnight Carliess, I'm going to shower and head to bed," checking his watch.

"Ok, I'm sleeping in here with the baby so Asia can get some rest. She took her medications so she will be sleep all night. I'll check on her a little later."

Kissing her on the lips, "Goodnight Robert."

"Goodnight Grandma," smiling while silently making his way

out the door.

"Ok, V.J. let's give you your nutrients for the night. It's a shame your mother didn't breastfeed you."

Vance Smith

"Hi Ms. Smith, he's not asleep yet?" The door open slightly, illuminating a small section of the room from the light in the hallway.

"No Vance but almost. You want to finish feeding him while I take my shower?"

"Yes Ma'am," reaching for him.

"Don't forget to burp him or his tummy will be upset tonight," she said, waiting for my look of confirmation.

"I won't," I walked gently to the rocking chair while holding V.J. in my arms.

"Hey shortie, it's Daddy. I can't believe you're finally here man," kissing his forehead. Looking at my son, *I can't believe how much he looks like me*. My heart began to smile.

"I wish my pops could see you V.J.," burping him.

"There you go lil' man," laying him down in his $2,500 golden crib.

It's only the finer things in life for my shortie. When we moved into this house we hired a designer to furnish the nursery. The wall reflected a mural of Sesame Street characters with a handmade rug that has his initials 'V.J.' stitched in the center. The vaulted ceiling was painted as the sky with clouds, he also has a baby carousel in the corner, reminiscent of a fair. His walk-in closet was completely full, including baby tennis shoes from Gucci, Louis Vuitton, Jordans, Fendi and more. I smiled while I turned on the baby monitor and slightly closed his door behind me. *This lil nigga spoiled, I can't wait until he starts walking and talking. Asia needs another baby because he's all mine.*

Checking on Asia, she's knocked out in our king sized bed sleeping with the angels. She didn't even move when I kissed her cheek. I head back downstairs to watch the highlights of the game. Our family room is so cozy, anyone who comes over gets really comfortable and doesn't want to get up or leave. We have an eighty inch T.V. custom made into the wall, a fireplace that's operated by remote, an oversized burgundy sectional couch with tons of throw pillows and two ottomans. Our entertainment breeding ground continued with a bose stereo system that connected to surround sound throughout the first floor living quarters. A built in saltwater fish tank and a wet bar, which is one of three throughout the house. We have a wet bar in the den and basement as well. The family room also houses a top of the line security system of the entire estate. Like the shit on scarface. *Let a nigga try to run up in my crib, it's on!*

I light up a blunt and chill, taking it to the head. Inhaling the smoke and releasing it slowly. These smoke clouds were keeping me company while everyone slept.

"That's what I'm talking about," talking to the T.V., high as hell. This shit I was smoking, was no joke. It reminded me of that song Asia played for me when we were in California by some bay area locals, a rap duo. *'Don't give me no bammer weed!'* that shit was dope and true. California had a few rappers that I admired, of course they had some talented artist in the lime light but they also had a few underground cats that was bomb too. Asia played a group, I don't remember what they were called but one of the members was named 'Darkskin' from Osceola Point Proven Records. I think he had a little group that was dope. They were going places with their CD and they even had a cousin who produced their beats and rapped. I brought a copy of their CD for back home so my partners can check them out.

After reminiscing for a while, I was starting to get tired. I don't know if I was high, exhausted, or hallucinating or all of them at once because Ms. Smith came into the room looking and smiling like an angel. She stood right in front of me with a soft, pink, see-through nightie draped on her shoulders and her nipples were erect. A bikini wax aligned her pussy perfectly and she had an hourglass shape that, to be in her forties, she could still shut some women down in their twenties and thirties. Her jet black hair came over her shoulders and down her back, reaching her buttocks. This was enough to have me captivated, but it was her eyes that had me hypnotized. Once you looked into them, you couldn't turn away. Her eyes were like looking into an ocean on a beach in Hawaii, Bali or some other island. They looked like they were blue, green, with a touch of gray. Absolutely beautiful.

She took my hands and pulled me up. I wanted to say something but no words would come out, like my vocal cords had been cut. She laid me down by the fireplace and removed my pants while still staring me in the eyes. Then she placed the softest kiss on my lips that took my breath away. She then kissed my earlobe and kissed my neck, sucking on my adams apple. I've never had anyone do that before. She made her way down to my dick and instead of sucking it, she lifted it up with one hand and massaged my balls with the other. She gently blew air on my dick that sent waves through my body. She then kissed that fine line from my balls to my ass that had me grabbing the carpet. She licked my precum like some ice cream and put my whole entire dick in her mouth.

She was sucking like the ice cream was melting. Before I knew it, I was busting in her mouth. She swallowed it like she was drinking a glass of wine. Like a lioness, she climbed on top of me and eased herself down real slow. She was looking me dead in my eyes again, I couldn't even breathe, her pussy felt like a vice grip around my dick. She contracted every muscle she had while easing down onto me. She came down and went back up, only keeping the head inside her, going faster and faster, contracting and contracting, driving me completely out of my mind. Shape shifting with ease, the lioness left the den and I was introduced to the spider.

She placed both her legs on my shoulders and grabbed my wrists, guiding my hands to her butt. She then bounced up and down with the help of my hands gripping her ass, never losing eye contact. This shit was feeling way too good, my emotions had taken over. I felt a little lightheaded so I closed my eyes and when I opened them I had tears forming out the sides, it felt that good. *I have to be dreaming, this shit can't be happening. Damn that was some good weed.*

As the tears slide down my face, I started to feel like I was about to bust again and I just closed my eyes. When I woke up, it was three in the morning, the TV was turned off and I was laying on the floor by the fireplace, in the dark with my hand on my dick. *Damn that was a hell of a dream I had or that voodoo shit is a motherfucker. I have to get me some more of that weed. I can't really remember if I fucked my woman's mom or it was some sort of hypnosis.*

I get myself together and head to bed. I kiss Asia on the cheek and hold her tight from behind. *I hope that was a dream because if it wasn't, her momma is a bonafide freak.*

I can see why niggas shoot bitches in the head. I could feel my shit getting hard just thinking about it. I prayed that I was dreaming and could return to that same dream as I drifted off to sleep, smiling. The following morning, Asia's mom brought us breakfast in bed. I try not to look at her, she did look at me a little funny but maybe I'm tripping. I'm just going to have to avoid her ass while she's here. I can't play these head games, a nigga will go crazy. If I wasn't a believer in that voodoo shit before, I do now. The eyes don't lie.

I take a shower and get dressed.

"Baby you look nice, where are you going?" Asia asks. I did look good if I can say so myself. It was December 28th and practically freezing outside. I wore a gray wool turtleneck with dark blue jeans, gray and black leather Kenneth Cole boots, my long gray double breasted trench coat with my gray messenger cap that snapped in the front – feeling like a million bucks.

"You like the way your man looks baby?" I ask her.

"Always Vance but where are you going?"

"I have some runs to make and I'm going by my moms, my auntie is in town remember?"

"Oh yea, is she coming by to see V.J.?"

"Yes Asia, and you know my mom is definitely coming over. She's not going to miss a day without seeing her grandson. I'll call to check on you and shortie later. Give daddy some sugar," I leaned in and kissed her like I would never see her again.

"Damn Vance, what was that all about," looking at me weird, she seemed perplexed by my demeanor.

"Damn a nigga can't kiss you now? Be glad a nigga still tonguing you down, most niggas can't kiss like I do," laughing.

"Bring me a plate from your mom's house Vance, please."

"I think she cooked some food for you to bring over here for your parents."

"Oh ok, I'll just eat when she brings the food over here, my mom acts like V.J. is her baby, she won't let me do nothing. You would think you and her made that baby," laughing.

Shit, we may have made our own last night, "Asia please gone with all that!" trying to sound irritated. "I'll holler at you later."

"Bye Baby Daddy," laughing.

"Bye Baby Mama," I said and proceeded to walk into the nursery to say bye to my son, he was sleep in his crib but he wasn't alone.

"Don't wake him Vance, I just fed him and put him to sleep."

"I'm not going to wake him Ms. Smith – "

"Please call me Carliess. I told you Ms. Smith is so formal and we're past that..." she was speaking seductively. I didn't respond. I kissed my son and walked out. *This is going to be a long week for me, I can see this now.* I jumped in my benz and rolled out to the spot.

Pulling up, all my homies were posted right in front, "What's up nigga! Congratulations on your son!" my boy Lazy says.

"Thanks bro," giving him dab.

"Pass the blunt, stingy nigga," I said to Boobie.

"Here man," releasing smoke from his nostrils as he passed me the joint.

"What's up, you going out tonight nigga? Are you wifed up now?" laughing.

"Nigga, if I recall –" hitting the blunt, "you're the only nigga who had a big ass wedding, not me." blowing the smoke out. "And if I want to go out nigga, I can." Hitting the blunt again, "I run this shit," I said, blowing smoke in his face.

"Whatever you say boss, let's take a ride to Loveland music store – " interrupted by his own cough, Boobie continues.

"I need that Nas CD, some nigga stole mine. It's ok though, we'll tell our homies and catch up with them later."

"Hey Lazy, you got my dough nigga?"

"Fo'sho homie, your deposit slip is always the same. Payday every Friday," laughing.

"That's what's up," I pass Lazy the rest of the burning ember and get back into my car. I motion for my partner-in-crime to get in, then Boobie and I jetted out.

"Did you get every niggas deposit this week?" I ask Boobie.

"Yeah, everybody straight on theirs, you know I only give them so much. Those lil' niggas are only sixteen."

"Shit we started at their age, it's in the blood with some niggas. Either you got it or you don't."

"Word," Boobie said.

"Fire it up homie," I said while Boobie lit up another blunt.

I take a pull, "This shit right here is the truth," exhaling. "Nigga this shit last night had me fucking my girls mom and shit."

"WHAT NIGGA! Asia's' mother? You must was on some shit other than weed. How did you wind up fucking her moms and shit?"

"Nigga I don't know, Asia was sleep in our room She took her medication that knocks her out and her old man always goes to bed early, I guess he's a hard sleeper," laughing.

"Nigga, I don't care how hard niggas sleep, y'all was all in the same house, now I know your house is phat nigga but damn how you pull that one off? You got to be the only nigga I know to do some shit like that and get away with it. Is her mama fine as hell too?"

I was still hitting the blunt and couldn't even respond, I was tripping – *Damn I did fuck my woman's mother.*

"What if Asia would have caught us nigga?"

"The shit is ill to me too."

"I was high as fuck in the family room, chilling, Just finished feeding my shortie when moms comes into the room, damn near naked and ish."

"Word?"

"Word...she pulls me off the couch and takes a nigga pants off and shit. Then she starts blowing me and shit –"

"Her mom's gave brains nigga? Are you serious? How was it? The best you ever had?"

"The shit had me stuck, I don't know if it was this shit here we're smoking or shock. But either way I couldn't stop her, she must of hypnotized a nigga with her eyes –"

"What color are her eyes?"

"Blue, green, some shit like that. But she's fine ass a motherfucker to be in her forties."

"Well nigga you said that right, 'mother-fucker'," laughing.

"Oh I did say that shit," laughing.

"Nigga this shit ain't even funny dawg, she rode a nigga and put me to sleep. All I remember was the shit felt so damn good, like having an orgy with virgins," my eyes rolled to the back of my head at the thought.

"Damn like that nigga?" Boobie's eye's was getting wider.

"Like that dawg. Her ass is from New Orleans, I think she did some voodoo shit on me," shaking my head while I switched lanes.

"I can't believe her mom gets down like that, pops must not be laying down the pipe like he should."

"I don't know but what I do know is I'm staying away from her ass while she's here before I wind up in the crazy house —"

"Or the morgue nigga, if Asia finds out," laughing.

"I know, that shit ain't funny," laughing with him.

"You play some dangerous games Vance, you need to start going to church with all the shit you do behind closed doors."

"I be trying to be right but shit always presents itself."

"I know, my lil chick on the side kept calling last night. Lisa was like, turn that shit off or call the bitch back and tell her you're at home with your wife nigga, before I do. And when I talked to her today, she was like why you didn't call back and I had to check her punk ass. I told her, 'Bitch I know you called the first time, why did you call a hundred and one times more? If I don't answer the first time, what makes you think I'm answering at all? For you to keep calling isn't going to make me call your ass back, it's only going to make me not call you at all - fuck jocking a nigga and shit. Let a nigga jock you'!" Boobie said, laughing.

"I hate that shit too! Monique calls me so much and leaves all kinds of fowl messages nigga. I had to change my battery. Speaking of Monique, she was at the spot before you pulled up. She's hot about my shortie being born —"

"I know she asked all the homies had they seen him, what he looked liked and that's fucked up that she lost her baby and you don't give a fuck and blah blah blah. Nigga, I think she needs some kind of help," solemnly speaking.

"Well she better hurry up and get it because I don't want to hear that B.S. about my lil nigga period. He's here and he's here to stay. She act like I made her lose the baby. Shit, I was laid up and damn near dead. I hate that it happened but it did now, move on."

"Well nigga, get her pregnant again," laughing.

"That shit ain't funny, I ain't fooling with that girl like that. I been told her stupid ass to kick rocks. She's straight financially, so I don't know what to do. Shit, I'm with who I want to be with and that's final."

"Dude, she just can't get over it that easy!"

"She better try shit, she has other niggas she fucks with. I saw her with that nigga Carlos before."

"Carlos from College Park?"

"Yeah, that nigga," nodding my head.

"He has a slew of women, I tried to fuck one at his broads at a party but she wouldn't budge," Boobie revealed.

"Word?"

"Word. Plus they say that nigga has about thirteen kids with all different baby mamas!"

"He's a busy man," laughing.

"Yeah but he can afford them, that nigga balling out of control in the game."

"Well I just hope he has something to fall back on when niggas get caught up because it's just a matter of time," pulling up at the music store.

"Are you coming nigga?"

"Naw I got a call to make, go ahead," pulling out my phone.

"Hello?" Asia answered.

"What it do baby?"

"Hey Vance, me and my mom were just talking about you."

Oh shit, "Really? What about me?"

"Nothing, just that V.J. looks more like you than me and he's going to be chocolate because his ears are dark."

Whew, thank you lord, "That's my strong genes baby and my right stroke," laughing.

"Funny, where are you at?"

"At the music store, you need some CD's?" I asked.

"I could use some rap and mixed oldies."

"Alright, I got you baby and I love you too." Hanging up the phone, I walked in the store with my agenda set.

"Nigga what brings you in Mr. Telephone man?"

"I need a couple CD's, some old school rap and classic oldies."

"What's up Vance, good to see you."

"What's up girl, how you been?"

"I've been better, why you never called me? I gave you my number the last time you were in here buying CD's for your woman."

I looked at Boobie and he shrugged his shoulders, as if to say - *don't look at me nigga*. "I've been kinda busy lately give me a minute, I'll call you. Is the number still the same?'

"Yea, try using it," giving me an alluring look.

"I will, how much I owe you?"

"Sixty bucks."

"Here's a hundred, keep the change. Happy holidays."

"Same to you, call me," she says while we're walking out.

"That's why I didn't want to come in," shaking my head. "Baby stalker in there," pointing towards the store.

"Nigga she's cute."

"Well you get at her and let her stalk your ass and see what Lisa does. I don't need no more drama in my life."

"Is that why you bought that no more drama CD nigga? To remind you of that?" laughing.

"Fuck you, that's for Asia."

"Asia don't need no more drama either. Shit and fucking her mother doesn't help the matters,," Boobie said frankly.

"Shut up nigga and fire up another blunt. Put on '*99 Problems but a bitch ain't one*'," laughing, handing him the CD.

"Take me to my car, I'm going home to wifey," Boobie says.

"All right, bet. I have to go by moms, my aunt is in town. I'll just holler at you tomorrow." After I drop Boobie off, I pull up to my mom's crib and instantly recognize Monique's car parked out front. *I hope she ain't on no B.S. today, I'm not in the mood.*

"Hey Vance, look at you looking like a million bucks! Boy, come give your favorite auntie some sugar!"

"Hey Auntie," planting a wet kiss on her cheek.

"I hear you got a fine baby boy, congratulations!"

"Thanks, he looks just like me," speaking produly.

"I heard, I'm going to see him later after I make my rounds,"

"Well don't come at midnight because I know how you are with your rounds," laughing.

"No your mama said we'll go around 5pm so she can bring dinner and we can eat at your house."

"What's up Vance, am I invited to your new house for dinner nigga?"

"What's up Monique, I thought that was your car out there."

"What's up Vance," kissing my cheek.

"Hey Vantrice, hows my nephew doing?"

"He's good," still looking at Monique's messy ass.

"Yeah, how's your baby doing Vance? I want to see him to make sure he's yours. You know that bitch was a tramp before you met her," sticking her tongue out at me.

"Monique don't disrespect my son's mother or my mom's house. I'm going to put your messy ass outta here, I'm serious. And who are you to tell me if my son looks like me or not. I don't need no approval from you –!" my voice was rising and getting louder, matching my temperament.

"Calm down out here you two," Mom interjected, coming from the kitchen.

"Monique, I asked you not to start with Vance when he comes. Now I understand that you're upset but it is what it is, the boy has a baby now and you're going to have to accept that! All this cussing and fussing in my damn house, I won't tolerate. Y'all can't talk like two adults around here? Shit and don't be arguing over my grandson – " Mom was setting us straight with a spatula in her hand before Monique spoke up.

"I wasn't arguing with your stupid son. I was asking him if I was invited to his new crib since he forgot about the one I live in, all alone now, since he went off and had a lil' baby and all," Monique says angrily.

"You know damn well that you're not invited over his and Asia's house, what type of question is that? You're trying to be funny honey but you better be careful before I let Vance go upside your senseless head with all that nonsense you're talking. You would probably go over there and try to kill everybody in the house," laughing while she returned to the kitchen to put that spatula back to work.

Monique rolls her eyes, "So Vance, can I ask you a question?"

"Momma I'm going out in the back to smoke a blunt," reaching into my pocket for the goods.

"Let me hit that!" Vantrice asked, trailing behind me.

"Come on," I responded to Vantrice.

"I'll see you in a minute Auntie," we walked out to the backyard with Monique right on our heels.

"It's so nice to be back here, peaceful, huh?" Vantrice asked.

"Yes it's nice, that's why I bought it for Mama so we can have big barbeques in the summer and ride jet skis and shit on the lake."

This house was going into foreclosure from a couple who was going through a divorce. I paid a little next to nothing for it and gave it to my mom and sister. Her first house was in the hood and she didn't want to move, I had to damn near bribe her to move out. But as a compromise, she still owns the first house. She says it's for memories. Memories of what – drive-bys, crackheads, and struggles we went through as kids? Even though my daddy was caked up, mom's wasn't. He made sure we had everything but we were still just hood rich. Not wealthy or affluent as other privileged families. I loved the hood, the schools, my people's – everything about it represents me. But as I got older and started getting money, I had to move out of the hood and head to the suburbs because some niggas get jealous and shit and we can't have that.

"So Vance can I ask you question?" Monique just couldn't waste any time.

"What is it Monique? Damn, you sure can shake a nigga out of his reverie," passing the blunt to Vantrice. "This the truth girl, I hope you can handle this," laughing.

"Boy please," Vantrice starts hitting the blunt.

"What's up Monique? What's on your mind?"

"What would have happened if I hadn't lost our baby?" Monique asked and for the first time, she actually sounded sincere.

"I don't know what you mean. I would have been there for my baby, if that's what you mean," looking her in the eyes, trying to read what is was she really wanted from me.

"No, what about us Vance?" the desperation in her voiced joined her sincerity.

I was hoping she wouldn't bring that shit up again, "Look Monique, I care about you. You my nigga when you not on that B.S. But how can I put this..." I paused, searching to find what I wanted to say in the right way. It was like years of a partnership resided on the next words I shared, I could feel her soul hanging on to my every word like her heart depended on it. "We share a special relationship. We've known each other since we were kids but that's it.

I could see the puppy dog eyes forming, but I had to let her know. There was no sign of weakness to be displayed at this moment so I continued on, "We're not kids anymore and we outgrew each other. We're twenty-seven now but we're always going to be cool – "

"I'm stepping back in Vance, I'll see you later, bye Monique," Vantrice said before heading back to the house and leaving me out here alone with the wolves.

The lone wolf started to release her fangs, "What you mean cool nigga?" As soon as she spoke, I immediately saw a change in her demeanor. She started off sincere, and now the werewolf was coming out to play. "We've been together for over ten years, we're not cool!"

"Monique calm down ma' and quit saying we've been together because it wasn't all like that. We fucked around for over ten years but I always did my own thing. I've never disrespected you because that's not me, but make no mistake about it, I had other women and you knew that."

"But we lived together Vance, we were going to have a child but no! Once your half breed bitch with colored eyes pops up pregnant it was 'Fuck Monique!' I don't think so nigga, I ain't goin' out like that," she spat. The woman's fury was exposed.

"Monique, once again, quit disrespecting my shortie's mom and Asia didn't have anything to do with my decision to stop fucking with you like that! It was bound to happen with or without her. You do way to much and draw too much attention to yourself. And all that clowning shit is for kids. You need to carry yourself like a lady, not some hood rat with an expensive car. You need to bring it down a couple notches ma' and I wasn't feeling all that shit. Fighting everybody you saw me talking to, you don't know if its business or not. Slashing tires and breaking windows, that type of shit can get your ass left. Everybody ain't having your shit. I tolerated it for as long as I could."

"But a nigga had to move on and I'm not tripping off no house ma. I been told you it's yours, I wouldn't do you like that. I've already spoke to my attorney's about changing the title to your name. I mean you deserve that and it ain't like you're broke Monique. You got mad paper that you just need to invest with wisely. Open up a business or something. I've been telling you that for years. But no you want to floss, taking all of your friends for leeches shopping, all-expense paid trips and all that B.S."

"Vance, I ain't even trying to hear what you're talking about," she said and with that, the conversation was over.

20

PAYBACK IS A MOTHERFUCKER

Vance Smith

"Go deeper baby," hitting it from the back, I pull Asia's ass up and ram my dick into her soul.

"Oh baby, this feels so good," she moans.

"This my pussy baby?"

"Yes Daddy! Oh yes, ohhhh."

"Damn baby this pussy is the bomb...fuck you're going to make me cum," hitting her ass like a home run, straight out the ball park.

"Oh baby, that's my spot."

"Daddy knows where your spot is love, here cums daddy!"

"I'm coming too baby!" The whole time we were fucking, my cell phone was ringing and now the house phone - *disrespectful motherfuckers.*

"Oh baby that was the shit," catching my breath.

"That was good baby, I'm exhausted."

"Come here," wrapping my arms around her, planting kisses on her face.

"I love you baby and thank you for my beautiful son," I said, kissing her lips.

"You're welcome and thank you for donating sperm to the sperm bank. Feel free to drop by anytime," Asia says jokingly.

"I just made another donation," we laughed as my wit amused us both.

"I wonder who the fuck was calling the house at this time of the morning? It better had been an emergency because my cell was blowing up too. Let me check my messages and see who wants to get cussed out if it's some bullshit," getting up, reaching for my cell phone.

"It's Boobie '911', let me call this nigga back."

"What's up nigga, it's three in the morning! Who died?"

"Nigga you ain't going to believe this shit here," he replied.

"What? You put that word out for anyone with any information about the hit to contact our folks?"

"Right nigga and well I just got a call from our peoples. She said she knows who ordered that shit but she wants her bread to get the fuck out of town."

"Word!"

"Word nigga!"

"How much were you offering for that a meal ticket nigga?"

"One million nigga, that's right and if they hand delivered, two meals."

"Well I want this info' like yesterday nigga before they get scared or some shit. I have about half a mil' here at the crib, what you got on you?"

"Nigga I don't keep that kinda' dough at the crib and you shouldn't either."

"Nigga fuck that! I have business and establishments. I can have five mil' on me like it's nothing. If the bad guys take it, they have to give it back. I'm too legit, too legit to quit," laughing.

"Nigga you a fool for that throwback but what you want to do?"

"I'll grab what I have and give her that and write a bitch a check for the rest," laughing, "I'll be at your house in about thirty minutes. Oh, and nigga don't call the crib that late no more, those are the hours we fuck nigga!"

"Oh! So what are love making hours nigga?"

"Baby."

"What Vance," Asia asked, her voice dragged because she was half asleep.

"Boobie asked what hours do we make love?"

"You woke me up for that?" looking at me crazy.

"Answer the question because I don't know," trying not to laugh.

"Umm tell him everytime he calls you in the morning," putting the covers over her head, the sun was starting to come up.

"You heard her nigga, stop calling so fucking early in the morning! I'm on my way," hanging up without saying 'bye'.

"Baby," I turn my attention to Asia.

"What Vance? I'm tired," her voice muffled through the covers.

"I'm going make a run and go take care of something that can't wait but I promise to be back before you get up, ok? Baby you hear me?"

"Yes, I do have ears unfortunately. Be careful, I love you and be home in time to ummm make love," smiling at me, she dropped the covers to get one final look before drifting back off to sleep.

"I will," kissing her cheek. I jump in the shower and throw on a black hoodie, black Dickies and a black skull cap. Just in case I needed it, I packed an extra change of clothing and my leather bomber jacket before I went to get the money out my safe.

I also grabbed my money machine to count the dough so she knew I wasn't playing. When I pull up to Boobie's, he's standing at the door and ran to the car to get in.

"What's good Nigga?"

Joking with him I say, "You're good, you're awesome!"

Boobie looks at me as if I spoke to him in another language, "Gone with that white shit, 'awesome.' Nigga, I'm hood, I'm grimy and I'm gangsta'. Those are your choice words pertaining to me," hitting his chest. "Not totally awesome," laughing.

"All right, how did you get this information?"

"Like I said, motherfuckas' are hungry right now and with a mil' ticket on the table, niggas digging deep to get that information so they can eat. But they know they have to come correct with their information and it's going to get confirmed before any payout. I've been hearing lil' shit here and there, but nothing solid until this bitch claims she heard it from the horse's mouth and she knew a lot of details. So we'll just see what's up."

"Where is she?" I asked, ready to get this show on the road now that I've been properly debriefed.

"She's at a motel by the airport, the bitch is ready to jet. She's serious," giving me a stern look.

"I hope this ain't no set up nigga, you got heat?"

"Always, one in my sock and my baby on my hip," tapping his hand against the metal hidden under his jeans. "How about you?"

"Shit I'm working on my eighth life nigga, of course. For one, they got me and I can't let that happen again. And to make sure of that, this little pussycat is taking out generations for each round nigga," pointing to my automatic sniper rifle that rested in the back seat. "I'm killing grandmas, ma's, daddies, nigga if the dog move, I'm killing it. Anything that's a part of the family has to go –"

"Damn like that?" Boobie asked.

"Like that nigga, the whole family tree."

"Now that's gangsta homie," he nodded in respect.

"Word. Which hotel did the bitch say she was at?" I asked while signaling to change lines.

"Motel 6 off the highway."

"That one over there?" I noticed the big blue and red sign after getting off the exit.

"Yeah, that's it. Room sixty-nine."

"Sixty-nine? This bitch think she getting fucked or

something," laughing as we pulled in. Instinctively, I began to survey my surroundings, observing the parameters. There weren't too many cars in the lot and I could see the room from where we parked, the light was on.

"Do you have her cell number?" I asks.

"Yeah, let me hit her up," reaching for his phone.

"Hello. Hey, where did you say you were at again? The Motel 6 off the highway by the airport right?" Boobie asked. We were walking up to the door with our shit ready to put a nigga or bitch to sleep, whoever was a threat.

"You by yourself ma'?" he asked when we approached the door.

"Yeah, I'm leaving first thing tomorrow morning."

"Open the door."

"Damn why the guns?" she surveyed the guests we brought to the party.

"Shut up before you wake your neighbors," slamming the door behind us.

"Sit down," I instructed her. "Check the room," spinning my finger in a 360 degree rotation. Boobie was a big nigga, so if he had to knock a nigga out, he could. He was 6'3", 250 lbs solid, a brown pretty boy lookin' nigga. But don't let the pretty boy face fool you. He loved putting niggas to sleep, especially this kind of shit, payback type shit. I still had my gun pointed to her head with the infrared light, if she blinked wrong, it was curtains for her.

"It's clear nigga, she's good."

"Alright lil' mama, tell me something good," I say.

She seemed a bit more at ease and dropped her hands from the surrender position, "Well I was seeing this dude name Dirty," still shaking in fear.

"Can I get a cigarette before I finish?" she asks.

I nod my head, 'yes' and hand her a lighter.

"Well Dirty was talking to his brother Big Mike and some

other cats about how they killed a bitch names Essence and a nigga name Vance over some money. They said Essence used to work for Milo and then cut him loose after someone put a bug in her ear about some work she was doing for him. They said Milo bought the work for $150 a profile but Essence was doing all the work and giving that nigga $15,000 for each piece and they said she was doing two, sometimes three profiles a week – totaling $45,000 at a time.

She took another drag of the cigarette, "So since she met this nigga Vance, he put her up on game - Like that nigga spending $150 per profile and profiting up to 45K in return when she could buy her own work for $150 and keep all the money she made. Plus he had a hook up for her to get the work so she didn't need to fuck with Milo at all. That meant Milo was taking a $540K a year loss and he wasn't having that so he ordered the hit to take them both out." We were both standing there with both our mouths open. We couldn't believe the shit we just heard. *Damn, did that nigga have her house bugged or something? That's exactly what I told her when I meet her six months ago.*

"I'd be damned. So ma' you telling me them niggas were running their mouths like diarrhea when you were around?"

"Well not really, I went to the store when his friends first came over but when I returned, I was in the kitchen putting shit away and the basement door was open so I just stood there listening to them without their knowledge. And after I heard what I heard, I ran back to my car and called his cell to tell him I forgot something at the store and I needed a few more dollars. And he needed to bring it out to me. It was all a ploy to seem as if I had never returned to the house. But I've been holding this in for some months, scared to death. He was just too excited about blowing that chicks brains out and opening up that niggas guts. I knew he was crazy," She took a moment to grab her breath and smash her half smoked cigarette into the ashtray.

I was beyond heated but I held my composure, "So ma' they killed the girl and the nigga too?"

"Yes, that's what he said," looking up at us. "Why are they still alive?" she asked.

"No they're dead, both of them. I was just wondering," presenting an honest composure.

"Did they say they made sure they were dead before leaving?"

"I'm not sure, I told you guys everything I witnessed during their conversation."

"Well thanks for that information, but unfortunately I can't get you all your money until tomorrow. Is that going to be a problem?"

"Hell yea it's a problem! I wanted to be on a plane, far away from here, first thing in the morning."

"You don't think Dirty or Big Mike will come looking for you if you just up and left?"

"I've left that nigga plenty of times and always come back, but this time is different," she said and her colors started showing clear.

Oh really. I looked at Boobie and he looked at me as if we could read each other's mind, we both pulled our triggers and put holes in her ass like Swiss cheese. Thank god for silencers, or the whole motel would have woke up. Shit, we could have woke the dead with that jump off. There was no sense in keeping any witnesses around and she said it herself, she always went back to him. So we made sure that she left him for good. I'll send the money to her family, they'll have to spend it on her anyways. So in essence, she'll still receive the reward money, she just won't be able to spend it like she wanted too. While driving back to Boobie's house, we rode in silence, with only the sounds of one another's lungs reaching a higher place after he rolled up a blunt and put it in rotation. I put on some DMX to keep my adrenaline going. *'Tell me what you want from a nigga!',* driving with the volume on high, beating the streets up at 6am. After I dropped him off, I went to my mom's house to dispose of my clothing because of the evident blood splatter. Disposal of all evidence is an unwritten hood proverb, and it's kept me out of the systematic cage that they call prison up until now. Adding layers to the haystack, I knew buying this house on the lake would come in handy and it did, more times than I can count on my hands. Whether it was burnt clothes or burnt bodies, that river held many dark secrets that only myself and I knew about. And I planned on keeping it that way.

21

I AIN'T NO JOKE

While still digesting the news I got about those bum ass niggas who tried to murk me, I had to keep my perspectives in order and strategize efficiently. I didn't want a messy job, if it was going to be done, it would need to be done correctly. Plus, I am still recuperating from my injuries. I called a club house meeting with my squad – 'Speak No Evil, Hear No Evil, See No Evil.' Whoever came up with that philosophy was the shit in my book – I would dap them up saying, "Good looking my nigga, mad props for that one!"

"What's up Vance, we're all here," one of my boys said.

"What's good fellas!" As I looked around the table, all my niggas were riders and I was proud of that. Boobie, my ace, my brother from another mother, we've been cool since the kindergarten, so you know this is some real love shit. Even when I transferred in the sixth grade and went to school by my pops house, he transferred too. He had my back, side and front without even asking. This dude could fool a pastor with a pretty boy face and style. But I've seen him take out families with no remorse and he's even taken one for the team. His specialty is snapping a niggas neck, 'crack' and it's over. Nobody wants to go head up with this nigga because if he gets the best of you, it's a wrap and this nigga stayed strapped like he was apart of the secret service for the president. He was like an American Express commercial, never leave home without it.

And next up is my other partner in crime, Dude, who was the quiet one out of the group. He was a short nigga, about 5'7" but buff as hell and stocky. He didn't talk much, just listened. We've been friends since our teenage years and he's no joke either. You never see him coming but he's always there, ready to take a nigga out of his misery. No questions asked. That's one of the qualities that I liked about him from the beginning – he ain't got shit to say.

Last but not least was Gibson, he's the genius of the bunch.

He was too smart for his own good. Before we had accountants and shit like that, he handled all of the business on his end. To deem him as business savvy would be an understatement. He's quick with numbers and can put a plan together, instantly. He's very talented in a lot of areas, except for his temper. He gets mad real quick, over just about anything. He killed a nigga at a club for accidentally stepping on his shoe and he can't keep a woman for too long because he has a bad attitude. But he's a cool brother once you get to know him. He's been dating this chick name Rashaun for about six months now and that's the longest I've ever seen him in a relationship out of the whole ten years I've known him.

I was surrounded by a table of wolves. But what good is pack without their alpha wolf? To top things off, of course, there was me – Vance Smith. The head nigga in charge with jet black melanin, hazel eyes, a pussycat-ally cat type of guy. I do what I do because I can. That's my motto. I'll say I'm very conservative in style with a republican attitude. I'm a go-getter. I brought this group together at sixteen years old when my uncle got raided by the police and I was sitting in his car, waiting on my ride home. My uncle and his peeps were making a delivery and you know what kind of delivery – it wasn't no pizza. I knew he had some work under both front seats of the car so I quickly put two bricks in my backpack. All I had in it was my hoodie and I never brought books home, I always had girls do my work. But my mom always though I had homework because I had my backpack. They took my uncle down because they had indictments for him, plus his stupid ass had more work in his trunk that I didn't know about at the time. Luckily, the po-po's never searched me. They let my black ass go and told me to run home and tell my parents that my uncle was going down. And at the same time, I was about to come up.

I opened up shop and been moving work ever since. I gave my uncle his share and profited off the rest. Now ten years later, I'm reaping the benefits of a hustler. Everywhere I go, I make people look – 'Is that so and so in that benz' or 'That's the nigga that owns the club or restaurant.' – and that's how I wanted to keep it. A lot of people thought I was some rich kid because my father owned a restaurant but the truth is, it was very profitable at first but I invested money into it and opened up the bar that he always dreamed about, in his name. My contributions allotted to the status he achieved before he parted. His job just paid the bills and kept food in the refrigerator but we didn't have a big house with fancy cars and shit, we were hood rich. But now a nigga is alright.

I'm worth an estimate of about twenty million, that includes drug money and business ventures. I could get out of the game but for what? The game is good to me and for me. I'll quit when I get tired, but until then, bring it on nigga! Bring it on! And by the way, since we're reflecting on our talents. I'll take a nigga down with my eyes closed. I dreamed about that kind of shit. What I can't do, my beretta can with the help of a little red light. I'll help you get to the maker or to hell, whichever you choose, I'll take you there. We sat around the table passing blunts, contemplating our next move.

"Vance you straight as far as security goes right?"

"I'm good," looking around at all my boys. It felt good to know you had someone you could really rely on if any situation arose.

These were my true homies, like brothers. They weren't just some niggas I was getting money with. When I got hit, they got hit too. Blood for blood. Ride or die. If I would have been taken out that night, this meeting would have went down a little different. Instead of executing a plan for revenge, some niggas entire family would have been executed. Generations gone, completely. You think Bush started a war, that wouldn't have been shit compared to what they would have done. I hate to admit it but we've done shit that's only supposed to happen in movies. But sometimes that's the price you pay for being in the game. But this was different all together. These few wanna-be gangsters, let a nigga live - why? That's the million dollar question. Why not check my pulse or make sure I'm not breathing, shit pop a nigga in the head. Do what you came to do, don't half step. That's why I roll like I roll, with true soldiers. We're all on the same page with this shit. We all know what time it is. We're here nigga, eye to eye. They need to watch some of those gangster flicks or playbacks of the game like they do in football locker rooms. Can't repeat no losses. Sure enough they did take out Essence and did a hell of a job at that. Every time I close my eyes I pictured her fine ass splattered across her bed with human membranes everywhere. Some of that shit even got on me but the minute I jumped to the floor to reach for my shit, I got hit. Instead of spraying her they should have sprayed me. But that's neither here nor there now. It's show time.

"I have my security tighten up," I responded, "My moms and Vantrice have a shadow and of course, my girl. She always did and didn't know," I said sarcastically, "and not for security reasons either." They bursted out laughing.

"You a jealous ass nigga blood," Gibson cuts at me.

"Naw man it ain't even like that but you can never be too careful man. I'm just tryna' protect my shortie. If she wanted to do her thang, more power to her ass but nigga truthfully - I ain't ever had woman who would want another dick after mine. This dick," holding my crotch, "is like Christmas day. It brings joy to the world," I yelled, high as hell and laughing at my own speech.

"Ok Saint Dick!!" one of my boys hollers back and we all fell out from our joking galore.

"You niggas is stupid!" Boobie says, "This weed got you niggas turning into Def Comedy Jam and shit. But Vance you got a point because Monique lunatic ass won't let it go. She's holding on for dear life. Now that shit is crazy."

"I don't know why," Dude paused, hitting the blunt, "she knows she doesn't have a chance going up against Asia's fine ass. It's not too many woman't I've seen that do, except for my bitch. She'll give

Asia a run for her money," and continues to smoke boastfully.

Now he had a point, Dude's girl, Egypt was bad. She was caramel with big brown eyes, about 5'2" and thick as hell. She wore about a size nine in clothes but it was all in the right places. I guess she weighed about 140lbs with a nice round ass. Her hair hung down her back and it was all hers. But her demeanor is what I liked the most, she was cool as fuck. No drama. She didn't mind if Dude went to strip clubs, she encouraged it when we did boys night and she didn't call every five minutes.

She was even cool to be around, very secure within herself and acted like a lady at all times. She was gangta' for that.

"I remember she got into it once at the club with this chick that Dude was creeping with. She let him talk privately with the chick and wasn't even tripping. But when she went to dance floor with this nigga, Dude went off. He was trying to cut in and shit, it was hilarious. Then the chick came over trying to say something to Egypt and Egypt checked her ass real quick. It went something like, 'you think you're all that because you got a degree, you stuck-up as bitch!' and Egypt politely retorts, 'I do have several degrees and one in whooping a bitch's ass and I got it from the school of hard knocks' she spat as she stared the girl down. But instead of Egypt beating her down, Dude stepped in because she had called Egypt at bitch and the whole night we couldn't stop laughing at his buster ass for trying to be slick".

"Stop bringing that shit up Vance!" Dude replied.

"Well nigga,I'm just saying the shit was funny!"

"Haha, yea nigga very funny. You had some episodes your damn self. Don't make me go there nigga!" Dude said, threatening me and laughing at the same time.

"Shit we all had some episodes if that's the case. We talking about bad bitches and shit, we're hella off topic -"

"So back to the meeting at hand. How do y'all want to do this thang?" Gibson asked, "messy or clean nigga because once again it's on!" he slammed one of his hand guns down on the table to emphasize the fact that he meant every word.

We began to brainstorm, throwing different concepts and schemes around but Gibson had the best idea, as usual.

"Nigga I say we hit them niggas on your anniversary."

"My anniversary?"

"Yeah, the one year anniversary of when you were shot."

"Oh...that long?" I asked.

"Nigga that ain't too long, plus I know they won't be expecting it. Their guards will be down because right now, they're expecting retaliation from your end. But when it doesn't happen, they slip up and then BAM! Like a thief in the night, we hit they ass up," Everyone looked at him like 'good idea nigga', he always came up brilliant shit like that. This nigga was a genius I swear.

"Ok, but we hit the two bragging-mouth motherfuckers first because if we take out the head nigga, they'll all go into hiding. We can do a drive-by on them punk ass niggas and take a few others out as well. Then the nigga who ordered the hit won't think it was intentional. Then give him a surprise going away bash. Let's do a drive-by like we did the Hardy boys," laughing.

As he spoke, I liked that idea more and more. This shit sounded so good it made my dick get hard just thinking about it. We rolled another blunt and smoked it. By the time the last ash fell into the tray, we were all in agreeance and giving each other pounds.

"One love niggas, one love," and with that, the meeting was adjourned.

22

LET'S TALK

Asia Smith

Vance had been home from the hospital for about a couple months now and had recovered quite well. Today was going to be just him and me relaxing at home. His mom had the baby for the weekend. She just wouldn't take 'no' for an answer and Vance said to let him go and when we start missing him, we could check up on him. He hadn't been gone for more than twenty-four hours yet and we both called about twenty-four times. His mom said if we called one more time she was going to turn her ringer off.

"Baby..." poking his ribs while he slept, "I can't sleep. I miss V.J."

"I miss him too Asia but I'm tired as hell. Shit, we were up all night gambling."

We hosted a card game at our house last night. It was our first gathering in our new home since we moved in a couple months ago. All of Vance's friends came and some brought their women and lady friends for me to entertain. We had plenty of drinks and of course, Vance had purple – one of the best party favors for this occasion – blunts continued to be fired up all night. The food was catered from one of the soul food restaurants owned by Vance, you know black folks love to have some soul food. The entertainment atmosphere was amplified by the music that was played throughout the house.

"Shit, the last couple that left was around five this morning and it's only 8 a.m. now," gazing up to the clock on the wall and dropping his head down heavily onto the pillow.

"Baby, I'm not tired, let's talk!"

"Asia please, just give me one more hour," grabbing me by my waist, pulling me close to him, "and we can talk then, Ok? I'm tired, I'm high, I'm sleepy and you should be too Superwoman!"

"I can't. I'm not tired yet," I lay my head on his chest, "I'm trying..." whining.

"Ok, move your big head and let me sit up," he grabbed about four throw pillows and placed them behind to prop himself up.

Rubbing his eyes, "So what do you want to talk about baby, at dark-thirty in the morning?"

"I don't know, I just want to talk. These past couple of months have been crazy, the baby, you getting shot, moving into this new house, Christmas and New Year's. Let's talk about new year's resolutions," I said, attempting to lure the cheese on the mouse trap. I really wanted to talk about him being at Essence's house but I didn't know how to bring it up.

"Resolutions, huh?"

"Well Asia, tell me what's yours since you want to talk so badly."

"Well for starters, being truthful to each other, trusting one another, and being the best parents we can be."

"That's not a resolution Asia, we're already that. Resolution means to resolve, it's an action to resolve a solution. So that can't be your new year's resolution. You have to replace that one with something else."

"Ok, Vance. No cheating. Can that be one?"

"Yes, but who cheats? You cheated on me before Asia?" asking solemnly.

"No Vance, I haven't."

"Come on Asia, you said be truthful and I know of at least one time you cheated."

"Nigga I never cheat when I'm in a relationship. Now if I'm not in one, that's different."

"So what are you talking about?"

I know I've never cheated on him, not with a man anyways. "Why you smiling Vance? I'm serious."

"Me too. If I ask you a question, you promise to tell the truth?"

"Yes of course."

"You never once cheated on me in our whole two years, even when you were mad as hell at me?"

"No Vance, but we can't say the same about you can we? You had two women pregnant at the same time," I said, getting mad now.

"Come here," kissing me, "No stop Vance, I'm serious."

"You're the one who wanted to talk so don't get mad. Plus, I never said I didn't cheat, that was you."

"So you cheated on me Vance?" poking my lips out.

"Sort of…"

"What the fuck is sort of, Vance? You sort of fucked Monique, that's how she got pregnant," looking at him, waiting for an answer.

"Come on ma', you knew about her from the beginning. That's not cheating. Cheating is when you don't know about a person."

"Oh I see, like you being at Essence house that night was that cheating?" *He knew eventually I would get around to asking about that night, he just didn't know when I would ask.*

Taking a deep breath, "Yes Asia, that would be considered cheating. But that night I didn't cheat."

"But you would have if that wouldn't have happened."

"Asia, she's dead and gone. Please let the girl R.I.P."

"I want to know Vance, I'm dying to know."

"That's not the right word to use under the circumstances. But if you really want to know, I'll tell you since we're being so honest this year. But first answer the question Asia, who gave head better, her or me?" *Oh no this nigga didn't go there, he knew all this time.* "Remember Asia to tell the truth, the whole truth and nothing more."

"I mean Vance, that's different. How long have you known? And why you never said anything?"

"Don't answer a question with a question Asia."

"Your head is better baby," I said, lying. Shit, she had me reaching for shit that wasn't even there. I started to question my own sexuality. Her head should have been taught in sex-ed class. She was the truth with that tongue. I can't even front she found my spot like a GPS.

"And how about why you and her were robbing banks. She told me you made over $180K, without me knowing, in a year's time Asia. I still don't understand why you were doing that dumb shit when I can give you anything you want, without ever asking," he said, looking perplexed.

"First of all mister, she was out of line for telling my damn business, pillow talking and shit. And you asked me why I did what I did...I let her give me head because I was mad at you for being with that bitch Monique. And for the record, we were into identity theft, not robbing banks –"

"Y'all went into banks, using other people's identity and took money out their accounts. That's not robbing a bank Asia?"

"No it's not. I didn't have a gun!"

"So what! You weren't that person either so that's robbery."

"No it's not Vance."

"So what's it called? Ms. Know it all?"

"Identity theft!"

"What did you do with all the money Asia?"

"I spent some, paid off my car –"

"Wait, your car had been paid off? I gave you that money a long time ago."

"I used it for something else."

"Like what? I want to know what you spent forty racks on, tell me? I'm glad you wanted to talk about resolutions because your ass need to start with the first two right now or I'm going to beat your ass in this king size bed. Now Asia Smith...start talking, I'm listening!"

"I am, dang why are you gettin' all serious on me?"

"I'm going to seriously beat your ass if you don't' start talking and say the right shit. What did you spend my money on back then?"

"I loaned it to my friend?"

"Your friend who? And please don't say who I think you're going to say because why does that nigga need to borrow money from you? That you got from me? Please tell me you didn't give my money to some nigga."

"No! It wasn't Rusty I know you think that. I wouldn't do that Vance, I'm serious."

"I hope not, but with you, it ain't no tellin'! Who then?"

"It was Essence –"

"Hell naw Asia, she had her own money. Come again?"

"No seriously, she got caught up and I bailed her out with ten percent. I even have the receipt to prove it. It's inside my jewelry box."

"Go get it," he said, pointing in that direction, not dropping his gaze from my eyes.

Jumping out of bed, walking into my walk in closet, I pull out my custom made jewelry box and grab the receipt, "See!" handing it to him, "see look for yourself."

"So did she pay you back?"

"Yes, the next day."

"So why didn't you pay off your car like you were supposed to?"

"I don't know, I just didn't. But that's why I was hitting all the banks because she was getting hot, they started recognizing her even with wigs on and shit. So I took over and hit the banks and we split the dough. And when you found out, you made me quit. Remember?"

"Yeah I do remember, but you didn't quit that day. She told me you at least did three more before you decided to stop... just greedy," he said ashamedly, shaking his head.

Wasn't this the pot calling the kettle black? As if his wealth wasn't a reflection of one of the seven deadly sins. We were two sides of the same coin, he just couldn't bear to see me as a hustler, in his mind – there was only one hustler in this relationship.

"Well baby, I couldn't. I had a couple more pieces of work I had to finish first. But you reaped benefits too. All the shopping I did, I always looked out for you and my sister."

"Well that's nice to know, but Asia you didn't have to."

He paused, seemingly as if his ego took some sort of hit from this ordeal, "How many times did we go shopping and I spent thousands on shoes for your ass. Jimmy Choo's, Christian Louboutin, Gucci, Giuseppe shit. One hundred thousand and five hundred here, two thousand and five hundred there. Not to mention five thousand dollar bags. Shit, I've dropped thirty racks on you alone shopping at one time easily. And I have all kinds of tailored made suits and shoes that exceed well into the hundred thousand range. My accountant said, last year alone, I spent close to 1.5 million and that's not including this brand new joint we live in and the new truck I bought you. My son's trusts and investment accounts. Shit, I have three million in a trust set up for him. I took it out my personal account alone. So about the time that nigga hit eighteen, interest alone will put him in the richest kids in America club. And don't forget my business, I'm like Richie Rich the cartoon character but in real life. So baby, you hit jackpot with a nigga like me. You better recognize! Giving me a son was the best thing you could do in life besides marrying a ball player or something. Plus them niggas have broads in every state they play in. So you should be counting your blessings that you're in the presence of a nigga with my status. Now suck my dick baby," laughing and his ego dropped the mic.

"Fuck you Vance. You ain't all that homie, don't get it twisted boo. I was far from broke when I met you. Don't forget I come from a family of money too. Now suck my dick nigga! Who's laughing now?"

"That's why I love your ass girl. You keep it straight gangsta," he said, still laughing at our banter.

"You know a nigga couldn't fuck with a weak ass bitch, always crying and shit, who doesn't have any balls. That shit is a straight turn off. Square bitches can't even keep my dick hard."

"Whatever nigga, I am square," crossing my arms.

"Yea you got some *square* footage on that pussy baby, that's about it," laughing.

"I'm tired now, let's go to sleep."

"Oh no, not so fast speedy Gonzalez, remember you wanted to talk? Baby Oprah don't get tired on my now," he said, laying my head on my lap.

"Oh you want me to rub your head? Nigga, you ain't slick," rubbing my fingers through his wavy hair, "V.J.is going to have pretty hair like this," I said.

"Your hair is like mine too but you never know, that lil' nigga might have nappy hair," he said, reaching down to massage my feet.

"Oh like Sonia – " I utter, trying to hold in my laughter.

"Don't talk about my momma girl. She has good hair, she just has to buy it," giggling.

"Give Daddy a kiss," he asked. Reaching down, I kiss them soft ass lips of his and he starts rubbing my titties.

"Stop Vance!"

"You know you don't mean that girl," massaging my nipples, "doesn't that feel good," putting one on his mouth.

"Yes it does," I whimper as he started sucking them both, "I love it when you suck them baby. Oh...give me those magic fingers." He slides his two fingers inside me and I open wide to accommodate them.

"Tell me you love me."

"I love you Daddy!"

"You want Daddy to make you feel good?"

"Um huh, please. Ohhh right there baby, put it in baby!"

We made love for about an hour before we fell fast asleep, lingering in our love juices.

23

ONE YEAR ANNIVERSARY

Vance Smith

The night before my one year anniversary of the shooting, my boys and I went to shoot hoops – it was a beautiful August day. We played two-on-two, Boobie was on my team with Dude and Gibson as our opponents.

"How much is this game worth today?" I asked.

"A rack nigga as usual and losers buy all the drinks," Boobie said confidently.

"Ain't shit funny nigga, let's do this!" Gibson replied, throwing the ball at my chest.

"Awe damn nigga like that? Don't be mad 'cause you niggas lost three nights in a row," mocking his demeanor.

"Shut up and ball!" He retorted.

We started hooping like NBA niggas and the bee's began to swarm. We always attracted a crowd of spectators from the hood. Mostly little niggas hanging out and fast ass lil girls who should be home because it was dark outside.

"Watch that three pointer nigga! Blam! Money in the bank!" I said proudly, giving Boobie a pound.

"That's what's up. Let's take these niggas to school," Boobie said, doing his best A.I. impersonation, zig zagging his way to the basket. But Dude short ass slapped the ball out his hand and dribbled down the court to shoot a three.

"Damn," I said, breathing heavily.

This shit is really physical. I don't know how them niggas in the NBA do it for a living, shit, they would have to pay me big bucks to just stay in shape for this shit – personal trainers, dietician, strenuous workouts, and not even considering the injuries. I grew a whole new level of respect for them cats, they're worth every dime they make and some, if it was up to me. We continued to hoop for about twenty more minutes before Dude hit his third three-pointer and closed game. *Shit*.

I had to give up a thousand dollars to each of them niggas and Boobie did too. I was so used to winning, they better be lucky I even had it on me. But I forgot I picked up money from a worker, so I as straight.

While walking to the bleachers to holler at my young nigga, I see this little chick that's been trying to get my attention for months now and finally got her courage up, I guess.

"Hi Vance. Good game, you were ballin' out there tonight!"

I looked at her but didn't respond, she was cute and all but seemed a little young for me. I said, 'Excuse me' to her and told my young nigga to let me holler at him for a minute.

"What's up Vance? That shit was mad crazy, you niggas be trying to kill each other out there on the court," he said enthusiastically. You could see the excitement in his eyes, the kool-aid smile on his face. I could smell the lust he exuded, in hopes of trading places or ages with one of my boys so he could participate.

"I know, there's no rules nor ref', so we kinda' get physical but it's all in fun," I retorted, "But what's up Dre, how did you do today?" I asked him.

"Oh me and my peeps were cool. I need another bird though, we're almost out."

"Like that? That was fast."

I couldn't believe these young niggas were getting money like that. They were buying more dope from me than some older cats that's been in the game and turning it over faster too. These young little niggas was hungry, you could see it in their eyes. I didn't judge them because I was the same way at their age. People look down on drug dealers but we can't help it.

The majority of the time these youngsters live with their mom in the projects on welfare and if she's not on welfare and working simultaneously, she's barely making ends meet. One should ask themselves, or their government rather, how can an able bodied working adult have a full time job, yet doesn't have the means to support herself nor her family with basic necessities.

Although I'm from the streets, I wish everyone would have went to college and got a degree. Could you imagine that? If everyone from the hood went to college, there wouldn't even be enough jobs for these niggas. They'll make up some excuse like there are too many African Americans with a formal education and not enough jobs or some shit like that. They'll have limits and shit on niggas. Every city, state to state, has a hood in the projects per say where niggas are getting mad money from the dope game. If all of that came to end, 'White-y' would be the supplying our people with narcotics, which they already do. They'd probably try to bring back slavery or some shit like that.

But I've also dealt with a lot of white clients in this game, so it's not really based on color. It's just depends on what avenue you take to start hustling. Whether its drugs, or white collar crime - big executives in big corporations rob their companies for billions but we're the ones who are looked at like animals and crooks wherever we go. But it's twice as hard for a black man to make it in this society, they make it harder for us to get ahead and if selling a little dope is going to help a brother support his family and get ahead, then why not? Shit the dope game have sent plenty of niggas to college and opened plenty of black owned business. So you judge me because I want to send my son or daughter to college but I don't have a job that pays well except minimum wage, and the philosophy behind all of this is, my child shouldn't be able to go receive a higher education because we aren't rich?

Hell no, with my philosophy, they can attend the same schools as the rich kids but on a full scholarship from the hood. Shit, after all, black folks don't make the drugs we just distribute them. The people making and supplying the hood should be the one's to blame, not us. We're just the middleman. Taking from the rich and giving to the poor. Why do you think Robin last name was 'Hood'? I'm just doing my part in helping out.

"Well Dre, I'll have my people meet you, same time same place.

"Good looking," he says giving me a pound.

"Oh Vance this might be inappropriate but my sister asked me to tell you that she thinks you're all that," laughing.

"Was that your sister who spoke to me before I started talking to you?"

"Yeah, her name is Tashay but we call her 'Shay' for short. She comes and watch y'all play sometimes. I told her you're too old for her," laughing again.

"Hold old is she?"

"Sixteen going on twenty one," he dropped his head while shaking it from side to side.

"Tell her I said she cute as hell but yeah man, too young. Plus, I'm engaged."

"I told her that you have a son but she doesn't care, you know how these young girls are now-a-days."

I didn't respond, I just walked to my truck where niggas were waiting to get paid.

"About time nigga, we was waiting on you," Dude said.

"Not over $1000 nigga," I snap back

"Anyway, we have to go to the clubhouse."

"I could have given it to you there."

"Break me off now," Gibson said, "I'm flat broke and starving. I'm going to grab a bite to eat and meet you niggas at the spot," rubbing his stomach.

"So what if y'all would have lost?" I ask.

"We didn't though, that's all that matters." I just shook my head and paid them fools $1000 each.

"Bet, see y'all in twenty minutes," Gibson said before he ran over to his benz. Come to think about it, I was hungry too. I'm not sure what I want to eat but my stomach is screaming 'help'!

Laughing to myself, *let me see if Asia's hungry too. I'll grab her something and bring it home.* I jumped into my truck and turned on an old school mixtape before I called home.

"Hello. What's up baby, you hungry?"

"I ate while I was out."

"What you eat?"

"Pizza."

"Pizza, that's it? What did V.J. eat?"

"Everything his greedy self saw," laughing.

"Is he sleep? Because I don't hear him."

"I don't know, he's not here."

"Where is he?" I asked impulsively.

"Where else? Your mommas house, she called fifty times asking me to bring him over. She said that she missed him and I reminded her that V.J. just left her house two days ago."

"Well she loves her grandson," I said smiling.

"That's not love, that's obsession," laughing.

"I agree but that's her first grandson."

"Well now she has a granddaughter, I thought she would chill a little on V.J."

"Please, she still jocks me Asia, you know that! She calls me at least ten times a day. I have to send her to voicemail most of the time."

"Well kid, it's just you and me tonight," Asia says, I could feel her grinning through the phone.

I reply, "That's a good thing, right? I know something we can get into," laughing.

"I bet you do Vance," sounding sexy.

"I can't wait to see you baby. See you in a few," I say before hanging up.

After I pulled up to the seafood restaurant, I ordered my food and waited out front, observing the night sky. Some people clock out when it gets dark, for me, it's all a part of my nature. When my food was ready, I headed to the clubhouse to go over the details for tomorrow and then headed home for some loving from my girl. When V.J. is gone, we get buck wild because when that little dude is home, he's right between us, no questions asked. He refuses to sleep in his room and will throw a fit if we make him. His nickname is 'Bossy' because that's what he is. He reminds me so much of myself, looks like me and acts just like me.

It was amazing. He kept me laughing. I just pray he doesn't inherit my I-don't-give-a-fuck demeanor. I want him to be a square nigga, but I doubt it, not with his linage – especially both parents with Asia's feisty ass.

Tomorrow came quicker than I thought, I looked over at the clock when it read 6:30 AM, I don't even remember what time we finally made it to sleep but we were at it like wild animals for about two hours. As soon as I got out the shower, she tackled me on the bed and went for hers. Then it was my turn to tackle her. That went on for about two more hours, then we fell asleep in each other's arms.

Looking over at her, Asia slept so peacefully with her hair all wild. I grabbed my phone and used my camera to capture the moment. *A picture is worth a thousand words, this will go into my private collection with the rest.* I always took pictures of her in the most compromising positions.

I laid back down and started kissing the back of her neck and rubbing on her breasts. She rubs her ass against my dick, *she's woke now*. I slid it in and hit it from the side, she lifts one leg up so I can go deeper. I fuck the shit out of her, knowing that this may be the last time. I seriously doubt it but you never know the outcome until it's presents itself in real time. With the mission on my mind, I gave it to her and she threw it back at me. This pussy was my motivation to bring my ass home in one piece, that and my shortie. So once again...it's on.

24

RIDE OR DIE FOR MY NIGGAS

Vance Smith

"It's 4pm, everybody ready nigga?" Boobie asked.

We all nod our heads in unison. The moving truck was parked around the corner from where the hit would take place. Everything was a go. Our mule had given us information on these clown niggas and it just so happens that they were having some sort of block party in their hood for a fallen homeboy. These fools were from College Park, straight out of the projects. I knew cats from there that were balling but I never heard of these dudes. It didn't matter anyways after today because they'll be throwing another block party for the same occasion, different names. I was listening to DMX all day to set the mood. Dude's younger brother was the driver of the moving truck.

He let the fork lift down and we rolled our BMW bikes down and rived them up. We all had on black leather Harley Jackets, black jeans, black boots and burners. The only difference was I had on my silver helmet and everyone else had black helmets, which would all be disposed of after the ride. I put on my favorite CD to explain our mission, and kept it on repeat. *'Fuck them other niggas cuz' I'm down for my nigga! What! Fuck them other niggas!* And off we went, four niggas on bikes, ready to give it to them. We were all strapped with semi-automatic weapons around our shoulders, fully loaded, delivering the business.

As we approach the crowded street, there were people everywhere. We wanted to make sure we killed the right niggas and avoid harming any kids in our attempt. It was a good thing they had a playground and jumper set up over by the picnic grounds and out of the way so we could give our best performance without being remorseful for innocent kids getting hit accidentally.

Gibson gave the signal as he spotted them niggas drinking and smoking, standing by a sideshow of cars. We rode by and my music was loud bumping *'Fuck them other niggas.'* But I heard some female say, 'Who is them niggas on the bikes?' staring in awe.

Right on cue, we lit they asses up. Our crew rode by, shooting directly at our targets and hit a few cars and an innocent bystander along the way. I emptied my clip on them niggas. It sounded like a fourth of July fireworks show. We rode up the street to our second checkpoint around the corner, only slowing down when we reached the lift where we turned our bikes off and removed the weight of our helmets. Lil Mo' concluded our mission when he put the lift back up, closed the door of the truck and started the ignition. Off we went in a moving truck with four niggas, on four bikes, with four semi-automatic weapons inside - who just finished a professional hit. No one would suspect we were inside an Uhaul moving truck, but we were. This is how we rolled if we had to. I'm sure no one even paid attention but our license plates read 'RIP Another Mission Accomplished With One More to Go'.

Later that night, while watching the news the inevitable happened – 'Breaking Story, another senseless drive-by killing in College Park, four dead, and seven critically wounded. There were six shooters. A female witness reports that they were riding Harley motorcycles. The motive at this time is still unknown. Stay tuned.' I changed the channel – *Six killers, Harley bikes, I hope they find them. That's not a description of us.*

It's funny how the media intentionally and aggressively seeks to portray the black community as riddled in violence. They never tend to dig a little deeper and uncover the truth. The truth is, they are bigger monsters than we are – we are solely in survival mode. On the other hand, they perpetuate these images for their own greed and control. We can never forget how we ended up in the hood, by way of the south, by way of America, by way of a ship, by way of Africa. I can only imagine the violence our ancestors endured from the hands of the oppressors. And now they try to portray us as a 'violent' people, when it is solely they're systematic extension of the 13th amendment.

25

V.J. TURNS ONE

Vance Smith

"Monique, what are you doing here?" I asked, *Why is she looking at my like I'm the one who's crazy?*

"It's V.J.'s first birthday isn't it?"

"Um, yeah. And?"

I could feel my forehead wrinkling up while asking this dumb ass broad questions and my heart was pulsating 100 mph. I know Asia is over there sitting with her sister and mother, looking over here like 'what the fuck! Did he invite her to my son's first birthday party or what?'. *I'm not going to hear the last of this.*

"Monique, my son's party is for family and friends. Since you're neither of those and you weren't invited, don't see why you are here?"

Looking perplexed, "Vance stop it. Our kids would have been siblings so that does make me family, sort of. I just want to give V.J. his gift I bought," she plead, holding a big ass box.

"It isn't a bomb is it?" shaking it and placing my ear to listen for anything that didn't sound like a child's toy. I was laughing but dead serious.

"You are so crazy Vance. Where is the birthday boy anyways?" she asked, looking around.

There was so much to see with all of the kids playing, getting their faces painted and enjoying the clown who made balloons. Other kids were lined up at the cotton candy and candy apple machines, eagerly waiting. I spot V.J. dancing with one of his older cousins who was holding his two little hands in hers and rocking to the beat.

I point in his direction, "He's the lil' handsome one in the True Religion jeans and Argyle sweater," smiling.

I sounded like a proud father, sometimes it felt so unreal how enamored my seed made me feel about love and life.

"He's so cute, he looks just like you but with curly hair."

"I know but anyways Monique —"

"You know you're hella disrespectful for showing up at my grandson's birthday party don't you?" my mom yelled, looking pissed off.

"Hi to you too Sonia. Thanks for inviting me."

"Inviting you to a child's birthday party? Monique you ought to be ashamed of yourself, showing up and disrupting my grandson's party," crossing her arms. If Monique couldn't pick up my mom's tone, she could definitely read her hostile body language.

"Well I'm not, is that a problem Sonia?" Monique hissed.

"Mom, Monique was just leaving," I interjected, ushering her to the door, "thanks for the gift. I'll make sure to send you a thank you card."

"Fuck you Vance. If I hadn't lost the baby, would you have invited us?" solemnly asking.

"I don't know Monique but you stopped by uninvited anyway, so it really doesn't matter, does it?"

"We need to talk Vance, Ok. "

"I'll call you, I have to go," I state firmly, progressively closing the door.

"I miss you Vance," she said and tried to look at me but she slowly started drifting her eyes towards the ground when my eyes didn't meet hers.

Stepping outside and cracking the door behind me,

"Monique I'm going to say this as nicely as possible. Do not make me act the color of my skin at my son's birthday party," raising my voice.

Asia must have reached her boiling point and couldn't take it anymore because she started walking towards us rapidly.

Asia looked me directly in my eyes, "You had your moment and it passed, say goodbye to your guest and return to your son's birthday party or you can leave with her," she walked away as quickly as she came, switching her hips in some tight ass Gucci jeans that hugged her fat ass. All of her assets, including her ass, had grown from the baby weight. After Monique received a triple threat, she finally got the message and ski-skirted out of here with the quickness.

I walked to the gift table to set the box down that Monique gave me for V.J. and before I could set it down Asia stepped in, "What do you think you're doing?" Asia asked, looking me up and down.

"Huh, what?"

"This is a gift from V.J.'s brother or sister."

"What brother or sister nigga. V.J. is an only child the last time I checked," mugging me.

"You know what I mean Asia, damn."

"No I don't know what you mean but what I do know is my son doesn't want or need anything from Monique or any other women you had dealings with, now or ever. Is that understood?" she questioned, still grilling me.

"So what am I supposed to do with it then?"

"Figure it out Sherlock, but it's not to sit at the gift table with his other gifts and you're not bringing it home so maybe you should give it back...oh my bad, she already left the building or you can just trash it. I don't know, I'll leave that up to you," she said as she was pointing her index finger towards my chest.

"You seem like a highly intelligent brother to me. Figure it out," and walked away again, switching that ass.

She needs some dick, that's why she's acting like that, my poor baby is having withdrawals. The power of this shit I got is immeasurable, literally and figuratively – smiling to myself. My skills had motherfuckers crashing parties and shit. This shit has to stop.

I walked towards my son who's was now trying to get inside the jumper full of kids with his fresh Gucci sneakers still on. *And nobody better not say anything to him about it either or I'm going to whip their parents ass*, laughing to myself. My little nigga can do what he wants on his birthday. Hell, anyday for that matter. It's his world, they're just existing in it. I see Sonia has everything in order, controlling as usual. So I stroll over to the table with my boys.

"Man, what was that all about with Monique showing up?" Boobie asked gravely.

"Nigga, I don't know the bitch is trying to get me killed crashing my baby's birthday party and shit!"

"That wasn't cool at all."

"Right," I said and told the homies, "Let's get the fuck outta' here while we still have a chance," laughing.

"You should have seen the look on Asia's face when Monique came in, she looked like she'd seen a ghost."

"Shit! She even had me scared for a minute," Boobie said.

"Yeah, that crazy bitch was talking about she's bringing V.J. a gift from his would-have-been brother or sister. She won't let that shit go. I think she needs some help and shit. She really popped up uninvited, I'm not going to be able to live this one down. Hell, the whole family might jump a nigga tonight," I said and the whole table laughed in unison.

"Goodluck nigga, don't call us for backup. You're on your own with this one homie, women are vicious."

"But peep game, she had the audacity to say she miss a nigga and shit. I almost slapped the shit out of her ass but I had to realize where I was at," I said.

"That's a disrespectful ass bitch, all at your son's party and shit." Boobie said.

"Damn nigga that's some stalker ass shit."

"Remember that broad from Miami that came to my house?" Dude said.

"Oh yeah, them broad's we met that weekend. How did that bitch find out where you lived?"

"She said some internet type shit. But that shit was scary. I wanted to pop that bitch right there for ringing my doorbell like she was crazy and I probably would have if one of my nosey ass neighbors wasn't outside watering their grass and shit. But I told that bitch if she ever step foot in Atlanta again, I could promise her a spot on a milk carton and slammed my fucking door in that hoe face." Dude said.

We all burst out laughing again, "Dude you a fool nigga. But you was cupcaking with the bitch all weekend long."

"Fuck that cupcake, pancake shit. I didn't give a fuck nigga. If Egypt would have been home, she would have killed the both of us, no need to try to explain shit. And I would have told on all you niggas too. Y'all was doing too much that weekend just like me. Hell Vance, you even flew a bitch down for the weekend."

"Ok nigga, let's change the subject y'all doing too much reminiscing and shit. Let me go check on my shortie and my wife," getting up to go.

"Alright, you scary ass nigga and ironically you're always the first one to be doing something out of pocket."

"Fuck you niggas," walking away laughing.

"Because he knows the truth. He always want's a nigga on a hype with him from state to state. You know how that fool is, and how he's always been. But he'll kill a nigga over Asia's fine ass in a minute"

Unbeknownst to me, all my boys were watching me kiss Asia on the forehead, "Yeah them two are made for each other, they're both crazy," Boobie says laughing, "what would they do without each other? Probably die," everyone laughed in agreeance.

"I'm just as tired as V.J. but I'm glad his party's over so we can rest," Asia said, looking at me while turning the music down.

"Yeah it really turned out nice but that lil' nigga fell asleep before we could even cut his cake or open his gifts," laughing.

"He wouldn't have been able to open all those gifts anyway Vance. It took us two trucks loads to bring all the stuff home. We'll open them all tomorrow. Just like Christmas all over again only it's two days after."

"Well you're the one who went shopping like crazy for him. I told you not to buy all that shit but no you wouldn't listen," Asia hissed, "'It's my shorties first Christmas, my living room is going to be filled to capacity with gifts just for him,' do you remember that?" she asked, looking at me suspiciously.

"So! You bought hella shit too Asia! And my momma, your momma, both our sisters and the whole family. I didn't think he would get that much this year for his birthday."

"Next year, let's not have a party. Let's just go somewhere," I suggest, yawning. We had finally settled down, during our drive home, from the festivities but I sensed that my work for tonight was far from over.

"Oh no, don't get tired on me now, the night is still young," Asia said seductively, rubbing my hand on her thigh.

"Stop! I'm tired," I said but I was really battling between my exhaustion and my libido.

"But I do want to make your body shake the paint off the walls," laughing.

"Ump, huh. That's why Adam got in trouble with Eve, the power of a woman Vance...the powers we have over you creatures of the opposite sex," laughing.

"So that means it's on tonight? V.J. is gone with his other mothers and it's just me and you kid. Let's have our own party tonight," I said seductively.

"We'll see Vance, I'm going to sleep right now, drive safely," laughing.

"Pull your pants off and let me massage it," reaching over to her lap.

"Hell-to-the-naw Vance, wait until we get home," Asia said, shooing my hands away.

"So that means 'yes'? If so, I'm running all the lights, stop signs and having a police chase if I have to, to get some pussy tonight," I say, pressing my foot on the gas.

"You so stupid, I'm taking a power nap," Asia rolled over and closed her eyes.

"You're going to need it baby," I said, turning the music up to keep my company during the drive back home.

The following morning my phone had so many missed calls and messages, no one could even get through. All of them were from Monique. *This has got to stop and I'm going to put a stop to it today.* I cleared all my messages and headed to my mom's to pick up V.J. but not before I made a detour to Monique's house. When I pull up, I see a few cars in front that I don't recognize so I grab my gat just in case. I opened the front door, I still had the keys, and heard voices in the kitchen, so I headed that way – dropping a glass of milk on the floor.

"Oh shit Vance! You scared me!" Monique said looking frighten. Her sister and girlfriend were in the kitchen too, that explained the cars. One of them proceed to clean up the mess I just made.

"Monique we need to talk right now," I started walking towards the living room with her right on my heels.

"What's up Vance, I thought you forgot where we lived," sarcastically speaking.

"Monique there is no *we* and please come out of the twilight zone with this make believe relationship. Why are you blowing up my damn phone all night and leaving all those messages. What's wrong with you, huh?"

"Vance, I love you and I know you still love me. I understand you have a son now but we still do care about each other, nothing changed."

This bitch is either slow or retarded, and she can take her pick but I don't have time for this shit, shaking my head, "Monique check this out – again, we had what we had, it's past tense, it's over and done with!"

"I'm engaged to be married and I have a son by my fiancé. You didn't get the memo?"

She started looking spaced out after I spoke my peace, like she just smoked some purple. She put her head down and walked back into the kitchen where her nosey ass guest awaited her return. I hope she got the message but just in case she didn't, I walked into the kitchen and handed her the house keys. Her ugly ass sister and friend was looking at me pitifully, shaking their heads.

"That's fucked up Vance. You're treating her like this after all these years? Now you're acting all brand new," snapping at me.

"Who the hell you talking to Pinky? Brand new, bitch do you even know the definition of brand new! Let me define it for you! Brand new is what you need on your motherfuckin' head 'cause that shit you rockin' look like a rug instead of a weave. And brand new would be a new whip to floss in instead of that old ass drop top Volkswagen that's outside. Well actually both of those cars outside are extinct and in desperate need of a tow yard. So both of you bitches sitting up here in this one million dollar home with a granite kitchen, black on black appliances, three bedrooms, three bathrooms, a pool, den, and flat screens everywhere that I paid for and you're talking about 'brand new', you need to shut the fuck up and fall back. I don't see no nigga givin' y'all bitches shit. No crib, no cars, nada. So get 'brand new' to that!"

All their mouths were wide open, I could have parked my benz inside them.

They couldn't believe I came at them like that. *Next time they'll mind their motherfuckin' business or they'll just have to get the business again.* With that all said and done, I was out. It wasn't the fat lady that sang but it was me who spoke nothing but facts at an octave they couldn't handle.

26

THE BIGGEST HIT - HAWAII

Vance Smith

For over a year I've been wrestling with this demon trying to get him off my back. I've had nightmares and woke up sweating profusely. I've plotted and even came close but nothing felt quite right. But the perfect opportunity presented itself and only I knew about it. With the exception of the few that I included in my scheme.

"Baby you almost ready, our plane leaves in three hours?"

"I'm almost done with V.J.'s carry-on bag, he needs his favorite movies and toys to keep him content."

She's never on time and she's using our son as the excuse this time around. If we miss this flight, it's all her fault as usual. My mom, sister, newborn niece, uncle and my partners are all on their way to the airport. We're all going to Hawaii for our annual getaway but low and behold, Ms. Asia is never ready. She knew weeks, even months ago about this trip. She started shopping in January and it's almost September. It's been exactly two years since I got shot but the memory is still fresh in my head. My son is now walking and talking with his bad ass. V.J. is one and a half now and looks exactly like his daddy. This boy is going to break plenty of hearts.

"Da' Da' we go bye-bye?" walking in our room, holding his pacifier in one hand and a toy in another. My mom won't let us throw it away. She says he'll get rid of it when he's ready. He looks like a mini me. We're dressed alike today in a cream colored shirt, Burberry plaid shorts, and brown Burberry sneakers for him and Stan Smith for me. He also wore his smaller version of my brown ATL fitted cap.

We even had matching diamonds earrings in our ear. I picked him up and kissed his chubby cheeks. He slaps my hat playfully, "Stop hitting me V.J.," I say jokingly.

"Fight fight, Daddy!" he retorts.

That's all this little nigga wants to do is fight, he had the blood of a warrior, it was ingrained in his genetics from many who came before him.

"You're momma better hurry up before she makes us miss our plane -"

"Shut up! We aren't going to miss shit," she said, smiling while she walked into the room. "You two are looking like identical twins," her face lit up anytime she saw us together.

"Hater!" I say, jokingly, "Your momma is a hatter V.J., she's just mad because she doesn't look as good as us," laughing.

She rolled her eyes, "Whatever Vance," and looked at me sideways like she's the one who's been ready and it's my fault that we're running late.

"Did you pack everything Asia because I don't want to hear no shit on the plane. It's not like we can turn the motherfucker around and fly back to get what you forgot. Just make sure you have all his movies, this is a long flight."

"I have all of his movies, toys, snacks, books, even a spare pacifier," Asia responded.

Shit his ass has more stuff than me, "unbelievable," I say under my breath, "Ok let's roll we're already late, shit everybody is waiting on us."

I put V.J. down and make my way to grab the bags. We already had most of our luggage shipped last week because somebody I know, I won't say no names, had more shit than the queen. So we had no choice but to have it shipped because we couldn't put all of that luggage on the plane. Plus, I own a condo over there so our luggages are waiting for us when we arrive.

I put V.J. in his car seat, Asia buckles up and off we go - the alibi in tact as soon as we touchdown.

The flight was long as hell but smooth, as smooth as any type of transportation system that allows you to coast along the lines of this earth, riding gently between the intersection of humanity and the greater universe. V.J. slept most of the way, which I figured he would since he cocked blocked all night. He had us up watching cartoons until the sun made its way to our front door. While on the plane, I watched my version of cartoons but I wouldn't say this were for kids or the weak minded. First up was my favorite movie of all time, Scarface - the portrayal of the ultimate hustler. I followed up with the movie Belly and tried to fall asleep halfway through watching Denzel on Training Day. These three movies were top tier in my book, and in that order. Fuck all the academy award ass shit, those movies aren't what real men are made of. *I need some shit that's gangta' with little twist.*

I look over to my future wife, the woman I spend every day with, yet we still hadn't set a date to our wedding. You know how black folks are - if it ain't broke, don't fix it. Deep into her slumber, she rested while looking like a million bucks, my money draped her in the finest attire. They address her by 'Ms. Smith' in the Gucci store when we walk in, not to mention all the boutiques that we frequent as well, where the treatment is comparative. And Nieman Marcus calls her personally and emails her when new shipments come in. I told her she's going to have to start working at one of my spots by the way she spends money. She cashes out on things like she's the one making the money and shit. She told me she works on her knees every chance she gets and pushed out a big head son, that's all the work she needed to do - compensation for life. She thinks she's the Elizabeth Taylor of this era but that's my woman and I love that woman, I would die for that woman, I would give my all for that woman. I don't know why I complain about her, I just do.

I get up and walk towards the back to go to the restroom, I hit Boobie on the head along the way. Lisa was knocked out too.

"What you watching?" I ask him.

"It was watching me actually," he said, yawning, "but it's reruns of Martin, that nigga is hilarious."

I shake my head in agreeance, walking away. When I finish in the restroom, I sit and chop it up with my mom for a minute. She seemed to be one of the few who weren't drifting with wind of their dreams.

"Did y'all remember to bring V.J. pacifier?" she asks.

"Yes Mother we did, Asia even has a spare just in case and we also brought his boxing game so we can play. That's why that bad ass nigga likes to fight now, playing boxing games and shit like he's training to be a heavyweight," laughing.

"Hate all you want Vance, my grandson is going to know how to protect himself from these knuckle heads out in these streets," my mom said, tightening her lips.

"Mama, it's ok. Calm down and yes he's going to know how to protect himself. Did you forget whose son he is?"

She rolled her eyes, "Vance please, you better gone with that rubbish, now move so I can take me a nap before we land," her hands waved up and down in the 'move along' motion.

I go back to my seat only to witness that my family was still sleeping, V.J. was in the middle as usual in his carseat and Asia head was resting on it. *This is what it's all about.* Life isn't complete unless you share it with the ones you love. It's cool being single but I wouldn't trade them in for all the money in the world. I prefer the family life any day. I wish Asia would have another baby, expand the nest. *Shit, I might work on that while were here on vacation.*

"Vance you're tired, go to sleep," I say, rambling to myself. I close my eyes and sleep the rest of the plane ride until we land.

We had cars waiting for us when we touched down, Asia and I headed to our condo. My mom, V.J., Vantrice and Vashaun, my niece, jumped in their cars as well and in their respective directions.

My uncle and his wife went to my dad's condo. My dad, Boobie and I collectively bought them all at the same time when we came down here for business and I'm glad that we did because the market in Hawaii has skyrocketed since we purchased ours. We all lived in the same building but on different floors. We settled in and got situated before showering and getting dressed to meet up at the Luau that we scheduled for the family. The night was perfect and we were having a ball - eating, drinking, partying and reminiscing about my dad. I sure did miss him, especially at a time like this. He would have loved V.J., his first grandson. The manifestation of the third generation of men, V.J. reminded me a lot of my father with some of the expressions he made.

V.J. bounced up and down as he danced with one of the Hawaiian women, we all started laughing. I could feel the stillness of the wooden log beneath, the fire that blazed in front of us keeping my skin comforted by warmth as I watched my son mimic the culture of the South Pacific islanders, moving his hips from side to side in a rhythmic attempt. Of course my mom was videotaping the entire performance and Asia flashed her digital camera under the night sky to capture the moment as well. I felt proud at this moment but guilt subtly crept in because I knew what was about to transpire. My happiness was being replaced with anger, this anger I had no control over. Just looking at my son and to think a nigga tried to take me away from him, from ever being apart of his life, invigorated my soul. He slept on my chest when he was born, I even cut his umbilical cord, I was there for his first smile, memories where he peed on me while I changed his diaper and he wet up my shirt to the point where Asia and I laughed hysterically. His first birthday, first tooth, first haircut and first words.

He said 'Da-Da' before 'Mama', hurting Asia' feelings. He was my son, my seed, my shortie, my mini-me, Vance Smith III. I knew I had to do what I had to do to make sure that person would never interfere with anything else pertaining to my son, my life, and my family again. Some things were inevitable and this was one of them.

I looked around at my family, my friends, my future and I saw happiness for many years to come but at this moment in my life, something or someone could change all of that and it wasn't the creator. No, God had no part of this that had been done and that had to be done. My only assurance was to repent and ask for forgiveness later on in my life. The God I grew up with was a God of second chances but with me it took a few more times but he understood the makings of a man. He understood me, he created me and understood my struggles and he knew I had to protect my family.

I brought my mind back to the present moment and continued in the festivities. We were enjoying ourselves until the wee hours of the morning. My mom, Vantrice and the kids headed back to the room for bed and the rest of us stayed out, the night was still young. We were on vacation, that's what you did while vacationing. I had a plane to catch at sunrise but I didn't care if I didn't even sleep a wink tonight. I would still make my plane and still get the job done beauce this is what I do.

Before showering, I kissed Asia again before leaving out. She was knocked out cold, too many island drinks had consumed her. When she wakes up, I'll be in another state physically and mentally handling business as usual. My driver takes us to a private jet that I hired, waiting to take us to Las Vegas, Nevada. Boobie and I board the plane and lay our heads back from the exhaustion that carried over from last night's events.

When we wake up, we'll be in Vegas, all arrangements had been made - people were in place, our ride to and from where we needed to go and return, we'll be back in Honolulu like we never left. I looked at my Rolex and said, "ten hours, plenty of time to relax." I fell asleep shortly after and Boobie did the same.

"Las Vegas, what happens in Vegas, stays in Vegas," that's what we said getting off the plane.

"Damn it's hot!" I said, using my hand to block the raze of the sun.

"Nigga it's about 108 degrees and it's only 2pm!" Boobie replied, "that's why I couldn't live in this hot ass state plus it's too much going on here." I had to agree, too damn hot and muggy for me. I only enjoyed Vegas at night, I couldn't tolerate the day life.

My people were waiting for us as expected. We talked, went over business and headed to have some drinks. It was shortly after 6pm and we had to be back to our jet by 9:30pm in order to be back on the island first thing in the morning. A couple reserved the chartered plane directly after our mission and my folks had everything taken care of for me up to the very last details. After we arrived, as planned, all I had to do was show up for the surprise party. No one but me would go inside, this had to be done solo. Then when I came out they would come inside because there were just some things a man would had to do on his own, self gratification.

Riding on the elevator of one of these plush condos, I considered looking into buying one, I didn't have any property in Vegas and the blueprints of these homes were phenomenal. The amount of square footage for the price and the accommodations you couldn't beat. For a cool one million, I think they were worth every dime.

We all rode in silence, why? I don't know? I guess surprises gave everybody a little anxiety. The elevator doors opened and we walked to the penthouse.

"Well, I'll be damn a penthouse. He really went all out," I almost cracked a smile. He is going to be so surprised, I opened the door and counted on three fingers, 'one', 'two', 'three' - and quietly walked inside. The living room was dark with just a bit of light coming through the balcony window. And the window was open, I suppose for fresh air and it smelled good in here like French vanilla. *They must have some flavored candles burning.* I walk past one room, the lights were off and it was empty. I hear voices coming from another room in the back, I gently walk towards the voices, my feet floating like clouds placing one foot in front of the other. My heart was beating like it wanted to escape but couldn't find an opening. Panicking, I take a deep breath without exhaling and before I realize it, I'm standing in the doorway watching two individuals conversing with their backs turned towards the wall, *perfect.*

I politely say, "surprise!"

They both turn to look at me, "Vance, what are you doing here?"

I looked at her, wanting to answer but no words would come

out, not at that moment anyway. I quickly turn back to him with a smirk on my face, immediately my voice box started working.

"Surprised to see me nigga?" I ask rhetorically.

"Thought a nigga was dead huh? Nigga you should know I'm a cat with nine lives, a pussycat nigga, an alleycat type of dude and if you want something done, you have to do it yourself! That way you know it's done right you bitch-ass-nigga!."

He opened his mouth to say something but my bullet silenced him. All I heard was India screaming and hollering with no prevail, screaming my name. I put my lips to hers and slipped my tongue her mouth. Why? I don't know? But that was the first thing that came to my mind. I didn't want her screaming and take the chance of someone hearing her, especially because she was clearly screaming my name which was a death sentence. My adrenaline took over and my tongue maneuvered through her mouth, I held on to her for dear life, kissing her. She reciprocated the gesture. She grabbed hold of my neck and started crying, she wouldn't let go. I laid her down and continued to kiss her, our tongues were doing dances together until they became one. She had a towel wrapped around her like she had just gotten out of the shower. The French vanilla aroma was coming from the folds of her melanin, breathing off her body. I caressed her breast and then kissed them.

I wasn't myself in this moment, I don't know who I was - a monster who just killed another monster with no remorse - not Vance, not a father, not a man in love with his fiancée's twin sister.

India and Asia were identical twin sisters who shared everything and now they shared me...I entered India gently, she was tight but soaking wet, I took my time and went real slow. I kissed her mouth, she kissed me back. She was still crying as we moved in unison and that shit was lovely, we weren't fucking, we were making love. I did love her, she was my woman's twin sister. She did love me, I was her big brother. What we were doing was so wrong but it felt so right. I had an image of their mother, and then Asia, then India would appear - a threesome without the three being present. These were sacred jewels like black diamonds, a rarity. I don't know what kind of voodoo they possessed but they had a hold on me, all three of them. I couldn't stop if I wanted to. We made love and came together, it was beautiful, just like the faces of all of them.

I kissed her mouth and told her, "I love you."

She replied, "I love you too."

She opened her eyes, still crying but only small tears now. I got up to get dressed and told her to do the same. It felt like eternity had passed us, my mind was still not quite right but I knew we had to leave in a hurry. This nigga had a safe here, I knew because India told Asia everything about Milo, all the places they visited while doing their thing with the banks. Everywhere that nigga laid his head, every move he made, I knew without him even knowing that I was hot on his tracks.

India helped me delete Milo's existence without even knowing it. Over the past year, I had known Milo's ins and outs, I even knew when the nigga shitted and scratched his ass, and how many breaths he took when he slept. That's how close I was to him without him even knowing. Like a fly on the wall, I just had to wait for the right moment and the right time to put things in motion. If everything wasn't done correctly, it could have cost me everything. Patience is a virtue and I learned the meaning of that tonight. Everything happens when it's supposed to, not before nor after.

Milo was opening the safe on the wall when I interrupted with the surprise party, which saved me the trouble of trying to get into it later. I grabbed the stacks of money and put them in my bag. *I thought that nigga only kept a few thousand on him at a time but this stupid ass nigga had two million in cash.* The money was right there in my face but I didn't want any of it nor did I need it, but the money would go to a good cause nonetheless. With all the suffering he made my family go through, this monetary contribution will be invested in the Negro college fund for a community of underprivileged kids that didn't have hope or faith that they would go to college and also those who didn't have father. Which is exactly how he tried to do my son, navigating the earth as a fatherless child.

This money would stop India from continuing her career in identity theft and risking her freedom for this sucka' ass nigga. This money would help several causes, all in the name of respect. If you respect the game, it will respect you back. Death before dishonor was the code. But he didn't respect that, he lived and died by his own rules.

India got dressed, holding her bag, and ready to leave this madness behind her - leaving yet another lover dead and her heart broken. *I'll do my best to soothe her pain and undo her hurt.* But I was hurting also, my soul had done some unspeakable things that were morally wrong but I was a man, a strong man with weak flesh. We would all get over this sooner or later but now wasn't the time to reflect on this or any other matter, now was time for closure.

As I walked out the door holding India's hand, my boys went in behind us to clean up the mess. India, Boobie and I headed back to the airport with only thirty minutes until take off. I left a token of my appreciation for my peoples back in the condo, a hefty one at that. I didn't count it but estimated it to be about a million strong.

It pays to be a boss, I was the nigga you love to hate. The nigga by any means necessary, the nigga that would be heading back to the islands to enjoy family and friends once again. We couldn't wait to leave this nightmare behind us.

India laid on my chest and quietly wept as I held her, not as a lover but as her brother consoling her until she fell asleep. Boobie and I chopped it up, we couldn't wait to get back and get our partying on. Hawaii was such a beautiful place to me, I took pleasure in the beautiful things in life.

27

WE'RE BACK

Vance Smith

Once we got back on the island, it was like we never left. I booked India a beachfront suite, overlooking the water, to help soothe her mind. Tranquility and relaxation is what she needed for a speedy recovery. We returned over twenty four hours ago and she still hadn't left her room.

"Baby you're back, did you take care of business?"

"Hey baby, what's good? Give daddy a kiss," she kissed me with a twirl of the tongue.

"I missed you baby, I'm glad everything is Ok. Where is my sister at? Why did you bring her here?"

"It's too much going on here Asia, my mom and the kids, she needs her rest. Plus there's no privacy, she's tired because we've been flying all night. What did you do while Daddy was gone?" getting undressed, heading for the shower.

"What we always do, party and shop! Shit what else is there to do on a beautiful island besides fuck and you weren't here —"

"Well I'm here now, want to join me in the shower," I asked with a devilish smile?

"Nope, I'm going to the bar and after I'm going to check on my sister. She's at the beachfront, right?"

"Right. I'm going to bed Asia after I shower, I'm tired," running the water and checking the temperature before stepping in. "I'll see you when you get back," my voice echoed through the shower chamber into the suite.

"Well it's going to be late because Vantrice and I are going clubbing tonight. I won't check on India until the morning —"

"Why Asia? That's your damn sister!" yelling from the bathroom with the shower door propped open.

"I know who she is but I'm not ready to see her *like that* again. Remember...this is the second time she's lost an intimate friend Vance," India stopped for a moment of silence, as if she was taking it all in herself.

"Plus she's probably not ready to talk about it. You said she was in shock, right?"

"Not actually in shock Asia but damn that's your sister, she needs you!" solemnly speaking.

"She's your sister too, so you go check on her. I'm not ready! You know how emotional I get!"

"I just told your stupid ass I'm tired, didn't I?" I ask, peaking my head further out the shower, trying to get a glimpse.

"Vance please just make sure she's resting tonight. I'll see her in the morning. I'm about to go before you upset me more than I already am. This shit is a lot to bear," walking out the bathroom, through the bedroom and out the front door, slamming it.

"Bitch!" I finish showering and put on a wife beater, shorts and sandals. My hair was still damp from washing it, so I put on a cap.

Staring in the mirror, "Not bad looking," I say, speaking to myself, "but nigga you look tired" I uttered, giving myself a deep, reflective look in the eyes as the mirror glanced back at me. After taking a deep breath, walking out the door, and riding the elevator down, I couldn't stop yawning. *Damn a nigga is really tired. I'm going to shoot over to check on India and come right back to go to bed.*

"Selfish ass sister of hers," I whispered under my breath.

Walking to the beach felt good. Hawaii's night air was perfect, I took my sandals off and carried them in my hand. I looked up at India's beachfront room only to see that one light was on. *Shit, she's probably fucking sleep, I'll just make sure she's comfortable then call it a night.* When I get to her door, I take out the spare key and insert it into the keyhole.

I heard her music playing as I got closer, it sounded like Jazz - *I didn't know India like jazz music, umph you learn something new every day.* I open the door, there was no light to welcome me but I heard the shower running.

"India!" I yell out, no answer. I walk to the bedroom, only candles were lit, no artificial lights were on.

"India you ok?" I say walking towards the bathroom, the door was open. I can hear her in the shower crying, "India it's me, Vance, you ok?" I ask again, walking towards the shower because she's not answering me. The steam against the glass obstructed the view of her silhouette with fog and clouds dancing against the shower. I lightly tap on the glass shower doors, she opens the door and she's standing there, crying, and naked with her hair wet looking like an angel with tears covering her breasts. I'm frozen and can't move, *damn she's beautiful.* All my tiredness faded, she reached out and touched my face without saying a word.

I put my hands on hers, "You ok India? You didn't answer when I called your name. Why all the tears baby? You happy to see me?" I asked, trying to cheer her up but I knew she wasn't in the mood for humor. She stepped out the shower without turning it off and took my hand and led me to the bedroom. I kept telling myself, *don't do it Vance, she's vulnerable right now, she's not in her right frame of mind.* But my body had a mind of its own. She laid down on the bed and spread her legs, she stuck one finger inside herself and at that point, I was gone! The shit had me gone!

She looked so good playing with herself and crying. The shower running in the background had an aphrodisiac effect on me and the next thing I knew, I was naked as the day I was born and she had my dick in her mouth, and I died and went to heaven. But what we were doing was so damn wrong, we had two free passes, don't pass go – we were going straight to hell, doors will be open, can't wait to see you there.

I just killed a motherfucker less than twenty four hours ago, fucked my sister-in-law and now I'm about to fuck her again. And I didn't have a care in the world at this moment, the shit felt too good to care about anything. It was like a good dose of morphine when you need to alleviate the pain. Losing control, I grabbed her wet, curly hair to remove her from my dick because I was about to cum, but she wouldn't let go. So I gave her what she wanted, a welcome gift from the island's that slid right down her throat - my erupting volcano. My legs felt like rubber and I couldn't move like my body was having a stroke.

She released me, kissed my lips and sensually rubbed my natural, wavy hair. After moments of kissing and caressing, she brought me back to life, my woodie had grown again like Pinocchio was being interrogated for a guilty crime. She pushed me back on the bed and climbed on top. When she came down, I felt a tear in my eye. I don't even know where that shit came from but that's how good it felt, it was one of the good cries.

She rode me nice and slow, going to the top and sliding down like a stripper dancing on a pole in slow motion. The shit had me mesmerized - she had her eyes open the whole time but she wasn't looking at me, she was looking through me. I've never came twice simultaneously until tonight. It paralyzed me, she came so hard it felt like I opened a new hole inside her and it just kept pouring out. It felt so good, I didn't even feel bad about the encounter.

I'm seriously fucked up and need some serious counseling for this shit. But if I told the therapist my story, he or she would surely lock me up for being insane. There's no way three women could have you pussy-whipped beyond your control. To add insult to injury, these three women composed of a mother and her two twin daughters. My only explanation to this madness would be voodoo, which means, I'm starting to believe that I'm really going crazy. *I wonder if anyone else has experienced this type of shit. Why me? Why am I the lucky one?*

All of these thoughts were going through my mind while I was holding the twin sister of my fiancé, my son's mother, and for some reason I wasn't able to let her go, not wanting to let her go. I wanted to make love to her again and again. *Damn, I can see how my pops could die over this pussy. It's suicidal, detrimental to one's health. When it's my turn to go, this is how I want it to be, inside one of these women that I love to death.*

The next morning, I slid from under India as smooth as the sunrise, pulled the covers over her naked body and went to release myself in the bathroom. After finishing, I got in the shower which was still running from last night and to my surprise the shit was nice and hot, *damn.* I got dressed, kissed her on the forehead and walked out the room.

"Vance?"

"Huh?" I turn around, "I didn't know you were woke India?"

"Thank you for everything. Tell Asia to come by later, I feel a lot better," sitting up in bed.

"I will India, get your rest. We'll check on you a little later," and with that, I was out and left with my thoughts on my trek back to my condo, *this shit is ludicrous.* Once inside, Asia was sleep but woke up when I got in the bed.

"What time is it?" she asks.

"It's 6:30 in the morning," I responded.

"You stayed with India? That was nice," looking over at me.

"Yeah, she wasn't doing that well but now she's feeling better."

Asia grabbed both sides of my face, paralleling her lips in front of mine for an exchange, kissing me passionately before she said, "That's why I love you, you're always there when I need you. Thank you for taking care of my sister."

You just don't know how good I took care of her, kissing her back, "I'll always be there for y'all, always baby," holding her tight, not feeling one ounce of guilt. Rationalizing my actions, in my mind they were like one person but still different two people and I loved them both, as twistedly and chaotic as it seemed. I couldn't love one without the other and I love their mom for giving me both of them and giving me herself that night. Without her, there was no them. God works in mysterious ways.

After our greeting, we drifted back off to sleep, this time I was with the twin whom I have a family with. I was sound asleep until V.J. came running in three hours later. I looked at him and prayed as I pulled him up that he would never have to go through that, being emotionally attached to three beautiful women at the same time. I don't know if his poor heart could take it because mine barely did, they had taken my breath away.

The trip was almost over, we only had one more night on the big island and I was happy. I was ready to go home and climb into my own bed. We partied nonstop like the world was about to end soon. Over the course of our stay, my niggas and I took a few Hawaiian chicks down, drunk way too much and spent way too much money. It was 'hush money' used in the best way. India and Asia shopped like their lives depended on it, at my expense. I even ran out of money and ordered my accountant wire me more. Milo's contributions were sent off and donated to various schools in the hood and a few charities like - 'Stop the Violence' and 'Guns Off the Street'. We didn't want the next generation to grow up with that grief. And when I asked Asia if she brought any money for the trip, I wasn't surprised when she told me she left her bank cards at home as usual. The whole tribe met at Benihanas for our last night to celebrate our departure.

"India are you coming back to Atlanta or going home tomorrow?" Lisa asked.

"I'm probably going to Miami for Milo's funeral in two days. I want to at least pay my respects."

"India do you want Boobie and I to go with you? You shouldn't be alone," looking at Asia for approval.

"That would be nice Vance, you sure you want to go? I mean y'all weren't associates or anything," India glanced at Asia too, following my initial stare.

"No India he's right, someone should go with you. I would but V.J. has a doctor's appointment and Sonia didn't you say that you had an appointment the same day?"

"Yes, I have to get a mammogram or else I would take him," Sonia said.

"No, it's good. Boobie will you roll with me to Miami?"

"I got you dog, it's good. I'll rest tomorrow, we can fly out the following day. Baby is that cool?" Boobie asked Lisa.

"Yes of course, she can't go by herself under these circumstances. I'll even go for support if you like India."

"Thanks Lisa, the more the merrier."

We ordered our drinks and dinner and it was settled. We were going to Milo's homecoming, the homecoming that I made possible, *R.I.P. nigga,* I laughed to myself at the thought.

28

WHILE LOCKED UP THEY WON'T LET ME OUT

India Smith

––––––––––––––––––––––––––––––––––––

After all the reminiscing that I've done, I snapped back to reality once I heard, "Ms. Smith, there's a package on your bed and it's very confidential," winking his eye. The deputy monitored my next movements as I returned to my cell, coming from the shower only to be welcomed by an empty set of four cold iron walls.

"What the hell is this big black gorilla lookin' nigga talking about," I said to myself, starring at the mystery mail. *I hope he didn't leave a box of love notes because that just isn't cool.* When I get back to my room, I don't see a package, *what the fuck was he talking about? Maybe I'm getting a new roommate since the other one moved, whatever.*

I started putting my toiletry supplies away, to get ready for bed. I always took a late shower to help me sleep better. When I got into my bunk, I felt something under my pillow. I didn't want to take it out now and risk someone seeing me so I decided to wait until lights out. As soon as the deputies did their last count and turned the lights off, I removed the package from under the pillow like a thief in the night. It was a cell phone, *well I'll be damn.* I knew some girls in here had phones but I guess the word gets around. You had to pay the deputy a grand to sneak one in. But I hadn't spoken to anyone about me getting one, but obviously someone else did. The phone was set to vibrate and it came with two ear pieces like headphones so I could talk while I was in bed and the police would just think it was my iPod.

Once I turned on the phone, I noticed I already had one missed call and it was from my sister. I laughed to myself, *I should have known she was behind this stunt. But how? Well, I'll find out soon enough won't I?* I put the covers over my face to the point where anyone walking by could only see my hair, and with this disguise, I called Asia back.

"What took you so long to call back India?"

"That's the greeting I get? Not the 'I miss you, I love you,' and that good stuff?" I asked.

"You know all that, but I do miss you though..."

"I miss your crazy butt too Asia. How did you manage this?"

Asia releases a brief sinister giggle, "Vance knows someone who knows someone and you know how that goes —"

"Hey baby sis, keep your head up!" I heard Vance yell in the background.

"Let me speak to him so I can thank him."

Vance deep baritone voice was followed by a few scuffling sounds, "Hey sis, how they treating you?"

"So far, so good. Thank you so much Vance for the kind gift. I really do appreciate it."

"No problem, anything for you. I tried to give your parents the bread to get you out but they declined. They're putting up their property."

"I know and that takes a minute, especially with the amount of the bail."

"Have patience, you'll be home in no time and we'll go celebrate," laughing.

"Where's V.J. at? I miss him so much."

"His bad ass is at his granny's house, probably tearing shit up. That lil' boy is hella bad!"

"Well Vance, considering his parents..." I said while trying to manage the perfect medium of speaking auditability yet quietly.

"I know sis, his mom is crazy huh?" he laughed, "you ain't had no problems with them females in there have you?" changing the subject.

"No, they're cool just nosey. Everybody wants to know what I'm in here for. I just say, 'mistaken identity', wasn't me," laughing.

"You a fool for that one. Hold on sis, your sister is looking at me sideways. I love you."

"I love you too brother."

"Damn move, move Vance I'm serious," Asia said followed by more scuffling sounds, "Hello, hello India?"

"Yes."

"You alright?"

"I'm good Asia, it's not as bad as I thought it would be. The food is even alright. We had steaks the other night."

"Forreal?" sounding shocked.

"Yeah it was small and wasn't filet mignon but it was still steak."

"I heard the county jail food is horrible."

"Yea that's what they say but the feds give out more time, that's why it's better I suppose. Plus they have more money to play with."

"Asking for a five million dollar bail is ludicrous," Asia said, I could feel her shaking her head through the phone.

"Yes, I agree. How long has V.J. been at Vance's mom

house?"

"That bad ass kid won't leave her house. Every time I pick him up, he cries and throws a fit! So I kiss him and say goodbye. His granny has him spoiled rotten and it doesn't help that she's a big-ol' kid herself," laughing.

"Don't start Asia!"

"Ok ok, but she remodeled her backyard for him and he loves it. Vance sister said she don't do shit for her baby. Which isn't fair, but she does show favoritism and Vantrice knows that V.J. is her favorite." Asia says.

"That's not ok Asia. Has mommie and daddy seen him lately?"

"No! When I come down next week, I'm bringing him, hollering and all," laughing. "You sure you don't need anything India?" she asked concerned, her tone changed like the seasons.

"No, I'm straight thanks. I have money for commissary and mom sent me some Triple Crown books," adjusting my body weight in the bed, it was starting to get too hot under here.

"Oh you straight then but those books are going to make your ass horny," laughing, "they puts it down in those books and I love them."

"Yeah me too Asia. That's why I had mommie send me some."

"Well India, keep the phone on vibrate all the time and if you get a missed call, call me back when you can."

"I will...thanks again Asia, I love you."

"I love you more, that's what big sisters are for. Also I spoke to your attorney, we have it all figured out how this is going to go down. Did he run it by you yet?" my sister asked.

"No, he's coming tomorrow."

"Well good, I'll let him explain it, but don't trip we got you."

"I love you Asia."

"I love you too and don't worry about anything, Mom is

getting you out as soon as the ink dries on the dotted lines."

"I know."

"Be safe please."

"Always. I wouldn't do anything to jeopardize me from coming home. Plus, I have a security guard watching me 24/7," laughing, hinting towards something we both knew. Vance was behind Mr. Protect and Serve, "but it's good because I can sleep better at night knowing that."

"I'll call you back tomorrow. Hugs and kisses."

"Same here, goodnight Asia. Thanks again," after hanging up the phone, I released the vault and stuck my head out the covers, the coast was clear and I could now breathe some much needed fresh air.

I talked to my sister every day, sometimes two times a day until I got bailed out. I even had a chance to talk to my nephew, he's so cute. He said, 'I'm coming to see you Auntie.' He's talking so clear now, I could understand him without any remnants of a 'baby talk' dialect. I couldn't wait to see him and that day came exactly one month after my arrest. My bail was posted and I was free to go home. 'Thank you Lord' is what I prayed while leaving the federal building in Dublin, Ca. I didn't look back because I knew I would never step foot in that place again, hopefully.

29

TESTIMONIES

India Smith

    While sitting in court, during several testimonies from the prosecutor's 'witnesses', I would write notes to my attorney. He told me to never have an outburst and just write everything down, so I did. I would write 'bitch quit lying' and hold it up for them to see and quickly put it back down. I had a whole folder of shit and when needed, I would pull them out. My attorney just shook his head. He would write notes to me occasionally, asking me to clarify what a witness said and I would always reply with one of my little love notes. At first he didn't quite get it but eventually he caught on. My notes consisted of:

        1. *"BITCH STOP LYING"*
        2. *"DIE BITCH"*
        3. *"YOU MAD BECAUSE I WOULDN'T FUCK WITH YOU"*
        4. *"HATER"*
        5. *"LAUGH NOW CRY LATER"*

    Once, a witness snitched to the judge, "She just called me a bitch," pointing at me. I started playing with my nails like I wasn't even paying attention, like what's all the fuss about?

    The judge said, "Don't look in her direction, stay focused on the questions please."

I played the game for two whole weeks until it started to bore me. They were still testifying against my ass no matter what. Some of these people really wanted me to go down in the history books. They were lying on me like some Christopher Columbus discovered America type shit. And now here I was, in the 'United States of Lies', facing lying witnesses, on this stolen land for stolen identities, and I'm the criminal here? I think not but this was incredible. And I just I remembered that my ex-is supposed to testify the next day.

Why? I don't know? His dumb ass didn't know shit about nothing. All he knew was that I had my own spot, car, and money in the bank. I was a college student at the time so my parents took care of me. The prosecutor asked him all this bull shit that didn't mean anything:

Q: "So Mr. Sean Hilton, how long did you date Ms. Smith?"

A: "For about six months." He was lying, it was only two.

Q: "And how did you two meet?"

A: "At school, Stanford University."

Q: "What was your major?"

A: "Business administration." Pinocchio's nose inched a bit longer, he was on a football school with an undeclared major.

Q: "And tell us here in the courtroom why you believe Ms. Smith committed identity theft while she was dating you?"

A: "Because my license came up missing and someone got a ticket in my name and tried to use my credit but I didn't have any at the time." The last lie put me over the edge and instead of writing a note I vented mentally, *you're such a liar. I can't wait to bust your ass out nigga.*

"No more questions your honor," the prosecutor retreated to her desk in the courtroom, and up next was my well paid defense attorney to continue with the witness.

Q: "Sean Hilton, that's an interesting name. Do you have any relations to the Hilton family son?"

A: "No sir."

Q: "I see, so you dated my client for six months, is that right young man?"

A: "Yes, about that."

Q: "Is that 'yes' to six months or is it about six months, maybe two-three months, four-five months, which one is it?"

A: "I'm not really sure, I think six or five maybe four months."

Q: "You're not sure Mr. Hilton, is that correct?"

A: "Yes."

Q: "Ok, did you ever meet her family, sister, brother, parents or anyone while dating?"

A: "No."

Q: "And someone stole your driver's license?"

A: "Yes."

Q: "Now make sure you think before answering son, ok?"

A: "Ok."

Q: "How do you think Ms. Smith could have gotten a ticket or credit or anything else in your name, aren't you a man?"

A: "I am a man!" He yells and gets a sharp stare from his attorney after he told him to calm down.

Q: "Mr. Hilton what I'm saying is my client is a female, there is a difference. Only a blind cop or crazy person would mistake Ms. Smith to be a man in order to get a ticket in your name and I wouldn't think a cop that blind would be on a highway by himself writing tickets. Do you get my point?"

A: "Yes."

"Also, she doesn't really sound like a man. We'll hear her rebuttal momentarily and we'll let the jury decide for themselves. No more questions your honor," he said, while shaking his head at Sean's stupid ass. When my attorney asked me why he was testifying in court - I told the jurors the only reason that I could think of, he was a big fat liar which was one of the real reasons we broke up.

"And it wasn't no six months like he stated on the stand, it was only two. It didn't take me that long to realize he wasn't shit. He lied when told me he was a part of the Hilton family and he was biracial, half white. He lied when he said he came from money but he never had any. I later found out that his mom was on section 8, living in a three bedroom apartment with six kids, all with different fathers. And he didn't even know his dad. She named him Sean Hilton so he could make it through school with people thinking he was important. His brother name is Mikeal Jordan and I know for damn sure that he's not a junior and his momma had to audacity to spell the name incorrectly, it's pronounced 'Mi-Kel'. But it was his sister that took home the cake, she was named Loreatha Franklin, apparently named after her grandmother Aretha, or something. His mother was crazy and so was he, the apple didn't fall far from the tree." The court room started laughing.

"Order in the court!" The judge said.

Q: "Is that why you two love birds broke up Ms. Smith? Because you thought he was crazy?"

A: "No, excuse me for a moment Daddy," looking over at my parents sitting tense as can be, "the truth is I didn't like him because he had a small penis like the size of my pinkie finger and he didn't know how to give head."

Q: "Ok Ms. Smith, what's your point?"

A: "And he sure in the hell didn't have any money either. So I started dating his roommate who happens to be an NFL player now but they were both on the football team scholarship and I would spend the night in their dorm, me and his roommate would have sex like our lives depended on it, all night. So I guess he got mad and he swore to get revenge some how and I guess this is how he thought he was going to do it…"

Sean was hotter than fish grease. He was so mad that he walked out the courtroom wearing shame at sleeve and didn't look back only to avoid the eyes of whom had witness his embarrassing demise. The song *'Look back at it'* popped into my head while stepping down going back to my seat, *'Look back at you for what? I'm trying to concentrate on bussing me a nut'. The next time I see that lil' dick as nigga he better not speak.* I laughed to myself, that's the perfect song for him. There are just songs for certain people and that was definitely the song for him, hands down. I pray no more of my exes show up in court trying to testify against me because my father would surely have a heart attack and I would be charged with murder. For my plea, I would plead insanity.

But my mom was a different story, women were the backbone of the human race and in my race of freedom mom inevitable played her part. We have to stick together and her way of comforting me was smiling at everything, giving me that glimmer of peace and hope throughout the trial.

30

CLOSING ARGUMENTS

India Smith

While sitting in court sandwiched by my two attorneys, I noticed how eager the D.A. was ready to wrap things up. She kept smiling at me, looking over at our table like she had this thing in the bag. I was a little nervous but kept my faith that the truth would prevail. My palms were getting sweaty and I kept looking over my shoulder at my two beautiful parents who were always sitting in the front pew, along with hundreds of spectators and haters waiting for my verdict to be guilty. Only my attorneys and I knew we had a surprise witness, but I didn't see them and it was almost two. *Maybe it was traffic or something,* now I was starting to get worried. As the prosecutors took their time with the closing arguments.

"Ladies and gentleman of the jurors, this day has finally come to make that important decision that will impact not one but all victims in this case, which are a several hundred and I'm sure there's more out there I don't know about but this verdict will affect our communities and other communities, cities and states everywhere. This case has national attention and it should have because it has brought thousands, maybe millions of Americans to realize how severe identity theft has become. It doesn't just affect the person whose identity was taken but if affects all of us as a whole community. We have to stick together and come to a resolution to end this from happening to any of us in the near future."

"You! You! And You!" pointing to the jurors like a parent talking to a child that did something wrong, "if this woman is not found guilty on all charges she will, and I repeat, she will go out and commit these very same crimes again but this time it might be you or your spouse or sister or brother or even your parents. Can you imagine what your parents would have to go through it that happens to them? Credit ruined! For all those years it took them to establish good credit, substantial amount of bills that they didn't acquire, life savings gone down the drain after working thirty five years to save it, retirement money gone and for what? I'll tell you for what, expensive shopping sprees to Gucci, Louis Vuitton, Prada, Versace, and all the rich and famous stores on your account. Thank you 'such and such' and thank you 'such and such' and the list goes on and on. I don't know why when she was doing all of this shopping and shit - oh excuse my language, she didn't pick up thank you cards and mail them out to each person who actually bought her that bull shit -"

Banging his gavel like a drummer, the judge quickly interjected, "That's enough with the language counselor. Did she steal your identity ma'am?" the court fell out in laughter but me. This lady is crazy, but she was good and she almost sold me.

She finished up with jurors, "We have shown you tons and tons of evidence, literally, against this person - receipts from every store, airline tickets, gas receipts, a few fake credit cards and fake I.D.'s she used to obtain goods. Ms. Smith lived her life like the rich and famous but at other people's expense. These people were her suga' daddies and mama's without even knowing it...at least she could have given them a kiss for all their contributions."

She paused, "Oh I forgot, she did. She said *kiss* my ass, laughing all the way to the bank and she was good at it too,"

Gavel hits again, "You know better," the judge said, giving her a piercing stare.

"Ok judge," the D.A. said, she was still one on. Looking at me directly in the face, she continued, "She got away with it for years, living in expensive lofts, driving expensive cars, partying with the rich like she inherited the life. B.S.! She stole a lifestyle that wasn't hers to take. But don't get me wrong, she does come from a good family, very respectful but that wasn't enough for her. She wanted more - "

With all of these allegations, it wasn't even enough of me to go around. I know y'all don't believe that shit do you? Neither do I, that's why a whole lot of motherfuckas are still behind bars, swole, tatted up. But shout out to the D.A., I'm rooting for you but I doubt she would win this war.

My attorney hand gestured from the back of the courtroom for the next witness to come up front. To everyone's surprise, walking up to take the oath, dressed just like me and looking identical to me was Asia. The courtroom went into a frenzy, "Ohhh, ahhhh," the D.A. almost shitted on herself. I knew she did because she never got up afterward, she just put her head down from embarrassment. The whole time I mentioned I had a sister, but I never said she was an identical twin.

"Do you swear to tell the whole truth and nothing but the truth?"

"I do."

"You may be seated," and from there my attorney began with questioning.

Q: "Can you state your name for the record?"

A: "Asia Monet Smith."

Q: "Ok Asia, how are you related to the defendant?"

A: "She's my identical twin sister, I'm older by three minutes," smiling at me. She had the same outfit on, only hers was blue and mine was black. A pinstripe trouser pants suit with suspenders by Dolce and Gabana with a white dress shirt and tie - *you know we had to be clean despite what people were thinking.* Our parents were the one's who actually purchased the outfits but we already had the shoes. We wore black Gucci pointed silver heel boots, our hair was bone straight with a part down the middle and Asia had on blue contacts.

This worked out perfectly and added a bit of detail I needed for my own freedom because a few witnesses reported seeing me at a few bank jobs and they identified me by saying I had blue eyes. My eyes are hazel with a hint of light brown, so it couldn't be me. *If the gloves don't fit, you must acquit*, I kept thinking to myself. Asia's eyes were a little lighter than mine so she pulled that blue shit off perfectly. *'Hi haters, bye haters,'* I started singing to myself.

"Asia," my attorney said, "Your twin sister, India Smith, is being accused of some serious charges. They say they have boat loads of evidence against her."

Q: "Do you believe your twin sister, whom you've known all of your life committed these crimes she's being charged with? Think about the question before you answer please." Asia looked at me and I looked back at her and blew her a kiss and she caught it. Then she looked at the bitch ass DA and said,

A: "She didn't commit any of those heinous crimes because I did them," the crowd went wild. The judge even looked at her with disbelief and hit his gavel against the submissive wood.

"Order in this court!" Nobody even paid him any attention, the news reporters were on fire and the cameras and lights were flashing violently, it was some surreal shit. I looked at my parents and I could have sworn they were doing the cabbage patch but maybe I was seeing things. In all of the commotion, I could only make out a few blurred images from the partial blindness I was experiencing from the lights. When the court settled and came to order, there weren't as many people present anymore. You could hear people on their cell phones, crying and screaming outside. The judge asked the jurors did they have a verdict. They had been whisked away after my sister's testimony and they did indeed have a verdict.

All the hearts beating in the room synchronized for this pivotal moment, as if we were watching the countdown to our fate, "We the jurors find India Mashay Smith...NOT GUILTY!"

"Thank you jurors," the judge said and walked out talking

under his breathe, "this was a damn circus." He forgot his audible mic was still on.

"Ms. Smith, you're free to go," his words unlocked the key. I ran to hug my sister for dear life and she was running to embrace me in return. But there was a dimming shadow amongst our light, the prosecutor D.A. was pissed.

She told my sister, "I will get you bitches if it's the last thing that I do!"

Asia responded, "Eat a dick you punk ass bitch and get over it!" we both looked at each other and joined in unison, "HATER!"

31

EPILOGUE

India Smith

Well one year to exact day of my trial, a miracle happened, "Asia hurry up out of the bathroom! We only have twenty minutes."

"I'm trying but I can't stop vomiting, it keeps coming up."

Knocking on the door, "What did you eat last night?" my mom asks her.

"Nothing different mom. I think it's my nerves."

"Ok, open the door Asia so I can help you."

"I can't get up, every time I try, I get nausea and throw up..."

"Well just take your time princess but we do have a wedding to host dear."

"I know mom, I'm the bride," Asia said, trying to get up but this time she was successful.

Opening the bathroom door, "Now look at my baby, you look just like I did on my wedding day. Beautiful! Even though you're not feeling well."

Taking Asia by the hand, "Come sit down on the bed. I'll get you a warm towel and your toothbrush. Are you going to be ok to get married today Asia? If not, we'll have to tell the guests."

"I'm feeling a little better mom, thanks. I just probably needed to get whatever it was out of my stomach."

"You're probably right dear, here you go let me wash your face," placing a soft towel against the bride's cheeks, gliding over her nose and around her eyelids, "your hair is so lovely. She did an excellent job with it. You're just so beautiful," her words got caught in her throat.

"Mom please don't start crying. That's all we need right now!"

"Oh hush India, you were crying earlier."

"Yea but that was before our makeup was done plus she's my twin," I said, sounding ridiculous.

"And she's my daughter," laughing, "and you're both twin monsters. But she looks so beautiful getting married. I'm going to be emotional with you too India, when it's your turn."

"Mom I'm never getting married, I don't need no man ok. I'm strong, powerful —"

"And single!" Mom says, laughing and cutting me off.

KNOCK! KNOCK! KNOCK! The sound rattled off the walls and bounced from the door to our ears, scaring us as well all jumped.

"It's almost showtime!"

"Yes Maria, we'll be down in a few minutes. Asia has to put on her dress and touch up her make up, then we'll be down."

"Ok Ms. Smith, thank you," closing the slowly door behind herself.

"You're welcome," redirecting her attention, "Sweetheart are you ready?"

"Yes mom, help me with my dress," slipping on a vintage lavender diamond encrusted Vera Wang corset with a silk A-line bottom with a tail. I could hardly tell Asia was four months pregnant with twins.

"Say cheese," I said with taking a picture with my digital camera, standing next to the photographers who were taping every moment of Asia's wedding day. The makeup consultant touched us all up and we walked out and down the stairs where Daddy was waiting for us patiently. I could tell from the look in his eyes how pleased he was as a father and how proud he was of his daughters.

"You look beautiful," kissing Asia on the forehead, "you're beautiful as the day you were both born."

"Thank you Daddy, you look nice yourself. You ready to give me away?" she asked with a hint of innocents.

"Well Asia, actually, I'm not giving you away sweetheart. I'm extending you to be someone's wife but you'll always be my baby girl."

"Don't make me cry Daddy," Asia said.

It was already too late for me, "I'm already there," I say, wiping the corner of my eye.

Our father was something special, "And India you look stunning as well."

"Thanks Daddy," I retort. "And what about me Mom?" I asks.

"You look beautiful also," giving me a quick glance and smile.

"Yes she does," Asia says.

"Listen girls, I love you both but I only have eyes for one woman today and she's on my arm."

We stood together as a family and took one more picture. Then my mom and I hurried outside to await their royal arrival along with the other guests. The backyards was beautiful and the weather sent a good omen with endless warmth and sunshine.

My parents went all out for this wedding, it looked like something in a fairytale - big tents, balloons, ice sculptures, wine fountains, and open bar on both ends of the garden. Our parent's chef wore a uniform with an earpiece along with other hired hostess and servers. Even the tables were special ordered from Tanzania with Asia and Vance's initials on the drapery. The wedding cake was a high castle that lit up and stood at about four feet high. In regards to the dining experience, let's not even talk about the menu. You would have thought this was the anniversary of Atlantis with the endless amounts of gourmet lobster, crab salad, filet mignon, salmon, pasta and the list went on. They even had a weight watchers table and vegetarian table for those with dietary restrictions. If you had a sweet tooth, you would be delighted to find the dessert table with slices of red velvet, carrot, vanilla and chocolate cake. It was spectacular. They even had a portable glass dance floor with their initials for the after party. They didn't leave anything out. But what we weren't expecting was that as my beautiful sister and my dad were making their grand entrance, I peeked at Vance for a second and saw tears in his eyes. That touched me so deeply.

My sister was finally happy and so was I. All two hundred or so family and friends stood for the arrival of the bride when suddenly Vance's ex-girlfriend Monique ran out from the inside of my parents' home, screaming with a gun.

"Bitch you stole my husband!!" and when the sound of bullets ended, Monique had shot and killed my twin sister and her unborn twins. Up until this point, I thought we had put everything behind us. But life is so full of surprises. You can never really prepare yourself for everything or schedule life altering events. The focus had shifted from a beautiful wedding to a dreadful massacre in one single moment. Monique's actions made you look at life differently - call it lover's remorse or a woman scorned, I just knew that I entered this world with someone who will no longer stand beside me and I will bear the weight of her legacy alone.

Made in the USA
Columbia, SC
02 July 2017